Terry Stiastny

The majority of Terry Stiastny's journalistic career was spent reporting for BBC News, which she left in 2012. During her time at the BBC, she worked in Berlin and Brussels, covered politics in Westminster and spent many years on BBC Radio 4 news programmes. She was educated at the University of Oxford, studying PPE at Balliol College and International Relations (MPhil) at St Antony's College. She lives in London with her husband and two sons. Her first book, *Acts of Omission*, won the Paddy Power Political Fiction Book of the Year Award 2014.

Also by Terry Stiastny

Acts of Omission

Conflicts of Interest

TERRY STIASTNY

JOHN MURRAY

First published in Great Britain in 2017 by John Murray (Publishers)
An Hachette UK Company

First published in paperback in 2018

I

A CIP catalogue record for this title is available from the British Library

ISBN 978-1-444-79439-7
Ebook ISBN 978-1-444-79438-0

Typeset in Bembo by Palimpsest Book Production Ltd, Falkirk, Stirlingshire

Printed and bound by Clays Ltd, Elcograf S.p.A.

John Murray policy is to use papers that are natural, renewable
and recyclable products and made from wood grown in sustainable
forests. The logging and manufacturing processes are expected to conform to
the environmental regulations of the country of origin.

John Murray (Publishers)
Carmelite House
50 Victoria Embankment
London EC4Y 0DZ

www.johnmurray.co.uk

For Gareth

I

August 2010

IT WAS EITHER nine or ten. The church bell always missed the top of the hour by a few minutes, but then it chimed twice. It gave you a second chance. Lawrence looked down at the space on his wrist where his watch used to be, where the skin was a smoother texture, the hairs rubbed away, still paler than the rest of the arm even now, in the late summer. He listened again for the second peal of bells, counting them this time to be sure. Ten.

He was relieved to see his favourite table still vacant and he claimed it, placing his baguette down. Although the laminated surface was chipped and it wobbled, despite the folded beer mat wedged beneath one of its legs, it was the best table. Sunlight was filtered through the wisteria that scrambled over the wrought-iron canopy sheltering the terrace and he could lean against the warm plaster of the cafe's wall and see everything going on in the square.

Lawrence lifted the bread up automatically as Elodie swept by, allowing her to give his table a cursory wipe with a cloth. Tattoos had crept further down her outstretched arm, as though the rose pattern was growing of its own accord. He scarcely needed to order these days; Elodie asked, with an upward inflection and a raised eyebrow, if it was the *petit crème* and he nodded in reply.

It was busier than usual for a Sunday morning, even in August. At the other end of the terrace, a family with three children were settling in to their seats in a flurry. They were Dutch, judging by the language as the mother lifted a toddler into one chair and separated two squabbling blond boys. It was a while before Elodie placed Lawrence's coffee on his table. She took the couple of euros he offered and went to stand over the Dutch family as they decided what to order.

He took a sip of his coffee and surveyed the square. There was a sense of purpose and expectation among the inhabitants of the village that morning. Strands of bunting, in French tricolour and the Provençal red and yellow, had been strung across from the town hall to the plane tree that sheltered the square. On the far side, beneath the thick stone walls of the old town, a few people were unfolding trestle tables, unloading cardboard boxes from the backs of small vans, setting out their displays. A yellow poster tacked to the tree trunk set out the order of the festive day: the *vide-grenier*, the games of boules, the meal in the evening and the dancing to follow.

It was usually a peaceful place now, undisturbed, but it had been a vicious little town in its time. A plaque on the fortifications told some of the history, that the walls were built when village was fighting against rival village, believers against heretics, enemies thrown from the tops of the walls. Every day when he passed the war memorial in the village and saw the weathered stone carving of a sad-eyed soldier, the plinth lined with surnames that were still familiar nearby, he was reminded that it wasn't so long ago. There, too, were the crosses of Lorraine that marked where the Resistance fighters fell. Everywhere was a war zone once, if you looked hard enough.

On the side of the square to Lawrence's right, opposite the town hall, the bakery was busy. The bell above the door sounded as each customer entered and left. An elderly lady emerged, carrying a large white cake box quartered with narrow blue ribbon. She wore a navy dress, a formal Sunday outfit. She held the box in front of her as she walked across the square towards the gate in the old town walls.

The bells started to chime again, no longer sounding the hour but a more tuneful peal. The church was at the top of the hill in the old town, at the end of a coil of streets that wound their way around to the centre. The lady with her cake box started to walk more quickly, picking up her feet over the uneven cobbles, the bells reminding her that she had to hurry.

It was as she approached the arched gateway in the walls that Lawrence heard the shots. The first shot cracked above the noise of the church bells. A second shot fired, then a third. He knew that sound, but he had to be mistaken. There couldn't be gunshots here, not on a Sunday morning in August, as an old lady carried her cakes home from the bakery. It must have been a motorbike backfiring. He told himself sternly, as he'd often had to do before, not to be so stupid, not to imagine things, not to overreact.

Then a fourth shot came and he stopped counting. It was a rifle shot, that much he knew, coming from the old village behind the walls, from near his own house, and there was more than one gunman. Lawrence screwed his eyes closed. He did not want to see what he expected to see. He did not want to see the woman, her cake box thrown aside, her body prostrate on the cobbles, her legs splayed and her black shoes at an unnatural angle to one another. The images played out in his mind the way they hadn't done in a long time; he saw them, as always, in slow motion and close up, framed as though he were filming them.

It wasn't until he opened his eyes that he realised he was crouched on the floor beneath the table, kneeling on the dusty terrace. He grasped for the baguette, which had fallen on the ground beside him, as though it were a weapon. There was a warm, wet patch on his left shoulder. Lawrence sat back against the wall and reached his right hand up to his shirt. Near the neck, he thought. As he felt under the collar of his shirt, he realised that it didn't hurt as much as he thought it would. It scarcely hurt at all, a slight burning. But then, he knew, that was sometimes the way. It would hit him later. He pulled his hand

3

away and looked at it. It came away light brown, the colour of coffee. It was coffee.

He peered through the thicket of chair legs in front of him to see a procession of black trousers and thick-soled shoes, marching in step in the direction of the cafe. They had rounded the stone trough of the fountain beneath the plane tree. There were still shots, but they were intermittent now. He sat up and looked at the men. There were perhaps a dozen of them, in waistcoats and black felt trilbies, red neckerchiefs knotted around the collars of their white shirts. They carried hunting rifles. They may have been in unusual costumes but he recognised them all the same: they were the villagers and he knew them. They were not shooting at him, nor at anyone else. The rifles, loaded with blanks, were aimed at the sky.

Lawrence scrabbled to his feet, dusting off the knees of his beige chinos. He righted the bentwood chair he had been sitting on and stood his coffee cup back up in the pool of spilt liquid in its saucer. He tried to act as though nothing had happened.

Four of the men carried between them a carved figure of a saint, raised to shoulder height on a sort of wooden stretcher. The gilt folds of the saint's robes caught the sunlight and his hand was raised in benediction. Behind them, the village priest followed, white-robed with a red stole. This must happen every year, the saint being borne from the church through the village to bless the festival in his honour. Somehow Lawrence must have always missed it before.

He wondered where he had been to miss this ritual; it didn't take him long to arrive at the answer. People said that nothing happened in August, but too often it did. Princess Diana had died in August, after all. He remembered that interrupted holiday, the drive back to Paris through the night, leaving Harriet behind with the children, speeding down the empty autoroutes, only slowing down when he thought that it would be too stupid to crash trying to get to the scene of a car crash. The coup in Moscow broke in the middle of the summer holidays. Wars and disasters didn't take school holidays off, as he used to tell Harriet. Nor did they respect birthdays or anniversaries or dinner parties.

The huntsmen at the head of the parade fired off a last volley, then broke their guns and started to approach the cafe. Gilles, the patron, came out to greet them and Elodie followed behind, her tray laden with glasses of red wine. Gilles took a glass from the tray and offered it to the first man. It was Pascal, the village's mayor, a broad-chested man in his fifties with a drooping moustache. The traditional outfit, like something out of Pagnol, suited him.

More people had gathered in the square to watch, cyclists dismounting and leaning their bikes against the water trough. A man in Lycra shorts and a cycling team jersey held his phone up to film the scene. Pascal turned towards his audience and raised his glass in their direction. Pascal's accent was strong, a Provençal twang at the ends of his words. Lawrence could follow it, but sometimes with difficulty. Pascal spoke about the hunting season that was to start, the wine harvest to follow. He was marking the end of the summer, though it was still the middle of August. It was a season of endings and of beginnings, rituals that repeated themselves year after year. The visitors went home and for those who remained, more work began. This year, for the first time, Lawrence would not be leaving, and he had no work to do.

Pascal raised his glass in honour of the carved saint, asking his protection. If Lawrence had had any coffee left, he would have raised his cup to join the toast. He could do with something to bring him luck, to bless him, however superstitious that was.

Her tray empty, Elodie returned to the cafe. As she moved towards him, she gasped at the coffee trailing from Lawrence's saucer and still dripping off the edge of the table. Her eyes darted towards the coffee stain on his shoulder before she looked away again. She removed his cup and saucer and began to wipe up the mess. She asked him what had happened. For a moment, he struggled to remember the word for gunfire, but it came back to him, as unwelcome as the shots themselves. *La fusillade*, he said. It scared me, he admitted. I didn't know what it was.

Elodie laughed and shrugged and went back to the bar. He was surprised to see her return a minute later with a replacement coffee, along with a glass of cognac that she placed firmly on the table. Lawrence reached for his wallet but Elodie shook her head and insisted that it was on the house.

'It's good for the nerves,' she said. Lawrence took a first sip at the brandy. It was not the way he was supposed to deal with it, he knew that much. He had paid enough money over the years to people who told him that. All the same, it worked, at least for a while. What was the point of living in France, after all, if you couldn't, when necessary, drink brandy at ten o'clock on a Sunday morning? He was conducting the familiar argument in his head with an interlocutor who no longer cared either way; Harriet, no longer his wife, was not here to tell him otherwise. But there were other visitors who were due to arrive. He'd be back to normal by the time they came.

2

H<small>E WOULD HAVE</small> made it all the way to the fountain in the middle of the square, if it hadn't been for the slow, aimless people blocking his path. There were only a few metres to go. Martin's calves were burning with the effort of the last hill on the way into the village, but he wanted to push on, get where he was going. He came to a halt, dismounted and turned back to look for Julian. Julian was a hundred metres or so behind, his face even redder than usual, his cheeks puffed out. He was certainly trying hard, for someone not used to the effort, but Martin had his doubts about whether he'd make the distance, come September. Martin checked the small digital screen fixed to his handlebars – 70 kilometres. A bit slow, but that was down to Julian. They were late; he'd promised to be back with the breakfast before everyone was up, and they'd be up by now.

Julian caught up, hauled a heavy thigh over his crossbar.

'What's all this?' Julian asked, once he'd caught his breath.

'Not sure,' Martin replied. 'Local colour. Great, isn't it?' A man in a black felt hat and a waistcoat like an old-time French peasant, a rifle slung over his shoulder, was downing a glass of red wine, slurping it through a heavy salt-and-pepper moustache, the crowd applauding him. It was as though Martin had laid on the scene for Julian's benefit, a film-perfect image of French village life. Julian nodded his agreement and wiped the sweat from his forehead with his arm. He reached for his water bottle and took a long swig. The cleats on their shoes clacked on the cobbles as they made their way through the square. Julian went over to the fountain, where he bent forward and sluiced water over his head.

As he waited, Martin recognised the familiar figure on the cafe terrace. The way he sat never changed. His head was tilted back against the wall, the greying blond hair swept away from his forehead, his eyes closed, one arm outstretched on an empty chair. His ankle was crossed over his knee. His romantic poet pose. He still wore the desert boots, same as always.

Martin wheeled his bike over and propped it against a wall.

'Wake up, Leith. You're on in ten.'

Lawrence's eyes blinked open. He rocked forward on his chair and looked around him. His eyes were that same clear blue but more watery than before.

'Trust you, Elliot,' Lawrence said as he stood up. They threw their arms around each other, the same hug they always gave when it had been a while. These days, it had usually been a while. Lawrence clapped a hand onto Martin's back where he felt clammy, the sweat starting to cool. His breath had a tang of alcohol and Martin noticed an empty cognac glass on the table.

'You look well,' Martin said, more quickly than he should have done. 'Still got all your own hair.' Lawrence tugged at a strand near his temples, as if to prove that it was.

'And you've got even less,' Lawrence observed, indicating Martin's stubbled scalp. It was an old routine. Lawrence looked better than Martin had expected. The year-round tan helped, even though it had made the wrinkles at the corners of his eyes more pronounced. Lawrence had all the time he wanted to sit in the sun and wouldn't care about the effects. He had put on weight, too. He had never stinted on good food and wine; he just couldn't carry it so well any more. Everything had slipped, betraying a lack of muscle and exercise.

'When did you get in?' Lawrence asked. The question reminded Martin of hotel bars and airport lounges, of Lawrence's erratic map reading. It was a long time since they'd been on the road together.

'Yesterday afternoon,' Martin said.

'How's the house?'

'Fantastic, thanks. Transformed. Can't wait for you to see it. You're coming, this evening, aren't you?' Iona would have reminded him, but he wanted to make sure. Though if he was already on the brandy at ten in the morning, it might not be such a good idea. 'Are you OK?' Martin continued, lowering his voice as Julian approached. He nodded towards the brown stain on Lawrence's shoulder.

'Oh, that.' Lawrence glanced down at the mark. 'It's nothing. I was a bit startled. They were firing rifles. It's a traditional thing. Gave me a bit of a jump.'

'So your coffee missed your mouth? By quite some way?'

Lawrence shrugged.

'Julian,' Martin began. 'You've met Lawrence Leith, haven't you? Lawrence, Julian Heathcote. Julian and Victoria are staying with us.'

'I don't think we have,' Julian said, extending a fleshy hand. His arm was freckled and had reddened in the morning sun. 'But I know your work, of course. Big fan.' Martin willed him not to ask what Lawrence was doing these days. Yet Julian blundered on.

'Where are you off to next? Plenty of trouble spots on your list, I expect.'

Lawrence shook his head. 'I'm giving the trouble spots a miss for now. Who needs trouble spots when you've got this?' He gestured towards the square.

'That's true,' said Julian. At least Lawrence had managed to be gracious. Before he'd left London, his bitterness and tendency to harangue people and blame others for his failures had become tiresome. He seemed to have mellowed in the sunshine. Martin knew he'd been right to get out of that business early enough. There weren't many old journalists and there were even fewer happy old ones. Lawrence may have scoffed at him once for selling out, but he didn't scoff any more.

9

'Listen, there's going to be a bunch of grumpy children up at the house wondering where we've got to with their pains au chocolat, so we'd better get to the bakery before they run out. But we'll see you later, won't we?' Lawrence nodded his assent.

'Great to meet you,' Julian said to Lawrence.

Julian reached the bakery door first and held it open. Martin stepped inside and inhaled the warm scent of fresh bread. The woman behind the counter moved slowly, taping a square of paper on the diagonal around each pair of loaves, twirling the corners of the bag that held the croissants and pains au chocolat in a way that Martin hadn't seen shopkeepers do since his childhood. He slid a twenty-euro note onto the dish on top of the glass vitrine and waited for her to count out his change. With each slow movement she made, his feet itched with impatience. He could already feel his muscles cramping up, needing to move again. He wanted to get back to the house and into a warm shower. He felt a vibration against the small of his back, his phone buzzing in the pocket of his cycling jersey; he ignored it.

Martin liked the image of himself cycling along idly, carrying his fresh bread home. One day there would be more time for that. One day that would be all he would do; he'd be able to stop. That time was still far away, though, the time when he would be able to come down here and do nothing but take in the view. It was all right for Lawrence; that choice had been forced upon him.

3

L AWRENCE THREW HIS coffee-stained shirt into the laundry basket and opened the wardrobe, pulling a clean navy polo shirt from the pile. The window was open and there was a breeze. He looked out across rows of terracotta rooftops, to where the hill below the village dropped away to the plain beyond. The slopes were striped with vineyards, the vines full and green, dropping with black grapes soon to be harvested. When he had arrived at the beginning of the year, there had been nothing but the pruned black stumps of the old vines, like gnarled hands reaching up out of the earth. Somewhere in that direction, across the valley, was Martin's house, though he couldn't see it from there.

Through the arched stone gate that led into the old town, among the low houses that jostled against each other, it was quiet. The windows of the houses were low, screened by net curtains. In the evenings you heard the murmur of televisions and on Sundays families gathered for lunch.

Lawrence had just set the needle on the old record player, the one he had taken with him, since no one else wanted it. The notes of the double bass began, then Brassens's guitar, then his clear rolling voice as he sang 'Les Copains d'Abord'.

> *Au rendez-vous des bons copains,*
> *Y'avait pas souvent de lapins.*

The phone rang. Reluctantly, he answered the call. It was Iona, her voice bright. They were all coming down to the village, to go to the flea market, and he would join them, wouldn't he? She hardly waited for him to agree before she rang off. Lawrence looked up at the framed poster that he had reinstated on the wall, the one Harriet had always disliked. Brel, Brassens and Ferré, in black and white, sitting around a table, sometime in the sixties. Each of them sat in front of a microphone but this was no neat recording studio; the table was scattered with empty glasses and beer bottles, a heavy cut-glass ashtray. Brassens was smoking a pipe, the other two, cigarettes. The three men looked happy, at ease in each others' company. *Les Copains d'Abord.*

The sun angled in through the thin curtains across the doors that led to the tiny courtyard. The little room that was usually large enough for him felt too small. He would go out again and meet them.

'So, do you miss it?' Martin asked, as he picked up an old yellow Ricard jug from one of the trestle tables in the market and turned it around in his hands, inspecting it closely. The yellow glaze on the pottery was in good condition, as far as Lawrence could see, scarcely cracked or chipped.

Lawrence shook his head. It was a question he had got used to hearing, though few people came down here and asked it to his face.

'There are days,' he began. 'There are the big days, when I have a moment of wishing I was there. And then I stop and remember why I don't want to be there any more.'

'Like when you think someone's shooting at you?'

'I haven't been like that for a while,' Lawrence replied. 'I can't remember the last time. It's just that I didn't have a chance to prepare for it. I heard the noise and I just reacted.'

'Are you still talking to someone about it?' Martin persisted. 'Seeing anyone to help?'

'Not down here,' Lawrence said. 'I can't see the point. Being down here is good for me. No stress. No difficult situations.'

The tables were covered with old glassware and ashtrays, rust-spotted tins that had once held stock cubes or chocolate powder, metal coffee-grinders with crank handles. On a sheet in front of the stall, a blunt scythe lay next to a manual typewriter, a Polaroid camera alongside a rake with unevenly bent tines, all unwanted and obsolete.

Martin turned towards the stallholder, a man in his sixties with pockmarked skin and grey hair combed sharply back. Although Martin's French was still as terrible as it had always been, he managed to make himself understood. Lawrence might have been more correct, but Martin was the more persuasive. Martin asked how much for the pastis jug; the stallholder told him thirty euros. Martin indicated the circular tray and the matching glasses that completed the set and asked how much for all of it. He feigned shock at the price he was quoted and turned back to Lawrence.

'You should get back in the game, though. Even if not the same game. You're wasted down here.'

Lawrence shrugged and let Martin get on with his negotiation. He'd just offered fifteen euros, to the stallholder's exaggerated exasperation. Lawrence had seen this often enough before; Martin negotiated everything from taxi fares to hotel room rates. He had bargained with editors in London for more time for the reports he produced for Lawrence. Then he'd cut himself deals for ever better jobs. More often than not, the deal was concluded on Martin Elliot's terms.

The stallholder conceded at twenty, spreading his hands wide.

'The game's moved on,' Lawrence continued. 'I'm like this stuff.' He pointed towards the typewriter on the ground. 'Surplus to requirements. Out of date.'

'Only if you let yourself think like that,' Martin insisted. 'Plenty of people could use you. We could use you.'

'What for?' Lawrence asked. He was trying not to sound too dismissive. It was a conversation he had wanted to have, though he hadn't expected to start it here, in the village street, surrounded by second-hand junk.

'We can talk about it. You should have come to see me, before you chucked it all in.'

Martin said it as though that were a simple thing, but Lawrence had lost count of the drinks they'd been meant to have, the postponed lunches, the times he'd called to be told that Martin was out of the country on an urgent trip. It was a reversal; it used to be Lawrence who always had to cancel.

These days, Martin was screened from people he didn't need to meet. When he had started Elliot Associates, the name was printed on a small plaque by a buzzer that gave access to a tiny suite of offices, up a narrow flight of stairs in a Westminster backstreet. The address, Martin had said, was everything, even if he had to hold meetings in coffee shops. These days, the Elliot Associates logo was etched on perspex in the white-walled atrium of a tall office building near Cheapside. He had done even better in recent years; the greater the crisis, whether political or financial, the more people needed Martin's help and the more they were prepared to pay for Martin's advice. He restored reputations, improved images, wove more convincing stories for them. Although Lawrence could have used advice from Martin, he doubted he could afford it any more.

The stallholder put the jug and glasses into a plastic bag and handed Martin the tray. Martin turned to Lawrence.

'We'll have a chance to talk properly now I'm here,' he said. 'Really catch up. There's a couple of things I have in mind.'

Before Lawrence could find out what those things were, they were interrupted by the squeal of a falling child, a wail of pain. Martin rushed towards the little boy who had tripped on the cobblestones. His sister was standing over him, her fists on her hips.

'Finn was running too fast and he fell over,' she explained. Maisie spoke with conviction.

Martin passed the plastic bag and tray to Lawrence, then leant over his son and inspected the knee that the boy stuck out. He rubbed the boy's kneecap gently before picking him up and standing him back on his feet.

'Nothing broken?' he said. Finn sniffed and shook his head. He had strawberry-blond hair cut in a long fringe that hung into his eyes, a superhero cartoon on his green T-shirt. Maisie, his twin, stared directly at Lawrence. Her hair was the same shade as Finn's, though tied back in a loose ponytail.

'I've met you before,' she declared. 'You've been to our house.'

'That's right,' Lawrence agreed. 'But it was a long time ago.' She was not yet five and already she had some of her father's networking skills. It must have been over a year since he had seen the children.

Iona was not far behind them, treading carefully on the chunky soles of her sandals as though she too might trip over on the sloping street. She was wearing a dark-blue linen dress, her face shaded by a large straw hat with a floppy brim. She was a redhead with pale skin that didn't take well to the sun.

'I told him not to run, but he didn't listen.' Iona looked towards Lawrence. 'Just like someone else we know,' she said. They both laughed. She embraced Lawrence with a real warmth and a clatter of bangles, a kiss on each cheek, before letting him go and holding him by the shoulders at arm's length. 'You look so well, Lawrence. You really needed the change of scene.'

The trouble with being told you looked well was that it made you wonder quite how bad you had looked before. In London, no one had mentioned that he looked rough. Iona usually spoke before she thought, which was one of the qualities that endeared her to Lawrence. She seemed to come at everything from an unusual angle. He had always expected Martin to marry one of the many interchangeable girlfriends before Iona, a girl with a flowery name, a Daisy or a Poppy; instead, he had married this wonderfully spiky, arty woman who had little tolerance for bullshit. Though in fact, the first conversation Lawrence had ever had with her had been largely about elephant dung. When Martin had introduced them, in a dark bar off Brick Lane, they had begun by arguing about Chris Ofili's paintings, then about Africa. By the end of the evening, as Martin left with Iona, Lawrence told him that he was an idiot if he didn't marry her.

There was another woman standing next to Iona, a distant look on her face. Her dress was printed with large, splodgy flowers but the dress itself looked tight and formal, the kind of outfit Lawrence imagined was better suited to a garden party or a wedding than a holiday. She seemed familiar, but he couldn't quite place her. He wondered if he had met her before, or was she just someone he'd seen on TV or in a newspaper? The same thing often happened to Lawrence in reverse; he'd be greeted by a passer-by or a party guest who thought they knew him. He would look blank, stumble and apologise for not remembering them. Then it was the passer-by's turn to apologise, when they realised they had only seen him on the news. This woman, however, expected people to know who she was.

Iona noticed the silence and turned to introduce her companion.

'Lawrence, this is Victoria Loxton.'

'Lawrence Leith.' The name seemed to mean nothing to her. Victoria's hand was cold, her handshake professional. She was taller than Iona and stood straight, almost to attention. She had coarse blonde hair that skimmed her broad shoulders.

'Victoria's staying with us,' Iona added, aware that the introduction was not going well.

'I think I met your husband,' Lawrence said to Victoria. 'Julian? This morning. He'd been out for a bike ride, with Martin.'

'Right,' Victoria replied. She nodded slightly, smiled a thin, forced smile and moved on.

Lawrence waited until she had moved out of earshot and had paused to look at some old paperbacks.

'Who is she?' he whispered to Iona. This head-girlish woman wasn't Iona's kind of friend.

'She's awful,' Iona whispered back, the brim of her hat casting a shadow on both their faces. 'She's a government minister, as of earlier this year, and she's one of those people Martin acquires. It's really Julian he knows – he's a client and now they go cycling together. He has this business selling fruit stuff for kids, you know, snacks that are supposed to be healthy but are really junk with a posh label. I wouldn't let Maisie and Finn eat them except we keep getting free crateloads of the bloody stuff delivered from him.'

'Then what are they doing coming on holiday with you?'

'They're on their way to see some far smarter friends, further south. They said they were just dropping by but they haven't said when they're leaving.'

'Is she always that rude?'

'No, not always. She can be quite charming when she puts her mind to it. Or when she's had a glass of wine.'

'What's she got against me, then?' Lawrence lowered his voice further.

'She probably knows who you are. Knows you're a journalist, I mean.'

'Was a journalist,' he corrected. 'And she gave a pretty good impression of never having seen me in her life.'

'As far as she's concerned, I expect, once a journalist, always a journalist.'

'What does she think I'm going to do? A feature on her holidays?'

Before Iona could answer, a long-legged teenage girl in cut-off denim shorts and black-framed glasses approached them. Freya was already as tall as her mother. She had an armful of comic-books with her, Tintins and Asterixes.

'Can I have twenty euros?' she asked Iona.

'What for?'

'These.' She held up the cartoon books.

'Twenty euros?' Iona queried.

'I won't spend it all,' Freya said. 'Plus, they're educational. They're in French.'

Iona dug in one of the large pockets of her dress for her purse and handed over the money. 'As long as you read the words, as well as copy the pictures.'

Freya gave a skyward look, as though her plan had been rumbled. She waved a vague hand in Lawrence's direction and muttered 'Hi', before wandering back to pay for the books.

'Another artist?' Lawrence asked Iona. This time it was Iona's turn to roll her eyes.

'Heaven help me,' she said. 'But I know the worst thing I can do is tell her she needs to think about a more sensible career. She's stubborn. Like her dad.'

'You did OK,' Lawrence reminded her. 'And these kids are far more sensible than we were at their age.' Iona nodded. Lawrence had only ever known Freya's father, Seb Anderson, by reputation. He was more notorious for his behaviour than his art, though his stumbling out of bars, his punching of photographers, his propensity for public feuds, were part of what had made his art so marketable. He remembered Freya at Martin and Iona's wedding, a little girl not much older than the twins were now, skipping happily around the room in a red velvet dress.

'She seems to have her head screwed on,' Iona agreed. 'But you never know.'

They gathered at the bottom of the hill and their loud English voices seemed to echo from the walls. Lawrence had become used to eavesdropping on tourists, not being one of them. He saw them as he saw the other visitors, as overdressed and conspicuous, heedless of their surroundings.

Lawrence had never felt he belonged. In childhood he had been moved around, army posting to army posting, to boarding school and then home to somewhere that wasn't home. Then he had repeated the pattern, moving every few years from one country to another; Germany to Egypt, France to America. When they returned to London, although they had called it going home, he was restless and dissatisfied. After Harriet had thrown him out, the home he had was gone.

It was just as well he had kept the house in France. It had not, he would readily admit, been the most sensible of purchases at the time. They'd been based in Paris and had come here on holiday, bought the cottage on impulse because they could hardly believe how cheap it was. The children had been tiny then, Josh still only a baby, Lizzie in nursery school. It had all seemed like an adventure. Then, when they'd gone to the States, they rarely managed to visit the place. When they were back in Europe there were too many claims on their time, relatives to see and friends to catch up with; the house had been rented out, when they could find tenants. By the time they came back, the children had outgrown it, demanding to stay somewhere with a pool, complaining about a house they saw as poky and boring. Harriet, too, had said it was time to get rid of the place, to sell it, however small the profit. She wanted to use the money to help them buy somewhere better in London, a bigger house for all of them. It had been one of the things they argued about, an item on a list of grievances that had grown ever longer. But, Lawrence thought, occasionally intransigence had its benefits. The house was still here, and when he and Harriet had split up, it seemed the obvious place to come.

Martin was showing Iona his purchases, seeking her approval. They would stand here and dither, Lawrence knew, for some time longer.

'I'll leave you to it,' he said, indicating the direction of his house.

'You're coming later?' Iona asked. Lawrence nodded, though he was dreading later. She must have caught the expression on his face. 'It'll be fine. Just a few people, drinks and stuff. You'll probably know them.' It was what Iona always said about her parties, that they were nothing much. It was always an understatement and he had learned to be prepared.

4

THE SWIFTS GLIDED on the currents of warm air, swooping down towards the blue water, barely grazing the surface of the swimming pool before soaring high again. Martin admired their accuracy, the way they glanced off their target without crashing. They rose and dropped and rose again, taking what must have been the smallest sips of water from the pool. Was it all as effortless, as natural as it looked? Swifts never stopped flying, he had read once. They lived on the wing, slept on the wing, only landing on the ground in order to breed. Their whole lives were in the air.

The pool was calm and empty, the protesting children gone, the damp towels and the scattered toys tidied away. The sun was starting to fall behind the oak trees and the Mediterranean pines, but the air was still warm. Martin had come down to the poolside, on the terrace below the house, to take a moment by himself before the guests arrived. He stretched himself out on one of the sunloungers, extending his aching legs. He took his BlackBerry out of his pocket, muted it, and laid it down on the flagstones. He could still feel an imagined vibration against his leg, the buzz of a phantom incoming message. He forced himself to look at the view, to resist the urge to check his messages, if only for a few minutes. They never stopped, not for Sundays, not for holidays, not for August. He had already spent a couple of hours dealing with problems that needed solving, situations that had to be kept under control. Iona told him that he needed to delegate more, to trust other people to handle things on his behalf; what she didn't understand was that people paid him for his expertise and they weren't paying that kind of money to have someone junior handle their crises.

The view was brochure-perfect. The hillside sloped down away from the pool towards an olive grove with a vineyard beyond it. In the distance were wooded hills and the outline of Mont Ventoux, the scree on its summit looking like unseasonal snow. From above where he sat he heard a crunch of tyres on gravel, a car approaching along the drive. Martin bent forward to retrieve his BlackBerry before he stood up. There was no more time to gaze into the distance; guests were here and he was needed.

There were three of them on the terrace. As Martin walked along the path back towards the house, he saw Iona rush out to greet them. There was a flurry of handshakes and kisses. Iona extended a hand in Martin's direction, indicating his approach. He waved back and hurried over. He could tell from the look she shot him that she wanted him there, that these were people she was not at ease with. The French visitors all looked pressed, formal, slightly on edge.

Sylvie greeted him first, holding out a small bony hand, presenting each cheek to be kissed. Despite the heat, she wore a pink-and-white tweed jacket that was most likely a real Chanel. A pink silk scarf was knotted around her throat. She threw up her hands, gesturing towards the house.

'I would hardly know it's the same place. It's . . .' She paused briefly, searching for the correct English word. 'Unrecognisable!'

'Do you like it?' Iona asked, a touch of anxiety in her voice.

'But of course,' Sylvie insisted.

Martin hoped that Sylvie would have been too polite to say if she had disapproved, at least so soon. The house was indeed unrecognisable. The pink ochre-tinted plaster of the walls had been filled in and smoothed over, the peeling paint of the lavender-blue shutters sanded away and renewed.

The first time Martin had seen the house, he had nearly turned back before he got to it. The approach was a sharp turn away from the main road, down a rutted track that rose between fruit trees to one side and vines to the other, past farm buildings with rusty machinery and old pallets scattered outside. They had pulled up at dark-green metal gates flecked with rust spots and he could see nothing beyond them, the house obscured by a tall evergreen hedge. The gates had been chained shut and it was not until they had been unchained and pushed back that he saw the house. It was everything he could want: a perfect oblong of a house like a child's drawing, with that view over the valley and the hills beyond.

Behind Sylvie stood her brother Christophe, appraising the house. Martin held out his hand and Christophe shook it.

'Not bad,' Christophe nodded. Martin clapped a hand onto Christophe's shoulder and led him further along the terrace, to where a tray of drinks was set out in the shade of a white awning. The edge of the terrace was dotted with young olive trees in huge earthenware pots. New wisteria and vines were starting to climb up the wrought-iron trellis; the long-established, twisted plants that had been there before had turned out to be infested with disease.

Christophe handed a glass of champagne to his wife. Isabelle hung back from the other two, looking at the house more intently. She was in a pristine white sleeveless dress. Martin approached her.

'What do you think?'

They walked over to the double doors that opened onto the terrace from the main living room and looked into the room, which was white-painted now with long dark beams running the length of the ceiling, a brightly coloured print and a 1930s poster of Mont Ventoux on the walls.

'It looks so different,' Isabelle began. She dropped her voice a fraction. 'So much better. Lighter. Cleaner. All that dust and darkness gone. Those horrible old long velvet curtains.'

Then she asked, 'Are you happy?'

'With the house?' Martin replied. Isabelle smiled one of her thin, nervy smiles. 'Yes,' Martin continued. 'We're very happy with the house.'

He steered Isabelle back to the terrace, where Maître Aubert, the lawyer, and his wife, Marie, newly arrived, joined her. There were introductions to be made, connections to be created. It should have been nothing, a small gathering like this. An *apéritif* and a few snacks. No caterers, no table settings. It wasn't like in London, where his summer and Christmas parties had developed their own traditions, even made the diary columns. It was all publicity. This was private. He felt a critical gaze from his French guests that unsettled him but he determined to ignore it. This was his house now, his rules.

Martin sought out Christophe Vernet, to introduce him to Julian. Julian brushed crumbs from his hand onto the back of his trousers and then stuck it out towards Christophe. Christophe held out a fastidious hand in return.

'Julian's staying with us,' Martin remarked. 'He's got a really interesting food business.' The two of them had more in common than appearances would suggest: the money; the old, landed families; the strong women around them. The two men had begun talking about wine and olives and he left them to it.

Martin picked up a glass of champagne and toyed with it, taking a small sip as he surveyed the guests on the terrace. There were moments when he had to remind himself this eighteenth-century *bastide* really belonged to him. He hadn't even had a passport until he was nineteen, and he still kept that first hard-backed navy booklet, the black-and-white photo inside showing a youth with a dark lick of floppy hair. He remembered the Interrail ticket he'd bought that summer and the first time he had boarded a ferry at Dover, and the oily smell of the boat. He had always wanted to go somewhere with no cold wind, little rain, where you didn't have to keep moving to keep warm; somewhere that wasn't bracing.

He looked up and saw Lawrence shuffling around the corner

of the house, a bottle of wine in one hand. He wore a familiar cream linen jacket which no longer fitted him well. He had made an effort, at least. Martin picked a second glass of champagne from the silver tray and carried it in Lawrence's direction.

Martin loved these moments, the moments where everything was possible. He raised his glass to the good life.

5

IT WAS THE first time Lawrence had seen the house properly, though he had tried to get a glimpse of it before. Once, the gates had been open and he had gone a little way up the drive, as though he was there by accident. Tradesmen's vans had been parked on the drive and the sound of sawing came from inside. Most of the house was covered in scaffolding. A painter had stopped work to look at him and Lawrence had turned back towards the road before being asked who he was. The drive then had been potholed; now a thick layer of gravel crunched under his feet and the vans had been replaced by the cars of the guests. The lavender bushes along the side of the drive still gave off their scent even though the flowers were over and they had been cut back. Tall, resinous Mediterranean pine trees overhung the approach to the house. It was still warm enough for a few cicadas to be chirping their hoarse sound from the branches. There was a cypress tree – traditionally a symbol of hospitality – at the end of the drive, pruned back to a neat pencil point.

His last invitation to one of Martin's parties had arrived in November. Ever since they had moved back to London, Lawrence had noticed that Harriet received more invitations than he did. He was becoming the plus one, if he went at all. He had put it down to the fact that the kind of people Harriet met were more likely to throw parties, were more likely to value the gossip she brought and the possibility of a mention in her newspaper column. Lawrence had tended to avoid the few well-intentioned but dull gatherings he was invited to, where people would want to involve him in worthy conversations about the state of the world. The state of the world was not much good and there was little that a glass of warm wine would do to remedy that.

It had begun as a childish argument about whose friend Martin really was. Lawrence had noticed a snippet in the newspaper mentioning Martin Elliot and the sought-after invitations to his twice-yearly parties. He'd been sitting in the kitchen, tilting his chair back on its rear legs, and tossed the invitation across the kitchen table to Harriet as she returned home from work, saying that their sought-after invitation was here. He'd thought it was a joke.

'They are sought after,' Harriet replied, scooping the invitation up and placing it carefully at the centre of the mantelpiece.

'Really? Who seeks them?' Lawrence had never thought much about it.

'Everyone,' Harriet said, as though this was patently a stupid question. 'You're lucky to make the cut.'

Lawrence had taken this as a joke too before he looked at her and realised she was completely in earnest, her face set hard. He laughed anyway. Once, it would have been the kind of thing they laughed about together, the ridiculousness of their friends taking themselves too seriously. Yet Harriet seemed to have lost her sense of humour in the months before.

'What do you mean, I'm lucky to make the cut? He's one of my oldest friends.'

'Yes, and have you noticed that the people he sees now aren't his old friends. They're his new friends. Unless his old friends have kept the pace, which you clearly haven't.'

Lawrence was winded by her comments, gasping for words and for breath as though she had punched him. It wasn't even six months since he had left his job and Harriet had been growing impatient with him and his insistence that he needed some time to decide what to do. She jabbed him with a follow-up while he was still unsteady.

'If it weren't for me, we'd have fallen off the bottom of the list, I guarantee. And I've told you before about rocking the chair on its legs like that. You'll break it.'

Lawrence had rocked the chair forward again, but not to do as Harriet had told him. He stood up and grabbed the back of the chair, one hand on each upright, and raised it over his head. Then he swung the chair down and smashed it onto the beige tiles of the kitchen floor. The chair split apart, the seat coming away from the legs and leaving one back leg lying broken across a cracked tile. Lawrence kicked the remnants of the chair for good measure.

'Happy now?' he shouted. 'That'll give you something to put in your column.'

She hadn't put that incident in the column at the time, though he suspected she might have done by now. He had stopped reading it, except when he hit a low point after a glass of wine too many in the evening and would look it up on the newspaper's website, trying to restrain himself from commenting below the line. The more Harriet wrote about her life after him, the more popular she had become. He was alluded to by a pseudonym, but the worst thing was that everyone knew who she had been married to. Everyone now knew his failings as a husband, as a father, as an unemployed journalist.

Lawrence had gone to Martin's Christmas party, out of spite as much as anything else. He and Harriet had circled the room, avoiding each other. He had drunk too much and provoked bitter arguments about the Middle East. By an uneasy family Christmas lunch, the dining chair and the cracked tile had been replaced, and in the first days of the new year he had moved out.

Lawrence rounded the corner onto an immaculate terrace that gave onto a lawn, a perfect rectangle of turquoise swimming pool below it, and beyond that a view towards the village and the distant hills. The sun was sliding lower in the sky and the shadows of the trees were lengthening.

Julian, the portly cyclist who was apparently something important in the world of fruit, was speaking English, too loud, to a dark-haired man with a pale-blue sweater knotted around his shoulders. Two women were standing further along the terrace, beside one of the terracotta planters. The one with her back to him was Victoria, though after that morning's encounter, Lawrence was not anxious to talk to her again. She was inclining her head down towards the other woman, involved in what looked like a serious conversation. The smaller woman's face was mostly obscured from Lawrence's view by Victoria's sunburnt shoulder and by a branch of the young olive tree that stood in its pot, but he could make out her high cheekbones and her sharply cut blonde bob. Lawrence shifted sideways so he could see her better, trying to remember where he had met her before. She was out of her usual context here. Sometimes he thought he had simply met so many people, in so many places, that he had used up all his available memory, like a defunct computer.

Her name returned with the first sip of his champagne. Martin had fetched Lawrence in from the edge of the gathering, accepted his offering of a bottle of wine, placed the glass in his hand.

'Isn't that Sylvie Barroux?' Lawrence asked. 'Talking to your friend Victoria?'

Martin looked surprised.

'Do you know her? Or just know of her?'

'I know her. Well, I knew her. When I was here.'

'When you were Paris correspondent? Of course. You know she's back in the government again?'

That was exactly the kind of thing Martin would know, and it was something Lawrence should have had at his fingertips. He didn't have time to ask Martin how she came to be here, standing on his terrace, drinking his champagne, before Martin had wheeled him round to be presented.

The Sylvie Barroux he had first encountered fifteen years earlier had left Lawrence stumbling over his words, fumbling for the interview questions he had prepared with a dry throat and a teenage gaucheness; it was not going to be much different this time. She had scarcely aged. Her hair was a few shades lighter, more determinedly sprayed in place, but her skin was still taut and there were only the faintest wrinkles. French politicians seemed to have a far greater longevity than their British counterparts, surviving defeat and disgrace and returning. His excuse for interviewing her as often as he could was that she spoke flawless English with a smoky French accent, and that she was one of the few French ministers happy to talk to the British media. His colleagues back at the office, and Harriet, at home, would tease him about it, accuse him of flirting desperately with her. He protested, although it was true. The first time they met, they sat in two spindly, gilt-framed Louis Quinze chairs with white silk seats at the ministry, and Lawrence had struggled to keep his eyes looking into hers. She crossed one leg over the other and leaned in towards him as she answered his mumbled questions. Afterwards, her microphone removed, she touched a hand on his arm as she said goodbye and then swept out of the room, an entourage enfolding her. As he and the cameraman packed away the cables and the tapes, they exchanged glances.

'Wow,' said Jake, who could never resist training his lens on the most attractive woman in any shot.

'Amazing,' Lawrence agreed.

'But did you notice,' Jake continued, 'it was as if she only came alive for the camera. As soon as we stopped rolling . . .' He clicked his fingers. 'She was gone.'

Lawrence shrugged and handed Jake his own microphone cable back.

'We're not in her league.'

'Well, you know what they say,' Jake had begun, looking around to see if any of her entourage were still in the room, waiting to usher them out. 'They say that she and the President . . .'

'Really?' Lawrence's voice had been far louder than he meant it to be. An aide reappeared through the double doors, as if in response, and looked pointedly at her watch. 'Tell me later.'

When Lawrence had repeated the gossip to Harriet that evening, she had already heard it, from a parent at school who claimed to have seen the presidential motorcade pull up in a nearby street where Sylvie Barroux lived. Lawrence had never been sure whether the rumours were true or not.

Martin was already making the reintroduction.

'I want to introduce an old friend of mine, Lawrence Leith,' he began. Victoria and Sylvie did not look as though they wanted to be interrupted, though they were prepared to make an exception for their host. 'In fact, I believe you have actually met him before. Lawrence tells me he often interviewed you, Madame Barroux, several years ago.' Martin paused for a response. Receiving none, he carried on. 'Though of course neither of you look old enough for that to be true.'

There was a moment of forced, polite laughter. Sylvie stared at Lawrence and he felt just as gauche as he had all those years before. There was a long pause. Lawrence was about to start with the old standby question, to ask her how she knew Martin — it was something that he did, for once, want to know — when Sylvie's face cracked into a smile.

Sylvie stretched out her bouclé-clad arm and placed a hand on Lawrence's shoulder. She leant forward and kissed Lawrence on each cheek, adding a third kiss that he had not expected.

'We're in the south,' she said, explaining the extra kiss. 'How many years is it now?'

'Ten years,' Lawrence replied. 'Ten years since I left Paris.'

'You went to America,' Sylvie said. 'Is that right? Washington? Where do you live now?'

'Here,' he said.

'Here in France? You're back in Paris? Why have we not seen you?'

'No, here in the village, in Saint-Barthélemy.'

'You live here?' Sylvie seemed hardly able to believe this. 'All year?' Lawrence nodded. It hadn't even been a whole year yet, but the more he said that he was here permanently, the more he was able to believe it. He had been here when the summer visitors arrived, driving into town with their people-carriers and their fractious children, uncramping their legs from the long drive down the busy motorways. This year, he would still be there when they left again, when the school stationery would replace the barbecues and the swimming-pool toys in the supermarkets and everyone else would go back to work.

'And you?' Lawrence enquired.

'This is my district, my . . .' She was searching for the correct English word and Victoria supplied it for her.

'Constituency?'

'That's it, constituency.' If Lawrence had known, he had forgotten. 'And my family is from here. We have always lived here.' Once she mentioned it, Lawrence had a recollection that Sylvie's father had been a politician before her. He knew, from the photo spreads in *Paris Match*, that she was married to Michel Barroux, a flamboyant academic who Lawrence wrote off as a pontificating fraud, a man full of exaggerated hand gestures and an overdeveloped sense of his own cultural significance. He remembered seeing them pictured against the backdrop of some huge villa and thinking that it was easy to think grand thoughts about the future of modern capitalism if you had a house like that. Lawrence hoped that Michel Barroux wasn't here at the party.

Victoria suddenly seemed more interested in him, now that he was obviously on air-kissing terms with her French counterpart.

'I thought I hadn't seen you lately,' Victoria interrupted. 'On TV.' So she had known who he was. Or Martin had reminded her. Lawrence toyed with all the euphemisms that he usually gave people on occasions such as this: he took early retirement; he had decided he needed a change of scene; it was time to do something else.

'They decided my face didn't fit any more,' Lawrence replied. 'That it was time for someone newer, someone fresher.'

'But that's terrible!' Victoria exclaimed. 'You were really good.'

'Kind of you to say so.' Lawrence shrugged.

'It's a tough old business,' Victoria said, with a new sympathy.

'Not as tough as yours,' he replied. For the first time, her smile reached her eyes. Lawrence changed the subject. 'But, anyway, Madame Barroux—'

'Sylvie,' she insisted.

'How are things politically at the moment? Are you worried about the Front National, down here?' It might not have been the right subject for a polite drinks party, but Sylvie pounced on it nevertheless.

He nodded at all the right points as she spoke, but his attention was drifting away. Standing at the top of the steps that led down towards the pool was a woman he recognised from the village. 'The Parisienne', the bakery assistant had called her, behind her back, though Lawrence had privately nicknamed her Anna Karina. She had the same wide-set eyes as the New Wave star, though darker, and Lawrence had a kind of hopeless, distant crush on her. Trust Martin to know her already, to have been able to invite her to his house for drinks when he had barely arrived in the village.

Sylvie had excused herself to speak to someone else.

He wasn't sure whether it was the fact that he approached her when she was seemingly deep in thought, but 'Anna' almost jumped as he introduced himself. Lawrence held out an arm to steady her as she wobbled on the edge of the step. From a distance she always seemed calm, sure of herself. Closer to, there was an uncertainty. Her eyes darted from side to side, as though she was preoccupied. Perhaps she was just hoping to escape, looking for someone else to talk to. She wore a stiff white dress and her collarbones stood in relief against her chest. Her name, he discovered, was Isabelle.

'We can speak English, if that's easier,' she suggested. Lawrence was crestfallen. His French was perfectly good for most purposes, certainly good enough for social chat at a drinks party. Isabelle's English was perfect, her accent no different from his own.

'I should be speaking French,' he said apologetically.

'No,' she insisted. 'Please don't.' She was emphatic. 'I grew up speaking English and I don't get to speak it often enough. At work, sometimes. At home, almost never. So you have to correct me if I'm speaking like it's still the nineteen eighties.'

'Where are you from, then?' Lawrence would have put money on Isabelle being nothing but French. She rolled her eyes.

'How long have you got?' Her mother was British, she said, her father French, but she had grown up in Switzerland, as her father had worked for the United Nations in Geneva.

'International school,' she explained. 'Everyone was the child of a diplomat or a banker or something like that. It was like breathing thin air, like being at the top of a mountain. People lived in a very exclusive, rarefied world and they thought it was normal, that everyone lived like them.'

As far as he could see, she had not moved that far from the mountain-top world of her childhood. Here, behind the tall gates and screened by the hedges, were people who moved in the same circles even if they didn't live in the same countries.

'I've seen you in the village,' Lawrence said and instantly regretted it. It made him sound creepy. Perhaps he was. She was younger than him after all, in her late thirties at most. 'Are you staying near here?'

'We come every year,' she said. She sounded resigned to the habit, rather than delighted by it. 'Family tradition.'

'Visiting your parents?'

Isabelle shook her head.

'My husband's family.'

He should not have been so disappointed.

As if her husband had been listening for a mention of himself, he appeared from behind her and laid a proprietorial arm across her shoulders. That wasn't the only reason Lawrence took an instant dislike to him, but it was certainly the main one. He was too neat, too constrained. Everything about him was precise, from the parting in his dark hair to the creases of his beige trousers. Even his dark-pink polo shirt with its expensive logo was ironed as crisply as a uniform. Isabelle introduced him; Lawrence shook hands reluctantly with Christophe Vernet and carried on talking to his wife, asking her what she did.

'I'm a doctor. I trained in London, but we live in Paris. I travel a lot. I've been helping to run an NGO, a medical charity.'

Lawrence leaned in with unfeigned interest. At least this was the kind of thing he understood.

'So which area do you specialise in? Which part of the world are you going to be working in?'

She was an eye surgeon by training and she planned to set up mobile clinics; everything needed for the surgery would be transported to countries that didn't have facilities. She and other doctors like her would carry out the operations, training their colleagues in developing countries. They had started in Africa and were planning to expand.

Christophe seemed disengaged from what she was saying, contributing little. He had a bored air, as though he had heard this all too many times before. Sylvie swooped in and extracted him, with a perfunctory apology.

'There's such a demand,' Isabelle was saying. 'Such an unmet need. The thing we have to be careful about is getting too big, too quickly. It's really important that we know about the places where we're working.' Her hands and her face became more expressive as she warmed to her subject.

He was irritated when he felt someone else standing by his left shoulder, listening in on the conversation and waiting for their moment to break in. Isabelle had noticed him first and stepped aside slightly, allowing Martin to join them. Trust Martin to break in, just when he was starting to enjoy himself.

'Isabelle's been telling me about her charity . . .' Lawrence began.

'It's great, isn't it?' Of course, Martin already knew. He was always a step ahead. He had already met Isabelle, he already knew Sylvie. He turned up in the village where Lawrence had been living for months and was on good enough terms to throw a house-warming party.

He turned towards Isabelle as though a new idea had just struck him. 'You might not know,' he began, 'and Lawrence is probably too modest to tell you . . .' They exchanged glances – modesty was not something Lawrence used to be known for. 'But he is actually a very well-known journalist in the UK. Very eminent.'

'Well, perhaps I used to be. Not any more.'

Martin waved his hand as if to brush away Lawrence's protestations.

'He's spent a lot of time in the developing world, haven't you?'

Lawrence nodded his assent. That was certainly true, though there had been less of it in the last few years.

'And what are you doing now?' Isabelle asked. The question he hated and the one he would have to supply an answer to, for the second time in one evening. He was just trying to choose his formulation when Martin supplied one for him, ready-made.

'Lawrence has been taking a bit of time off for the last few months, enjoying the life down here.'

He was good, Lawrence thought. He had to credit him with that. It was what people paid him for, after all: coming up with neat phrases that glossed over the problems beneath.

'So you've got time – spare time?' Isabelle asked.

Lawrence shrugged. 'I suppose so.'

Isabelle and Martin exchanged a look.

'You could be just what I need, then.' Isabelle smiled at Lawrence. 'Isn't he?' This question was directed towards Martin. Martin ran his hand over the back of his scalp in a way Lawrence recognised, the way he did when he was coming up with a plan.

'I've been looking for someone to help me with a project,' Isabelle began. 'We have this medical agency, but there are so many agencies out there that it's hard to get our message out. We're quite new, and we're getting better known in the French-speaking countries but the English-speaking world is harder. We're looking for someone who could help us.' She inclined her head, waiting for him to volunteer his help.

'Help you to do what, exactly?'

'Someone who could communicate what it is we do, tell a story about it. Someone who people would listen to. We don't want a celebrity, we want someone serious.'

'Lawrence has got that,' Martin said. 'Gravitas. Authority. People trust him.' He turned towards Lawrence. 'What do you think?'

He was being bounced into something he had not expected.

'I'm sure you have the best intentions,' Lawrence said. 'But does it really help?'

Isabelle started to work on him, the way he imagined she worked on reluctant donors. She had the numbers, she offered him evidence. She didn't speak in platitudes, but about real people and how she had helped them.

'Come and see for yourself,' Isabelle concluded. 'Come to one of our Africa projects and see it, objectively, dispassionately. Say what you think.'

Beside her, Martin nodded.

'That would be good. That would be really strong. No pre-written script. Tell people what you see.'

'You're talking as though I've said yes,' Lawrence said. 'I haven't.' It was a tactic he had seen Martin use before: he assumed agreement and often got it, before the person he was asking had even noticed. He wasn't going to let that happen to him.

It was too late for Lawrence to start finding himself a cause. He had always mistrusted people with causes.

'I need another drink,' he said, holding his glass in Martin's direction. 'Before I can think about it.'

6

THE PEOPLE IN the village square seemed to be enjoying themselves without effort. Long-married couples were dancing together, cheek-to-cheek dancing with the correct steps. The cafe's tables were crowded, extra chairs spread out around the square. Martin spotted two people getting up to leave their table and he dashed for it. He sat in a wobbly chair and beckoned Lawrence to come and sit beside him. Whatever Lawrence's faults, he was someone it was easy to go for a drink with, he always had been. The evening up at the house had been hard work, harder than he had expected. He was relieved that the visitors had excused themselves early; he too had made his excuses and wandered down to the village with Lawrence.

The waitress, a striking young woman with a pierced nose and tattoos of roses on her arm, brought them a carafe of red wine. She knew Lawrence, patting him on the shoulder affectionately as she took his order.

'Cheers, neighbour,' he said. Martin smiled. Lawrence had been coming here long before it was fashionable. They had visited him once, years ago, in his tiny little place behind the fortifications, passing through on the way to the coast.

'To good neighbours,' Martin echoed, chinking his glass against Lawrence's.

'Just like old times,' Lawrence said.

'Except you'd have made a lot more fuss about the wine, in old times.'

'That's true,' Lawrence acknowledged, taking another swig of the rough-edged local red. The first time that Martin had travelled with Lawrence, he had been called aside by another producer in the office, a guy called Simon who was usually the first to the airport in any crisis. Martin had been checking his passport, the currency he had collected in its plastic envelope, the address of the hotel and the local TV station they would send their piece from. He thought he had it all covered.

'One thing before you go,' Simon had said. Martin waited for the important advice. 'Don't let Leith choose the wine. You'll be there all evening and you'll never get it back on expenses.' It had been good advice. Lawrence had been the more sophisticated of the two of them, the one who had lived in more countries than Martin could keep track of, who always had an anecdote or a piece of trivia to hand about wherever they found themselves. Lawrence was only the older by two years but it was as though he had lived far longer. Whichever city they arrived in, Lawrence not only had been there before but he knew where to find the best restaurants and what to order. Martin wasn't sure at which point the balance had started to tip in his direction. They had been through a lot together, it was true, but it was all a long time ago. It would be easy to leave it all back there, if it weren't for the occasional reminders.

'This place would have made a great location,' Martin said.

Lawrence nodded. 'We'd have started with the music,' he said. 'And the dancing feet. Then the couples' faces. The bunting. Nice opening sequence. Hardly even needs any words from me.'

'Always better that way,' Martin agreed.

'What's the story?' Lawrence asked and for a moment Martin forgot what the question meant.

'It could be anything,' he said at last. 'State of the nation. Generic France story.'

'Olly would have done it well,' Lawrence said, refilling Martin's glass.

'Olly always did it well,' Martin said. 'He was the best.'

They paused, thinking of their absent friend. The band on

the stage finished the song, the accordion drawing out one last long chord, and the dancers stopped to applaud. Martin put his glass down to join in the clapping.

'About Olly,' Martin began, as the band struck up the next song, allowing his words to travel no further than Lawrence. 'Did you get a letter?'

'Eventually,' Lawrence said. 'It took a while to get here. Harriet sent it on.'

'And?'

'I don't know. I feel as though I should. You got one too, then?'

It had been the last thing he needed. There was more than enough going on in his life and a request to give evidence at the International Criminal Court was an unnecessary complication. It wasn't even as though it was about Olly Dawson's actual case. Olly's death was incidental, as far as the lawyers were concerned. It was the kind of thing that happened in wars: innocent bystanders got killed. The case was about some of the other things that had happened, that probably happened in most wars there had ever been.

'Yes, I got one,' Martin said. 'I don't know either. I'm not sure how it would help, this long after the fact. I don't know how much I even remember. Not well enough to say in a court of law. It was a long time ago.'

'I remember it,' Lawrence said. 'There are plenty of things I've forgotten. There are whole cities, whole countries I've pretty much forgotten being in, but that place I remember. Even when I don't want to.' Martin noticed that he avoided even saying the name.

'Like this morning?' Martin asked.

'Like this morning. From what I gather, it's not so much about what we remember, it's more about what Olly filmed. The footage of the child soldiers. It's evidence.'

Martin drank some more of the wine.

'There are better ways to help. Isabelle was serious, you know,' he prompted. 'You are going to take her up on it, aren't you?' Lawrence was still seemingly insouciant.

'I'll think about it,' he said.

Lawrence had too much time to think about things. He seemed to have given up. He was only just fifty and he had plenty of good years left in him, if he chose to use them. The danger was that if he sat down here, watching the world go by, the world would just go by. There would be no way back for him. There were plenty more people out there, younger, keener, ready to hustle for what they wanted. Of course he felt bad for Lawrence after everything that had happened between him and Harriet, but he had to move on. He couldn't wallow in self-pity for ever.

'Say yes,' Martin insisted. 'Why would you not do it? We'll pay you for it.'

'We?' Lawrence queried.

'I'm working with her. Advising them.'

'Why does that not surprise me?' Lawrence asked. It was a rhetorical question and Martin let it go. Lawrence drew a packet of cigarettes and a lighter from the inside pocket of his jacket and lit a cigarette. He offered one to Martin.

'You're smoking again?'

'Just now and then. I know I shouldn't.' Lawrence looked like a schoolboy who'd been caught breaking the rules.

'Are you sure you want me?' Lawrence went on, 'For this charity thing, I mean?'

'I wouldn't ask you if I didn't mean it,' Martin said. There were plenty of other people he could have asked. 'But I need to be sure that you're committed to it. It would be a few weeks' work, that's all. It would be a good rate.'

'What if I can't remember how to do it?'

'Don't be silly. It's like riding a bike. You never forget.'

'And I don't know if I want to get back into all that.'

'All that what?'

'Human misery. I've had enough of human misery.'

'Well, unfortunately it goes on, regardless of you. And this time you'd be trying to do something to alleviate it, rather than just watching it. I'm sure that's what Olly would have said. Help the little kids, the people losing their sight, rather than chase some abstract idea of justice.'

'He wasn't one for abstract ideas, was he?'

Martin shook his head. 'Isabelle's amazing, you know,' he went on. This, at least, was something that they could agree on. Martin had noticed Lawrence's puppyish stare when he saw Isabelle, the way his eyes widened and he tried to stand taller, to pull his stomach in.

'Yes,' Lawrence agreed. 'It's a shame she's married to that awful man. At least, he looks awful.'

'Christophe?' Martin said. 'I know what you mean, but he's OK. You know he's Sylvie Barroux's brother?'

Lawrence shook his head. 'Small world,' he observed.

It was, Martin thought. At least it was, if you made it that way.

Martin felt the buzz of the BlackBerry in his pocket. He pulled it out, angling the screen so that Lawrence couldn't read it, tapped out a quick holding reply and then stowed it away again.

'Who calls you at this time of the evening?' Lawrence asked. 'It's the weekend and you're on holiday.'

'It doesn't stop,' Martin said. 'Just, you know, emails and so on.'

'You can relax now,' Lawrence said. 'You've got everything you could want, surely?'

'You'd think so, wouldn't you,' Martin said. 'Have you been talking to Iona? Because that's what she always says. But there's a lot going on. I'm trying to sell the company, for a start.' It would have been churlish to say it to Lawrence, but there was always more. The other thing about riding a bike was that you had to keep propelling yourself forward. Freewheeling didn't get you far enough.

'To whom?' Lawrence asked.

Martin shrugged. 'That all depends. You put it up for sale and get a whole load of advisers who go through the books and see who might want to buy it, who'll give you the best deal and the best price.'

'A bit like selling your house?' Lawrence offered.

'A bit,' Martin said. 'Except they're looking at the numbers rather than the state of the foundations.'

'So this time next year you could retire,' Lawrence suggested. 'Buy a bigger vineyard. Produce your own olive oil.'

'One day,' Martin said. 'Not yet, though.'

'The thing with you,' Lawrence began, pausing for another sip of wine, 'is that you wouldn't be content with that. Château Elliot would have to be the best, you'd have to win all the prizes, get it stocked by all the best wine merchants. Make it a brand. And you'd probably manage it, knowing you. You'd never be happy with it just being some kind of hobby.'

Lawrence still knew him quite well, he realised. He wouldn't be able to stop. He found it hard to understand how people switched off, even for a few weeks. There were so many people who said to him that life was too short, as though that was a reason to get less done. If life was short, then why waste it on views and flowers and the other things he was supposed to stop to enjoy? Life being short was all the more reason to get on with it.

'I've just got too much on my plate right now to think that far ahead. And that's why I can't get involved in – you know, legal cases. I have a duty to people. A duty of confidentiality to my clients. And a duty to get the best deal I can for my employees and investors. I have to be discreet, otherwise people can't trust me. They need to be able to tell me things, without thinking they're going to hear them somewhere else. I can't become the story.'

Lawrence, on the other hand, though he would never have admitted it, always wanted to be the story. You didn't spend half your life standing in front of the camera, telling people your version of events, if you didn't.

'What about you, though?' Martin asked. Lawrence usually liked talking about himself. 'Where do you go from here?'

'I'm not going anywhere,' Lawrence insisted. As he topped up both glasses, splashes of wine spilt onto the table.

'Your life, I mean. How are you going to occupy your time?' Lawrence shrugged, as though time would just occupy itself. Martin persisted. 'Have you met anyone, down here?'

'How do you mean?' Lawrence volleyed back, though Martin was certain that he knew perfectly well what he was suggesting.

'You know,' he said. 'A girlfriend. A companion. Whatever we're supposed to say, at our age.'

Lawrence shook his head and tapped ash into the ashtray. 'It's hard,' he said. 'Though I haven't made much of an effort in that direction. I mean, I wouldn't even know where to look. It's a small place. I thought when I left – when she chucked me out – that it would all be different, you know. I was with Harriet for twenty years. Two children. I thought I'd feel free, that I'd get to do whatever I wanted, but I found I was used to having them around. I miss them being with me, but I can't go back.' Lawrence scanned the crowd as though he might find a suitable partner there. 'At our age,' he continued, 'where do you start? At least when I was a student down here, everyone was my own age. Even then, it wasn't how I'd imagined it. I spent the afternoons in the cinema watching old films. I'd just sit, like I'm sitting now, in cafes, watching other people enjoy their lives.'

'That's not how I remember you,' Martin observed. Lawrence used to have a certain charm that he didn't hesitate to employ. Lawrence shrugged. 'You've got to start by meeting people. Then you'll meet other people. You know that. Like you say, it's a game you've been out of for twenty years.'

'Like riding a bike, you said just now.' Lawrence had recovered his composure and looked round. He helped himself to more wine, draining the last of the carafe. He held up the empty container as the waitress walked past and gestured for more. Martin tried to protest that he'd had enough, that he scarcely drank these days, but Lawrence ignored him. A full carafe was set before them.

'There's something . . .' Martin began. He hesitated for a moment. He shouldn't really be telling Lawrence, but he wanted to tell someone. There was something in him that wanted his opinion. The whole habit of discretion was getting too much; sometimes things spilled over. 'But it mustn't go any further.' Lawrence cast a glance around the square again.

'Where would it go?'

'Don't tell Harriet,' Martin said. He realised his voice was becoming too loud, even against the music. 'Especially not Harriet.' Lawrence used to be quick to spread rumours, especially ones that Martin had known to be untrue; sometimes he knew because he had started them himself.

'I don't tell Harriet anything,' Lawrence said. 'We don't speak much. We send each other emails, occasionally. About money or the children or both.'

'Or anyone you used to work with.'

'I don't hear much from them either. Unless they're looking for holiday destinations. And then when I tell them I only have the one spare room they lose interest pretty quickly.'

'Because if this gets out, it means it won't happen.'

'Go on, you've got to tell me now.'

'They've offered me a peerage.'

'A what?' Martin wasn't sure whether Lawrence hadn't heard what he said or whether he hadn't believed it.

'A lord. A member of the House of Lords. A peer of the realm.'

'I know what a lord is, thanks,' Lawrence said in a snappy tone. 'Seriously?'

Martin nodded. He found it hard to believe himself. What had started as a half-joking suggestion had become gradually more serious, turning from an offhand remark over lunch to an offer discussed at discreet meetings.

'Lord Elliot,' Lawrence sounded the title out, the way Martin had done himself, looking in the mirror while shaving. 'Lord Elliot of where?'

'I have a couple of ideas,' Martin said. 'Places I used to go on holiday, as a kid. Places near home. But I can't tell you, until the Queen says it's OK.'

'Really? The Queen?'

'Seriously. Because you have to go to this weird place and talk to some strange Dickensian characters about it and then you're sworn to secrecy unless and until the Queen approves the title.'

'What happens if you tell?'

'I didn't ask. The Tower, I expect.'

Lawrence seemed to be fumbling for the right questions to ask, the correct phraseology.

'And which kind of lord are you?'

'Just a life peer, you know. We don't really do hereditaries, these days.'

'Obviously. I meant are you cross-bench, opposition?'

'Government.'

Lawrence nearly spluttered on his wine. He wiped his mouth with the back of his hand. 'Since when? I mean, since when are you one of them?'

'I wouldn't have said I'm one of them, exactly. More that they're trying to reach out. They're trying to be inclusive, that's what they said. Non-partisan. Detoxify the brand.'

'And that's what you do. Detoxify brands.'

'Well, I try to avoid them getting toxic in the first place, if I can. But yes.'

'So what are you going to do, exactly? Wear robes and claim expenses?'

Lawrence was starting to get tiresome. He was asking the naive questions that he knew everyone would ask sooner or later, but Martin thought Lawrence would have had a better idea of how things worked. He must have met enough peers in his time, travelled around on enough junkets and pontificated to the world about how things ought to be run. Either he was feigning ignorance, to make some kind of point, or he really didn't know.

'It's a proper job, you know. There's no need to be so sarcastic. And it's not as if I haven't got enough to do already.' As if to prove his own point, he added, 'And they're giving me some sort of official role, though it's not finalised yet.'

'What does Lady Elliot think of all this?' That was a question that required a swig of red wine.

'Lady Elliot is not best pleased,' he confessed. 'And if you call her Lady Elliot, even as a joke, she'll take a swing at you.'

'Does Iona not like it, not even secretly?' Lawrence persisted. 'Not even for booking restaurant tables?'

'Iona's quite capable of getting a good restaurant booking in her own right already,' Martin said. She took enough art collectors out to dinner to make it well worth the restaurants' while. Martin hadn't thought of turning the title down for more than a few minutes. Why refuse an honour that said you had made it, you had succeeded, you belonged? It was something that no one could take away. Investments and everything else could go down as well as up, but a peerage held its value. Lawrence shared the last of the wine between them.

'Sorry,' he said. 'I should have said congratulations, straight away. Very rude of me. Here's to you, Lord Elliot.' Lawrence had those old-school manners that usually won out.

'I'm not, yet,' Martin said as he put the glass to his lips, suddenly superstitious. 'But thank you.'

The band was finishing. It was getting late. Martin had promised Iona he would come straight back to the house and he wasn't sure how much time had gone by. The sky was dark and the square only illuminated by a string of light bulbs fixed between the tree and the cafe. He drank down the wine and then stood to go. He would have to take the most direct route back; he'd be in enough trouble already. Lawrence stood up to say goodbye and they hugged each other close.

He watched Lawrence walk across the square, towards the

archway that led into the old town and his little house. Martin turned in the opposite direction and started to head down the narrow street, barely wide enough for a car to pass, that led out of the village and back towards the house on the hill. His house, he corrected himself. It was still hard to think of it as his house.

7

THE NORTH WIND was stirring the trees as he parked his dented Renault alongside a Range Rover and a four-wheel drive BMW. Lawrence didn't usually have much time for the local superstition that the mistral drove people crazy, made them behave unpredictably, but the phone call that had summoned him seemed to bear it out. He rounded the house to the shelter of the terrace and looked for Iona.

At the poolside, Maisie was wielding a huge pump-action water pistol; Finn was taunting her until she retaliated, catching him full in the face with a jet of water. Finn howled and ran to his mother, who perched on the edge of a sunlounger. There was another woman in the pool, in a blue swimsuit and red swimming cap, ploughing up and down in a smooth crawl that barely disturbed the surface of the water. It must have been Victoria.

Iona's legs were tucked under her as though she might need to spring up at any moment. She hugged Finn and ruffled his hair, but her voice was sharp.

'Stop whining, Finn. That's what happens if you annoy your sister.' Lawrence hung back for a moment. Finn turned towards him, tugging his swimming goggles up onto his head. The little boy glowered.

'It's that man from the village,' he said. 'Daddy's friend.'

Iona jumped up and came over to Lawrence.

'So he's not back yet?' Lawrence asked. She shook her head and moved away, tilting her head to show that Lawrence should follow. He remembered he was holding a packet of rice. He held it out towards her.

'Oh,' she said. 'It's not what I'd expected.' It was red rice from the Camargue. 'I'm sorry, I mean it's far too good for what I need it for.'

Lawrence shrugged. 'It's all I had. Do you want to tell me what's going on?' He had barely surfaced when Iona had rung, even though it was already around lunchtime. He'd been pottering around the kitchen, making coffee to clear his head. The anxiety in her voice had made him leave the coffee undrunk.

'Let's go inside,' Iona said, taking the packet from him.

She called across to Freya, who was lying on a lounger on the far side of the pool. Iona had to call several times before Freya pulled one white bud from her ear, raised the brim of her sunhat, and acknowledged her mother.

'Keep an eye on the twins!' Iona shouted. 'I'm going indoors.' Freya nodded and put her headphones back in. 'Victoria would save them, I hope,' Iona observed. 'Even at the cost of interrupting her hundreds of lengths. Trying to relive her glory days. Former national champion, apparently.'

They entered the kitchen through a pair of doors that stood ajar. Iona took a bright yellow bowl down from a shelf and poured in Lawrence's rice. Then she lifted a tea towel that was folded over something on the counter and picked it up delicately.

'What is it?' Lawrence asked. Iona showed him the BlackBerry swaddled in red-and-white gingham. The screen was grey and dead.

'Have you taken the battery out?' Lawrence had lost count of the number of phones he had ruined during his career. He was reading the last rites over this one, not confident of its survival.

Iona fiddled with the back of the machine until it came open and then prised the battery out. She wiped drops of water from the inside of the casing and buried the phone under the rice.

'Do you think it will work?' she asked. There was a hope in her eyes that Lawrence hated to dash.

'It's worth a try,' he said. 'You have to be patient. So this is why you can't call him. Do you want to tell me what happened?'

They went into the cool, parquet-floored living room. There was a large, white fireplace at the far end. Above the sofa where Iona sat down, Lawrence recognised a Patrick Caulfield print, a still life of wine bottles and polka-dotted red plates against a blue background of vines, an illustration of the life you hoped for in a house like this one.

'I threw it in the pool.' Iona didn't hedge around with her answers, once they came.

'Why?'

'When he got back last night, after he'd been out with you, he didn't seem to think he'd put anyone to any trouble, he just expected me to have done it all – fed the guests, put the children to bed, cleared up after the party. Instead of apologising, he started getting out his stupid machine and checking his emails and messages.' Iona stood up again, unable to settle. 'So I – well, I said some things I shouldn't have said, and it all got heated, and in the end I took his fucking BlackBerry and I chucked it in the deep end.'

'What sort of things?'

'That he was working too much, that he never switched off, that even holidays were work for him.' She paced the room, her bare feet slapping on the wooden floor. 'That I had to spend my time, even on holiday, entertaining his clients, his political mates, when he didn't spend enough time with the children as it was. And that . . .'

'And that what?' Lawrence prompted her.

'And that it's a bit odd that one of his new clients, contacts, whatever she is, is a stunning Frenchwoman who supposedly helps starving orphans.'

'Isabelle?'

'Oh, you noticed her too.'

Lawrence gave an apologetic shrug. 'I think they're blind people. And she's married.'

'Whatever. She's French. She wouldn't care.'

'What did he say to all this?'

Iona was in full spate, scarcely needing Lawrence's prompts. 'He said that his working so hard meant we had this house and this pool and a new car to get here with. He said he had to invite people here, because that's what oiled the wheels; it was the same here as in London. He owed people hospitality, he said. I told him that we earned plenty of money from the gallery when times were good and that I didn't feel the need to invite a bunch of art collectors to stay with us.'

'And so what happened after that?'

'He spent ages trying to fish the BlackBerry out of the pool with Finn's fishing net. He was about to dive in for it, fully dressed, but I yelled at him even more, told him not to be so stupid. He was drunk and clumsy. So you know how they say you're not supposed to go to bed on an argument?' Lawrence nodded. 'Well, we did. We weren't speaking, by then. When I woke up, he was gone.'

'I never managed to keep to that rule either, for what it's worth. What time was it that he left?'

'Finn woke me up. It must have been about half-past seven. I sent him downstairs to put a DVD on and I went back to sleep. I thought Martin was just somewhere in the house, but I think he must already have gone.' She was twisting her fingers together, clasping her hands and releasing them again.

'Would this help?' Lawrence asked, drawing out his packet of cigarettes.

'I really shouldn't,' Iona replied. She reached over and took one. 'But not in the house.'

She opened a pair of double doors giving onto the terrace. Lawrence squinted against the glare of the sun. Iona accepted a light and walked out, scanning the horizon.

'This isn't like him,' Iona said, as if to herself. 'He flares up. It blows over. He doesn't take it out on us like this.' That had been true of the old Martin, Lawrence thought. They'd argued often enough, but it never lasted.

'Where do you think he's gone?' he asked.

'The bike's gone. It was the first thing I looked for when I couldn't find him.'

'So, he's probably just gone on a long ride. Might do him good, clear the air.' Lawrence felt he had been dragged up there under false pretences. Iona seemed to think he bore some responsibility for Martin's behaviour, but he couldn't see how that was true.

'Not this long.'

'How long is normal?'

'A couple of hours, I suppose. Longer, sometimes. But not seven hours. You're better off asking Julian about the cycling . . . But don't say anything about last night. Though they must have heard,' she added. Lawrence nodded his agreement.

Julian was on the terrace beneath a sunshade, reading. Lawrence walked over to him. He splayed his book down on the table as Lawrence took a chair. A curly-haired blond boy of about three was playing at Julian's feet, running a plastic truck back and forth along the flagstones.

'Raffy, can you be quiet?' Julian asked his son, as the boy rammed his toy truck into the table-leg.

'Iona's a bit concerned about Martin,' Lawrence began. Julian nodded. 'When you and Martin go out for your bike rides, how far do you usually go? And for how long?'

'It depends,' Julian said. 'We're training for this London to Paris ride at the moment, so quite a long way. Three hours, maybe four. Martin's fitter than I am, though.'

'So seven hours – could he be out for seven hours? If he had a puncture or something?' He still imagined that Martin would arrive back any minute, wraparound shades on his head, sweat coursing down his back, the cleats of his cycling shoes clattering on the patio, downing water and acting as if nothing had happened.

'Not likely,' Julian replied. 'Though he always wants to push himself further. You know Martin. But this would be too far, even for him. Something must have happened.'

'Were you planning to go with him today?'

'I should have done. But I didn't fancy it this morning. Bit of a dusty head after last night, truth be told.' He took a long sip of water.

'Did he look for you? Knock on your door?'

Julian shook his head. Drops of sweat were standing out on his brow. There was a pale stripe across his forehead where his cycling helmet had shielded his skin from the sun; below the white was a redder stripe where no amount of sunblock had prevented the sunburn. The whole effect was to make Julian look like a wedge of Neapolitan ice cream that was beginning to melt.

'Not that I heard. Sleep of the dead.'

'And did you have a plan, a route mapped out ahead of time?'

'Martin might have. Basically, I went where he told me to go. We hadn't discussed it much. I know he wants to do the Ventoux, while he's here. I said I wasn't up to it. Even he said he'd leave it until the end of the holiday, until we'd done a few more hills.'

'You think he's gone up Mont Ventoux?'

'I don't think so. He was planning to do it once Victoria and I had left. I was pretty relieved, I have to say. In the heat there's been.' Julian lowered his voice. 'Are they OK?' he asked. Lawrence pulled a puzzled expression, as though he didn't know what Julian meant. 'Martin and Iona,' Julian continued. 'Is there more to this? I heard . . .'

He didn't have a chance to say what he had heard. Iona was bringing the twins indoors, against their protests. Victoria followed behind them, shaking her hair loose from the swimming cap. Maisie had her hands cupped together, concealing something inside. She brought it over to show Lawrence and Julian. Maisie lifted her top hand like a half-shell to reveal her treasure. As she did so, a creature leapt for freedom, a flash of red wings beneath a brown exterior. It landed on the table and then sprang away again, onto the flagstones where Raffy started to chase it away. Maisie looked crestfallen.

'It was a cricket,' she explained. 'I caught it but now it's escaped.' She chased after Raffy, who was searching the flower bed for the creature.

'When's Daddy back from his bike ride?' Finn demanded.

'Did you see Daddy this morning, Finn, when you got up?' Lawrence asked, trying to disguise the question as a casual enquiry.

The boy shook his head. 'I want to go for a bike ride too.'

Iona ushered the twins indoors.

'What do you think we should do?' she asked as he followed her inside.

'He's on his way back,' Lawrence said. 'I'm sure he'll be home, any minute now.' If he kept repeating it, he would believe it.

They climbed the curving wooden staircase and entered the bedroom, where the shutters were still closed. On a small table beneath the window was a handful of change and a set of keys. Iona stood over the table, inspecting what was there, trying to remember what had been there before, like Kim's game.

'He's taken his wallet,' she said. 'That's always here. And so's the phone, usually.'

'What would he have been wearing?' he asked. Iona crossed to the dark wooden armoire and opened the doors. One of the shelves held a neatly folded pile of cycling jerseys in bright colours, covered with names and logos, alongside a pile of Lycra shorts. She ran a hand down the pile of tops.

'I've no idea,' she said. 'He has so many. I couldn't tell you which one's gone.'

She stepped back and sank down onto the bed, propping her elbows on her knees and sinking her face into her hands. She began to cry. 'It's all my fault,' she sobbed.

'It's not your fault,' Lawrence reassured her. He sat down next to her and draped an arm around her shoulders. 'He'll be back, any moment. You'll have forgotten it all, by tomorrow.'

The repetition was still not helping Lawrence believe what he was saying. It would be just his luck for Martin to walk in now, as he was sitting on the white linen sheets of their unmade bed, his arm around Martin's tearful wife.

A fat drop of rain splashed into a heavy blot on the dusty windscreen. It was quickly followed by another. At first, Lawrence thought it was a passing shower, but the black-blue bruise of the clouds ahead told him otherwise. The windscreen wipers screeched across the glass. The whole car was protesting, struggling against the gradient, the gears grinding as he urged it further up the winding road. He changed down a gear to get the car around another hairpin bend. The peak of the Mont Ventoux always loomed over the landscape, its strange moonscape summit covered in white scree. He hadn't driven this road in years. Unlike Martin, he didn't believe that because a mountain was there was sufficient reason to ascend it, let alone on a bike. There were three routes to the top and Lawrence chose one of the hard ones, on the assumption that was what Martin would have done.

The weather closed in as he drove, the wind that gave the mountain its name growing stronger the further he went. There were few cyclists on the road; the change in the weather was enough to make anyone give up. According to Julian, it was too late in the day for anyone still to be attempting the ascent. All the same, Lawrence scrutinised each one he passed.

He had stopped briefly in the village of Malaucène, looking for Martin among the cyclists who were sitting in cafes, treating themselves to large helpings of carbohydrates washed down with cold beer. There were countless middle-aged men in Lycra and sunglasses; it was easy to dismiss the ones who sat together in large groups, the ones speaking German or Dutch. He wished that Martin didn't have the ability to fit in, to adjust his image so well. He saw shaven-headed, stringy men by the dozen, though never the right one. This whole cycling thing was a silly fad, as far as Lawrence could see, another way of pretending you weren't getting old.

If it were only down to him, he would have turned back. But

Martin might be out there somewhere and he had to keep looking. He didn't get to make the choice. As he turned another sharp bend, he saw the flashing light of a police motorbike. An officer was pulling a red metal barrier down across the road. A sign said the route to the summit was closed. Lawrence pulled up and lowered the window, the rain slanting in, and shouted out to the gendarme, asking him whether there had been an accident on the road ahead. The officer shook his head but ignored the further questions that Lawrence asked. He waggled a black-gloved finger at Lawrence and indicated that he should head back down the hill. Lawrence turned the car around, crunching the gears and nudging into the verge.

He hated returning without having found Martin. The thought of having missed him, left him on the road, awoke troubling memories.

When he saw Iona, he spread out his hands in apology and shook his head.

'No sign,' he said.

Outside the kitchen, Julian was lighting the charcoal on a barbecue, watching the flames flare up and then die down. The rain had evaporated from the paving stones but the earth smelt damp and the air was clearer.

'I don't know what to do,' Iona said. She repeated it as they walked towards the house, under her breath.

Victoria emerged from the patio doors with two mugs on a tray; she handed one to Iona and they sat down.

'We should start making some calls,' Lawrence volunteered. 'Report him missing. Ask if there have been any accidents.' Disasters were his area of expertise. He knew the stages to be gone through: call the police, call the hospitals.

'What else can we do?' Victoria asked. She took naturally to the role of chairing a meeting.

Lawrence found his reporter's instincts sputtering into life again, like an old car that took a few goes to start.

'We need to talk to the other people he knows, the people

who were here last night. The locals – well, the Parisians. In case they've seen him. Or in case they know which strings to pull around here, who to ask for favours. Victoria – do you know how to get hold of Sylvie Barroux?'

'Not directly. I mean, I could through the office, but this isn't official.'

Julian turned away from the barbecue to face them.

'You don't think . . .' he began, before pausing again.

'We don't think what?' Iona asked.

'Nothing.' Julian turned his back again and made a play of poking at the coals.

'Say what you were going to say,' insisted Victoria. Julian looked towards them reluctantly, wiping his hands on a blue apron.

'I mean, don't take this the wrong way, Iona, but is it possible he's just . . . gone?'

'Gone how?' Iona asked. Lawrence was glad that she put down her mug of tea, otherwise he feared she might throw it at Julian.

'Left,' he explained. 'Run off. Done a disappearing act.'

Iona's eyes narrowed behind the heavy black frames of her glasses.

'What makes you say that?'

He put his hands up in a gesture of surrender.

'Nothing.' He turned towards his wife. 'I shouldn't have said anything.' Victoria shook her head, a tiny gesture she must have hoped wouldn't be seen, suggesting that he should not.

'Is there any reason you think that?' Iona repeated, her voice slow with suppressed anger.

'No,' he insisted. 'Nothing. It's just – you know – men, midlife crisis. Sometimes they do stupid things. Sometimes they do things you don't expect.'

'Because if there is anything you know,' Iona said, 'and that I don't, you'd better tell me now.' She clutched her mug of tea again.

Victoria intervened.

'I really don't think there could be. But is it the kind of thing he might do? In anger, maybe? Just walk out? Not want to be found?' It was her way of saying that she had overheard the argument.

Iona thought about this for a moment before replying.

'It's not like him. We had a row, it's true, but we often have rows. If he were going, he would say that he was going. He would – I don't know – have someone call him a cab. Not pretend to go off on a bike. He would tell me. He doesn't hide from things.' She looked to Lawrence for reassurance. 'Don't you think?'

'It's true. Martin tells you what he thinks. He always tells you.'

He found himself delegated to make the calls. He had the best French, Victoria observed, wrapping the work up in a compliment. It was a frustrating task; offices were closed, phones went unanswered. If there was a good time to try to deal with French officials, an early evening in the middle of August was certainly not it. Most of the contacts he needed would have been in Martin's defunct BlackBerry. Lawrence tried another number that rang out and he cursed Martin again as he waited in vain for a reply. He borrowed an iPad from Julian and started searching further. The more he dug, the less it seemed to be about Martin. It became about the search itself, the story, the long-neglected need to find things out.

Lawrence sat at the head of the table, among Martin's family and his guests, wearing his friend's expensive sweater. It was a fine grey cashmere jumper that Iona had insisted he borrow when she noticed that he was shivering. He was trying, as Martin would have done, to keep the conversation going. He forced a laugh as Victoria told a story of something amusing her son, Rafferty, had said while touring the Roman ruins that afternoon. He feigned interest in Julian's chatter about his barbecue marinade and how he hoped to create a new product line. Martin's absence was not mentioned once they sat down to eat.

Freya laid a half-eaten chicken drumstick down on her plate. She finished chewing her mouthful and looked around the table.

'Can we stop all this?' Freya declared.

'Stop what, darling?' Iona asked.

'All this pretending. We're all pretending that nothing has happened, that it's all going to be fine. We don't know that. None of us know that. None of us know anything.'

Iona tried to hush her, stretching an arm across the table in her daughter's direction. Freya ignored her. 'Martin might be dead, for all we know.'

Iona shook her head, pointed at the twins. Maisie, next to Freya, was starting to look more interested in what was going on.

'Don't say that, Freya. I don't want them to hear you say that.'

'But it's true.' She lowered her voice only slightly. 'He might have been hit by a lorry. Anything might have happened. And no one's doing anything about it.'

'That's not fair,' Iona said. 'We're trying. Lawrence is trying. He spent all afternoon—'

'Well, he's the only one,' Freya interrupted. 'And he's not getting very far, from what I can see. It's as if you don't care. He's not even my real dad and I'm the only one who seems to care.'

She shoved back her chair and left the table, running into the house. Her pink flip-flops smacked against the flagstones and she wiped the sleeve of her hoodie across her face. Iona shook her head in exasperation and got up to follow her.

Lawrence turned towards Victoria.

'We're going to need your help,' he said. 'You're someone who can get things done.'

'Doing what?' Victoria asked.

'There are strings that you can pull and we can't,' Lawrence said. 'We'll go to the police in the morning, I'll call the consulate again, but you can go further up the food chain. Get on to the Foreign Office. If the call comes from you, they'll do something about it. You know the right people. You've got influence. Use it.'

Victoria had a distant expression, the air of someone calculating a set of possible outcomes.

'I'm not sure it will make anything happen any faster,' she said.

'It will. Of course it will. You tell them who Martin is, and you impress on them that we need help urgently. You need to tell them how important he is.'

'You mean the business?'

'I don't just mean the business. I mean the peerage. I mean that he's going to be working for the government. He's practically one of your colleagues.'

Victoria's jaw dropped slightly, her mouth opening to show her large, bright teeth.

'How do you know about that? You're not supposed to know about that.'

'Martin told me. Last night. He'd had a bit to drink and he swore me to secrecy. Don't worry, I'm not going to put it in the public domain. But it doesn't mean you can't use it to put pressure on a few diplomats.' She nodded slightly, not enough to convince Lawrence that she would do as he had said. 'Think of it this way,' he continued. 'It's potentially a lot worse if you don't. Say something really bad has happened to him and the word gets out that you did nothing. And word will get out . . .' He paused long enough to let his implication sink in. 'The story would be that you just sat here, staying in his house, drinking his wine, and you didn't help him when you could have. Think how that would look.'

It was the old test, Lawrence thought. Not whether you would do the right thing, but how it would look if it got into the papers. Lawrence didn't care whether it was the correct thing to do, according to some bureaucrat or book of procedure. He cared that Martin was found. Victoria was a woman who had seemed, so far, to glide through life from one success to another: public school to university; the City to politics. She did not know, Lawrence imagined, what it was like to leave a friend behind when it really mattered, for it all to go wrong, beyond repair or redemption. He hoped she would never have to know.

'OK,' Victoria said. She looked at her watch, an expensive sliver of brushed steel and gold, as if to say it was too late to call people. It wasn't. These people called and texted each other all the time, even on holiday.

'What about Patrick?' Lawrence prompted.

'Which Patrick?' she said. He wondered how many Patricks she knew.

'Patrick Chambers. He's one of yours, isn't he? I mean, someone you're on good terms with.'

While he was looking for other contact numbers, Lawrence hadn't been above running a couple of quick searches for Victoria's name. That of Patrick Chambers often seemed to be mentioned in the same articles. He'd worked alongside Victoria in opposition, another adviser who had become a minister, in his case in the Foreign Office. He seemed often to be quoted as saying that Victoria was one to watch, a rising star. She returned the compliment. They were clearly political allies; Lawrence wondered idly whether there was any more to it than that.

'Patrick's a friend, yes.' She raised an eyebrow.

'Then call Patrick. A word from him to the embassy, the consulate in Marseille would help. Even a word from someone who says the word comes from him.' Lawrence lowered his voice so that the children would not hear.

'He's been gone for twelve hours. It's starting to be a long time. Too long.'

8

THEY WERE OUTSIDE the Gendarmerie Nationale, housed in a modern concrete block at the edge of the town, as soon as it opened in the morning. The young police officer who took Martin's details was polite and apologetic, commiserating with Iona but saying that there was little he would be able to do. It had been twenty-four hours, they insisted, assuming that the length of time he'd been gone would worry the officer.

'*Je suis désolé*,' he shrugged, in a way that Lawrence recognised to mean not that he was genuinely upset but merely stating the rules. He wasn't sure whether to address Lawrence or Iona and his gaze flicked between the two of them. Lawrence shifted uncomfortably in his plastic chair. He translated for Iona.

'He says that since Martin is an adult there's not much they can do, unless we suspect that he has been the victim of a crime, or unless there's anything physically or mentally wrong with him. Which we don't think, do we?'

'I'm not sure I know, any more,' Iona said. Behind her glasses, her eyes were red. Without make-up, her pale eyelashes almost disappeared against her face. She obviously hadn't slept much.

Without meaning to, Lawrence told the officer that Martin and his wife had argued the night before his disappearance. The policeman had given him a knowing shrug and raised one eyebrow, as if to ask whether Lawrence had been the cause of the argument.

'Ask him if they're actually going to look for him,' Iona urged. 'And check the hospitals, check any other reports.'

Lawrence put her question into French.

'He says they'll check if any reports come in.' Lawrence paused. 'But no, it doesn't sound like they'll actively do much to find him. He's not a priority case. It's down to us, I think.'

Lawrence slid a picture of Martin across the desk. It was from his company website and showed Martin in three-quarter profile, arms folded, the confident face of a man you could trust with your crises. The gendarme put the picture on a pile with his other papers, scarcely looking at it.

As they returned to the waiting room, Maisie and Finn looked up expectantly, as though their father would have been found at the police station, like a lost toy. Their faces were cast down again when Lawrence and Iona appeared without him.

Lawrence walked with them to the cafe where Iona had promised the children breakfast. They pushed their way through slow, market-day crowds. On a normal day, they would have stopped to admire the tables with the warm reds and browns of spices arrayed in sacks, bunches of lavender and packets of herbs. One stall was heaped with green cantaloupes, a couple of them cut open like gaping mouths to reveal the orange flesh inside. The stallholder held a cube of melon out to Finn on the point of a pocket-knife and Finn tasted it, licking the juice from his lips. Iona tugged him away as he tried to insist they should buy some.

Lawrence checked his watch. He'd dug it out of a drawer that morning, because time seemed to matter again. He envied the locals who had time to stop and exchange gossip in the street while the crowd eddied around them. Tourists shuffled and ambled, pointed and took photographs; cyclists nudged their bikes through the throng, their bright shirts stretched taut. Each time he saw one he couldn't help but look up in expectation. He gauged their height, their build, their hair. He recalled the description they had given the police: forty-eight years old; 180 centimetres tall; slim; dark hair shaved back to the scalp; brown eyes. He grasped at the hope that a cyclist matching it would turn towards them, raising a hand in greeting and charming them into believing his excuses.

He announced his arrival into the entryphone, a gimlet-eyed camera inspecting him. The name Barroux on the letterbox was printed so small that you would have to strain to read it. Nothing else he'd tried had worked: late-night calls to a number for one of Sylvie's former aides that he'd found in an old contacts book; calls to her local office. Lawrence was grateful for the new technology that had allowed him to unearth an address but sometimes nothing but the old method, the foot jammed in the door, would work.

He detected surprise in the crackly, answering voice but the white gates ground open. The gravel drive beyond led past a smooth lawn up to a low, green-plastered villa. Most of its shutters were pulled closed. Lawrence climbed a small flight of stone stairs to the terrace that ran around the house.

He found them there, still at breakfast, sitting in the shade. Sylvie was at the head of the table, Isabelle to one side, Christophe opposite her.

'I'm sorry to disturb you,' Lawrence said as he approached. Christophe stood up to shake hands with cold formality. 'It's about Martin Elliot. He's gone missing.'

Sylvie raised her eyebrows in surprise and indicated that he should sit down.

'We have searched for him,' Lawrence continued, his words rushing in to fill the others' silence. 'We've just been to report him missing to the police, but they say they can't do much. We wondered if there was anything you could do to help.'

Sylvie paused before answering. 'What can I do?' she asked. Her inflection made the question hard to interpret. He wasn't sure whether Sylvie meant it as an expression of powerlessness or as an offer of assistance. In any case, Lawrence had been hoping she would volunteer something that she could offer, rather than expect him to supply the answer. Flatter her, he reminded himself. Appeal to her sense of importance.

'Well, as the *conseiller* for this district, I know you must have excellent relationships with the authorities. I'm sure everyone concerned will be doing an outstanding job, but they must be very busy at this time of year, with all the tourists.' Sylvie nodded her head slightly, agreeing that this was the case. 'Perhaps if you could speak to a few people – in the police, maybe, or in the emergency services – we could be sure that they were aware of the importance of Martin's case.'

Sylvie nodded again. She understood perfectly well what he was asking, even though he was putting it in a more diplomatic way than he had with Victoria.

Christophe stared at Lawrence from across the table.

'Do you think there's anything suspicious about his disappearance?'

'I can't imagine why there would be,' Lawrence replied. He had lain awake the night before, conjuring up disgruntled clients, creditors, people whose reputations Martin had not been able to salvage. None of the stories he told himself rang true.

'There's nothing the police can do, if an adult's gone missing,' Christophe continued. 'Unless you have reason to believe there's something more to it. Here in France, that's how it is. You might not understand that.'

'I do understand that,' Lawrence said. 'I know how it works. But I also know that he's my friend and that his family is worried sick about him.' Lawrence also knew that the way things worked officially was not the same way they worked in practice. Christophe must have known that too.

'I will speak to some contacts,' Sylvie said.

'When did you say you last saw him?' Isabelle spoke for the first time. She was sipping espresso from a white china cup, as straight-backed as the wrought-iron chair she sat on. All three of them seemed strangely calm, despite Lawrence's interruption and the news about Martin.

'I haven't seen him since Sunday night. We had a drink together in the village, after the party. But he went home after that. He had – he spoke to his wife. Then she says he left early in the morning to ride his bike and no one has seen him since.'

Isabelle was holding her coffee cup in her right hand; her other hand was clasped around her thin bicep, as though she was protecting herself.

'And he's not answering his phone?' she asked.

'He didn't have his phone with him.' Isabelle raised an eyebrow.

'I'm sure this kind of thing happens often,' Christophe said. 'Particularly at this time of year, with so many tourists around. People aren't used to the heat, the roads.'

'He's not just a tourist,' Lawrence protested. 'He has a house here. He's a friend of yours. He invited you to his house.'

'Of course,' Christophe said. 'It used to be our house, in fact. But as far as the authorities are concerned, that doesn't change anything.' Sylvie shot her brother a look, as if there was something he needed to add. Christophe nodded. 'And, of course, we're anxious that there shouldn't be any publicity. Concerning us, I mean.'

'We might need there to be publicity,' Lawrence said. He hadn't yet considered putting the word out that way, but he could see that it might come to that. 'We might need to appeal for information.'

'As a family, we like to keep things private.'

Lawrence looked over towards Sylvie, addressing his comments to her. 'But you're a public figure,' he protested. 'You're very well known.'

'That's public life,' Sylvie said. 'Which is different. Private life is another matter. We don't want any intrusion. We have a right to our privacy.'

He felt more unwelcome than ever. Their politeness didn't extend to offering him a cup of coffee, not even a glass of water to ease his throat and make the silences less awkward.

'I'll do what I need to do, to make sure Martin is found,'

Lawrence declared. 'At this stage, I can't see why we would need to mention you.'

Lawrence had the feeling that the interview was over. He looked at Sylvie again, then across to Isabelle.

'I'll leave you my number. In case you hear anything that might be useful. Martin's family are very distressed.'

'I'm sure they are,' Sylvie replied. 'Of course, leave us your details.' She looked around the table as though some way of taking down Lawrence's number would present itself, but saw nothing.

Isabelle stood up. 'Come with me,' she instructed Lawrence.

He followed her into the shade of the house, into a fussy room, full of ornaments, whose decor had evidently not changed in decades. She found a notepad and a pen on a side table and handed them to him.

'I didn't know it had been your family's house,' Lawrence said as he scribbled down his number.

'I shouldn't say this,' Isabelle replied, 'but I was glad when they took on that house. It belonged to my mother-in-law and it used to be like this.' Isabelle indicated the room they were in. 'Full of dust and trinkets. She was a nasty, bitter woman, even though she had little to be bitter about. When she died all the bitterness seemed to pass on to the children, Sylvie and Christophe and the others, all the husbands and wives. So they all fell out with each other about who should inherit it. It all became too complicated. It was the best thing, to sell it. People here still complain that it's been sold to an outsider, but I think that's the best way.' She paused for a moment. 'But that's just between us, OK?'

She took the pad from Lawrence, ripped off the top sheet and started to write a number down. 'I need to know what has happened to Martin, once you find out.'

'Is this to do with your project, with the fundraising, the film? Because I'm sure he'll be back in touch about it, as soon as he can. And if not . . .' Lawrence corrected himself. 'I'm sure there are colleagues of Martin's who are well briefed on it, who'll be able to work with you.' Lawrence wasn't entirely sure how these things worked, but he found himself wanting to reassure her.

'It's partly that,' she said, handing him the piece of paper with her number on it. 'But also that I want to know he's all right.' She started to usher Lawrence back out of the room. In the hearing of the others, she continued, as though she was carrying on a previous sentence. 'So we're here for another few days. And if not, you can reach us in Paris.' She held out a hand for Lawrence to shake. He took it, noticing that they all seemed to have reverted to formality, even though they had been friendlier at Martin's party. Perhaps it was the effect that Martin's absence had on people; he brought them together and when he was not there, they broke apart again. He turned to go.

'Many thanks, again,' he said. 'And I'll look forward to hearing from you, if you have any news.'

There was a muted chorus of goodbyes behind him. Lawrence left, the gravel of the drive crunching beneath his desert boots, with little expectation that he would hear anything from them at all.

9

THE BUZZING WAS loud and it seemed to surround him, as though a swarm of bees was circling his head. It was continuous, a hum with a mechanical, metallic tone to it. His eyelids were heavy and resistant but he managed to crack them open. He couldn't see anything. There was something close to his face, a white wall.

Then the knocking started. It sent vibrations through his whole body. He wanted it to stop, wanted the rhythmical, repetitive hammering to end. Like a bad dream, none of it made sense.

There was shouting, words directed at him that he didn't understand. He felt something hot and painful course into the back of his hand. Then he wasn't able to open his eyes any longer and all he saw was the glow of lights burnt onto the insides of his eyelids, dark circles and paler stripes of light that began to fade.

He found himself in a room that he did not recognise, a room with a window that was screened by a white blind. He was in a bed with a thin blanket over his legs and wearing what he realised was a hospital gown. His left wrist was in a cast, a sling holding the arm in place, and there was a cannula in his right hand, connected to a drip that hung above him in a plastic bag.

His head was groggy and his thoughts slow, memories surfacing briefly, like fish in a murky pond, only to disappear beneath the surface again. He tried to capture a thought as it rose, like one of the fish, swiping at it clumsily, but it escaped him. All he could think clearly at that minute was that his legs itched and that he could not reach down to his shins to scratch them. He tried to kick the blanket and the sheet away, wriggle his legs free of their constriction.

His legs didn't look like his own. His own legs were muscular, tanned from days out on the bike. These legs seemed thinner and paler, covered in grazes and bruises like Finn's. The left shin had long, livid scratches across it, stains of yellow iodine spreading around the cuts. Someone had shaved patches of his leg in order to clean the wounds. He couldn't see much of his right leg; it was wrapped in gauze with an oblong pad of dressing beneath, a yellowish-red patch beginning to spread onto the dressing from whatever was seeping out of his leg. At least he could move them. He lay back on the pillows. Even this small effort exhausted him. It was an unwelcome, unfamiliar sensation, that of being so deeply tired. His first instinct was to get up and leave, to go home, but he could not see how that would be possible.

He tried to concentrate again, to remember how he had come to be here. It must have been the bike, but what had happened was blurry. The last thing he remembered was the force of the wind on the mountain buffeting him, his efforts to keep the bike under control. He'd tried to pull himself back on course, to keep going uphill. He remembered that his arm on the brake lever had not done what he told it to. The fingers of his right hand were alternately numb and tingling, a dart of intermittent pain shooting down from his elbow to his fingertips. It was as though he had forgotten how to ride his bike, something he had known since he was six years old, something you never forgot. He closed his eyes and resolved to put his mind to it when he felt stronger.

He woke at the sound of the door opening and two women entering. One had dark hair, tied back from her face, cat's-eye-shaped glasses over dark eyes, olive skin. His eyes still felt puffy and it took a while for him to see distinctly. It was Isabelle. He was sure that it was Isabelle, even though he had never seen

70

Isabelle wear glasses. He smiled at her, though, the way Isabelle always made him smile. He was happy to see her. She would be able to explain it all to him. She smiled back; she must have been happy to see him too.

He patted the edge of the bed with his plastered hand, indicating that she should come and sit down. Isabelle did not sit down, though, nor did she come over to touch him. Martin wanted her to be close, wanted at the very least a kiss on the forehead, a stroke on the arm, a hand on his head. He would have wanted her to hug him, wrap him in those thin, taut arms, but he felt too fragile for that. Instead, she walked to the end of the bed and picked up a folder. She said something in French that he didn't understand. Sometimes she did that. She forgot which language she was speaking, said something to him in French by mistake. When he asked what she had said, she would clasp her hand over her mouth, apologise, and switch to English. He waited, but the switch to English did not come.

'*Bonjour, monsieur,*' she said. He managed a weak '*Bonjour*' in return.

'*Monsieur?*' she repeated, with an upward inflection, a question implied. He wasn't sure what answer he was supposed to supply. Why was she speaking to him like this? He studied Isabelle more closely.

It wasn't her. The woman spoke to him again, more slowly.

'*Vous êtes Monsieur . . .? Votre nom?*' This much he understood.

'Martin,' he replied.

'*Monsieur Martin,*' she repeated, taking a pen out of a pocket and writing his name down on one of her forms. Martin didn't have the strength to correct her. Monsieur Martin would do for now.

The doctor, who could have been Isabelle, looked like Isabelle, but was not her, watched while the nurse began checking him over. She attached a plastic clip to his finger and watched numbers flash on a machine nearby, then noted them down. The numbers seemed to meet with her approval. Next, she attached a blood-pressure cuff to his upper arm. Martin winced as she inflated it, tried to clench his hand against the pain. The more awake he was, the more pain he felt in his shoulder and chest. He saw the doctor wince as well, as if in sympathy, but he realised that her grimace was directed towards the numbers on the screen. He tried to relax his arm again, hoping that being less tense would make the glowing red numbers click downwards, but it was too late for that.

The nurse started to speak to him, chattering away as she made her observations, and once more he didn't understand what she was saying. Something was very elevated, he made out. His blood pressure, he assumed. He shook his head, trying to indicate that he didn't speak enough French to follow.

'*Anglais?*' The words came slowly. '*Vous parlez anglais? S'il vous plaît?*' The nurse did not reply.

'A little,' the doctor answered. 'You have had an accident,' she continued, her English careful and correct. 'As you see, you have a fracture of the wrist, also of the . . .' She paused, searching for the right word. '*Clavicule?*'

She pointed a finger towards the base of his neck, not touching the skin.

'The collarbone,' he volunteered.

'Yes.'

'I need to go home,' Martin said. It suddenly seemed the most urgent thing. The doctor made a calming gesture with her hands, as though she was soothing an impatient child.

'Not yet,' she said. 'Do you remember it, the accident?' she asked.

'I was on my bike,' he ventured. She nodded and waited for him to continue. 'I remember the wind on the mountain and my arm – I couldn't control it, or the bike.'

'And then?' she prompted.

Another tiny moment came back to him, like a short clip of a film. He saw his front tyre on the white limestone scree at the side of the road, felt the bike tipping over the edge onto the hillside below. There had been blurry flashes of green and grey and blue, trees and rock and sky, as he tumbled over.

'I went off the edge of the road.'

'Was there a car, something like that?'

Martin tried to shrug but the action sent a shooting pain through his shoulder. That came back to him too; his shoulder landing on sharp stone, his head striking something hard. The doctor indicated his head.

'It's good that you were wearing your . . .' She hesitated again.

'Helmet?'

'That's it, helmet. If not . . .' She shrugged and left the sentence unfinished, in either language.

'We need to do some more tests,' she said, folding the medical notes away and replacing them at the foot of the bed. Martin opened his mouth to protest, to ask all the questions he needed answered, but the right words didn't come.

'You need to rest,' Isabelle's doppelgänger instructed in the same strict voice that Isabelle herself used with him, telling him why things would not happen the way he wanted them to.

She left the room and closed the door behind her. He hadn't managed to ask where he was, or if anyone knew he was here. There were people who needed him, things he had to do. He fumbled, trying to reach the table at the bedside, hoping to find his phone there. Another thought floated up to the surface and he glimpsed a black gadget sinking through blue water, against the light that illuminated the pool. He remembered what had happened to his phone.

10

DR ARNAUD STOOD in the ward with her arms folded, reluctant to allow them any further. The patient was tired, she protested, needed to rest. In any case, if they were not sure that this man was their relative, it would be unorthodox to allow them to visit him. It was one of those bureaucratic paradoxes that Lawrence had come across often enough before. Surely the only way of finding out, Lawrence argued, was to see the patient.

Lawrence half expected the Mr Martin, unfortunate victim of a bicycle accident, found in an Avignon hospital with no identification, but speaking English, to be someone else. The message from the consulate had been apologetic in its uncertainty, as though they didn't want to get Iona's hopes up. Whatever Victoria had said to them seemed to have made some difference; there had been regular calls from junior officials at the British Embassy over the last two days that gave little information, though with the politest of manners.

'We could send someone with you,' the woman at the consulate had offered. 'If that would help?' Iona and Lawrence said that it would not be necessary. As the doctor obstructed them, Lawrence wished they had accepted the offer.

They had heard nothing from Sylvie.

Dr Arnaud inspected the picture that Iona handed to her and gave it back again, saying only that it could be him. She disappeared into the room.

'How bad do you think he is?' Iona whispered to Lawrence.

'At least if it's him, you'll have him back. Even if not quite in one piece,' he replied.

The door cracked open again.

'He says that is the correct name,' the doctor said, holding the door open.

Martin did not, it had to be said, look much like his picture. His face was pale except where the bruises and the grazes showed. His eyelids were swollen and half-closed, the bruises around his eyes aubergine-purple, with dark, almost black shadows beneath his eye sockets. It would have been hard to recognise him with only the picture to go on; the knowing half-smile and the confident raised eyebrow had gone. Ragged grey-black stubble had sprouted across his scalp; around his chin and jaw it revealed patches of grey at the corners of his mouth. He looked old. All that work, all that effort to stay young, and one accident could overturn it in a minute.

Iona rushed up to the bed and sat down on the edge of the mattress, taking care to avoid Martin's bandaged legs.

'Look at you!' she exclaimed. It was the kind of thing you said to a child, one with grazed knees or a dirty face. Lawrence hung back; although Martin acknowledged him briefly, a quick flicker of a gaze, he felt awkward. He needed to leave the two of them together.

As he turned to leave the room, he asked Dr Arnaud what had happened.

'He was found by another cyclist, on the road up to the Mont Ventoux. He had come off his bicycle and somehow fallen off the road and onto the mountainside. The cyclist who found him luckily saw some debris on the road; some sunglasses, a water bottle. Then he spotted him and called the *pompiers*. The ambulancemen told us it was hard work to get him. He'd fallen a long way down and it was a steep slope.'

'He was lucky, then.'

The doctor gave Lawrence a quizzical look, as though he had chosen the wrong word. They stepped out into the corridor.

'Well, in some ways, I suppose. He was lucky to be found in time.'

'How long was he on the mountain?'

'We don't know. They brought him here on Monday evening, I think. He came in the air ambulance. I saw him first on Tuesday morning, when I came in for my shift.'

'And what condition is he in?'

The doctor pulled herself up short, realising that she was perhaps telling him too much. There was something about Dr Arnaud that reminded him of Isabelle, that same slightly formal manner and the sense that she was holding herself back.

'Are you a member of the family?'

'I'm a close friend of the family,' Lawrence said. 'And the only one who speaks reasonable French.' She seemed reassured, and continued.

'I'll need to explain this to his wife,' she said. 'You'll have to help me with that, because my English isn't good enough. The broken bones will heal, it's mostly a matter of time, though one of my colleagues thinks he might need surgery to fix his collarbone. But what worries me more is what caused the accident.'

'In what way?' Lawrence asked.

'He doesn't remember what happened, except that he was trying to get to the top of the mountain. Was he fit, before the accident?'

'Very fit,' Lawrence said. 'He exercised regularly, hardly drank, he's not overweight. He looked after himself.'

'Because we think there might have been some damage to the brain and we need to know what caused it.'

'Well, if he landed on his head . . .' Lawrence said.

'Yes, of course. He had a helmet on, which helped. But it's possible that it was the other way around.'

'What do you mean?'

'That something happened in his brain first, an attack, and then that caused him to lose control of the bike.'

'How serious is that?'

'We don't know. We need to do some more tests. But for the time being we should keep him here, under observation.'

Lawrence had more questions but they were interrupted by Iona, emerging from the room. She pulled the door shut behind her and her face dropped as she released all the effort that held her brave expression in place. She slumped down onto the metal bench in the corridor. Her fingers tugged at the fabric of her baggy denim dress. Then she tipped forward and sank her elbows onto her knees, the palms of her hands covering her eyes and her fingers pushing up into her red hair. Lawrence saw her shoulders shake as she began to cry.

He walked over and put a cautious hand on her shoulder.

'It's OK now,' he said. 'I know he looks rough, but he's going to be OK.'

Iona looked up at him, her face crumpled and her eyes reddened. All the strain of the last few days was written in those tired eyes.

'He's such a fucking idiot,' she said. 'I ought to feel sorry for him but I'm just angry that he's a fucking moron, that he put everything at risk, that he had everyone chasing around after him. I am so furious with him that I can't tell you. He's a selfish fucking idiot.'

Lawrence sat down next to her.

'It's OK,' he repeated. 'It's OK to be angry with him. You've had a rough few days.'

The doctor hovered, a sheaf of paperwork in her hand, then interrupted them, speaking to Iona but looking to Lawrence to translate.

'Your husband will be well, madame. But the important thing is that he needs to rest. To allow time to recover completely. And to avoid stress.'

Lawrence translated this and Iona laughed a sharp, bitter laugh. The doctor looked disconcerted and turned to Lawrence for an explanation. 'I'm not joking,' she said.

'I know,' he said. 'It's just that – Mr Elliot is not someone who rests. He doesn't know how to relax.'

'He needs to learn,' the doctor said.

Lawrence asked the doctor whether he could talk to the patient and she nodded.

As Lawrence entered the room, Martin had his head turned towards the window. Lawrence coughed, trying to get his attention without startling him.

'How are you feeling?' Lawrence ventured. Martin's head moved slowly on the pillow.

'Been better,' he croaked. His words came out slowly and slightly slurred. He always spoke fast, his words and ideas tripping over one another in their rush from his mouth. You could rely on him to keep talking in any situation. He talked his way into things and he talked his way out of them.

'The doctor says you're going to make a good recovery,' said Lawrence. 'You've got to take it easy for a while. I know that's the last thing you want to hear, but it's true.'

'I have to get out of here,' Martin insisted, every word an effort.

'You will, soon enough. Just not yet. You have to be patient.'

Martin shook his head slightly, though the effort of the gesture seemed to hurt him.

'I can't stay here.'

'You don't have any choice about it. Iona's fine, the children are fine. They'll stay here until you're ready to come home. I'm helping them. Try not to worry. Everything's being taken care of.'

Martin said nothing.

'Is there anything you need?' Lawrence asked. 'Clothes, a book?'

'A phone,' Martin said, immediately. 'Any phone. A pay as you go is fine.'

'I'm not sure,' Lawrence said. 'Iona would kill me. And the doctors say you need to avoid stress. They want you to relax.'

'I need it,' Martin insisted. There was an anger in his voice that Lawrence wasn't used to hearing. 'I need a bloody phone.'

Lawrence glanced towards the door, wondering if his shout had been loud enough for Iona and the doctor to hear, out in the corridor.

'It's OK,' Lawrence reassured him. 'I'll talk to the office. I'll let them know that you've had an accident, that you'll be back on your feet by the time you would have got back from holiday. It can all wait, everything can wait.'

Martin grimaced again, whether from pain or from the frustration of not being in control Lawrence couldn't tell.

'What happened?' he said at last. 'What do they say happened?'

'You don't remember?'

'No. I was just on the road, on the hill and then . . . nothing. I mean, something. Something made me fall, but I don't know what. It wasn't just the wind.'

Lawrence wasn't sure how much Martin needed to know.

'They're not sure. They need to do some tests. You might have overdone it; exhaustion, dehydration. It might be nothing more than that.'

Even in his weakened state, Martin could tell that Lawrence was omitting information that he wanted.

'But they don't think it is? They don't think it's nothing.'

'They don't know. But whatever it is, it won't get better by you worrying about it. Resting is all that will help.' Lawrence thought he was probably wearing him out, that it was time to leave. 'We'll come and visit tomorrow, one or other of us. The children will be so happy to know we've found you.'

Martin spoke again, but his thoughts were lagging behind.

'Tell people it was just the fall. Nothing else.' He made a weak gesture towards his head, indicating that he didn't want Lawrence to go into the other reasons, whatever they might turn out to be.

Lawrence made to leave.

'It's going to be OK,' he assured him.

Martin spoke another few scratchy words. 'Tell Isabelle,' he said. 'Please, tell Isabelle.'

'We will,' Lawrence said. 'But, you know, don't worry about the project, the bike race, all that. Other people will look after it – it'll be fine. We asked them to help look for you, you know. Her and Sylvie and Christophe, because we thought they'd know people, have influence.' Lawrence was rambling, filling the spaces where Martin's words would normally be. Martin was giving him an unusual look, a pleading look. He would almost have said there were tears welling in his eyes. Maybe the doctor needed to give him some more painkillers. But he knew it wasn't that kind of pain.

'Just tell her,' he whispered. 'Please.'

Lawrence had to hold back his reaction. He didn't want his envy, his disappointment to show in his face.

'I'll tell her,' he said. He raised his hand to say goodbye and opened the door of Martin's room, stepping out into the corridor where Iona was waiting.

II

LAWRENCE WAS ON the point of ordering a second cup of coffee when she arrived. She was late and for a while he hoped she would not come at all. She would go back to Paris, Martin would go home, he would be the go-between who never passed on the message and it would all fizzle out. Martin had to learn to be grateful for what he had, instead of always wanting more. He'd already had one lucky escape.

She strode across the square, arms swinging, then stopped to look around. He waved a hand to her and she approached him, wearing dark glasses even though it wasn't yet bright enough to need them. Where he sat, the light was dappled through the leaves of the plane tree and it was still cool in the shade. He was wearing Martin's grey jumper that he hadn't got round to returning.

He needed the money, he told himself. That was why he was doing Martin this favour, when he knew in other ways it was wrong. Martin owed him. He owed him the work, at least. But he needed Isabelle in order that the work would happen, so he had to go along with the deceit.

Isabelle was dressed for exercise but she didn't seem to have broken sweat. She sat down at the table, taking the chair next to him but sitting on the edge of the seat as though she might leave at any second. She raised a finger to call Elodie over and asked for an espresso. He added a *cafe crème* to the order. Isabelle folded her hands into her lap.

'So?' she began. 'What happened?'

He had sent her a brief text, almost abrupt, saying that Martin was alive and in hospital in Avignon. She had replied straight away, suggesting that they meet here, early in the morning. Even at this hour, the village was awake and observant and little passed without someone being aware of it.

'He's had a bad accident, but they say he's going to be OK,' Lawrence said.

'What happened, exactly?' She was hurrying him on and he was reluctant to be rushed.

'The British consul called us – called his wife, I mean.' Lawrence relented for a moment. He was going to have to stop himself being outright cruel.

'What injuries does he have?' she said quickly.

Lawrence began to list them as if he were a junior doctor on the night shift, handing over to his superior.

'Broken collarbone, broken wrist. Very badly bruised around the face.' Isabelle nodded, as if all of this was to be expected. 'He doesn't look great,' Lawrence observed. He tried to stop himself again, but these thoughts kept escaping him, out loud.

'It sounds like a typical bike accident,' she observed. 'How long will he be in hospital?'

'That's the thing,' Lawrence said, pausing as Elodie returned with the coffees. He doubted that she understood that much English, but he could easily have been wrong. 'They want to keep him in for tests. They think he might have had some kind of attack, something that caused him to come off the bike in the first place. A transient—'

'Ischaemic attack?' Isabelle volunteered.

'Yes, that's it. A TIA. But like I say, they're not completely sure.'

Isabelle took it in clinically, professionally.

'And where was he, when they found him?'

'He'd tried to cycle up Mont Ventoux, like an idiot. I went up there to look for him, but I had to turn back, because of the storm. He'd gone right off the road, a different road from the one I'd taken. Another cyclist saw him and he was airlifted to hospital.'

'Which hospital is it?' she said. 'I should go and visit him.'

'No, you shouldn't,' Lawrence protested, his voice harsher than he meant it to be. Her hand, holding the small white coffee cup, stopped halfway to her mouth.

'I could talk to the doctors. I could make sure he's well looked after. There are probably people there who know me.'

'That's even more reason for you not to go,' Lawrence said. 'He's being looked after perfectly well. I know he wants to see you, but he's supposed to rest. Not to have any stress.'

'And you think me being there would be stressful for him?'

'Of course it would. It must have been stressful enough already, before the accident – hiding things, deceiving people. No wonder—'

'You're saying it's my fault, somehow?' Isabelle's voice was indignant.

'I'm not saying that.' But now that he'd said it, he thought it might well be true.

'When did he tell you?'

'He didn't. He didn't have to. He said I had to get a message to you, and the way he said it, I just knew. I've known him long enough.'

'We were supposed to meet,' she said. 'He said there was something he wanted to talk about. I don't know what it was.'

'When?' Lawrence asked.

'That morning. The morning he went off. But I couldn't get hold of him. I thought maybe he'd changed his mind.' Isabelle paused. 'Does this – does he do this kind of thing often?' She stared into the coffee cup, avoiding Lawrence's gaze.

'Have affairs, you mean?' She still wouldn't look up. Once again, Lawrence reproached himself for rubbing it in. Even if she was reluctant to show it, Isabelle was also upset. They were all upset and angry in varying degrees. It was the downside of Martin's ability to draw people in; they still felt attached to his world, even if they did not want to be.

'If that's what you want to call it.'

'What else should I call it?' Isabelle shrugged and didn't answer. 'I don't think so,' Lawrence went on. 'Not any more. Not since he was married. At least, not as far as I know. How long have you known each other?'

'We've known each other a while – a few years – but nothing happened until earlier this year.'

'And?' Lawrence prompted her. 'What did you think was going to happen? Did you have – plans?'

'Not seriously,' she said.

'What does that mean?'

Isabelle pushed her sunglasses up from her face and stared directly at Lawrence.

'It means that there were times we imagined it, leaving our families, starting somewhere new. Moving away somewhere. And then we saw sense again and realised it would never happen, that there was too much we would both have to give up. His children, for instance.'

'Do you have children?'

She shook her head and changed the subject. 'He was the only person for a long while who talked to me, about myself. He was interested in me, really interested. In what I did, what I thought.' That was what Martin always did. That was his secret. His enthusiasm and his curiosity were never feigned. But he wasn't going to disabuse her. 'So many of the people I know, in Paris or here, only know me for who I am related to, who my husband is or my sister-in-law, my father-in-law when he was alive. I thought I wanted that. I wanted to belong to a family like theirs, one that had roots somewhere, a place in society. They have codes of behaviour, ways of doing things that have been done the same way for generations. I never had that and I was fascinated by it. But now I'm not so sure.'

'But you get away from that already,' Lawrence suggested. 'You go off to your projects, to the developing world. When you go to – I don't know – Africa, India – I shouldn't think they care who your in-laws are, do they?'

'That's true. But I'm only dropping in and out of their world. I'm no better than any other rich woman with a charity project. They do functions, I do operations.'

She was being disingenuous. He was getting into the bad habit of sitting up late at night, his teeth on edge from too much caffeine, looking up the people in Martin's life online. There were pictures to be found of Isabelle and Christophe in evening-wear, appearing at charity events. In all the pictures except one, she wore the strained, taut expression she had when he had first met her. He recognised it now as a fear of being caught out in one way or another. There was an image she had to keep up and it was proving harder, not easier, with time. The only picture that was different was the one he had found on the aid agency's website. Despite her surroundings, Isabelle was still pristine, in a white T-shirt with a logo, a stethoscope slung around her neck. She was talking to a mother holding a child in her arms, a hand extended towards the baby to keep it amused. For once, she didn't look anxious. She had an expression of genuine concern, kindness. They were on the veranda of a wooden hut and there was green foliage out of focus beyond the railing of the balcony. She was somewhere she wanted to be.

Isabelle finished the espresso and looked at her watch.

'I have to get back. Christophe will wonder where I've got to.'

'Promise me something,' Lawrence said.

Before she put the sunglasses back over her eyes, she gave him a furrowed, quizzical look. She was not going to promise anything before she knew what it might be.

'Leave him alone,' Lawrence said. 'I've known him for twenty years. I've known his wife for . . .' He had to pause to count how long it had been. 'For ten years. Anything else now, anything drastic – well, it won't help him. It could make him worse. Whatever might happen in the future can wait.'

'I understand,' Isabelle replied. It was the cool, professional voice again. 'But you'll tell him you spoke to me?' Lawrence nodded. She was composing a message to pass on. 'Send him my – tell him I want him to get well soon. That I know he will.'

She stood up to leave and Lawrence got to his feet to say goodbye.

'And we just bumped into each other, if anyone asks,' she said. She flicked her head in the direction of the shady interior of the cafe, the regulars sitting at the bar who noticed everything. 'I was passing and you wanted to let me know that we didn't need to search.'

'Of course,' Lawrence said.

She turned to go, striding across the square in the direction of the bakery. He had sometimes imagined sitting here, talking to the woman he now knew to be Isabelle; but this had not been the conversation he would have foreseen.

12

EACH TIME A door had opened, he hoped that it might be Isabelle. Martin did wonder, in the hours when he lay awake listening to the strange bleeps of machines and the rhythms of the hospital corridors, whether Lawrence had actually passed on the message, as he claimed to have done.

'She says she hopes you get well soon,' Lawrence said as he sat in the chair at his bedside, having handed over his offerings of books and fruit and boiled sweets.

'Is that all?' Martin had asked. He had hoped for more.

'She was very cagey, very reserved,' Lawrence had replied. 'Maybe it's because she doesn't know me very well.' Lawrence avoided his gaze and the obvious question. There were still some things that they just understood about one another. At first Martin had been too weak for explanations and now he did not want to volunteer one. It was one of Lawrence's redeeming qualities; if he never expected the best of people, then at least he was never surprised to learn the worst.

He wished Isabelle had come. She could have done, if she had really tried. She could have said she was going to Avignon, to do some shopping or visit the sights. Perhaps she was already back in Paris. In her absence, he asked, every morning, whether today he would be allowed home.

In the late morning, Dr Arnaud arrived in his room with a rare smile.

'You can go home today,' she said. 'We'll call your family, so that they can come to collect you.'

Waiting for someone to arrive was the longest wait of all. He hated waiting. If anyone asked him the reasons he gave up journalism, his impatience would have been near the top of the list. Waiting for press conferences that were delayed, waiting for people to return your calls, waiting for things to be ready on someone else's terms. He wanted to be inside the room, deciding what happened and when. He hated being subject, as he was now, to decisions that other people made.

For a moment, he considered trying to get himself home. He was convinced that he could manage it. There must be a way of getting a taxi. Then he realised how he would look: he wore an old shirt that was half buttoned over his sling; a pair of pyjama trousers, blue and yellow plastic pool shoes on his feet. He was unshaven, tufts of greying hair sprouting from his head and chin. It was hardly the image he wanted the world to have of him. He wanted to look like a well man, even if he no longer was one. That idea dissipated, the way all his ideas seemed to at the moment.

Martin kept telling himself that once he left, it would all be back to normal. Iona said that she had called the office, told them that everything could wait until he was back, but it wasn't that simple. She didn't know he had managed to speak to them himself, shuffling in his plastic shoes to the phone in the corridor.

'Sorry if I sound a bit slow,' he had told Lucy Fox. 'They've got me on some pretty heavy painkillers.' Lucy was smart and there was a risk she would detect, even at a distance, that all was not as well as he claimed it to be. He'd tried to avoid taking his pills, but the nurses had spotted it and stood over him.

'Iona told me you came off your bike,' Lucy said. 'Broke a few bones.' It was good to hear her voice again; Lucy's soft West Country accent could fool those who didn't know better into thinking she was naive. She would soon set them right; the endearments she used could just as easily be swapped for vivid and fluent swearing.

'They'll mend,' Martin said, trying to sound upbeat. He didn't mention the metal pins that now held his collarbone together, let alone the less visible damage.

Lucy ran him through a few issues that had come up, with her usual efficiency. Normally he would have provided answers straight away. His first instinct now was to put things off, tell her that it was August and there was a lot that could be pushed back until September. He congratulated himself again on having hired her. Lucy Fox had worked in Downing Street, under the last government; she had left a year or so before the election, beating the rush to the door. MPs that Martin spoke to had been terrified of her, the way she could charm and cajole them into doing what was required of them. The only thing he worried about, with Lucy holding the fort, was that he would get back to find her name over the door instead of his. Still, there were things that even Lucy did not yet know.

'I've had your lawyers on,' Lucy added. 'Asking about the request to give evidence. What should I tell them?'

'Tell them I'm in hospital, recovering from an accident. Knock it back. They'll have to wait.'

'Are you OK?' Lucy asked. 'Are you going to be well enough to come straight back to work?' Not much got past her.

'I'll be fine,' he said, a little too quickly.

He had filled hours of empty time trying to force himself into remembering. The ride came back to him and he relived it, telling himself the story with a different ending, imagining he was still outdoors with all the freedom of the road. He could feel again the exertion in his calves on the long incline, saw the sunflowers and the orchards in the valley, the pines alongside the road as it rose. He felt the wind that he'd fought against as he emerged from the shelter of the trees, the anger as other cyclists had overtaken him.

Martin still recalled nothing that came after the fall. Not the

Dutch cyclist who had found him, not the helicopter, not the flight to hospital. He thought about what had happened to his bike. It had been a beautiful, lightweight carbon-fibre machine, expensive, but worth it.

'You can replace a bike,' Iona snapped. 'We can't replace you.'

It was true enough, but she didn't understand what it meant. It reminded him of the bike he'd had as a teenager, the same dropped handlebars, the same sense of being able to get on it and escape from whatever was troubling him. When things were difficult, he rode until they no longer were. He'd bought that bike on a whim one day, when a young employee had asked him to sponsor a London to Brighton ride. Instead of just stumping up the sponsorship, he did the ride himself. Iona was just pregnant then, sick and anxious, with what they did not yet know would be the twins.

The doctor had looked at him askance when he asked how long it would be before he could get back on a bike, but he needed to have something to aim for, a target to reach. He was told it would be eight weeks until he was fit again. He counted the weeks forward. The middle of September, the middle of October. There was no way he would be riding from London to Paris, he reluctantly conceded. The others would have to go without him. It was galling to think it, after all the work he had put in; not just the training but the organisation, the sponsors, the participants he had encouraged to sign up. He wasn't someone who watched from the sidelines.

When Iona arrived, he was already in the chair beside the bed, his plastic carrier bag containing his possessions in his lap. He tried to leap up, but conceded that he had to get to his feet slowly.

'Where are Maisie and Finn?' he asked. As far as Martin was concerned, hospitals were places you went to welcome people into the world or to see them out of it, and they were to be avoided at all costs between those extremes. The summer that he had seen both, five years ago, had almost overwhelmed him; he would have given anything for the events to have happened the other way around, the twins to have been born a few weeks before his father died, instead of a few weeks after. Sometimes you didn't get to construct the narrative in the way you wanted it to happen; sometimes the narrative constructed you.

'They're in the car,' she said. 'Lawrence is with them, and Freya. Probably filling them with sweets.'

'Can we go?' he asked.

She took one look at him and laughed. 'You don't want to go out looking like that,' she told him. 'I've brought you some better clothes.' She pulled out some clothes from a canvas bag: a clean linen shirt, a pair of chinos, boxer shorts, deck shoes. Iona struggled to get him into the shirt. She undid the sling around his neck and he tried to hold his broken wrist in place with his better arm. Every movement was difficult.

'It's like dressing the twins, when they were tiny,' Iona exclaimed in frustration. 'In fact, you're worse. You're not bendy, like them. Just hold still.'

'You're doing it wrong,' he protested.

'Well, how should I know?' Iona demanded. 'I'm not a nurse. I haven't done this before.'

'You're hurting me.'

'I didn't mean to.' She bit her lip and looked as though she was biting back tears.

'I'm sorry,' Martin said. 'I just can't get used to this, being so helpless.'

'It'll be fine,' she reassured him in the same gentle voice she used for the twins.

Even being helped to dress was hard work. Martin slipped his bare feet into the deck shoes and eased himself out of the chair. Iona offered him an arm to take but he refused it. He wanted to walk out of the hospital without help. At the end of a corridor he could glimpse the warm light of the outdoors, tantalising him.

Outside it was bright, the sun reflecting on the white building and the paths surrounding it. From somewhere, there was the smell of rosemary mingled with the dust of the road. Martin stood still, tried to steady himself. That smell made him feel suddenly sick.

13

LONDON STRETCHED AWAY below him, the park sloping downwards towards the river. The Wren domes of the Old Royal Naval College marked out the edge of the Thames. It was a warm morning, by London standards, but a few grey clouds whipped across the sky and there was a stiff September breeze. It was nine months since Lawrence had been back and the city had recovered its power to astonish him. He saw it once again as a stranger, as a returning traveller. Beyond the river were the towers of Canary Wharf, shoving against each other, competing to reach higher. Cranes reached above the sites of future tall buildings.

It was a view he hadn't often seen from the south side of the river. He had a dim recollection of having been here before, as a child, and struggled to remember who had been with him, whether it was a school outing or a rare trip to London with his parents. There were no skyscrapers then; the only cranes were those of the docks, their jibs pointing skywards, already falling into disuse.

He had been taken to see Nelson's coat, the uniform he had been wearing at Trafalgar. That much was clearly imprinted on his memory. It must have been a school trip, he thought now, because he had had to draw the coat, with its bullet hole and the bloodstain around it. A wound that changed history should have left a bigger mark, he had thought.

He turned back from the view to inspect the cyclists starting to gather outside the Observatory. There was a large banner marking the starting line, dozens of cyclists in matching tops that bore the logos of the sponsors; among the symbols, Lawrence could make out that of Elliot Associates and a swirling script that denoted Julian's fruit snacks. The mark of Isabelle's aid agency was prominent on the banner and on the front of the royal-blue cycling jerseys.

'Don't you wish you were giving it a go?' Julian had asked, as they greeted each other near the meeting point. Lawrence shook his head.

'Rather you than me,' he said. 'Have you thought of taking the train? It only takes two hours and you can have a glass of wine and look out of the window.'

Julian didn't seem to realise, at first, that he was joking. He assumed a rueful expression.

'Wish I'd thought of that when I signed on the dotted line. At least I didn't take Martin's way out, though – a bit drastic, wasn't it?' Julian laughed at his own joke. Lawrence managed a smile. It was easy for Julian to say that, when all he'd had to do was a bit of babysitting, when he hadn't spent hours visiting the hospital or helping Martin to get home; when he hadn't known how close a call it had been. In fact, Victoria and Julian hadn't visited Martin in hospital at all, not even when they had been spending the day at the Palais des Papes, which was just down the road. By the time Martin came back from hospital, they had left, pleading that they were expected by other friends on the coast who they couldn't let down. Iona had been happy to see them go.

'I feel as if she's judging me,' she had confided in Lawrence, one evening after they had gone, as the two of them sat on the terrace. Martin had gone to bed, trying to recover his strength before the journey home. 'As if I'm not to be trusted.'

'I don't think she trusts anyone,' Lawrence replied. 'At least, anyone who's not in her inner circle. Anyone she hasn't known since school or college. You know what those people are like. If you're part of their clique, if you belong, then anything goes.

If you're not, there's this wariness about them.' He had taken another sip of rosé. 'If anything, she's probably afraid of you. You're in a different world, one she doesn't understand and doesn't belong in.'

A young black woman in a blue T-shirt with the Heathcote's slogan on the front came up to them, holding out a box full of fruit and nut bars.

'Free energy bar?' she asked Julian. 'They're very good for you. Slow-burning·and delicious. They'll keep you going for the ride.' The woman had a broad smile that persuaded Lawrence to accept her offer, even though he had no intention of eating it. Julian took one as well.

'I know,' he said, 'I make them.' The woman's smile flickered for a moment with nerves. 'You're doing a great job, though.' She smiled again and moved on.

An anxious female voice started calling through a loudspeaker for the riders to line up for a photograph.

'Well, good luck,' Lawrence said. 'Probably "break a leg" isn't the thing to say, under the circumstances.'

'Probably not,' Julian replied. 'But thanks.'

Lawrence waved him goodbye. The cyclists stood in rows on the esplanade that gave out onto the city below. There was a clicking of cameras and phones, shouts of 'over here'. Professionally done, Lawrence noted. Proper camera crews.

Martin stood at the centre of the group with Victoria Loxton alongside him. He was no longer wearing the sling and looked his usual self again. It would have been hard to notice anything wrong with him, but Lawrence knew where to look. There was a blue tubular bandage on his left wrist and the faint pale marks of cuts above an eyebrow.

Once the photos were taken, the voice over the loudspeaker directed everyone to the starting line. Martin walked over to a small green gazebo where he took the microphone. He began with an apology and a gesture towards his bandaged hand.

'I wish I could be out there with you today,' he said to the crowd of riders and supporters. 'Unfortunately, I had an accident while I was training and my broken bones are still healing.' There was a smatter of heckling from the crowd, led by Julian. 'I know some of you think I had a lucky break. Like many of you, I've been threatened with divorce if I do the ride. Unlike many of you, I think this time my wife actually meant it.' There was sporadic laughter. Most of the riders were men, most of the spectators women and a few small children, too young to be at school. Lawrence knew that Iona wasn't there and he wondered how many would relate the comments back to her. 'But in any case, this is going to be a wonderful ride for a wonderful cause, and even if I can't be with you on the road I'll be there to welcome you in Paris with a glass of champagne. Here to send you on your way is our guest of honour, Victoria Loxton.'

The crowd applauded, the cyclists releasing their handlebars to clap. Martin handed the microphone over to Victoria. She was in her politician's uniform, a collarless jacket with a brooch on one lapel, a slim skirt and high heels. She took the microphone and thanked him. Her voice resounded through the speaker.

'Martin – we're all so grateful for your fantastic efforts in organising this event and we're sure you'll be back on your bike for next year's ride – let's make this an annual event. I only have a few words to say, as I know you're waiting for the precise Greenwich time to start – but I'm sure you all know what excellent work the agency does in tackling vision problems in some of the world's poorest countries and I'm delighted to add my support to the money you'll be raising over the next few days with your valiant efforts. So without any further ado – the best of British luck to all of you and off you go!'

There was a clatter of shoes clicking into pedals, a squeak of wheels, and the cyclists started to move away, pedalling off towards the smooth wide avenue beneath rows of chestnut trees. The supporters cheered them on their way and started to disperse. Lawrence started to amble downhill towards the river.

★

As the hybrid car hummed its way along the Embankment, Lawrence watched the buildings that he passed on the river, trying to work out what had changed since he was last in London. The waters closed over your head quickly if you had gone. The city did not notice one person leaving when there were always others to take your place. He didn't have a home here now and that was all that seemed to count, where you lived and how much your house was worth.

He recalled with particular bitterness one of Harriet's columns when she wrote about life as a homecoming expat in London. It blamed him for this failure as well as his many others, which she had shared with her readers.

We arrived back from America and this time we were the huddled masses, it began. He had to admit, however reluctantly, that it was a good opening line. *We yearn to breathe free*, the article had continued, *but even breathing in north London now appears to be beyond our price range.* A quizzical-looking Harriet struck a pose among piles of packing cases to illustrate how their old Washington life would not fit the space allotted for their new, cramped life in London.

'You can't compare us with that,' Lawrence had protested. 'We're hardly the wretched refuse of a teeming shore. Emma Lazarus was talking about people who had escaped pogroms, people who were running from Cossacks wielding sabres, people starved out by a potato famine.' Lawrence thought of their modern equivalents, refugees washed up on Mediterranean coastlines, if they were lucky enough to get to shore, the people cowering in the backs of lorries, the people chased and starved from their homes, fleeing from war and disease, even those closer to home who would have envied them what they had. 'At least we have a house, even if it doesn't have enough bedrooms.'

Of course the house was small, particularly if you compared it with the detached colonial house with its large front lawn they'd lived in near Rock Creek Park in Washington. Josh missed nothing about it more than his basketball hoop above the garage. They had neither garage nor hoop any more and Josh twirled his basketball on a finger inside the house while Harriet warned him against breaking anything. He had been too young to remember much about the parquet-floored apartment in Paris with its wrought-iron balconies and cage lift, but Lizzie still remembered sliding across the wooden floors in her socks. What Harriet seemed to forget was that the company had been paying for those and now they were back in London they had to pay for themselves, and nor were they getting the rent that the house had earned them over recent years. They had left London with a baby and a toddler and returned to it with two teenagers. Every so often, either Lawrence or Harriet would suggest moving further away, out of London to the suburbs or beyond, and the other would refuse. The children were the most adamantly against moving.

'I've lived in two great cities of the world, and this is my third,' Lizzie protested. 'And I didn't come home to go and live in the sticks somewhere, with boring people and nothing to do.' Josh muttered his agreement. Harriet would have agreed that boring people and nothing to do were two of her greatest fears. She found herself more and more in demand back in London; she was the one wanting to be within a taxi ride of town in the evenings. They came to an impasse, in that argument as in many others.

The restaurant was washed with pale, milky light. Brisk feet passed by on the pavement above the frosted glass of the basement windows. The maître d' greeted Martin by name as they arrived, showing them to a table for four. Lawrence chose a seat with his back to the wall, facing into the room, the better to see the other diners.

'Come here often, then?' he asked Martin.

'Pretty often,' he replied. 'Once, twice a week maybe. It's reliable and easy for people to get to.'

Victoria was late, but she entered the restaurant as calmly as if she were not. She was accompanied by a young Asian woman, shorter than her, with shoulder-length black hair, who Lawrence had noticed at the start of the bike ride; she had been standing by Victoria's shoulder, but spent most of the time either with her ear to her phone or tapping away at its screen. She was finishing a call, apologising to someone at the other end that the basement room meant her signal would cut out.

'PMQs overran,' Victoria explained as she shook hands, without apology. 'Martin, you've met my adviser, Anjali, haven't you?' Martin nodded. 'Anjali Mehta, this is Lawrence Leith.'

'Great to meet you, Lawrence,' Anjali said as they sat down. She put her phone on the table, glancing at it and swiping a finger across the screen briefly before leaning forward to talk to him. 'I remember watching your pieces, when I was at college. They really made me interested in the news, made me care about it.'

'Thank you,' Lawrence said, taking the menu that the waitress handed him.

'In fact,' Anjali continued, 'in a way, you probably helped me get where I am today.'

'Really?'

'Oh yes,' Anjali smiled. She had bright, wide dark eyes with long lashes, shielded by tortoiseshell glasses. Lawrence made a rough calculation of her age – mid-twenties, he guessed. It was probably a few years since she had left college. 'I was already interested in development issues, but I think you made me realise how important it was to communicate them in ways people could understand.'

'That's very kind,' Lawrence said. It was a long time since anyone had praised his work. 'But you weren't tempted to go into journalism yourself?'

Anjali shook her head. 'It wasn't really for me. I did a Masters and a couple of internships, then started working for Victoria, when she was in opposition.'

'Great,' Lawrence said, trying to echo her enthusiasm. Anjali would go far, he had no doubt. She already had. She had chosen the inside track, the track of meetings in comfortable rooms and nice restaurants and the occasional air-conditioned summit conference centre. It was the sensible thing to do and he could hardly criticise her for it.

Lawrence had hoped to have a proper lunch, but he heard Victoria order grilled fish and salad, and Anjali just a starter, so he restrained himself. Victoria must have caught the slightly piqued look on his face. She ordered a bottle of sparkling water for the table, without asking whether anyone wanted wine.

'I have to watch what I eat,' she said. 'Too many lunches and everyone says you put on a stone in no time.'

Martin began exchanging gossip with Victoria, rumours of who was marked out for promotion, speculation about which brother would soon be running the opposition, asking what life was like in the coalition. Anjali was alert, though adding little, listening to what Victoria said in case her comments resurfaced somewhere they shouldn't. The restaurant was filling up. Lawrence recognised some of the faces, though probably not as many as he should have done.

Lawrence had never enjoyed lunches like this; he had endured the occasional lunch with people like the ones in this room: the diplomats and retired military men and former ministers who always had an opinion about what their successors were doing wrong and who had plenty of spare time in which to express it. They were of an older generation, for the most part, and they preferred to complain to him over lunches in gilded rooms with heavy carpets, in their clubs or in Parliament, though at least they always made sure there was some wine to hand and sometimes Lawrence would manage to get a decent story out of it.

The waitress set a large white plate down for Lawrence and he was glad he had chosen the most expensive item on the menu, whatever the others might have thought. Even that was only a few circles of lamb and swirls and drizzles of jus. It tasted good, at least, but he had to hold himself back and try to eat slowly. The conversation turned to the aid project that Lawrence still thought of as Isabelle's, the reason they were here.

His doubts had resurfaced as he watched the computer slides projected onto a screen in Martin's office. His eyelids began to droop as one of Martin's colleagues explained the campaign as if they were selling cans of baked beans. Isabelle hadn't needed to sell anything.

'Don't let on,' Martin had advised him as they sat in the back seat of the car that brought them to the restaurant, 'that you're not sure about this. They'll pick up on that. You're too transparent. Sound enquiring, by all means, sceptical, up to a point – but not up to your usual point.' Lawrence nodded and kept his counsel.

Anjali was in the middle of asking Martin something about social media when Lawrence's attention began to wander. Martin talked to Victoria and Anjali in a language that was strange to Lawrence, a language of priorities and outcomes and funding. At one of the tables towards the back of the room was a face that was possibly familiar. It was that of a man a couple of years younger than Lawrence with thin blond hair, clear-framed glasses and a small chin. There were plenty of men who looked like that, plenty of men who looked exactly like Ed Blake.

Lawrence tried to work out who the man's lunch companion was, in case that would help him. All he could see of him was his navy jacket, the back of his head, cropped dark-brown hair. It could have been anyone. Lawrence turned back to his noisettes of lamb and tried to forget about the distant table.

Victoria was talking to him, clearly having noticed that he was distracted. She had mentioned almost nothing about their meeting in France, the phone calls she had made asking for help to find Martin. It was as though those events had never happened. She had asked Martin once about his arm, whether it was healing well and when he hoped to be back on his bike, but that was it.

'. . . So, Lawrence, what's your interest in this project?'

Lawrence took a sip of the fizzy water and washed down a mouthful of lamb. It was one of the questions that Martin had prepped him for.

'From what I've learned of the project, it's doing really valuable work and I think it deserves a wider audience. Not just in France, but in the rest of the world. So I'm very keen to see their work for myself and if I can be useful in getting the message out there, then I'm very glad to be of help.'

Victoria nodded. Lawrence had the feeling that he was at a job interview, which, in a way, he was. At least it felt as though he had given the right answer. He didn't mention that they would be paying him for it and that the money would certainly be useful. He had tried not to let his eyes show his astonishment at the day rate that Martin had offered him. This kind of work paid far more than proper journalism did, these days. It was costing him more to live in France than he thought.

The waitress tried to suggest that they order desserts but the other three all shook their heads immediately. Lawrence didn't feel that he could even ask to see the menu. They all agreed on a round of espressos.

'Decaf espresso, please,' Martin asked. Lawrence was about to mock him for it and then he remembered that Martin had good reason to be careful of his health. Still, decaf espresso, if such a thing even existed, was an abomination.

Anjali started to check her phone again, the messages bleeping in with increasing frequency.

'Are we supposed to be somewhere?' Victoria asked.

'Not yet,' Anjali replied, checking one of the alerts.

He was drinking his coffee, with a momentary wave of homesickness for France and the cafe he thought of as his own, when he saw the man at the table on the far side of the room rise to leave. The restaurant was already thinning out, coats being retrieved, guests departing; the days of the long lunch were gone. Victoria had insisted on picking up the bill; that way, she didn't have to declare that she had accepted Martin's hospitality. If she didn't claim the cost back, the lunch went unrecorded.

The two men on the far side of the room were heading straight for their table. It was Ed Blake – of course it was – and he'd been lunching Patrick Chambers, Victoria's friend. There was no way to avoid them now.

Chambers was bright, presentable, the sort of minister who could answer any question in any interview and never say a word out of place, so much so that his words were entirely unmemorable. That was a quality that got you a long way, these days. He was also frighteningly young. He couldn't have been much over thirty.

Victoria stood up to greet her colleague.

'Are you going to be at the two thirty?' Chambers asked.

'You're heading up there already?' Victoria said, checking her watch.

Martin also rose from his chair, more slowly than he usually did. He came over to Chambers and patted him on the shoulder.

'I ought to have said thank you before now,' he said. 'Victoria tells me you were a great help, when I had my accident in France.'

'Glad to be of assistance,' Chambers replied. 'Though I'm not sure how much I did. A couple of calls. But if it speeded things up.'

'It certainly meant the family could find me. And Lawrence here, as well. He's been a rock.'

Patrick Chambers shook Lawrence's hand.

'We haven't met, have we? Though of course I know your name and your face.'

Ed Blake had been silent throughout this exchange, taking it in. Blake had a rounded, ageless face and if he was surprised to see Lawrence there was little sign of it in his expression.

'Are you back in London?' he asked Lawrence, as though that gave him cause for concern.

'Just passing through,' Lawrence said.

'Martin,' Blake said. 'Long time no see.' Martin nodded. To his credit, he didn't have much time for Ed Blake either. They both remembered him as a junior television researcher who could tell you the population of a country, its capital, who had the percentage swing of its recent election results and the name of its opposition leader at his fingertips but who would never, if he ever left the office, be able to find his way from the country's airport to the hotel. The trouble was, it was the pallid, office-bound people who did well, their political intelligence outweighing any need for practicality. Ed Blake, who read the power plays in the office as assiduously as he did *The Economist*, ended up as Lawrence's boss.

Blake studied the group at Lawrence's table before he turned back to Lawrence again.

'And in what capacity are you here?' There was an emphasis on the *you*, as though he could not understand why Lawrence would be lunching with a group of people of far greater status than him.

Lawrence felt prickles of sweat break out on the back of his neck, beneath his shirt collar. He ran a finger around beneath his collar, trying to think of a way to answer Blake that didn't involve punching him in the face. His answer needed to be quick, pithy, without hesitation.

'We're discussing a very interesting project,' he began. 'But I'm afraid I can't tell you anything more about it at the moment. It's all still confidential.'

That would do it. That would make Blake feel that Lawrence knew more than him, and there was nothing he loathed more. And at least he had shown that he could still string a sentence together, when it mattered.

'Oh, I see.' Blake was on the back foot, but he still looked to Martin for confirmation that Lawrence was to be believed. 'And is this something that we might be interested in?'

'It might well be,' Martin said. 'We'll be sure to let you know, as and when.'

Blake checked his phone, a quick pretence to show that he was in demand, needed elsewhere.

'Did you get my email?' Lawrence asked.

A crease appeared between Blake's eyebrows as he considered the question. He shook his head. 'Your email?' he repeated. Lawrence nodded.

'It was a while ago.'

'Remind me?'

'About the . . .' Lawrence hesitated for a moment. It wasn't something he wanted to discuss in Victoria and Patrick's presence. Martin wouldn't thank him for it. 'About the archive footage we were trying to get hold of.'

Ed Blake's face was still blank.

'I need to talk to you about it,' Lawrence said. He should never have assumed that Ed Blake would have done anything as straightforward as seeing an email and responding to it. At least, in this company, he couldn't decline.

'Of course,' Ed replied, with an artificial geniality. 'Let's have a coffee. We'll get something in the diary.'

'I'm only in London for a couple of days.'

'Sure, sure,' Ed said, eager to move on. 'We'll catch up. Call the office. It's the same number.' He inclined his head towards the phone again, a reflex action that had replaced looking at his watch but had the same meaning. 'Lovely to see you again, Lawrence. Give my love to Harriet.'

Lawrence couldn't work out whether that was a calculated slight or whether Ed Blake had just misspoken, through force of old habit. Everyone knew about Harriet. Particularly people like Ed Blake, who read every word of the newspapers. Ed Blake and Patrick Chambers bustled their way out of the restaurant, re-emerging into the world of rising stars.

No one mentioned Harriet and no one mentioned one of the incidents that Lawrence tried so hard to forget. Every time someone said that they had seen him on television, he never thought they were recalling the hundreds of times it had gone right; he only imagined them seeing the one time it went wrong. Martin certainly knew; they had talked about it since. Martin had reassured him that he would get over it, but he never had. Victoria probably knew. Even Anjali, who claimed to be a fan of his work, must have known. She had probably seen the clip on YouTube; thousands of people had.

It was Washington, the autumn of 2008, just when everything was starting to fall apart. It was an unusually warm evening for a Washington November and until that point, everything had been going well. He even thought he understood some of the economics he was talking about, although that wasn't really his subject. The report had been filed on time, London were happy, he stood looking down the barrel of the camera. He adjusted his tie, checked his microphone. Jeff, the cameraman, had given him a thumbs-up. Megan, the producer, looked up from her notebook and phone to make sure that everything was all right. His heart rate rose slightly as he heard his own words through his earpiece, the report playing out, the clips of Bush and Brown and Merkel talking about what they were going to do to save the world's economies from disaster. All was as it should have been.

Then he heard the presenter come to him.

'Over now to our correspondent Lawrence Leith, who's in Washington for us this evening. Lawrence, are the measures the G-20 has agreed going to be enough?'

And Lawrence said nothing. He opened his mouth to speak and no words came out. He had prepared it all. He knew what the question was going to be and what his answer should have been. He could remember the words to this day. He had tried to form them, *Emma, the presidents and prime ministers here hope so. Their futures, our futures, depend on that.* His mouth had opened and closed like a helpless goldfish. He couldn't even say the name Emma.

Emma, in London, had assumed that she couldn't hear him. She tried the question again.

'Lawrence, will these measures make a difference?'

The precious seconds of airtime were disappearing, the satellite time that they paid for by the minute. Lawrence heard other voices clamouring through his earpiece down the talkback line, demanding to know what was going on. He kept his eyes fixed straight and unblinking into the lens of the camera, but he had a distant impression of Megan putting the phone to her ear, moving away so that her shouts in response wouldn't be over-heard on the microphone.

'Emma . . .' he began at last, the name stuttering out. It was too late. 'The presidents . . .' He stopped again. Emma apologised to the viewers and moved on.

'I'm sorry, we seem to have problems hearing from Lawrence Leith in Washington but we'll try to come back to him later in the programme.' Lawrence put his hand to his earpiece as if to suggest that he could not hear her either, though he could hear every word.

They never came back to him, despite Megan shouting down the phone that they should. Miles Renfrew, the economics guy, had sauntered up, as if by chance, fresh from a briefing that he claimed was exclusive. He had stepped in to the spot where Lawrence stood and Lawrence had surrendered the microphone to him.

'What happened?' Megan had demanded afterwards, when Renfrew had explained it all to the viewers. 'What happened to you?'

'I don't know,' he replied. 'I just froze. It's never happened before.'

'I know,' she said. 'They're asking me if you were drunk.' She tapped the phone that was never out of her hand.

'I'm not. You know I'm not. I haven't touched a thing. It's five in the afternoon here and we've been working for forty-eight hours. Did you tell them that?'

'Yes and I told them it was nothing of the sort. Just stage fright. A rabbit in the headlights moment.'

He had been tired and he'd had a long trip, a long few days, but then so had everyone else. That was to be expected and it was no excuse. Regardless of the crises that swirled around him, the financial and the political ones, it was only his own crisis, this private one, that mattered to him now.

When Lawrence had returned home, Ed Blake called him into the office. He never said in so many words that it was all over, but it was clear from then on. He was quietly shunted aside, overlooked, the trips not agreed to, the ideas not commissioned. He was never the person they called when something happened. Ed Blake asked him, obliquely, whether he had given much thought to the future, as though it was an abstract concept rather than his real life. They made it clear that he would be expected, sooner rather than later, to move along, make space for younger, hungrier colleagues.

He had bumped into Emma Bailey once, in a corridor as she came out of the make-up room. She had put a red-nailed hand on his shoulder, peered at him from under her freshly curled eyelashes.

'Are you OK, Lawrence?' she had asked solicitously.

'Thanks,' he had replied, unable to repeat her name, because it would echo that awful moment. 'I'm fine. Thanks for asking.'

But he had not been fine, and although he may have moved away, he had not moved on.

Lawrence was at the coffee shop early, even though he knew Ed Blake would be late; he always was. His PA had conceded that Blake could leave the office, but only after Lawrence had used all the persuasion that he could muster. Lawrence wasn't going to go to the office. He wasn't interested in standing in the foyer to have people recognise him and mutter behind their hands about what he might be doing there.

He stood up as he saw Blake come in, apparently talking to himself in animated conversation. It was a moment before Lawrence noticed the earpiece attached to his phone. He waved across to him and managed to catch his eye. Blake didn't remove the earpiece as he ordered his coffee, barely acknowledging the barista. He sat down opposite and Lawrence waited to speak until he had removed the white earphone from his ear and coiled the cable away.

'How can I help you?' Blake asked. He wasn't bothering with any small talk.

'I don't know whether you've had this request through more official channels,' Lawrence began. Blake would have a reverence for official channels. 'But I've been asked to give evidence to the International Criminal Court. About what we saw on the trip to Congo, the one where Oliver Dawson was killed.'

'Yes,' Blake said. 'I'd heard.'

'There's a man called Faustin Kalombo,' Lawrence continued. 'He's accused of war crimes. It's a long list. Rape; sexual slavery; pillaging; using child soldiers.' Blake flinched as Lawrence ran through the list of charges.

'Why have they called you as a witness?' he asked.

'Because we were there. We filmed some of his soldiers, some of the children. We were on our way back when we were ambushed.'

'It was an awfully long time ago,' Blake observed.

'These things take an awfully long time,' Lawrence replied.

'Martin Elliot was there with you, wasn't he?' Lawrence nodded. 'Is he giving evidence?'

'He's been asked to, as well,' Lawrence replied. No point in admitting Martin's reluctance. 'I wanted to talk to you about the tapes.' Blake did his little quizzical face again. 'The tapes we filmed that day,' Lawrence continued. 'They're evidence. They show that the children were there, under arms. It could form part of the prosecution case.'

'I don't know,' Blake replied. 'Would we even still have them? They might have been wiped by now, thrown out.'

'I'm sure they're still there.' Lawrence knew they would have been kept. It had been hard enough to bring them back, after all. As far as he remembered, they had been filed away in the archives with a warning label stuck on the cassette, to remind people that they shouldn't be reused indiscriminately. Martin had insisted on it. They were the last shots Olly ever took and he was adamant that they shouldn't be turned into wallpaper, generic images used without a second thought, any time someone needed some pictures of Africa, some shots of child soldiers. He wasn't going to have them devalued like that.

Ed Blake took a small sip of his coffee.

'I'm not sure we'd allow the tapes to be used,' he said, after a pause. 'It might set a precedent. We shouldn't be seen to be – taking sides.' Lawrence shook his head.

'This isn't taking sides,' he said. 'This is just showing what happened. Bearing witness. It's what we're – what you're – supposed to do. It's what you're there for.'

'Can we be required to hand them over?' Blake asked.

'Ask the lawyers,' Lawrence replied.

'I don't think it's something we should be seen to do,' Blake went on. 'There have been cases, in the past, haven't there? What if it puts people at risk in the future, people in similar situations to yours back then? I've got to think about the safety of our teams in the field. Not to mention the publicity, the legal implications.' That was typical Blake – make out that it's about the safety of other journalists, appeal to Lawrence that way, but in the end it would come down to what people thought about Ed Blake himself. He didn't want to cause trouble; more precisely, he didn't want to be seen to cause trouble.

'Then don't be seen to do it,' Lawrence insisted. 'Make a public fuss about how you're not going to do it, and then do it anyway. People will only remember the public fuss.'

'It isn't that simple.' Blake was stalling him. It was that simple, if he wanted it to be.

'You'd be doing the right thing,' Lawrence repeated. He hated having to come to Ed Blake, of all people, as a supplicant. At least he wasn't having to ask a favour for himself. Lawrence thought of this instead as a favour for Olly Dawson, a favour for the boys they had filmed that day, for all the other victims.

'The cut story,' Blake said, thinking aloud. 'That might be possible. I mean, it's probably out there by now, anyway. There are probably ways to see it, online.'

'It's not enough,' Lawrence said. The few minutes that they had eventually put together, after they got home, showed very little. It was the hardest edit Lawrence had ever done, not because of the lack of material, but because it was too good, too painful. He had sat in the small edit suite next to Martin, another editor spooling through Olly Dawson's pictures, putting the sequences together when it should have been Olly doing it himself. Each time the editor took a tape from its hard plastic case to slide into the slot of the player, Lawrence saw those moments again, the tapes secreted beneath the vinyl seat of the car, the images of that evening on the road running back and forth in his head the way Olly's pictures went to and fro on the screens in front of him. Every shot Olly had taken was precise, clear, the sequences fitted together neatly. They scarcely needed Lawrence's words. He remembered the boy soldier's face and the close-up of his fearful eyes that contradicted the bravado of every word that he'd told them. He remembered the boy playing with a football, a few minutes of childhood recaptured before he was made to pick his weapon up again. There had been the end-shot, the boy standing to attention, acting older than he was. They had added a black screen at the end, a picture of Olly with his camera, his name and the dates of his abbreviated life. 'They'll need the rushes. There's stuff on there that we didn't use. There'll be people there who could be identified. It could all help.'

Ed Blake shook his head.

'I'd have to refer it up,' he said. 'To people higher up the food chain than me.' He glanced upwards, as though there were people in an upstairs office that he was invoking.

'Oh, come on,' Lawrence said. 'You could take the decision. You take bigger decisions than this. One quick call from you and it's done.'

'We'll see,' Blake said. He stood up and picked up his phone from the table, indicating that the meeting was over. He held out a hand to Lawrence. 'I'll be in touch.'

Lawrence was conscious of how little he now mattered to Blake. He was nothing more than a potential irritant, someone who might be able to cause him a problem if he wasn't handled correctly. He had been that before and he had been handled out of the way. Lawrence wasn't going to let that happen again. His old, long-forgotten desire to cause trouble had returned. He owed Blake nothing now; he owed Olly Dawson something.

14

Paris had gone back to work after its somnolent summer; the cars were thronging the avenues, the shops and restaurants open for business again. Martin laid a hand on the brown-painted metal of the safety railing and looked out at the city marked out in squares by the wire mesh of the grille in front of him. On the far side of the grey-blue river, the trees in the Tuileries were already starting to turn, their leaves a dark red against the green of the park. One long line of red-leaved trees followed the river's edge on the right bank, near where the tourist boats were moored alongside the embankment.

He walked further around the viewing platform to see where he should have been instead. The rest of them would probably be approaching the Bois de Boulogne by now, the distant green shape that he could just see, further to the west. He should have been feeling the sweat coursing down his back, the exhaustion in his legs, the exhilaration and the adrenalin of knowing he was going to make it and that soon it would all be over. Before much longer, they'd be coasting down the final avenue to arrive beneath the Eiffel Tower, below where he was standing now.

There were armed police officers standing at the bases of the tower's legs, scanning the tourists buying their tickets. Up on the viewing platform, there was a nervous atmosphere, a jumpiness. Whenever there was a loud noise, a creak or a crash, people looked around to see what might have happened. A couple of evenings earlier, even as the illuminations on the tower sparkled, it had been evacuated after a bomb scare. Martin had been at home when he received a text telling him to check the news. His first thought, he realised, was not whether anyone actually wanted to blow up the Eiffel Tower – though he was sure someone, somewhere did – but what it would mean for the bike ride if the place was closed for the next few days. They could finish at the Arc de Triomphe instead and it would look just as impressive; the echoes of the Tour de France might even be an improvement. Then he started working out what he'd do if there was some atrocity; the ride would have to be cancelled, or at least postponed. You couldn't have people riding into a city in mourning, celebrating their fantastic achievement while one of the world's most recognisable monuments had been attacked. It would be incongruous, in poor taste; it would attract ridicule. He came up with a backup plan, a couple of them for different eventualities. Only now he was standing up here in the wind and surveying the other tourists with suspicion, alert to every unusual noise, did he actually start to think about what would happen to him and to the other people here if it hadn't just been a warning or a hoax.

It had been easy to convince Iona that he needed to set off early, to spend the extra night in Paris before the cyclists arrived; all he had to do was to argue the opposite.

'It'll be fine,' he had mock-insisted. 'I'll catch the earliest Eurostar on Friday, I'll be there with half an hour to spare. If I rush across town, move quickly enough to get to the front of the taxi queue, I'll be there in time.'

'I don't think you should do that,' she said. 'There's no need to put yourself under pressure. In fact, you need to make sure you're not doing that to yourself.' Martin had waited. 'Why don't you go over the night before?' Iona had volunteered. 'Take it easy. Have a bit of spare time?' She would have expected him to say no, to insist that it was a waste of time and money to stay longer than necessary. Instead, he looked back across the breakfast table, as they compared diaries, as though it was her idea.

'I suppose I could,' he said, giving the impression of weighing the plan up. He had arrived, checked in at the hotel, had a shower, felt that sense of anticipation mixed with danger that he recollected from before his fall. It was the first time he had travelled alone since the accident and it had been easier than he imagined. Even with one good arm he could manage a trip of a couple of days, pulling a small wheeled suitcase behind him. Iona had worried about him, but then she always worried about him. He only remembered what he couldn't do when he tried to hoist his bag onto the luggage rack.

His phone rang and he stepped back from the edge of the viewing deck.

'I'm here,' she said. 'Where are you?'

Martin felt giddy and closed his eyes. This was not the good kind of fear, the fear that made the adrenalin pump and sharpened life's edges; it was the fear that made you step back, made you realise that life was going to get the better of you, sooner or later. It made him wonder whether this was the beginning of something worse. These days, he could not help but think of the worst that could happen. If you get those sensations again, they told him, you should take yourself to hospital. Straight away. Even if you think it might be nothing. Martin told himself firmly that it was perfectly normal to feel a sensation of vertigo when he was hundreds of metres above Paris.

'I'm up here,' he said. 'On the top deck. I'm on my way.' The lift ground its way downwards, the buildings getting larger, and Martin kept staring outwards, at the metal girders that slid upwards, past him.

Isabelle was standing at the very centre of the base of the tower, looking up. She was wearing black trousers and her legs looked skinnier than he remembered. She wore a white shirt, a grey cashmere wrap folded around her shoulders. Even the sight of her from a distance, her familiar outline, felt like a punch to the guts. It was painful but it was a better pain than he had become used to.

'I never come here,' she said as Martin approached. 'You don't, unless you're a tourist.' She said it as if they had met by chance, as if she was expecting someone to overhear them. She did not say that he was looking well, or even that he wasn't.

'I am a tourist,' Martin replied. He glanced from side to side as he went nearer. There was no one to see them. He kissed Isabelle on the lips, hugged her close and held on to her for all the moments that he could manage. 'What happened last night? Why did you cancel? I had to sit in our restaurant by myself.' He recalled the pitying look of the waiter in the little bistro with its lace-curtained windows, who had cleared away the second place setting.

'I know. I'm sorry. It's just that Christophe had a last-minute dinner that I had to attend. There was no chance of avoiding it.'

'You knew I was coming. You've known for a while. I came here early, so that we could spend time together, before the others arrived.'

'I said I was sorry. Sometimes things just happen and you can't get round them.' She pushed her hair out of her face, a reflex action that she did whenever she was uncertain. Martin tried to tell whether she was genuinely apologetic. Sometimes even he couldn't read her expressions.

They heard a loud hooting of car horns from the street and broke away from each other. They walked, carefully separate, towards the road that passed the tower's feet. A van plastered with logos was pulling up, the cyclists in their blue jerseys not far behind. Drivers leant out of their windows and cheered encouragement.

Martin mustered the face he had to assume for the team's arrival, the confident, happy expression they expected of him. A few supporters were lined up to welcome the cyclists. Martin knew many of them and he exchanged the same conversation with each. Yes, it was terribly bad luck. No, no lasting damage. He tried not to brood on the fact that Isabelle did not seem to care. Perhaps this was her way of telling him it was over. He stood and clapped, as best he could, a gentle tapping of one hand against the other rather than full-strength applause, as the cyclists pulled in, a few dozen of them. They had made it and he tried not to resent them all for it.

He caught sight of Julian Heathcote, somewhere towards the back of the pack. He stood astride his bike and was taking off his helmet to reveal damp red hair beneath, his face the russet of one of his own apples.

'Apple juice or beer?' Martin asked Julian as he watched him gulp down water from the bottle that had been attached to his bike frame.

'Sod the apple juice,' Julian gasped. 'I need a bloody beer.'

'It's good stuff, this apple juice, I've heard. Expensive.' Martin enjoyed teasing Julian.

'Beer,' he repeated. Martin waved over one of the young women who were handing out drinks and T-shirts to the finishers. Julian cracked open the can and took a long swig. Martin helped himself as well, even though he hadn't earned it.

'You made it, then,' Martin said, raising his beer can to Julian. 'Well done.'

'There was a point on one of the hills where I didn't think I would, to be honest,' Julian replied. 'It was bloody hellish. But you'll be with us next year, won't you?'

'You try and stop me,' Martin laughed.

'To next year,' Julian said, raising what was left of his beer in return.

'To next year,' Martin echoed.

He had to stay at the celebration dinner for the speeches. There was no option, since he had to make one of them, introduce the others. There had been cheering, applause, thumping of tables, though he was not sure anyone was really listening by that point. They had seemed to listen to Isabelle, who spoke in a soft voice that the people at the far end of the restaurant's private room would have strained to hear, but the stories she told did not need a loud voice. Her soft-spoken manner made her audience lean in, anxious not to miss what she said.

He had reassured her of that, the first time he heard her speak in public. They had been backstage at a conference, about to appear together on a panel. As a producer in a headset had fiddled with Isabelle's microphone, she had whispered in Martin's direction, 'Help me out, if I'm struggling. I'm dreadful at these things. I have so many ideas but I can't express them clearly.'

She had been great; brilliant, in fact. She talked about people and their lives and how they could be made better. Even the applause at the end of the session had not convinced her that she had come across well. She turned to Martin as they left the stage with an anxious look.

'How was I?'

'You were fantastic. Very impressive.'

'Really?' The smile that she gave him was worth the trip. As members of the audience crowded around her afterwards, pressing business cards on her, she began to believe she had done a good job, but the only person whose invitation for a drink she had accepted was Martin's.

The restaurant might have been beautiful, its private room with its panelled walls and its framed paintings immaculate, the food delicious, but it was time to leave. The bikes were safely in the vans, ready to be driven back to London. The cyclists, showered and hobbling, had hit the food and the wine greedily. Some of them were making a big weekend of it. The way they were walking – and drinking – now, though, he didn't imagine they would be getting far around the shops or the art galleries the next day. Martin declined the cake that he was offered and started to say his goodbyes. He pleaded tiredness and he got in return that sympathetic look he was starting to hate, the one that treated him as an invalid.

'I'm leaving now,' he told her. The plea for her to follow him was implicit.

'Not together,' she whispered.

'But you will come?' he urged.

'I'll try,' she replied. Isabelle never promised anything, in case it didn't happen. She rarely lied outright. All her evasions were in the things she did not say.

As he waited in the narrow hotel room, reclining on the bed against a pile of cushions, he wondered how long she would wait before she left. Fifteen minutes? Twenty? Half an hour? Long enough that people did not connect the two departures, short enough not to run into the others in the lobby downstairs. Perhaps she would not come at all.

He heard a text ping on his phone. All it said was *Room number?* He texted back: *406.* As soon as it had swished away, he made sure to delete her message and his reply. It was one lesson he had learned from the events of the summer, though he had ignored others: delete anything from his phone that he didn't want found. He had been lucky in that respect, that Iona had drowned his last BlackBerry in the pool. There had been things on it she should not have seen. The couple of minutes between the text arriving and the knock seemed like hours.

He opened the door to see Isabelle standing in the dimly lit corridor. She stepped into the room without saying anything and he closed the door behind her.

'I didn't know when I was going to see you again,' he said. 'Properly without other people.'

Their phone conversations had been hurried and brief and they had never really talked about what had happened in August. It was a subject that had hung over them, unsaid.

'When you didn't come past the house that morning,' she said, 'I was so angry with you. I thought you were realising it had all been a mistake. I thought you had come on holiday with your family and realised how foolish it was. Maybe you would have been right. After all, it was the second time. Because you didn't come the night before either.'

'That wasn't it, you know that. It was a mistake, a series of accidents.'

'I was so worried about you. I didn't know what could have happened.'

'Why didn't you come and visit me?'

'I couldn't get away. And, besides, your friend Lawrence said I shouldn't come.'

'He said that?'

'He spoke to me. He gave me your message. He asked Sylvie and Christophe to help find you. He did all the right things, but then he said I should leave you alone. At least until you were better.'

'And you listened to him?'

'I can make up my own mind. Maybe he was right.'

Martin turned away and walked further into the room. Isabelle followed him.

'Can I see your arm?' she asked. At first he held the arm in towards his ribs, protecting it with his other hand the way he had learned to do, reluctant to show it to her, but then he surrendered his wrist to her, stretching the damaged limb forward and supporting the forearm with his other hand. She sat down on the edge of the bed. Her fingers stroked his and he stretched the fingers and clenched them again, almost to show her that he could. Isabelle put her right hand up to his shoulder and pushed the cotton of his shirt away from his collarbone. She unbuttoned the first couple of buttons on his shirt, to see more.

'I've got scars,' he said. He both wanted her to see it and not to see it, the long, livid red dotted line that ran along from his shoulder towards his neck. There were still bumps and swellings along the ridge of the bone.

'Does it hurt?'

He could not help but flinch at her touch, even though her cool hands were soothing and exciting. 'Not now,' he said. 'But be careful with me.'

She raised her other hand to his face, pressing the side of her thumb onto his cheekbone, her fingertips against the base of his skull where it joined his neck. Then she leant in closer and kissed him.

15

IT WASN'T UNTIL Lawrence put his hand in his coat pocket to find his keys, a reflex action, that he remembered he no longer had any. He heard the doorbell echo inside and he waited. The house was still the same: the cracks on the black-and-white tiles in the porch; the straggly box hedge around the small front yard; the steps down to the basement flat that they had never managed to buy. Next door, there was scaffolding around the neighbours' house, a skip in the street, hoardings with an architect's name on. Sacks of rubble were piled up in the front yard. Lawrence looked across to the bay window of his former home to see if he could detect any signs of movement inside.

He was about to ring the doorbell again when Lizzie opened the door. Behind her, the hallway was piled high with plastic crates, new suitcases, a huge rucksack. A duvet was stuffed into a dustbin liner.

'Dad's here!' she shouted back into the house.

Her long chestnut hair swung over her shoulder as she leaned in to hug him. The top of her head came level with his eyebrows now. Lawrence hugged her back and then held his daughter at arm's length to inspect her. She had lost weight, which made her cheekbones seem more prominent and her face sharper, the roundness of childhood completely gone. Lizzie's scattering of freckles across her nose was darker, her face was tanned and blonde sun-streaks ran through her hair.

'You look great,' he said. 'That trip really must have suited you. Please tell me you haven't got a tattoo.'

'I haven't got a tattoo, Dad,' she said with a roll of the eyes that was more affectionate than it used to be. 'I had a henna one for a bit, but they come off.'

This was the little girl who had set off to her Parisian school with a backpack almost bigger than herself, her dark hair tied in bunches, who within a few weeks had spoken better French than either of her parents. Her French was probably still better than his and she would probably take the chance to prove it. She scarcely needed to study it, Lawrence thought.

He walked into the house, past Lizzie's heaps of possessions, into the living room. He wondered where Harriet and Josh were. Lizzie offered him a cup of tea, but he declined. It was strange to be treated as a guest here. So much was still the same: the plants, the family pictures on the mantelpiece. Lizzie coiled her legs, in skinny jeans, beneath her on the sofa. Lawrence didn't sit down; he paced the length of the living room, examining what he found there without touching anything.

All he had seen of his daughter for six months was an occasional picture attached to an email; he had seen her in front of temples with other young people he did not know, or with the Cambodian orphans she was teaching. Mostly the emails were happy, breezy, full of jokey observations. Once in a while she would send a longer message, one he wished she'd sent in a letter. Lawrence printed them off to read and to keep. There was one email that, he worked out, had been sent late at night, Phnom Penh time, arriving in the early French evening.

Lizzie had spent the day at Tuol Sleng. She wrote:

It was a school. It still looks like a school. It has a playground and classrooms, like any other school. And then you go inside and you see all the people who died, hundreds of pictures of them all, so many that they almost stop being real. Then you see how they died, how they were tortured. And it's all still there and it wasn't all that long ago.

Lawrence had never been to Tuol Sleng but he knew about it, that it was the prison where the Khmer Rouge had tortured and killed many of their victims. He must have been about Lizzie's age when it was going on. She signed off:

There's a translation there of one of the rules of the prison. It says 'You must immediately answer my questions without wasting time to reflect.' So without wanting to be a torturer, that's what I'm asking you. Why do people do things like that and how could you bear to go and see them, time after time, without being able to do anything about it?

Lawrence had replied straight away, as the torturers had commanded, even though he knew that it was late and she was probably out somewhere by the time he sent his response, drinking beer and trying to forget about it. He gave the answer that he had always given, without wasting time to reflect.

I wish I could tell you, Lizzie, why people do things like that. It's one of the great unsolvable puzzles of human history. If we could answer it, we'd win Nobel peace prizes and we'd be able to do something about it. Maybe you will. Evil? Power? Society? Your guess is as good as mine. I'm sure that's not an answer a torturer would be happy with, because it's not an answer at all. But as to your second question, how could I bear to see atrocities that I couldn't do anything about – I know it's a cliché but someone needs to witness things, someone needs to tell the world what is going on. Then, I'm afraid, you've got to leave it to the people with power to try to sort it out.

As he typed, he realised what an inadequate answer it would seem to Lizzie. At least, in a court of law, he would only have to bear witness to what he had seen, to what he could manage to remember, inadequate as that might be. They would only ask him what had happened, not why. It was an answer he had given often enough, to people who confronted him in trouble spots, demanding to know what help he brought.

'We'll let the world know,' he had said. 'Then they'll see what's happening.' And they'll change the channel and see if there's something funny on the other side, because they don't want to think about it that much. That's why we don't show them the worst things.

Lawrence envied Lizzie having years ahead of her to argue these questions, late student nights over coffee and wine. He hoped more than anything that she kept the sense of outrage, didn't let it dim and tarnish.

He heard shouting upstairs, Harriet trying to extract Josh from his room and get him to come downstairs. That much, at least, hadn't changed since he'd been away. Harriet clattered down the stairs and entered the living room. She addressed Lizzie first.

'Have you got everything?' she asked. 'Because I don't want to be halfway down the motorway and have you suddenly remember something.'

Lizzie shrugged and then stretched an arm out along the back of the cream sofa.

'I've got everything. And if not, I can live without it. Or buy it.'

Harriet seemed to notice his presence for the first time.

'You made it,' she said. He resented the assumption that he wouldn't have. Harriet seemed to have grown younger since he'd been away. She scarcely looked old enough to have a daughter who was leaving for university. The two women wore almost interchangeable outfits. Harriet's hair was blonder than before, better cut, her skin more taut. Harriet had come into her own in his absence and he wondered for how long he had been holding her back.

'We should be going,' she said. She turned back to the door and shouted up the stairs again. 'Josh, come down.'

Lawrence heard the answering shuffle of his son's large feet on the wooden stairs. Josh appeared in the doorway, reluctant to cross the threshold. He leant against the doorframe, almost filling the space. His shoulders were slouched under a baggy grey hoodie, his hands stuffed into the pockets of his jeans. He looked at Lawrence with a wary gaze from beneath the blond hair that fell over his eyes. Knowing Josh, he would not admit to how unsettled and upset he felt. Lawrence remembered him sitting, chubby legs crossed, on the floor of the Paris apartment as removal men packed their belongings into cardboard boxes, refusing to budge. He was staying there, he said, even if the others left. He had said much the same when they left Washington. Now the hallway was full of his sister's possessions, as it had been full of his father's just a few months before.

There were some old habits that it was easy to settle back into. Lawrence loaded the car, because he had always loaded the car. It was the same estate car with its familiar dents, including the one in the rear bumper where he had reversed into a bollard while arguing with Harriet about where to park. Lawrence enjoyed the sense of order he got from slotting the suitcases and the boxes containing books and coffee mugs into the most efficient places, tucking a desk lamp and a computer case into the gaps that remained. It was like solving a three-dimensional jigsaw puzzle. He had loaded in everything that Lizzie and Josh had brought down; he was about to close the boot when Lizzie presented him with one last item to pack. She came down the front steps with a large picture frame held out in front of her.

'Mum says I have to ask you if I can take this.'

'What is it?'

She turned the picture to face him. Jean Seberg and Jean-Paul Belmondo were, for a brief moment, strolling down the street in Tufnell Park instead of the Champs-Élysées. It was his *À Bout de Souffle* poster, the one he'd bought in a little shop in Paris when he himself was a student.

'I didn't know you liked that,' Lawrence said. For a moment he was going to say she couldn't have it, that he wanted it back instead. It would have looked good on the wall in France and he didn't know why he'd left it in London in the first place. 'It's an original, you know. It's even older than me. So you'd better look after it.' Lizzie looked hesitant, as though she was about to take it back into the house. 'Of course you can have it. Give it to me.' Lizzie handed him the frame and he turned it sideways, sliding it on top of the rest of the luggage. He leant further in, fussed around with a cushion and the duvet that he pretended to be using to protect the glass of the picture, when really he was trying to avoid Lizzie seeing that tears had sprung to his eyes.

Harriet came out of the front door, keys in hand, Josh behind her.

'I don't think I'm going to come, after all,' he said. 'I'll just stay here.'

'You are coming,' Harriet said. She tried to usher him out of the door so she could lock it after them. He shook his head, his gaze downward. Lawrence closed the car boot and walked up the steps towards them. Harriet would get angry and that would only make Josh even more reluctant to come. Conflict, as well as change, was something he tried to avoid.

'Are you driving?' he asked Harriet. He had usually driven, when he was around, but he was conscious that it was no longer his car. She nodded and moved to the side, to let him pass.

'Come on, Josh,' Lawrence said gently. 'It's strange for all of us. But it won't be the same without you.'

'It won't be the same without Lizzie,' Josh replied. 'And it isn't the same without you.'

'I know,' Lawrence said. It was the same look of disappointment he remembered in Josh's face from before, the look he saw when he had brought Josh another hasty airport present, an aeroplane in a cellophane-windowed box or another gold prism of Toblerone.

Lawrence put his hand on Josh's shoulder and urged him gently forward. Josh sidled down the steps towards the car and opened the rear door. Lizzie, who had been waiting on the pavement, followed him into the car. Harriet locked the front door and then climbed into the driver's seat. Lawrence sat in the passenger seat and slid the seat back to allow him to stretch his legs out.

'Dad!' Josh exclaimed from behind him. Lawrence shunted the seat forward again, realising that Josh's legs were now as long as his own and required just as much space. As he turned his head towards the rear seats he still expected to see two small excited faces, a little girl and a little boy, heading for a French holiday or an American road trip. Lawrence suddenly knew how much he had missed, how much time had passed when he had been absent.

Lawrence put the last crate of books down on the floor of Lizzie's new room.

'Did you really need all of these?' he asked.

'I'm going to do some work, Dad,' she replied. 'Unlike you.' All the students he had seen so far in the corridors of the hall of residence were similar to Lizzie and her friends. They were well groomed, eager, conscientious. The rebellious poses of his generation seemed to have gone. When Lawrence had arrived at his Cambridge college, it had barely taken a day before a bearded young man in a Che Guevara T-shirt had told Lawrence, on hearing where he went to school, that he would be first up against the wall come the revolution. The last Lawrence had heard of Jim Kavanagh, he was something big in the civil service.

Lizzie leant the film poster up against the wall and surveyed her room, its bookshelves and noticeboard yet to be filled. There was a desk below a narrow window that overlooked the gardens, a bed, not room for much more.

'It's pretty small, isn't it?' she observed. It felt cramped with the whole family clustering inside. Lawrence could see her sizing everything up: the room, the halls, the fellow students she did not yet know, trying to foresee the next few years of her life, to work out how these in turn would determine the rest of her future.

'It'll be fine,' Lawrence reassured her. 'Let's go and get some lunch.'

They waited for a table in the large, barnlike restaurant, as other parents finished feeding their student children what they imagined would be their last proper meal for weeks.

Once they sat down, the waitress slapped large laminated menus in front of them.

'I've been meaning to ask what happened to Martin Elliot in the summer,' Harriet said.

'What did you hear?' Lawrence replied. He was torn between wanting to show Harriet that he had privileged knowledge, that for once he was closer to the story than her, and worrying to what use she might put the information.

'I heard he was doing some crazy bike ride and came off on the mountainside, that he had to be rescued.'

'That's pretty much it,' Lawrence replied.

'But you were there, weren't you? There must have been more to it than that.'

'What makes you say that?'

'It's just that he seems to have taken ages to recover. I heard from someone who was on the bike ride, the London to Paris one.'

'Heard what?'

'That Martin's still in a bad way. Not himself. Bad tempered, not as charming as he usually is.'

Josh lifted his head from his menu to interrupt.

'Did Damian tell you that?' He laid a heavy emphasis on the 'Damian', drawing the word out into three long syllables. Harriet pretended to be perusing the menu and didn't answer him.

'Who's Damian?' Lawrence asked.

'Damian Charlton,' Josh said in a sing-song voice, teasing Harriet. 'He's Mum's boyfriend.'

'He's not my boyfriend,' Harriet replied, as though she was the teenager.

'Damian Charlton? The one who you used to say was a complete intellectual fraud? Damian Charlatan?'

'I never said that,' Harriet retorted. 'You used to say that.

Because you were jealous of him. You said anyone could stride around old battlefields, waving his hands to the camera and explaining it all, when the battle had finished hundreds of years before. Much harder when the guns were still firing, you used to say.' The colour had risen in Harriet's cheeks, enough to let on that despite her protestations Josh was right.

'Well, it is. Have you been to his castle?' Lawrence had never met Damian Charlton but it was true that he envied him, not just for his aristocratic privilege and his air of eternal youth.

'It's not a castle. It's a country estate.'

The waitress returned to take their order, interrupting their barbs. Lawrence tried to tell himself that it didn't matter if Harriet was seeing Damian Charlton. It was no longer any of his concern. He tried to be happy for her.

'Anyway, what did the viscount, or whatever he is, say about Martin?'

'He's only a baronet, for now. And he doesn't use the title. Damian said that Martin has got very tetchy, since the accident.'

'I think that's only to be expected,' Lawrence said. 'He had a bad bash on the head. It can affect you like that. He needs to take it easy, for a while, but knowing Martin . . .'

'. . . . he won't. He's incapable of it.' It was a long time since Harriet had finished one of his sentences for him and he realised that he missed it.

'He's frustrated, as well,' Lawrence continued. 'Hates to feel he's missing out.'

'So what actually happened?' Lizzie asked. She had still been away and had not heard much of the story.

'We had to look for him,' Lawrence said. 'It took a couple of days to find him. We had to pull out all the stops, call the consulate and the police. Victoria Loxton was there, she talked to some people in the Foreign Office.' Lawrence knew that he was name-dropping and that this was for Harriet's benefit, not Lizzie's. Harriet leant in, the way she always did when she was hoping to extract more information. She had a knack of getting people to tell her more than they meant to and it had served her well; they rarely realised how much they had said until it was too late. 'Did I tell you I'm going to be doing some work for him?'

Harriet raised her eyebrows slightly.

'For Martin? That's good. I always said you should do that.' Harriet's desire to be right about everything was still present.

'Doing what?' Lizzie asked, trying to deflect an argument, as she often had.

'It's some work making a film for an NGO, a French one. But I'm still not sure about it.'

'But that's great, Dad. You'd really be making a difference.' Lizzie was both surprised and enthused. 'What do they do, exactly?'

'Eye clinics, mostly. Mobile surgeries that go into places with no real infrastructure. Everything's shipped in: staff, equipment. All the kit pre-packed and sterile and ready to go.'

'So the more money you help raise, the more people will be able to see, right? And then able to work and look after their families? Rather than rely on the state in somewhere there's probably no functioning state to speak of.'

'Basically, yes.'

'So, do it.' To her, the question was settled.

'It's more complicated than that,' Lawrence objected. 'It's more to do with where they want me to go.'

'Where?' Harriet asked.

'Africa.'

'Where exactly in Africa?'

There was an uneasy silence as the waitress put the plates down in front of them. Lawrence picked up a knife to cut into his steak. Harriet hesitated over her large heap of salad.

'They want me to go to the DRC – to Congo.'

'Does it have to be there?' Harriet asked, her fork hovering above her plate. 'You could ask for a different location. Martin would understand.'

'I've tried that. But he's quite insistent. It needs to be the extreme case, apparently. Because otherwise people get compassion fatigue, don't see why they should give any money.'

Harriet poured water for all of them before she spoke.

'Compassion fatigue isn't real. It's a condition made up to justify people being mean. Not like what you—'

'It's also that I've been asked to go back and give evidence, at the Hague, about — what happened there before.' Lawrence interrupted her.

'But surely you should, Dad?' Lizzie persisted. 'Say yes to both. It's the right thing to do.' Lizzie paused, trying to remember the correct expression. 'It's about reconciliation. Coming to terms with the past. It helps.' Josh remained silent, cutting into his roast chicken. He did not say much, but he missed very little.

Harriet made to hush her.

'Your dad had a bad time there, a long time ago. It was a very long time ago. Maybe you should leave it there. Move on.' It was the kind of thing that Martin would have said.

'Bet you don't say that to Mr Charlton,' Lawrence observed. 'He'd be out of a job if it weren't for talking about things that happened a very long time ago.' He was being snarky but he couldn't help it.

'Dad,' Lizzie reproached him. 'Not now. I know about what happened,' she continued. 'You've told me about it before.' She addressed him rather than her mother. 'You had a friend who was killed, right? The cameraman?'

'Olly Dawson,' Lawrence agreed.

Lizzie continued, undeterred. 'And you'd be able to tell people about what happened to him? What do they want you to testify about, exactly?'

Lawrence ignored Harriet, across the table, as she shook her head at him. Lizzie and Josh were no longer tiny children. They were old enough for this sort of conversation.

'The militia commander's been indicted. He's accused of using child soldiers, selling girls into sex slavery, rape. We saw the child soldiers. We filmed them. And it was on the way back that Olly was killed.'

Lizzie chewed a mouthful of salmon before she spoke.

'Then you definitely should. What about the victims? Don't they deserve it?'

'Of course,' Lawrence acknowledged. 'But I don't know how much difference it would make. One testimony. A few minutes of film.'

'And what would Olly have told you to do?'

'He'd have asked how much they were paying me for the filming job. And then he'd have told me not to be a fucking idiot, of course I should go.'

16

THE RAIN RATTLED down on the corrugated-iron roof of the clinic, splashing from the metal onto the muddy ground below. They huddled on the veranda and wondered when it would stop. Still, at least it was warm. The winter in France was proving colder than Lawrence had expected, frost coating the vineyards and wood smoke from the chimneys pervading the village. He leant his elbows on the railing of the balcony and watched the sky to see if he could see a break in the clouds.

Amy Finch leant on the railing next to him. They were a mismatched team in many ways, but so far it seemed to be working. She took the little headphones out of her ears and shook her head.

'It's no good,' she said. 'Too much rain noise. We'll have to wait for it to stop.' She tilted her head up beneath the brim of her baseball cap to look at the sky.

Amy was petite and wiry and did not fit Lawrence's preconception of what a cameraperson should be like. The ones he had worked with had mostly been men, they had been tall enough to wield their cameras above crowds and press scrums. Olly Dawson had been like that. He kept trying not to think about Olly, but it was hard, especially here. Maybe, given what had happened before, being accompanied by a small blonde woman was better than being alongside a burly Aussie. He kept hearing Olly's sardonic voice in his ear, criticising him, teasing him. Amy was brisk and uncomplaining and knew what she was doing.

'Where's all the kit?' Lawrence had asked as they arrived in Nairobi, before they caught an onward flight to Kigali.

'Here,' Amy said. She was carrying a laptop case and a black nylon padded rucksack that held her camera.

'That's it?'

'That's most of it. There's one other box in the hold.' Lawrence must have looked unconvinced. 'It's all digital. Smaller, lighter. But it still works, don't worry.'

That was Amy: the new, digital version, compared to the analogue guys he had always worked with before. There were no more clunky plastic tapes to feed into the camera and store in boxes, just tiny memory cards whose contents she uploaded to her laptop. He had to stop himself again from thinking how that might have made a difference, the last time. Don't replay it in your head, they had told him. There's no point. You can't go back and change it.

Jason Evans was pacing the length of the veranda, his boots drumming out a rhythm as he marched up and down. He was never still, never off guard, but then that was his job. He was a compact, stocky Welsh ex-Marine in a dark polo shirt and combat trousers.

'Reckon the rain will stop soon, Jason?' Lawrence asked with a sidelong glance towards Amy. It was already becoming something of a joke between them: to see who could get anything more than a monosyllabic response from Jason. Jason had been watching the middle distance, the road and the trees beyond, the people he saw passing with boxes of fruit and vegetables for sale.

'Might do,' he agreed. Two whole words. Amy smiled at Lawrence.

Isabelle emerged from inside the office.

'Are we ready to go?' she asked Lawrence. 'We're meeting Celestine at her shop, like you wanted.'

There was a white Land Cruiser with the agency's logo on the doors and bonnet waiting outside and the four of them climbed in, Jason in the front passenger seat. Lawrence sat in the back, between Amy and Isabelle. He looked at Isabelle, wondering how she looked so clean and elegant, whatever the circumstances. She was wearing beige trousers, a white shirt, a linen jacket over the top, not a fleck of red mud on any of them. It was having the staff, he decided, uncharitably. Having people who sorted things out for you. Isabelle, in professional mode, had hardly mentioned anything about the summer. It was almost as if he were meeting her for the first time.

'Should I get some extra shots, while we drive?' Amy asked. She was curious, alert, seeing all of this for the first time. Lawrence was glad they had a fresh pair of eyes, ones that could bring the hope and optimism that he lacked. He had asked Amy, on the journey over, whether she had done anything like this before. She hadn't, she told him, but she wanted to do more of it, perhaps get into making documentaries. Mostly she did corporate work, lifestyle programmes for TV when she could get the contracts.

Amy slid the rear window of the car down and balanced her camera on the edge. The driver, Fabrice, pulled into the road. As they drove towards the centre of town, the roads became better, less rutted. The main boulevard was tarmacked and even had streetlights and a grassy central reservation with plants; other roads were still covered with red mud. In some places, the road was solidified lava, with heaps of black volcanic rock piled by the houses.

'You can't really see the volcano from here,' Isabelle said. 'It's up there, to the north. But you can still see the lava. It covered so much of the airport runway that they can't use it any more.'

Lawrence wondered what the people of this city had done to deserve it; the town having nearly been destroyed by a volcanic eruption eight years earlier was one of the lesser of their troubles, beyond war and constant, unpredictable violence. They all agreed that what they wanted the film to show was resilience rather than hopelessness, a sense that Isabelle's agency was enabling people to live their own lives, rather than being dependent on others. That was why they were heading to see one of Isabelle's patients at the shop she ran with her family. Help Celestine, so the narrative went, and you help not only her but her children, her extended family, her employees.

On one of the muddy avenues, Isabelle directed Fabrice to pull the four-wheel drive over in front of a parade of shops. The rain had stopped and the sky was clearing. Amy jumped down from the back of the vehicle and began sizing the place up, looking for possible shots. She persuaded Fabrice to move the car away from the front of the shop they were visiting and crossed over to the other side of the street. From here, the volcano loomed above the city. The flat top of the mountain was visible between breaking clouds and a ray of sunlight was streaming down. There was a coil of grey smoke from the volcano's crater. It was a great shot.

Amy set the camera up on its tripod, panned across from the distant volcano to the shops. They were in a single-storey concrete building, with pillars supporting the parapet that overhung the pavement. Their signs were hand-painted on the dirty cream render of the frontage. Celestine's shop was the *papeterie*, the stationer's. A young man on a two-wheeled, home-made wooden scooter, a *tshukudu*, kicked his way along the road in front of the shop. Amy held the camera steady until he had passed out of the frame, then picked her tripod up and headed back to the other side of the road.

Celestine Macuba's shop had a metal grille on the window. The owner was waiting in the doorway to greet them. She was probably in her fifties, wearing a bright pink blouse and a long skirt of green and orange printed cloth. Her stationery shop was small but neatly organised, with piles of exercise books, packets of paper, boxes of pens on shelves and behind her counter. She greeted them effusively and insisted on offering them drinks, summoning her youngest son from a back room with chilled cans of lemonade. Patrice was sixteen, she told them with pride, and he hoped to go to college if he passed his exams. Then he wanted to run a business of his own, she continued; a mobile phone shop or something to do with computers.

'Phones are good business here,' Lawrence observed, nodding to Patrice. They were a necessity here but they also conferred status; the more you had the better.

'Young people, they don't want all this,' Celestine said, gesturing towards her stock. 'They want everything to be electronic. But I tell them, when the electricity stops working, I still have my pens and my papers, but what do you have? Nothing.'

Amy bustled around, setting up the camera, moving a chair in front of the counter for Celestine to sit on. Patrice brought a chair for Lawrence. He settled down to do the interview. Isabelle was standing near the front of the shop, looking out of the window to the street beyond. Jason was in the doorway, keeping watch. Lawrence had noticed how he had checked out the whole shop, unobtrusively, making a play of going to chat to Patrice in the back room, in order to see what lay behind the shop, to check if there was another exit.

Celestine was thoughtful, well-spoken, had good English; everything you needed in an interviewee. She told him how her eyesight was getting worse, how it made it harder for her to run her business and look after her family.

'This wonderful doctor is going to help me,' she said, gesturing towards Isabelle. 'She'll help all of us get our lives back.'

Lawrence paused the interview when Celestine had finished speaking. He turned to Amy.

'Should I ask her to do that again? Say the name of the agency rather than talk about Isabelle?'

Amy raised her head from the eyepiece.

'No,' she replied. 'It's great like that. More natural. Don't try to coach her.'

'But if we can't see Isabelle?'

'It's fine,' Amy assured him. 'It'll work.'

They filmed Celestine behind her counter, a staged tidying

of her already immaculate shelves, and her flicking through a ledger book. Amy, in her soft-spoken voice, coaxed an initially reluctant Patrice into being filmed alongside his mother. He flashed Amy a smile and she had to ask him not to look directly at her or the camera, to keep his gaze on Celestine and to look as though he was listening to what she had to say.

Lawrence shook hands with Celestine as they prepared to leave.

'I'd wish you luck for the operation tomorrow,' he said, 'but I know you don't need it. You're in very safe hands.'

Isabelle came over to say goodbye, reminded Celestine what time she should arrive at the clinic in the morning.

It was going well, Lawrence told himself. It was all going well. History did not have to repeat itself. Sometimes you could rewrite the script, go for another take.

The sun was setting over the lake as they entered the restaurant. It had red and white gingham tablecloths, starched white linen napkins, gleaming glassware. The glass doors gave onto the terrace and the lake beyond. Shocking pink bougainvillea crept up a trellis on one of the walls and the lawn that ran down to the shore was studded with palm trees. As they arrived, the lights flickered and there was the juddering of a distant generator. Power, like so much else here, was unpredictable and unreliable.

They sat at a table outside. Jason pulled his chair away from the table so that he could check both directions, the approach from inside the restaurant and from the lake.

'It's beautiful, isn't it?' Amy said. 'I didn't expect it to be beautiful.'

'It's such a shame,' Isabelle agreed. 'The nature, the people, this place could have so much. And yet . . .'

The bar and the restaurant were filling up, but not with local people. The cars outside were the large four-wheel drives of aid agencies, hired by foreigners, their local drivers waiting for them. The snatches of conversation that Lawrence overheard were loud, in English and in French and in mixtures of the two, discussing supplies or when new colleagues were arriving or leaving; it was a place for gossip to be exchanged and business to be transacted. The atmosphere was familiar but Lawrence wasn't sure whether he liked it, that easy camaraderie of people in a strange place, picking up where they had left off in the last war, the last crisis.

'You've been here before, Lawrence, haven't you?' Isabelle asked. 'With Martin.'

He had told her. Lawrence wondered how much he had said, in how much detail.

'It was a long time ago,' he said, reluctant to say more. The others had never heard the story but he had repeated it too many times, told it to himself over and over in his head too often, hoping that it might end differently.

The waiter put large brown bottles of Primus beer on the table, the condensation dripping from their sides. Only Isabelle poured her beer into a glass.

'Martin said that one of your colleagues – one of your friends – was killed, and that the two of you were lucky to escape.'

Lucky. Martin had always thought he was lucky, then and since; Lawrence had always believed disaster was bound to strike him next. In all the discussions it had taken for Lawrence to be back here, the fixing, the to-and-fro of what it would be possible to do and when, the weeks of emails and permissions and bureaucracy, the waiting for the rains to finish, they had always skirted around what it meant to them. Martin had always side-stepped the conversation, saying he had enough on his plate. Recruiting Jason was the only time they had touched on the old subject; they had agreed they needed a decent security guard, someone who knew what they were doing. If anyone asked, Jason was the assistant, the sound man. Amy had showed him how to work the microphones, just in case.

'I don't know if we were lucky. We made some bad decisions. We got it wrong. We didn't all come back.'

Lawrence gulped down the cold beer.

'Who was he?' Isabelle asked. 'Your friend, the cameraman.' That was a question Lawrence could answer, one people asked too rarely.

'His name was Olly. Oliver Dawson. He was Australian. The best cameraman I ever worked with,' Lawrence said. He realised he might have offended Amy. 'Camera person. Present company excepted.'

'No offence taken,' Amy said, sipping her beer. 'Anyway, I haven't been doing this all that long. What made him so good?'

'He cared about the people he met, the people whose stories we were telling. He talked to them, especially the children. He was great with the children. He was this huge, tall guy – he must have been six foot five – but he got down to their level, played with them, made them feel at ease. I used to tell him he'd make a great dad, and he always said he wasn't ready, that he would give it all up one day and move back to Brisbane and raise a family. And he never did . . .'

The boy they had met that day was called Benjamin. He was nine years old, a skinny boy in baggy green shorts and a grubby T-shirt that had been white, a camouflage shirt that was too large for him buttoned over the top, the buttons in the wrong holes. The gun that he carried was too big for him as well. It was no toy. Benjamin and one of the other boys had been allowed to fall out of line for a few minutes and they had found a football nearby. At first he had been reluctant to talk to them, his eyes flicking sideways towards the adults. Lawrence had wondered what would have happened to him if he spoke out of turn.

'Can you show me some skills?' Olly asked and Benjamin was only too happy to oblige. He found a friend and the two of them played as though Lawrence, Martin and Olly had the power to select him for a London team, with neat passes, trick shots and headers. Olly shot Benjamin playing keepy-uppy for minutes on end, the camera on his feet and then on his face with its intent concentration. Martin had tapped Olly on the shoulder, saying that they had more than enough, that they would never use it all.

'Let him play,' Olly muttered. 'Let the kid play.'

'What went wrong?' Jason asked. It was the first time that Lawrence remembered him volunteering anything on the trip, let alone asking a question.

'We had got used to it,' Lawrence said. 'We had been going down the same road for a few days and we stopped thinking that there was anything to worry about. Then one day there was a roadblock.'

Jason nodded, as if this was the kind of story he had expected.

They had got what they needed for the day. They were all tired and heading back to the house where they were staying before it got dark and more dangerous. Jean-Baptiste, the driver, was bouncing the car across the potholes. Their fixer, Emmanuel, was speaking into one of his two mobile phones. Lawrence was wedged into the back seat of the four-wheel drive, his chino-clad leg pressing up against Olly's tanned, hairy leg in his shorts. Olly cradled the camera on his lap as though it were a baby. He took as much care of it as he would have done of any child, never letting it out of his sight, keeping it safe, wiped clean of dust. As they went over another pothole, Olly's head was jolted against the roof of the car and he swore out loud. Martin was next to Olly, applying a sticky label to a video tape and scrawling on it in Biro.

'I should have noticed that there wasn't any traffic coming the other way,' Lawrence said, 'that all the people seemed to have gone. But I didn't notice. None of us noticed.'

The stretch of road where Jean-Baptiste slowed down was narrow, the lake to their right, the forest starting a few metres away from the road to their left. Lawrence wondered at first why they had stopped. He saw, ahead of them, a pickup truck parked next to the verge. It had pulled up awkwardly, at an angle to the road, as though the driver had stopped on a momentary impulse. Two men in camouflage gear sat on the sides of the pick-up, one facing inwards towards the bed of the truck, the other, closer to the car, with his boots swinging out over the truck's side panels. Their clothes were less a uniform than a cobbled-together collection of items intended to give the impression of a uniform. One of the men wore camouflage trousers and heavy boots, but with an old red T-shirt. The other had a military shirt with epaulettes but wore beige trousers. He had a cartridge belt slung around his shoulders. Perhaps they only had one uniform to share between them, but they didn't want for guns. Each of the two men carried an AK-47. A third man, in a khaki beret, was the one clearly in charge. He sat in a plastic garden chair next to the truck, with an improvised armband around his bicep. That and the hat were his badges of authority but it was the way he sat that showed he was the commander, his heavy legs spread wide against the arms of the chair, one fist on his thigh.

Jean-Baptiste switched off the engine as the commander heaved himself up from his chair and approached them.

'*Ça va aller,*' Jean-Baptiste said. It'll be fine. Lawrence had rehearsed situations like this in the safety of training courses back home and he had been in them for real and until now he had always been fine. You could never be sure, though.

The commander leant in through the driver's window, his mirrored sunglasses masking his expression. Lawrence could smell the smoke on his breath as he asked Jean-Baptiste something that he didn't understand. Emmanuel answered the question for them. They were evidently discussing the passengers in the back seat. His palms open, Emmanuel indicated the letters 'TV' marked on the bonnet in strips of gaffer tape.

'What did he say?' Martin whispered to Emmanuel. Lawrence could tell that he was trying not to make any sudden movements.

'He wants to know who you are, where you are from.'

'And what did you tell him?'

'I said that you are journalists, from England. From the television.'

The soldier pulled his head back and stared through the rear window at the three of them. Lawrence could feel the sweat running faster down the back of his neck. The vinyl of the car seat squeaked as he shifted in his place. The commander tried to open the rear door; it was locked. His large hand reached around through Jean-Baptiste's open window and pulled the lock up from inside. Lawrence didn't try to stop him. He then tugged the handle again and swung the door open. A gust of heat from the road entered the car.

'It had happened to me before, often enough, in other places,' Lawrence recalled. 'I just thought we'd hand over a bribe and we'd be back on the road again. I didn't think much of it at first.'

The soldier beckoned them out of the car and again they didn't refuse. The two younger soldiers had climbed down from the back of the truck and were ambling towards where the officer stood. The one in the T-shirt was tall and gangly, his arms and legs loose as he strolled along. His eyes were as red as his shirt and Lawrence wondered if he was drunk or stoned. The other was smaller, stockier, and either angry or nervous, it was hard to tell which. Lawrence tried to remember where he had his most accessible bundle of dollars, one he could reach without it looking as if he was reaching for a weapon.

The three journalists stood in the road, facing the three soldiers. Emmanuel and Jean-Baptiste were allowed to stay in the car.

'Martin tried to talk our way out of trouble,' Lawrence said.

Isabelle nodded in recognition. 'It's what he always does,' she observed. 'It usually works.' She gave a glimmer of a smile and Lawrence wondered what she was remembering.

'It didn't work that time,' he said.

Martin tried first English and then his rudimentary French. He kept his eyes lowered and his gestures slow and submissive, the way they had learned to do. Other times, there had been answering laughs and the exclamation of names of football teams.

Instead, the commander gestured towards Olly. He was still

holding his camera in one hand. He held it by its top handle, low down, the lens carefully pointed away from the soldiers, towards the lake. He wasn't filming anything; he wasn't stupid. The commander ordered Olly to put the camera down on the ground and Olly complied, though Lawrence could see the slight contraction in his face as he laid the camera in the dust.

The commander directed a question towards Olly in French, asking what he was filming.

'Children,' he replied. '*Les enfants. Les petits.*' He held a broad hand out at hip height, the height of an imagined child's head.

The commander told his skinny junior to pick up the camera and look into the viewfinder. He held it unsteadily, not sure at first where to look or which buttons to press. Olly pointed to the buttons that would make the camera work, but there was nothing on the new tape for the soldier to see. If the stoned soldier managed to focus on the viewfinder, there would not even be the usual black-and-white image for him to look at. The tapes were in the car, stowed away in Martin's rucksack, in the footwell beneath his seat. The trouble was, if they offered one of those tapes to show the soldiers, there would be other images they would not be so keen to see. They were children, yes, but soldiers too.

'*Ça ne marche pas,*' the soldier said, giving up. '*Il n'y a rien.*'

Martin tried talking to them again, saying that they just wanted to go home. He called to Emmanuel, still in the car, trying to get him to come and explain. The soldier pointed his gun towards Emmanuel and told him to stay where he was.

'We are going home,' Martin said. 'You can have the camera. We are going home to our families.'

Lawrence was trying to keep thoughts of Harriet, of Josh and Lizzie, all back in Paris, out of his head.

'Is there a fee to pay to go through this checkpoint?' Martin asked. He was trying to offer them a bribe. It wasn't the most subtle of ways but it was better than digging in his pockets for the cash. The commander shook his head.

'Can I take the camera?' Olly asked. 'And then we'll go.' He took a pace forward. Lawrence never knew why he stepped forward like that. In his mind, when he replayed the scene that looped through his head, he stayed still and it was all different. Olly never drew himself up to his full height, setting his shoulders back, directly in front of the commander, the commander's beret barely reaching as high as Olly's chin. He never reached his arm down towards the camera, and nor did the commander.

It all happened, though. The commander took hold of the camera first and raised it in the air, throwing it down on the ground. Lawrence heard the crack of glass as the lens shattered.

'You can't do that!' Olly exclaimed, moving instinctively to retrieve it. The look on the commander's face said that he could do anything he chose to do. He made no more than a quick gesture and his two men stepped forward, pointing their weapons at Olly and gesturing to him to go towards the lakeside. Then they forced him to get down on his knees. Olly tried to fight them off, since there was no point any longer in trying to win them over any other way. There was not much point in fighting them either, but he wasn't going to give up.

'Let him go!' Lawrence shouted. 'Please let him go.' He hoped against all hope that this was a bluff, some kind of amusement for bored soldiers at the end of a long, hot day.

'We tried to save him,' Lawrence said. 'They were about to take Martin as well, because he was talking too much. If he'd kept talking, then . . .'

'Then what?' Isabelle asked. Lawrence shrugged and then shook his head. What happened next should have been clear, but sometimes what he remembered and what he told himself later blurred into one another.

'He doesn't always know when to stop,' he said. He allowed Isabelle to imagine the rest.

As he remembered it, Martin had been about to step forward, still speaking, when Lawrence grabbed him. He had sunk his fingers into Martin's forearm, pulling him back. At first, he strained to get away from Lawrence, but Lawrence whispered at him out of the corner of his mouth.

'It's too late,' he said. 'There's nothing more we can do.'

They had looked across at each other and understood that bravery would not help them. Only silence might work, and then not for Olly.

The commander strode over towards Olly and fired a single shot from a pistol into his head. That, the actual shot, was the thing that Lawrence could not see, however he recalled the moments before and after. Perhaps he had closed his eyes at the crucial moment. All he could see of Olly was the soles of his boots amid the undergrowth, part of his long legs trailing towards the ditch at the roadside. Lawrence was still holding on to Martin's wrist, more for comfort now than restraint.

'They decided that they didn't like us, didn't like Olly in particular, and they killed him.' Lawrence addressed his remarks to Jason, the least likely of his companions to react. 'We had to leave him, there on the road,' Lawrence continued. 'They wouldn't let us take his body.'

'You had to get away,' Isabelle said. 'I'm sure you did everything you could.'

Lawrence took a long swig of his beer, then traced a pattern in the condensation on the bottle with his finger. 'If we had done things differently. If we hadn't been in the wrong place at the wrong time. If I hadn't been racing to get back so we could start putting the piece together. It might all have been different.'

Amy was silent, looking into the distance, at the lake. Lawrence hadn't wanted to scare her, had spared her the details.

'You can't blame yourself,' Isabelle said. 'It was a dreadful time.' She seemed to look at him with a new respect.

'I do, though,' Lawrence replied. It was easy for other people to say, other people who hadn't had to meet Oliver Dawson's parents and tell them what had happened on that road, explain why he would never be coming home.

He blamed himself, too, for telling the world about it, before any of them were ready. Once, he had seen a recording of the broadcast he made when they got to the television station, the casual fluency as he spoke about Olly and the events on the road. No one else had seemed to see, not until much later, that he was in a state of shock.

'Sorry to bring you all down,' Lawrence said. 'Who wants another beer?' Without waiting for an answer, he went up to the bar and ordered another round.

The restaurant was filling up and the noise of music and chatter was rising. Isabelle's phone rang and she screwed up her nose when she saw the name on the screen. Lawrence tried to see who the call was from, but Isabelle picked up the phone and carried it away. Her face was contracted into a scowl. He wondered if it was Martin calling. He felt an involuntary twinge of envy. He hoped that at least Martin would ask after him, check that they were all safe.

He wanted Martin to be worried about them, but the more he thought about it, the more he realised that one of the reasons for Martin's success was that he didn't worry. Every misfortune that Martin suffered seemed only to make him believe he had been spared for some purpose. He had escaped being shot on the roadside, all those years ago, which had seemed to give him extra impetus, sharper focus. He had escaped again, a second time, on the hillside and again he disregarded it. It was an inconvenience, nothing more, one that could easily be overcome. Lawrence took the opposite view; the shot that was fired on the roadside could just as easily have been aimed at him. Every time he survived, it was only by chance and the fact of his survival meant that the odds next time shortened.

At the far edge of the lawn, Isabelle was pacing up and down between two palm trees. Her conversation was animated. She held the phone to her ear with one hand and waved the other hand, palm turned up to the sky in a beseeching, questioning gesture. He watched her end the call and turn away, staring out over the lake. She stood there for a while, still. After a few minutes, she raised her hands to her face, holding them there. Then she turned and walked up the lawn to where the rest of them were sitting.

'Everything OK?' Lawrence asked. Isabelle didn't answer.

'I need to get back,' she said. 'It's late and I have to operate tomorrow.'

She had scarcely touched the beer. They agreed on a time to meet in the morning and Isabelle stood up again to leave. Lawrence followed her into the entrance lobby, a show of politeness that was really something else.

'What's the matter?' he asked. Isabelle shook her head. 'Was that Martin?'

'Martin?' Isabelle looked at him with surprise. 'No, it wasn't.'

'Who was it?' Lawrence persisted. 'You seem upset.'

Isabelle assumed her haughty look again, the one he hated.

'I am upset,' she conceded. 'But it doesn't concern you.'

'It does concern me,' Lawrence said. 'I'm only trying to help, to see if there's anything I can do. You can tell me.' He put a hand on her shoulder and she recoiled. 'How are you getting back to the house?'

Isabelle lived, while she was working here, in a rented house with a group of other international aid workers. They were a mismatched bunch, she said, all nationalities and backgrounds. She had complained that some of the younger ones stayed up late, listening to music and talking into the early hours when she was trying to get to sleep.

'Fabrice will take me in the jeep,' she said. 'He's outside.'

'You shouldn't go on your own, after dark.'

'I won't be on my own. Fabrice will be driving.'

'I'll come with you, if you want,' Lawrence offered. 'It'll be safer.'

'I do this all the time,' Isabelle insisted.

'Yes, but it only needs to go wrong once.' Lawrence paused. 'Why don't you stay here?'

Isabelle was suddenly affronted. She pulled her shoulders back and raised her chin in a way he recognised, the way she did when someone had crossed her own indefinable line of propriety, the line he could never gauge correctly.

'What do you mean?' she retorted. 'Stay here with you? Do you really think that's going to happen? Is that why you're here?'

'That's not . . .' Lawrence stammered. It had sort of been what he meant, somewhere in the realm of distant possibilities. More unlikely things had happened, now and again, in hotels in far-flung places, on the road.

'You think I make a habit of it?' Isabelle continued in a harsh whisper. She was angry, but she didn't want to be overheard. 'Or is this some way of trying to get back at Martin, for having the life you want?'

'It's nothing like that,' Lawrence protested. 'I was just worried about you going out there on your own and – I don't know – it came out wrong. I'm sorry.'

He was crestfallen. Isabelle adjusted her jacket and started to walk towards the front door.

'I'll see you in the morning,' she said. 'Seven o'clock, like we said.'

'Send me a text, when you get back to the house,' Lawrence said. 'Please. So I know you're back safely.' Isabelle gave him a curt nod and strode out of the door. Lawrence stood in the lobby and weighed up staying longer with the others in the bar or going up to bed. It was an easy choice – he wouldn't be able to sleep, in any case.

17

A T LEAST HE didn't have to watch the operation. The mobile surgery was on the back of a truck, the size of a shipping container. It reminded Lawrence of an outside broadcast van, the kind of set-up that allowed concerts and sports to be live on TV. Isabelle had said there wasn't enough room for him inside, only for Amy. Lawrence pondered for a moment whether this was a calculated snub, after the evening before. He decided not to flatter himself that she cared either way; no doubt it was simply a matter of practicality. It would be finished before long, if all went according to plan.

Celestine had been cheerful, optimistic, though her daughter, Mireille, accompanying her to the clinic, had been more nervous. Jason was also tense, making phone calls and pacing up and down. Lawrence tried to eavesdrop on Jason's conversation, but he heard only monosyllables before Jason moved out of earshot. Lawrence wondered what he wasn't supposed to hear.

The door in the side of the truck opened and Isabelle came down the metal steps. Amy waited, framed in the door, getting a shot of Isabelle leaving. Lawrence hung back, making sure to stay out of the shot.

'How was it?' Lawrence asked.

'Good stuff,' Amy said. 'Not for the squeamish.'

'What makes you think I'm squeamish?'

'I can tell,' Amy said, smiling.

'We should do a quick answer with Isabelle now,' Lawrence

said, 'just saying how it went.' He called Isabelle back, explained what they needed. She was fluent and confident, happy that the operation had gone according to plan. She told them that Celestine would need a while to recover and then they would be able to talk to her.

The moment the interview was finished, Jason was at Lawrence's shoulder.

'We need to leave,' Jason said. As ever, he was abrupt, terse.

'What do you mean?'

'Somebody has informed me that we need to leave. We should get back across the border, into Rwanda.'

'What have they informed you?' Lawrence demanded.

'There have been threats against the team here.'

'Which team?' Jason was always taciturn, but now Lawrence wondered why he wouldn't tell him what he knew.

'All of you are at risk,' he said. 'And if you're asking my advice, which is what I'm here for, I'd say you need to get out straight away.'

'I have a patient just coming out of surgery,' Isabelle said. 'I can't leave . . . And in any case, we have our own procedures. I haven't had any information to suggest a threat.'

'What you do is up to you,' Jason told Isabelle. 'These other guys, I'm strongly suggesting that we go. Now.'

Isabelle started to move indoors, to the office.

'I need to call Paris,' she said. 'Find out if they have heard anything.'

'Don't do that,' Jason said.

'Why not? It's what I'm supposed to do. We have a plan in place and there are steps I need to take.'

'Don't make the call. It could put you in more danger.'

Isabelle hesitated. Lawrence led Jason away from the two women, further down the balcony.

'What the hell is going on?' he asked. 'And where is your information coming from?'

'Contacts. Reliable contacts. Trust me,' Jason insisted, 'I

wouldn't say it if I hadn't checked. There are people who want you out of here and they have the means to do it.'

'Out of here? As in far away, or as in dead?'

'Not as in far away.' Jason didn't seem prepared to say more.

'Why, though? What have they got against us?'

'It's not so much you. It's her.' He nodded towards the office door. 'Her husband, really. He's upset some important people.'

'Christophe?' Lawrence asked. 'Are you sure?'

One of Isabelle's assistants emerged from the office and Jason hushed him.

'What should we do?' Lawrence continued in a whisper. 'Can we at least go back to the hotel, get our stuff?'

'I wouldn't recommend it,' Jason said. 'It's the one place they know you'll be. And if you go there and check out, word will get round. Do you have your passport on you?' Lawrence did. It was an old habit and one he had not lost. They called Amy over and told her what they knew. Her bright, optimistic expression was transformed; Lawrence saw a look of real fear come over her face.

'Got your passport on you?' Jason asked. Amy shook her head.

'It's at the hotel, in the safe.'

'And the footage we've got so far, your kit?' Lawrence asked.

'That's here,' she said, 'in the car.'

'Amy's going to need to go to the hotel, then,' Lawrence said. 'Whether we like it or not. Why don't you go there with her, as if she had to collect something, don't check out, and meet here?'

Jason nodded. It was the best they could do. Lawrence tried to remember if there was anything in the hotel room that he would miss, that he'd ask them to bring, but there wasn't. Everything could be replaced.

'What about Celestine?' Amy asked. 'We need to get the pictures, when she comes round. To show that the operation has worked. To show how it changes her life. Without that, we don't have the end of the story.'

'We can't afford to stay,' Jason said.

Amy looked to Lawrence, expecting him to back her up. He shook his head.

'We can't risk it,' Lawrence said. 'We'll find a way.' He turned back to Jason. 'And you're absolutely sure this is serious?' Jason nodded, the look on his face saying everything Lawrence needed to know.

Sometimes, Lawrence thought, if you got the chance to go for a retake, you had to do it. This was the point at which you had a shot at rewriting the script, with a different ending. Isabelle was about to go into the mobile surgery. He had to catch her before she disappeared.

'You have to come with us,' Lawrence said. Isabelle shook her head and was about to move away. He grabbed her shoulder and she tried to brush him off, almost pushing him.

'Let me go!' she exclaimed.

'Jason won't tell you,' Lawrence said. 'He would leave you here. But I won't let him. You have to come. I don't understand exactly what it is, but it's to do with Christophe and so it's to do with you. I don't want to know what you know, right now, but if I get you out of here you have to tell me. And you have to come with us because I can't have it on my conscience to leave you behind.'

'So it's all about your conscience, is it?' Isabelle snapped. 'Because I have a conscience too and it tells me I should stay.'

'It's not about that,' Lawrence retorted. 'Unless you think me caring that you don't get killed is really all about me. I don't want to have to be the person, again, who calls your family, your friends, to tell them what happened.' He paused for a moment to see whether his words had any effect. 'You can't help anyone if you're dead,' Lawrence continued. 'Celestine, any other patients. I know it doesn't feel like you're helping them if you leave, but think of all the good work you're doing. They, all the other people you might treat, need you to be able to keep doing it.'

When Jason and Amy returned, it was in a different car, with a different driver.

'Where's Fabrice?' Isabelle asked.

'We need to use someone else,' Jason said. 'Fabrice knows where we've been, where we're going. We don't know who he might pass the information on to.'

'But I trust Fabrice,' Isabelle argued.

'You can't trust anyone, right now,' Jason said in a manner that would accept no contradiction.

The border crossing was busy with people milling about. Shacks on the Congolese side of the border ran right up to the red-and-white barricades marking the frontier. There was a small stretch of no-man's-land between the two border posts and even from a few metres away, Rwanda looked different. The official buildings were new, the houses better built, wider spaced. There was a new-looking gantry that stretched across the road, welcoming them to the country.

When they approached the crossing point, Lawrence felt his throat constrict. The lid of his right eye started to twitch. He was in the back seat of the car, Jason and the new driver, whose name he had not asked, in the front seats. They had driven slowly, as though there was nothing unusual in their journey. The seat felt hot beneath the backs of his thighs. He tried to breathe slowly, the way he had been told to do. He counted his breath in and he counted his breath out. He tried to focus on where he was, here and now. The trouble was that all these sensations, this place, were the ones that brought it all back. The sweat pooling on his back felt the same, the humid air smelt the same, the feeling of being wedged in the rear seat of a four-wheel drive car, approaching a barrier, was the same.

Jason opened the car door and got down onto the road. He stood watch as the others got out. Isabelle walked past Lawrence, ignoring him. She had not spoken to him since they left. Celestine had been awake, the operation had been a success. Isabelle had reassured her that she would come back, and left her in the care of a nurse.

They joined the queue at the customs office. Lawrence hoped the officials behind the desk would be bored, indifferent, undemanding. They were lucky; the woman in charge gave their passports a perfunctory check, stamped them 'Goma-Corniche' and waved them on. They called it the Grande Barrière, but there wasn't much to it really. The barrier across the road swung open. Lawrence held his breath as the driver started up the engine and drove slowly into the gap between Congo and Rwanda. The Rwandan officials decided to be more officious, fussing over entry visas. Lawrence did not argue. He would have paid whatever they asked to have that stamp in his passport, to see the barrier swing open.

Once they were back in the vehicle, Lawrence allowed himself to look back through the rear window. As he turned forward again, he caught sight of Isabelle's face. She had put her sunglasses on after they crossed the border but he could see there was a tear running down her cheek. His instinct was to reach out to comfort her and he stretched out his right hand, about to cover her hand in his. Then he thought again and withdrew it, folding his hands in his own lap instead.

For the whole journey, a two-hour drive, Isabelle had barely spoken. She had sipped from a plastic bottle of water and stared straight ahead, ignoring the steep, terraced hillsides of Rwanda, the patchwork of fields in shades of green, the farmers working the land.

Amy had filled the silence with her questions, asking about Rwanda and what had happened there, asking Lawrence if that was a story he had covered. It was one of the few big stories that Lawrence had been glad to miss. Josh had been due to be born, arriving late. In the days that Josh was overdue, thousands of people had been slaughtered. After he was born, Lawrence refused to go, no matter how much he put his career at risk by his intransigence. He also knew that if he had gone, Harriet would have left him.

'It looks so peaceful now,' Amy said as she looked out of

the window at the terraces and the forests. 'You would never think . . .'

'You wouldn't,' Lawrence agreed.

They passed a group of men in pink jumpsuits, picking litter from the roadside. Amy asked why they were dressed like that.

'They're people convicted of being involved in the genocide,' Lawrence said. 'They're on a release scheme. They wear the pink suits, to mark them out.'

Amy stared out of the window, silent.

The hotel they arrived at was a large modern building that could have been anywhere in the world but for the security guards at the gate who checked beneath the car. Lawrence went to his room, showered with a useless sliver of hotel soap, and for a moment regretted the essentials he had left behind in Goma. He phoned down to the reception to see if they could send up a toothbrush and a razor.

He phoned Isabelle's room but she didn't answer. After the third time, he gave up and resolved to go and find her. Shaved, clean, but still wearing the sweaty clothes he had left in, Lawrence walked down the hotel corridor. He thought of announcing himself as room service, in order to get her to open the door, but he didn't think Isabelle would react well.

He banged on the door of her room. He waited for a while, listening for sounds of movement on the other side of the door. After a while, he heard a shuffling noise.

'*Qui est-ce?*' Isabelle called out.

'It's Lawrence.' There was a long pause.

'What do you want?' Her voice sounded sleepy.

'I need to talk to you. About what happened. About why we had to leave.'

There was a soft padding of feet behind the door, then the sound of the lock being turned. She opened the door a crack, the chain still on.

'Is it just you?' she said.

'Just me.'

'Where are the others?'

'I don't know. I said I'd see them later, get something to eat.'

'I don't want to come down,' she said.

'I'm not asking you to come down,' Lawrence replied. 'And I don't want to have this conversation in the corridor or in the lobby. But we should have the conversation.'

She unchained the door and let him into her room, then locked the door again and put the chain back across. He followed her through the room, towards the balcony. Isabelle stepped tentatively onto the balcony, walking to the railing and looking from side to side before sitting down in a chair, her back to the wall. She had a packet of cigarettes in her hand which she put down on a small table in front of her.

'Do you think we're safe out here?' she began.

'Should be,' Lawrence said. 'There's enough security down there.'

'The kind of people we need to worry about are the kind of people that security let in,' Isabelle said.

'So, can you tell me what's going on? What's Christophe got to do with all this?'

'I don't know.' She gazed out into the distance again, as though she was waiting for someone to arrive. She picked up the cigarette packet, shook a lighter out from inside and lit a cigarette, without offering one to Lawrence.

'I didn't know you smoked,' he observed. 'You're a doctor.'

'I don't, usually.' Isabelle didn't attempt to justify herself.

'Can I have one?' She slid the packet across the table in his direction and Lawrence lit a cigarette for himself. 'But you know something,' Lawrence said. 'Something's happened. To do with Christophe.'

'I can't tell you,' Isabelle said, blowing out smoke.

'You can tell me. And if you don't, I'll find out. Jason knows at least part of it. But I want to hear it from you.'

There was a long silence before she spoke and Lawrence wondered whether she was just going to go quiet, the way she often did.

'Christophe has been arrested.'

'For what?' Lawrence couldn't help but interrupt, even though he knew he should simply let her speak.

'For not declaring his income to the tax authorities.'

'Tax evasion?'

Isabelle nodded.

'What happened?'

Isabelle reclined against the back of the chair and took another drag on the cigarette. 'He was on a train from Paris to Geneva. It was stopped at the Swiss border and the customs officials came on board to do a spot check. He was carrying cash, lots of cash. They took him in for questioning in a place called Bellegarde, the last town on the French side, discovered he had a Swiss bank account and that he hadn't declared it. I don't know how he could be so stupid.'

'Did you know?' Lawrence kept to himself the feeling that Isabelle was more angry at her husband getting caught than at what he might have done.

'No. I mean, I have a Swiss bank account but that's because I lived there as a child. It was just a savings account, for pocket money. I must have a few francs in it, nothing more. But I've never asked about the family money, the Vernet money I mean. They have a foundation and all sorts of companies. I always thought it was complicated and boring and I didn't need to understand it. Not that they would have told me that much, anyway. And then he told me that he had been under investigation for a while, but he'd thought it was just routine, a formality.'

Isabelle tapped ash into a chrome ashtray.

'When did all this happen?' Lawrence asked.

'It must have been three days ago. Christophe said he'd been trying to get hold of me, but he couldn't have been trying that hard.' Isabelle shrugged, as though this was only to be expected.

It was early evening and the sky over the city was growing dark, lights coming on in the buildings beyond the hotel's compound. Isabelle stood up and leant against the railing of the balcony, her back turned to Lawrence. At first, Lawrence thought she didn't want to show him that she was upset; it came to him that this was an evasion, that she hoped he would stop asking questions.

'Why would that matter?' he asked.

'What?' she snapped, not turning back to answer him.

'What has that got to do with us, here? Jason said it was something to do with Christophe. I don't imagine the French tax authorities—'

'I've let everyone down.' Her voice was starting to crack. 'They depend on me. I called the office, in Paris, and they were furious. They didn't believe what you'd been told.' She turned and walked away from him, to the furthest corner of the balcony.

'You did what you had to do,' Lawrence told her. 'It wasn't worth risking your own life for. Very little is.'

'Maybe this is. Maybe sometimes you just have to put yourself at risk in order to help others.'

'Like I said before, how does that help anyone? If you'd been killed, they'd have had to shut down anyway. The project would be over for ever.' He leaned forward and tapped his cigarette into the ashtray on the table between them. He realised that Isabelle had not answered his question.

'There has to be more to it,' Lawrence insisted. 'What else has Christophe done? Whatever it was, it put us all at risk. It could even have put your patients at risk, the people you're supposed to be helping.'

Isabelle stubbed the cigarette out on the balcony railing and took a couple of steps back towards her chair.

'What they're saying is . . . he's accused of . . .' Isabelle paused again, struggling to find the construction that she wanted. 'They're saying that he was sheltering assets that should have been frozen. That belonged to an individual who was the subject of sanctions.'

'What does that even mean?' Lawrence asked. 'What assets? Which individual, what sanctions?'

'Christophe handles investments for a lot of very wealthy

people. High net worth individuals, they call them. And now apparently they're saying that one of his clients was under international sanctions and Christophe shouldn't have had anything to do with him.'

'And who was he? The client, I mean?'

'He didn't say,' Isabelle said.

'But someone from Congo?'

'We didn't talk for long,' she said. 'Only a few minutes. I didn't ask for names.'

'But you'd have to have done something pretty bad to be placed under international sanctions, wouldn't you? I mean, these can't have been very nice people. What was he doing, dealing with them?'

'These things can be political,' Isabelle said. 'There are all sorts of accusations made against people. Sometimes it just means they were on the losing side. We forgive people a lot, if they win.'

'Do you know who it was?' Lawrence asked again.

'You think he'd tell me?' she snapped.

'I'm just saying that it sounds as if you deliberately didn't want to know.'

'Christophe deals with a lot of people. I don't know most of them.'

'But since you were working here, he might have discussed it with you?'

Isabelle shrugged and didn't answer. She folded her arms and rubbed her hands on her upper arms, although it didn't seem to have got any colder. She went into the room and returned with a grey wrap around her shoulders.

'It doesn't make sense to me,' Lawrence persisted. 'Do you really not talk about something like that? That he's doing business with someone powerful, in a lawless place where you're working.'

'Maybe he thought that it was better for me not to know. That knowing might put me in danger.'

She tugged the wrap tighter around herself. He knew that Christophe was taciturn enough, hiding himself behind the duty of confidentiality, but they must have talked about some things, between them, even if there were areas they avoided.

'But it's not like that, working in a place like this, is it? Things don't work without contacts. Clinics don't get set up. Supplies don't get through. The wheels need to be oiled. Palms need to be greased. And if you knew someone who could help, you would use that. You must have known.'

Isabelle laughed a sharp, bitter laugh. 'Oh, so you're the expert, all of a sudden? On the basis of what, two days' experience?'

'I've seen how it works in enough places,' Lawrence said. 'But, you know, maybe you're right. Maybe you don't talk to your husband about important things. It seems that you have some kind of don't-ask-don't-tell policy going on between you. About all sorts of issues.'

Isabelle stood up and threw a loose end of her wrap over her shoulder.

'That's enough. Get out.' She was almost in tears.

'I'm sorry. I shouldn't have said that.'

'Get out of my room.' She advanced towards him and he held his hands up in a gesture of surrender.

'I'm sorry. I'll go.'

He unchained the door and let himself out. Then he heard Isabelle lock the door again. Jason was walking towards him down the corridor. He stopped and gave Lawrence a lopsided smile. Lawrence had never seen him smile before.

'That's Isabelle's room, isn't it?' Lawrence didn't reply. Jason took it as an admission. 'Nice work, mate. Knew there was a reason you wanted to bring her out with us.'

'It's nothing like that,' Lawrence protested.

'Always the gentleman,' Jason said. 'No need. I won't tell.'

He started to walk off down the corridor with his rolling gait and Lawrence thought that the more he protested, the more Jason would believe it was true. Nothing was ever straightforward.

18

THE SNOW WAS falling in thick, heavy flakes. Martin scooped a heap of fresh white crystals from the wooden ledge of the balcony and scattered them to the ground below. There were people who came to hotels in the Swiss Alps for the good of their health. At least, there used to be. Perhaps there still were. For the first time in his life, Martin thought that perhaps he would rather be reclining in a lounge chair, a blanket tucked around his legs, with people giving him spa treatments. At this rate, he was going to need a sanatorium.

The phone in his pocket vibrated again, its noise muffled by the padding of his down jacket. It was a message from Victoria Loxton.

On my way. V.

Typically imperious and unapologetic, even though he had already been waiting five minutes in the cold. He shoved his hands back in his pockets.

Victoria appeared through the door to the terrace wearing a ski jacket, its fur-trimmed hood pulled up. She moved to a spot on the balcony where she couldn't be seen from inside the hotel.

'Is this going to be a problem for us?' she asked. Which of the problems? Martin wanted to ask, but he couldn't. That would make her realise quite how complicated things were.

'The Vernet issue?' Martin prompted her. There was no one on the terrace to overhear.

'Yes, that.'

'I think we can handle it,' he reassured her. 'Isabelle's not her husband's property, after all. I'd be surprised if she was aware of anything he's alleged to have done. People might assume that, but as far as I'm aware there's no evidence. And just because there are – questions – about the Vernet family's businesses, it doesn't imply anything about the charity. It's properly registered and above board. It's doing good work. Most people won't even make the connection between the two.'

'It's not always about the evidence, though, is it,' Victoria said. 'It's enough that the two things come in the same sentence. The questions are enough.' She lowered her voice another degree. 'He's supposed to have been looking after the assets of an alleged war criminal, someone who's under sanctions. We've been talking about how we're cracking down on that sort of thing; tax avoidance, dodgy money.' She gestured back indoors. 'I've got to go back out there and tell everyone about the work we're doing to fight money-laundering. It doesn't look good.'

'But as far as I've seen, the British papers have barely picked up on it yet, have they?' Martin asked. She would have seen more than he had. 'It's someone they've never heard of, supposedly looking after the money of someone else they don't care about.' Martin's breath made clouds in the cold air as he spoke. 'In any case,' he added, 'it's still at some distance from you. It's a pretty tenuous link.'

Victoria clasped and unclasped her gloved fingers.

'But it isn't, is it? Because I've met him. Met all three of them. At your house.'

'Again, who's to know that?'

'Well, Lawrence Leith, for a start.'

'He's an ex-journalist. And in any case, he's working with us now. He knows which side his bread is buttered.'

'You don't know who he talks to, though, do you. There's no such thing as an ex-journalist, anyway.'

'I'm one,' Martin offered. Victoria laughed, an abrupt laugh that ended almost as soon as it began. 'Does Anjali know?' he asked. 'About the people you met on holiday?'

'No, she doesn't. But she met Lawrence, remember, at lunch. And I think she knows how I'd met him before, about the accident. It came up in conversation.'

'Don't mention it to her,' Martin advised. 'Unless someone comes to her with a specific question. And in that case, you can brush it off. They're some people you had a passing chat with at a drinks party. You'd never met them before – unless you've met Sylvie in a professional, a ministerial context, which you don't have any choice about and which doesn't mean anything. They're friends of friends. Which is true, after all. Sylvie will be here, but I'm sure you can steer clear of her, if you need to.'

She nodded and stamped her feet against the cold.

'Better be going,' Victoria said. She turned to leave. 'Thanks,' she added, as an afterthought, over her shoulder. Martin's coat pocket kept pulsing with messages as he watched her go. He tried to manage both the phone, tucked between ear and shoulder, and the door handle; it was a manoeuvre he still couldn't manage. His mobility hadn't come back completely. As Iona kept reminding him, it wouldn't unless he did the exercises he was supposed to do, but as he kept insisting to her, he didn't have the time.

As he queued for the conference centre, there were other calls coming in, but it wasn't the place to have a private conversation. Iona, Isabelle, Lucy from the office. They were the ones that were going to demand a reply, the ones he had to deal with. He wanted to call Isabelle back first but now was not the time. This was a place he always associated with her. It usually gave him a buzz, the fact of so many influential people in the same spot, the chance that the person drinking a coffee next to you would be a chief executive or a government minister, but this year there was no chance that one of the people he would bump into would be her and all other potential encounters lost their charm. It wasn't that the halls weren't filled with elegant, articulate women whom he might have met; they were. It was just that he no longer wanted to meet anyone else. It was more painful still to think she was thousands of miles away and that Lawrence, of all people, was with her.

Martin had placed his phone into a grey plastic tray and was watching it slide along a conveyor belt and disappear into a scanner when he heard the inevitable ring. The security guard gave him a hostile look and seemed to spend longer than necessary examining his belongings. Martin could feel the other delegates shuffling behind him in their impatience. He retrieved the phone, his keys, a clutch of coins from the tray and looked to see whose call he had missed. It was Lawrence again.

He was fed up with Lawrence's constant desire to tell him everything he was doing. Lawrence seemed to be behaving as though Martin was still the producer, someone who had to take responsibility for him. He was having to do a lot of firefighting at the moment and, frankly, there were bigger fires to fight than Lawrence's. There was somewhere he needed to be, and at this rate, he was going to be late.

Further along the corridor there was a sudden commotion, a bow wave of movement that made everyone else turn and look, a disturbance drawing passers-by into its wake. The scrum was moving towards him at speed and although Martin tried to move out of the way, he wasn't fast enough.

A cameraman backed into him, the impact jarring his bad shoulder, a producer who had been grasping hold of the cameraman's jacket to guide him turning to glower at Martin as though it had been his fault that he had blocked their route. He heard the shouted questions that seemed incongruous, up here in the rarefied air. They came both in English and in French, languages lapping over one another.

At the centre of the commotion, as proud as the figurehead on a ship, was Sylvie Barroux. She wore a bright pink jacket and her blonde hair caught the light from the cameras. Her gaze was fixed on the middle distance. Martin stepped aside as reporters and producers elbowed their way past one another. Journalists jabbed their microphones under Sylvie's upturned nose; others wielded telescopic sound booms above her head like a guard of honour.

A young woman with an American accent, from one of the news agencies, shouted louder than the rest.

'How do you feel about your brother's arrest?' Sylvie said nothing. The producer in Martin thought it was the wrong question, not pointed enough. This wasn't about Sylvie's feelings.

A British voice shouted out, a tall man at the back of the scrum.

'Did you know he was breaching international sanctions? Do you have financial dealings with a war criminal?' Sylvie stared straight ahead, intent on keeping moving. What kind of a question was that? Not one that was going to get any kind of an answer.

Sylvie was approaching the room where she was expected, two men in suits beside her holding their arms wide, pushing the journalists away. One of them barged a reporter back with his shoulder, knocking her to the floor. The reporter remonstrated with him but he ignored her. Sylvie turned and gave the journalists a wide smile that didn't reach her eyes.

'I'm so glad you're all showing such a great interest in the issue of climate change. Now, if you'll excuse me, there are people waiting for me in here.' She passed through a set of double doors and disappeared from view. It was textbook stuff. Don't say anything. Don't engage. She behaved as if she were used to that kind of attention, even though French journalists weren't that aggressive.

'They don't do the kind of things your reporters are allowed to do,' Sylvie had said. 'They don't come round to your house, stand outside and shout at you. They're not allowed to intrude on your privacy. It's against the law.'

'Are you sure you want to go?' Martin had asked, when she had called him after Christophe's arrest. 'There'll be a lot of attention. A lot of questions that you won't be able to answer.' She was going to be in a public place, he had reminded her, in a different country. There would be hundreds of journalists there, from all over the world. Even French journalists, these days, were crossing lines they had never normally crossed before.

'I have to go,' she replied. 'It would be out of the question for me not to go.' It was the answer Martin had been expecting and he acknowledged that it was the right decision. Anything else would almost be an admission of guilt. Hence a brightly dressed, confident Sylvie, giving her best impression of having nothing to hide. She'd been around long enough, Martin realised, to know how it worked. She could also claim she knew nothing of Christophe's financial dealings, that the family's interests were handled by Christophe and lawyers.

Martin's phone buzzed. Lawrence again. What did he want now? Now that Sylvie had stepped into the conference room, he had no reason not to take the call.

'Did Isabelle get hold of you?' Lawrence began. 'Has she told you what happened? I've been trying to get hold of you since last night but you weren't picking up.'

'I haven't spoken to her,' Martin replied, suddenly worried. 'What? Are you OK? Is anyone hurt?'

Lightning didn't strike twice, Martin believed, but he understood now, in a way he never had before, how in a moment, life could change. All those missed calls might have meant something important. He had been going to call Isabelle back, he really had, but he wanted to do it in his own time.

'We're in Kigali,' Lawrence said. 'We're all fine. But we might not have been.'

'What the hell are you doing in Kigali? You're not supposed to have left yet. You're supposed to be there for what – another two days?'

'That's why I'm calling you. We had to evacuate in a hurry. The security guy told us we had to go.'

'Really? Why, what happened?'

'People were after us. After Isabelle, specifically. Something to do with Christophe and his dodgy business connections. Do you know why?'

'What did Isabelle say?'

'She wouldn't tell me much. That it was to do with an alleged war criminal, someone whose money you're not supposed to be able to touch. And Christophe has had his manicured mitts all over it, apparently.'

This was not a conversation Martin wanted to have, certainly not in a place where anyone might overhear him.

'I can't really talk,' he told Lawrence. 'It's just . . . I'm surrounded by people.'

'I don't give a fuck if you're having tea with the Queen,' Lawrence said. 'I was in a place where I was surrounded by people who wanted to kill me. I had to leave everything, drive across the border. It could have been like last time.'

'But it wasn't,' Martin interrupted. 'It wasn't like last time.'

'Yeah well, it could easily have been. Jason wanted us to leave Isabelle behind but I wouldn't let him. I couldn't leave her.'

'Who's Jason?'

'The security guy. He wouldn't tell me who these people were or why they were so angry, but I need to know. Do you know?'

'You haven't been reading the news, then?'

'Of course I haven't been reading the fucking news. I was in a country that barely has electricity. I know that Christophe was arrested because Isabelle told me.'

'Calm down, Lawrence. I was only asking.'

'Who was it?' Lawrence demanded.

'Who was who?'

Martin looked around him. There was no one nearby that he recognised but you couldn't be too careful. He cupped one hand in front of the phone so that no one could read his lips.

'The man Christophe was dealing with. Because there can't be many of them, can there? Is he our guy?'

'How do you mean, our guy?' Martin wasn't going to answer unless Lawrence asked the right questions.

'You know exactly. Was it Kalombo?'

There was no point in stalling him further. He would be able to find out; the name was out there already.

'Yes, it was.'

There was a pause at the other end of the line and Martin wondered for a moment if he'd lost the connection. It would have been a blessing if he had. Lawrence's voice returned.

'When did you know about this?'

'I heard about Christophe being arrested yesterday,' Martin replied.

'Did Isabelle know?'

That was a good question. Isabelle rarely let on everything that she knew, yet at the same time had a capacity to ignore facts that were not convenient. Isabelle had not actually been present at the meeting; he would have remembered.

He recalled that everything about Faustin Kalombo appeared to have changed. Kalombo had worn a double-breasted navy suit, cut to flatter his stocky build; it emphasised his broad shoulders and slimmed his heavy paunch. His gleaming, uncreased black shoes had hand-stitched uppers; they were the shoes of a man who rarely had to walk far. He certainly wasn't a man dressed for having to go out in the snow after his meetings were over. Kalombo had held out his broad hand in greeting, his smile open, his eyes friendly. For a moment, Martin considered refusing to shake his hand. He could have done it. He could have kept his hand by his side, greeted Kalombo effusively and hoped that no one noticed. But they were surrounded by people whose job was precisely to notice any perceived insult.

Kalombo's hand had remained outstretched for a second or two and then Martin took it. It was a robust handshake, one with a strength behind it that could have turned into force if it chose to. Martin broke eye contact and focused on Kalombo's watch instead. It was a watch that matched the scale of his large hand, a huge chronograph in rose gold with an abundance of buttons on the side, the kind of watch Martin glanced at in airport shops, wondering why rich men felt the need of them.

Martin told himself there were handshakes like this that changed things for the better, that consigned dark days to history. Kalombo released Martin's hand and they had spoken a few words, an exchange that Martin struggled to remember. It had been before Kalombo's arrest, before his extradition. He had still been free to travel anywhere that he wanted to and there were plenty of people who were happy to meet him, who were happy to let the past remain in the past, to accept his business. People who had invited him to conferences like this one, in previous years. Ones where he had talked about peace and reconciliation and then probably called in to the bank to visit his money on the way home.

'I don't know how much she knew,' Martin said. 'I don't think so.' Another thought occurred to him. 'Is she there now? With you?'

Martin was suddenly suspicious. He didn't put it past Lawrence to try it on with her, make some sort of clumsy, out-of-practice pass on the grounds that what happened on the road stayed on the road.

'No,' Lawrence said, his voice sullen. 'She's not – she wasn't happy that we had to leave. She's upset.' *So you did try*, Martin thought. *You did try and she told you where to go.*

'Are you happy with what you got, though?' Martin changed the subject.

'In what sense?' Lawrence sounded confused.

'The film. Have you got enough to make the film?'

'Well, we didn't get everything we wanted. But I think we got most of it. Could have done with a few shots more. Our patient recovering, for instance. But there are ways round that.'

'You didn't get the patient recovering? But isn't that kind of the whole point? That people recover?' Martin realised that he had raised his voice more than he meant to.

'Well, no, we didn't, but since the alternative was having someone – Kalombo's guys, I imagine, people who are unhappy that his money's been tracked down – find us and kill us, then we had to make the call to go without it.' Lawrence was indignant. 'We'll find a way,' he insisted. 'We'll get Celestine — the patient — to send us some pictures. Some stills or some video. Her son was good with technology, I'm sure he can work out how to upload a clip or two if he doesn't already know.'

'I don't know if that'll be good enough,' Martin said. 'And Victoria's questioning the whole thing now, because of the Christophe connection.'

'So what does that mean? You might not use it?'

'I'm not saying that,' Martin insisted, attempting to placate Lawrence. Martin had dealt with Lawrence's tantrums before. 'I'm sure we can work something out. I'm sure you'll get paid. Listen, Leith, I've got to go.'

'And maybe a thank-you would be in order?' Lawrence said. He was getting petulant now.

'Er, for what?'

'If I hadn't insisted on it, Isabelle would still be there. Your girlfriend could have been—'

'Yes, of course. Thank you. You did the right thing.' Martin didn't like Lawrence's tone — he sounded snide and bitter.

Lawrence muttered some grudging acknowledgement and he got him off the phone with a promise to see him in London before long, a promise that they would talk it all through.

The air inside the conference centre suddenly felt thick and stuffy. Martin wanted to be outside again in the snow, looking down from the mountain-top towards the valley, in the cold clean natural light, not this fluorescent, artificial place.

19

L AWRENCE LOOSENED HIS tie. He had always hated ties and it had been a good couple of years since he had worn one. A tie, proper shoes that had to be polished; these were things he had avoided whenever possible, but this occasion demanded them. It was just like a wedding. Shuffling sideways onto narrow benches, being overdressed, a requirement for stupid hats and even sillier costumes. All this for a ceremony that took a few minutes, where you could barely make out the important words.

The woman who would shortly become Lady Elliot sat next to him, as uncomfortable in her dress as she was with the title that the ceremony would confer on her. Iona hitched up her tights, rubbed one shoe against her calf and adjusted the brim of her hat so that she could see out from underneath it.

'You look great,' Lawrence had assured her as they climbed the stairs to the gallery.

Iona had rolled her eyes. 'I don't,' she said. 'I look like an idiot. And I hate this sort of thing.' She did look great, though. It was the first time in years that Lawrence had noticed her figure. The tailored green silk dress was a far cry from Iona's usual floaty, arty clothes and it made her look like a different woman, one who belonged in a different world. That was probably why she was so unhappy about it.

Beyond her was Martin's mother, Linda, in a pale violet outfit that Lawrence suspected was the same one she had worn to Martin and Iona's wedding. She sat with her hands folded in her lap, her handbag neatly stowed at her feet, reverent, watching the proceedings below. Prayers were being conducted and Lawrence noticed that Linda had her eyes closed in observance, muttering an *amen* under her breath.

There was a smattering of peers on the red benches below them, a respectable turnout of grey heads. The burble of chatter was stilled by the arrival of Black Rod. Black Rod, in his sombre coat and breeches, white jabot and frilly cuffs, brightened by a gold chain and a row of medals, was followed by another man, dressed like a herald. His tabard, quartered in red and blue, covered in gold harps and lions, reminded Lawrence of nothing so much as the White Rabbit in Tenniel's illustrations. It was an Alice in Wonderland world, the whole thing, full of absurdities.

Not the least absurd was Martin, the man who would, in a few minutes, become Lord Elliot of Saltburn. First came a baroness, robed in red with an ermine collar, a woman of around sixty with grey hair cut into a bob. As she bowed towards the throne, her name came to Lawrence because it fitted her so well: Lady Gray. Eleanor Gray, as was. Used to work for the Foreign Office. One of the great and the good, a Conservative peer these days. Martin followed a few paces behind her, his navy suit enfolded in scarlet robes. His shaven head was shiny, catching glints of the light. His robes had an ermine collar and broad gilt bands and joined at the neck with a black ribbon bow. The combination of the bare skull and the long robes made him look like some sort of medieval henchman. Lawrence nudged Iona and they caught each other's sideways glance before having to look away again, in case they both burst out in unseemly laughter. Lawrence bit his lip.

A third peer, a man with close-cropped grey hair and round glasses, followed behind Martin. Greg Castle, that was it, a former Labour MP. A fixer who'd been kicked upstairs once he could no longer fix things. Typical of Martin to keep in with both sides. Martin bowed and walked towards the clerk. The clerk read out the formal, antiquated words of the sovereign: the Queen, through her especial grace, had decided to advance, create and prefer her right trusty and well-beloved Martin Elliot. That was Martin – trusty and well beloved. He had advanced. He had created himself. He was preferred.

Martin would have the title to have and to hold unto him for his life, the clerk pronounced. Lawrence cast another glance at Iona. Despite herself, she was enthralled, watching the performance below as if she was watching Shakespeare at the Globe, leaning towards the railing so that she didn't miss anything. They'd come a long way since Martin and Iona's wedding, held in an art gallery in a converted warehouse in Hackney. Lawrence had only just made it there, getting in from Washington not long after international airspace reopened after 9/11, but their genuine happiness had made the journey worthwhile. By the grace of God and the Queen, Martin was duly installed as Lord of a small seaside town on the north Yorkshire coast. Martin, Baron Elliot, signed his name in a large volume and bowed again, carried on in his stately procession to shake hands with the Lord Speaker. A gentle rumble of 'Hear, hears' rolled around the red benches and Martin was gone, exiting the stage through an archway of dark wood beside the throne.

Lawrence and Iona stood aside when they took the photographs. The Robing Room was heavy with wood panelling, the ceiling gilded. Martin posed for his portrait in front of an ornate fireplace, beneath the huge frescoes on the walls; first him on his own, then with his supporters, Lady Grey and Lord Castle. Iona pointed out the pictures to Lawrence, muttering 'Victorian kitsch' as she indicated one.

'It's the virtue of hospitality,' she explained. King Arthur was wielding a sword above a prospective knight as a crowd of courtiers looked on. 'There are five virtues,' Iona said. 'There were supposed to be seven, but the artist died before he could paint the last two.'

'Which ones were those?'

'Courage and fidelity.' Lawrence bit his lip hard.

The photographer summoned Iona over for a joint portrait

with Martin. He lifted his camera up and tried to coax a smile out of her.

'It's serious,' he said, 'but it's not that serious. You're allowed to smile.' She smiled but it was a weak, thin smile. Lawrence moved into her eye line and pulled a face until she burst out laughing. 'That's better,' the photographer said, clicking several frames. 'Now all of you,' he said, summoning Lawrence and Martin's mother to join the group. Lawrence shook his head.

'You don't want me in it,' he said. This day wasn't about him, after all. He hadn't really wanted to come; he would have been happier staying in France. He was persuaded to join the picture and so shuffled into line.

He forced his face into a smile. I'm happy for Martin, he repeated silently to himself. He's worked for this, not inherited it. He's come a long way. Linda Elliot stood just to his left and Lawrence saw the pride in her face, combined with the wish that Martin's father could have been there to see the day.

Iona had called Lawrence when he hadn't responded to the invitation sent in the post.

'Martin really wants you to be there,' she insisted when Lawrence demurred. 'I really want you to be there.'

'Are you sure he does?' Lawrence asked. 'He's not very happy with me. And to be honest, I'm not very happy with him.' There was so much he could tell her that he wasn't prepared to tell her. Lawrence knew he had it in his power to tell her about Isabelle but he didn't want to take responsibility for that, for pulling the world down around Maisie and Finn, around Freya. He had seen how it unsettled Lizzie and Josh, however much they kept it to themselves. 'I don't think Martin understands how serious it was in Congo,' he told Iona. 'That we might not have come back.'

'He does understand,' Iona said. 'It's just that maybe he didn't put it all that well. He's under a lot of pressure.'

'Is this you apologising on his behalf?' Lawrence asked. 'Because you don't have to do that for him. In fact, I'd rather he did it himself.'

'I know. But please come.' There was a pause at the end of the line. 'He wouldn't be here, if it weren't for you. You helped save him, helped all of us. And we'll never forget that.'

'I didn't do that much,' Lawrence mumbled.

'You did,' Iona said. 'I wouldn't have known where to start, without you.' Lawrence began to believe that this was more than simply flattery. 'So that's why we want you to be there. To celebrate.'

Lawrence walked alongside Linda Elliot as they made their way towards the terrace for the reception. Martin had been whisked away for his robes to be put back into whichever mothballed box they came from. Their footsteps echoed through the long gallery, a painting of the death of Nelson on one side of them, Wellington meeting Blücher on the other. Mrs Elliot was small but she kept up a brisk pace. Her only physical resemblance to Martin was in her bright, dark eyes that fixed Lawrence closely as she spoke to him.

'I remember you from the wedding,' she said. 'Lawrence, isn't it? You used to work with Martin, on the TV. You made a very good speech.' Lawrence thanked her. 'You'd come from somewhere specially. America, wasn't it?'

'That's right,' Lawrence said, surprised that she had remembered.

'Yes,' Linda continued. 'I used to watch you on the news. But I don't seem to see you any more. What happened?'

'I left,' Lawrence said. 'Sort of retired.'

'That's a shame,' she said. 'I liked your reports. You seemed to care about people.' Linda went quiet for a while, taking in her surroundings. 'Martin didn't really tell me much about what happened on holiday, in France,' she said. 'But he said you were there. He said you were a great help, particularly for Iona and the children.'

'I made a few phone calls,' Lawrence said. 'Asked around to see who could help. It was the least I could do.'

'Is there something wrong with him that he's not telling me?'

'With Martin? What makes you say that?'

'I'm his mother. I still know when he's not telling me things.'

'He'll be OK,' Lawrence said. 'He overdid it. You know how he is. He took a bit of a bump to the head and I think that's taken some getting over. But he'll be fine, don't worry.' Beneath the brim of her hat, Linda looked unconvinced.

'He's never known how to stop,' she said. 'I remember once – Martin must have been about seven or eight – he had a new bike but we'd said he couldn't take it further than the end of the street on his own. So he cycled up and down the street for hours, until it was dark. He wouldn't come in or even break for a drink of water. He doesn't stop until something makes him.'

They reached the end of the gallery, the arched gilt doorways with crowns and roses set into them. Lawrence pushed one of the doors open.

'Which way do we go now?' he asked.

20

H E STEPPED FORWARD, the Writ of Summons in his hand, and presented it. The clerk read out the Letters Patent, a spell that would turn him into someone else, into Martin, Baron Elliot. He didn't need to believe in the magic for it to take its effect. His younger self would have hated this, the costume and the ceremony, the fusty vocabulary. These days, he had a grudging respect for its survival. The words of the clerk floated over him. He had a seat, a place and a voice. He took the Bible in his right hand and prayed, if anything, that his arm would not give way, that his hand would not tremble. He read out the oath from the card the clerk handed to him. He spoke and bowed his head in the right places and his arm did not quiver.

The other peers murmured a polite cheer and with that, he was one of them, among bishops and professors, politicians and soldiers, scientists and spies. As he left the chamber, he could feel the sweat start to prick at his scalp, but he had made it.

He was happier once he handed the trappings back, brushing down his suit that still retained a faint odour of mothballs from the robes. He made his way to the terrace room, and emerged into a space with a swagged white ceiling and glass doors that gave onto the river. The room was already starting to fill with people.

It had been worth it, all the time he had spent getting to know these people. It repaid the effort, the meals he had bought them and the wine he couldn't afford at the time, it repaid the long days and the interrupted holidays. It was a reward for all those cups of coffee, all those handwritten notes, the phone calls, the introductions. He had wired all these connections into place and now the circuit joined together, the energy flowing through the network. Make yourself useful, he had always been taught. Now he was useful, now they needed him.

A waitress handed him a glass of champagne and Martin paused to look around the room. He would give it a few minutes before he said a few words, let everyone have a drink and relax. The room filled up, the sound of chatter rising to the brass chandeliers, the fog of warm breath starting to collect on the inside of the patio doors. Victoria arrived, rushing in with her adviser, Anjali, declining champagne and taking a glass of sparkling water. She came up and gave him a hug, kissing him on both cheeks.

'I'm so delighted,' she said. 'I hope the wait wasn't too long. All the formalities, you know, they take their time. We're so excited to have you here. I know everyone is.'

Now she was here, her colleagues with her, it was the right moment. Martin excused himself and moved towards the small dais, covered in red carpet. He stood to one side of the lectern, in case he needed it as a prop for his elbow, if his arm was giving him trouble. He didn't have notes. Notes were for people who didn't know what they wanted to say. The swell of conversation started to fall as he looked around the room.

'I won't keep you for long,' he began, 'but I wanted to thank all of you for being here today.'

He saw the rows of faces turned towards him, Iona and his mother in the front rank, side by side. Patrick Chambers was standing next to Victoria and Anjali, which was a good sign. He only went where the power was perceived to be. People talked about Chambers as a strategic genius but his plotting and his tactics were always so close to the surface as to be visible, which disqualified him from genius, in Martin's view. A couple of Cabinet ministers had entered the room; they wouldn't stay long, just long enough to acknowledge that Martin was worth congratulating, before meetings and division bells called them away.

'I am greatly honoured and at the same time greatly humbled

to be here, in this place. I know most of you will say I'm not often overwhelmed by events but today I really am.' He paused for the ripple of laughter that he expected and which he got. 'I am overwhelmed to be a part of this ancient institution, I am overwhelmed that you are all here with me, I am overwhelmed by the responsibility of serving the House and the government.' There was a smattering of applause and he paused again. 'I was reminded this morning of the jokes that Harold Wilson and Alec Douglas-Home used to exchange some fifty years ago; Wilson used to tease Home about being the fourteenth Earl of Home – he in turn would point out that Wilson was probably the fourteenth Mr Wilson. Well, I am probably the fourteenth generation of Mr Elliots, quite definitely the first ever Lord Elliot, and the one thing I wish today – though he would probably have disapproved – is that the thirteenth Mr Elliot, my father, was here.' Martin still resented the tweedy genealogist who had asked him, while researching his prospective title, where his family came from, in that tone of voice that always made him feel chippy.

Another pause, involuntary, as Martin swallowed down the sob that he could feel rising in his throat. He had to avoid looking at his mother or he would lose it altogether. 'And as for the fifteenth generation, Miss and Master Elliot, well, they said they would rather be at school, because the classroom chicks are due to hatch and they didn't want to miss it. So I'm glad to see that they, at least, have got their priorities right.' There was another approving burble of laughter. Iona looked up at him with an unforced smile. 'So I need to thank everyone who has helped me be here today, first of all my wife Iona, who will not, in case you hadn't guessed, be changing the name of her business to the Lady Elliot gallery.' Iona gave him one of her quizzical looks, a raised eyebrow. 'Also, I am grateful to my mother, Linda, to whom I owe so much. Of course, I'd like to thank my sponsors who stood by my side as I was introduced to the Lords today, Lady Gray and Lord Castle, and to all my current and future colleagues.'

It was time to wind up; the audience's attention seemed to be slipping. Anjali had pulled a BlackBerry from her pocket and was showing something on the screen to Victoria, who pulled a disapproving face. 'And one final word of thanks – to Lawrence Leith, my friend and former colleague. Without him, I might not have returned in one piece from a rather unfortunate cycling accident on holiday, so I'm delighted he was able to join us today.'

Lawrence was leaning against a window frame, his tie loosened and his collar button undone. He was on the far side of the room from Harriet, who was there with Damian Charlton. Lawrence looked up at the mention of his name. Martin wound up, exhorting his guests to enjoy the drinks, waited for the applause and hear, hears to come. They came, but they seemed strangely muted. Perhaps that was what his guests thought was appropriate for these surroundings. He shouldn't have expected cheering. Martin stepped down from the dais and went to give Iona a hug.

'Well done,' she said. He hugged his mother, negotiating the awkward brim of her mauve hat.

'That was lovely,' she told him. 'Especially what you said about Dad.'

The chatter in the room was lower, as though it had been muffled. There seemed to be fewer people at the reception than there had been when he'd started to speak. He would have heard the jangle of the division bell, had it rung, calling a vote. 'I have to say hello to Patrick,' Martin said to Iona.

He edged his way through his guests towards where Victoria and Anjali were standing, Patrick Chambers alongside them. They were conducting an animated conversation in whispers. There must be some news story breaking; there was that anxious huddling, people pulling out their phones, looking at messages, curving their hands around screens. Martin broke into their closed circle, curious to find out what they were talking about. He stuck his right hand towards Patrick, conscious that the muscles of his arm were twitching.

'Thanks for dropping by,' he said to Patrick. 'Good to see you.'

Patrick looked at Martin with a startled expression, as if jolted by an unwelcome memory.

'Ah, yes, Martin,' he said in the tone of a headmaster calling a miscreant into his office. Martin noticed that he didn't use his new title, even in jest. 'Yes. Well done. Would you excuse me, just a minute?'

The circle of shoulders closed him out again and he stepped backwards. As he turned to go back to Iona, he saw that Patrick was walking away, towards the door. His champagne seemed to have gone flat in the glass in a moment. Chambers was fickle like that. One moment you were in, the next out, for no reason that he could yet discern.

Martin tapped his own pocket, where his BlackBerry usually was. It was no longer there. Iona had made sure that he had switched it off and left it somewhere out of reach. 'What if it rang?' she had said. 'In the Chamber? While you're reciting the oath?' He hadn't wanted to argue, not after what had happened last time they had disagreed over a phone. Someone would tell him what was going on. There were consequences, not least the impression that it would give to be drinking champagne on the Lords terrace if something terrible were happening somewhere. The news cycle moved so fast these days; one misstep and your reputation could be damaged beyond repair.

Lucy Fox was standing near the head of the stairs, her head bowed over a phone screen. She seemed to be shaking her head slightly from side to side. It must be bad.

'What's up?' Martin asked, trying to see what was on her screen.

'Nothing,' she said, putting the phone away in the bag that hung from her shoulder. 'Well, it's not nothing. It's just something that's not for right now.'

Martin rubbed his hand over the back of his scalp, feeling the ridges at the base of his skull with his fingers.

'What do you mean it's not for right now? Things are always for right now. If it matters, it matters now.'

Lucy patted her hand in a downward gesture, suggesting that he lower his voice.

'Not here. Not now.' Usually, when Lucy's voice was dangerously soft like this, Martin knew not to argue with her.

'This is what I pay you for. To tell me what's going on, when I need to know it.' Lucy shook her head in exasperation.

'Don't blame me if you decide you didn't want to know, after all.' She gestured to him to follow her downstairs. They huddled close together in a corridor, waiting for people to pass, before she took the phone back out of her bag and called up the screen she had been looking at. She handed the phone over to Martin. It was one of the gossip blogs, one of those that spread scurrilous, unsourced rumours, the kind the papers used to avoid touching.

'French Kissing' was the headline, and as soon as he saw the picture, it was obvious why. It would have been a great picture, if it wasn't a bit blurry and out of focus, snapped on a phone. If it wasn't a picture of him. He was beneath the Eiffel Tower and you could make out its iron lattice in the background. He was kissing Isabelle. It was unmistakably him and unmistakably her and they were plainly embracing each other, kissing full on the lips. Martin tried to think of ways to explain it away, to say that they were just friends, that it was a misperception.

He scrolled down the screen to the text below.

New crony peer in steamy clinch with stunning wife of scandal Frenchman.

It was as though they were running some kind of competition to see how many tabloid clichés they could get into one sentence.

Beautiful angel of mercy Isabelle Reynaud is married to Christophe Vernet, arrested over tax-dodging and sheltering the funds of an indicted war criminal. Someone's on a mercy mission here but we're not quite sure who it is . . .

He had seen enough. Martin handed the phone back to Lucy.

'It's bad, isn't it?' Lucy looked at it first through professional eyes. He tried to detach himself from the story, see it as he would have done if he were advising someone else, but found it impossible. 'It's pulling a lot of things together. Maybe they aren't all that closely related?' Lucy was trying to sound optimistic, to cheer him up, but that made it even worse. He knew what she would have said if they'd been talking about someone else. She'd have sworn a blue streak, said he's a fucking goner or words to that effect. 'We'll come up with a plan to handle it,' she assured him.

Right now he had no plan, no strategy, couldn't put anything in the boxes of a grid. He wanted to tell her and everyone else, that things weren't what they looked like. The trouble was that in his business, things *were* what they looked like. It was how they looked that mattered. And this looked, from any perspective, very, very bad.

21

L AWRENCE WONDERED HOW soon it would be polite to leave. He found himself repeating the same answers to the same questions and his conversation had soon run dry. The House of Lords' champagne was not bad but it was a bit early in the day for the waiters to be refilling the glasses so assiduously, especially when there were only canapés to accompany it. Lawrence had been avoiding Harriet, but that was no longer possible, and, despite himself, he was curious to meet Damian Charlton. Harriet was wearing a dress that made Lawrence feel he needed his eyes tested – it had a blurry print that looked like oil patterns in a puddle, purple and green splashes against a dark background. He noticed how Harriet's arms had become more muscular than he remembered, her shoulders more solid and sculpted. It must have taken work; he had seen an article she'd written recently about hiring a personal trainer, illustrated with a 'before' picture where Harriet was dressed in a baggy black T-shirt, and an 'after' photo where her gym kit was brand new. It was disingenuous, like so much of her stuff.

Damian Charlton stood behind her, a beanpole of a man in a light-blue suit. He was even taller in real life than he seemed on screen. They both held out awkward hands.

'I hear you and Martin go back a long way,' Damian Charlton ventured.

'Oh yes,' Lawrence said. 'I knew him when we were both still very green. He was my producer.'

'What was he like, back then?'

'Much like now,' Lawrence replied. 'Very driven. Very ambitious. He could always spot where the power lay.' Charlton nodded his overemphatic, television-interviewer's nod.

He should have known that Harriet would be there; she seemed to show up at everything, to judge by the columns he pretended not to read: at private views, book launches, parties where she met the names she could later drop. The risk for Harriet was in becoming so successful that she lost her stock-in-trade; the first columns she had written were about being an outsider, about trying to settle in and make new friends in a strange place, learning new customs. Then she'd written about life in London as a returning expat; later, on life as a single mother of teenagers. All of those predicaments created sympathy. Although life as an insider, a perennial party guest and the partner of a television celebrity may have posed problems, they weren't ones that her readers were likely to identify with. In December, Lawrence had read, alone in a cold house, about the difficulty of juggling so many clashing Christmas party invitations. He clicked the page closed and wondered whether he would find anyone in the cafe that evening to talk to, whether he would have to spend all evening talking to Gilles, the bar owner, about football.

'I wanted to talk to you about Lizzie. Have you heard from her lately?'

As she spoke, Harriet was rummaging in her handbag, searching for a buzzing phone. She found it, checked the screen, lifted her eyebrows in surprise and then stowed the phone back in her bag.

Lawrence tried to remember when he had last spoken to his daughter. Last week, the week before?

'A week or two ago, maybe?'

'How did she sound to you?'

'Fine, I think. A bit tired, maybe. But that's just being a student, isn't it? I probably caught her when she had a hangover. Why?'

'I don't know, exactly,' Harriet said, taking a sip of her drink.

Damian had stepped back, reluctant to intrude. 'She seems – yes, as you said – a bit subdued. Not her usual self.'

Harriet's phone set her bag shivering again and once more she pulled it out. It was starting to get on Lawrence's nerves. She took the call and muttered an apology.

'Sorry, I have to take this. Work.'

It was the kind of thing that Martin would have done. They were supposed to be talking about their daughter. He scanned the room to see if he could spot Martin. There he was, of course, heading straight for the politicians.

'Why would I go into politics?' Martin had said, years before, when Lawrence had wondered out loud about his future. 'It's so precarious, so fickle. You can work for years for something and then the voters decide they don't want you. I'd rather be in business. At least people are straightforward when they tell you they don't want what you're selling.' But he had ended up here anyway, conveniently bypassing the necessity of being elected. Martin had claimed, in his speech, to be humbled by his peerage, although that was what people said when they meant that they were glowing with pride, but knew it was unseemly to brag.

'I'm there, right now,' Harriet was saying. 'I can't really talk. But I'll give you a call, if I hear anything.'

People were already leaving. He guessed they had places to be, meetings to hold. Harriet ended her call and beckoned to him to follow her out onto the terrace. They found a spot where they were separated from the rest of the party by a sheet of glass. Beyond the windows he could see Damian Charlton inclining his head to talk to a far shorter guest, then glancing back through the window at them.

'Is this about Lizzie?' Lawrence asked. Harriet shook her head.

'Something else.' Her phone was still in her hand and she called something up. 'Have you seen this?'

Lawrence squinted, trying to make out the words and the picture. He was reluctant to admit he needed glasses. He slanted a palm to shield the screen from the sunlight, hoping that would make things clearer. There were two figures, a man and a woman, in what must have been Paris. It was a snatched kiss, the passers-by not seeming to notice. One passer-by, though, had taken the picture. He didn't need to read the caption to see who they were: the shaven-headed man in a blue jacket, jeans and an open-necked shirt, the dark-haired woman with the long neck and sunglasses on top of her head, wearing a swathe of grey fabric around her white shirt and skinny black trousers. It was Martin and Isabelle.

'Oh God,' Lawrence said, clasping a hand to his mouth.

'I know,' Harriet said. 'Did you read all of it?' He shook his head. He hadn't got much further than the picture.

'Hold it a bit closer,' Lawrence said. 'It's very small print.' He could make out most of the story, but it didn't tell him much more than he already knew. The story about Christophe and Sylvie hadn't made much headway in the British papers – a few down-page mentions on the foreign pages – let alone the TV news. Lawrence could imagine how the conversations with the news desks had gone.

'This really matters,' the correspondent would have said. 'It's a big deal over here. A government minister, suspected of involvement in money-laundering, and not only that, her brother laundering the assets of a suspected war criminal . . .' Then a pause at the other end of the line: 'Would I have heard of her?' 'Yes,' the correspondent would have said, 'she's very influential. And she's very elegant into the bargain. We have pictures of her.' There would have been a non-committal murmur and, 'File us some copy. But it's not going to play big.'

'Did you know?' Harriet asked.

'Did I know which bit?' Lawrence hedged. As soon as he'd said it, he realised he was admitting more than he had meant to.

'Is this the same woman?' As ever, Harriet assumed he knew what she meant, even though he often no longer did. She had always had a habit of launching into stories in the middle.

'The same as what?'

'The same one you went to Congo with? The one you were making the film about?'

'It wasn't really about her, as such. But yes, she's the same woman.'

'She's very attractive,' Harriet observed.

'Yes, she is,' Lawrence said.

'Just your type,' she laughed.

'Out of my league,' Lawrence replied. He raised his eyes from the phone and looked out into the distance, across the river.

'And Martin's league?' Again, Lawrence tried to ignore what she was driving at. 'I mean, have they got this right?'

'When is this supposed to have been taken?' Lawrence asked, trying to deflect her question. Harriet looked down at her phone again and swept her index finger up the screen until she found the answer.

'September. A charity bike ride, it says.' That figured. Lawrence looked closer at the picture and could just about make out the bandage on Martin's hand. So much for having gone to Paris to support the team.

'Who do you think would do this? Send it to the website, I mean?'

'I don't know,' Harriet said. 'There must have been plenty of people around, friends of the other riders, maybe. Plenty of people are envious of Martin, want to take him down a peg.'

'At least I wasn't there,' Lawrence said. 'He can't think it was me. You're my alibi.'

'Alibi?' Harriet wondered aloud.

'We were in Bristol, with Lizzie.'

'Why would he think it was you, anyway?'

'I don't know,' Lawrence said, finishing his drink. 'We had a bit of a disagreement. About the film, mostly.' He stopped himself from saying any more.

'How long has this been going on? The affair, I mean. Assuming it is what it looks like.'

'Harriet, stop fishing. I'm not going to say anything about anything. We're standing here drinking his champagne.' Lawrence swirled the last drop around in the base of his glass as though it might refill itself.

'Lawrence, don't be precious,' Harriet insisted. 'You know how it works as well as I do. You don't think that everyone will be on this already, doorstepping him, finding out all about her?'

'Does anyone really care about that sort of thing any more – affairs? Haven't we gone beyond that?'

'Affairs on their own, probably yes. But the rest of this is worse for him.' Harriet tapped an orange fingernail on her screen. 'That her husband's been arrested, that he's involved in money-laundering and tax evasion, supposedly. The links to a war criminal. Someone, it says here, who used child soldiers, raped women.'

'Really?' Lawrence queried. 'It's a tenuous connection, isn't it? I mean, Christophe would hardly be telling all this to the man who's – allegedly – shagging his wife.'

'Do you know him, then, if you're on first name terms? What's he like?'

'Christophe?'

Harriet nodded.

'I've only met him once or twice. He lives near Saint-Barthélemy. He's a cold fish. Very straitlaced, very proper, at least on the surface. From one of those old families who like to do things correctly, observe all the formalities. But listen, that's enough.'

'I remember Sylvie,' Harriet said. 'From when we were in Paris. I hadn't realised she was still around.'

'She's a survivor,' Lawrence said.

'Go on,' said Harriet. 'Just tell me if it's true. About this Isabelle. You must know.'

'I'm not saying anything. Anything I tell you, he'd know it came straight from me. And he still owes me money. I'm going back inside.'

'That film's never going to see the light of day, now, though, is it? Think how it would look: a film featuring the wife of a corrupt businessman, a woman supposedly having an affair with a lobbyist crony of government ministers. No matter how many good works she's been doing, they'll run a mile.' He hated to admit that Harriet was right. Once again, he had nearly got himself killed for nothing. None of it was going to work. 'If it's not true, just tell me it's not true,' Harriet said. He looked her in the eye and said nothing.

He turned and walked off the terrace, back into the room. He scanned the room for Martin, the dutiful need to thank his host outweighing the awkwardness. Iona was still there, chatting to Martin's mother. Lawrence imagined that she did not know.

'It's been lovely,' Lawrence said, excusing himself. He kissed Iona lightly on each cheek. For a moment, he wondered whether he should be the one to tell her, whether it would be a kindness to let her know now, before Martin had to, before she got home to find the phone ringing and the photographers starting to gather outside the house. It felt like a betrayal to allow her to remain in ignorance. No, he thought. If Martin had got himself into this situation, it wasn't Lawrence's responsibility to get him out of it. He didn't owe him that.

22

MARTIN TRIED TO remember where his new peg was, which of the brass hooks on the ornate metal coat racks belonged to him. It would have been just like a first day at school, if you had been to the kind of school that looked like this. He hadn't, but he remembered the awe he felt when he had arrived at Oxford and discovered that someone painted your name, by hand, in white calligraphy on a black board at the foot of your staircase, to show where you would live. Martin found his name on a cream card slotted into a brass holder on one of the racks by a diamond-latticed window. Iona, behind him, was laughing in wonderment at the cloakroom itself, the way she had laughed at so many of the quirks of the day. She idly picked up someone else's umbrella from a stand and twirled it around.

'It's so kitsch, isn't it?' she observed. 'It's like some fantastic museum, full of secret entrances and passageways.' She still didn't know. No one had told her, not yet. There was a part of him, a cowardly part, that wanted someone else to break the news; a well-intentioned friend, an accidental discovery. Then all he would have to do was react. They left the room, past another peer drifting into sleep on a red leather sofa.

The white-tied doorkeeper at the entrance wished him 'Good afternoon, my Lord.' As he pushed through the doors that led back out into Old Palace Yard, Martin wished that nothing would change, that this day could be preserved. He would have to tell her before they got home. There would be people waiting for them outside the house. Having found his phone and switched it back on, he discovered dozens of messages and missed calls. He switched it off again.

If this were someone else, he would snap into action. Front up, he would tell them. Go on the offensive. Get out there and get your version of events in front of people. Take back control. Be decisive. Be contrite, up to a point. Explain how things were going to change. He'd slipped up on evaluating the risks beforehand. It was a bit late to be preparing for a worst-case scenario. This was it.

They climbed into a taxi and headed back towards Parliament Square. Martin wanted to stop time at that moment, to keep going around the square. They stopped for a moment at a red light, a gaggle of foreign schoolchildren crossing the road ahead of them. Then the lights turned green and the cab moved on.

Martin made sure that the glass partition that separated them from the cab driver was closed, that the switches which would allow him to hear their conversation were off.

'Iona,' he began. 'There's something I need to tell you.'

There was no way the cab driver couldn't have heard the scream that ensued, or the swearing.

'Why are you telling me this now?' Iona demanded, once her initial blast of yelling had tailed off. 'Why do you have to ruin today? Which was already, in many ways, pretty awful, but at least I was proud of you. We were all proud of you.'

'The thing is,' he said, 'it's – it's kind of in the public domain.'

'What the hell do you mean, it's in the public domain?' He explained about the website.

'And you're telling me now,' she said, 'because everyone knows, is that right? Everyone in London knows. Everyone in that horrible room at the House of Lords. Everyone except me knows.'

He had no answer to that. The taxi had turned off the Embankment, heading away from the river.

'Who is she?' Iona demanded. 'Do I know her?'

He had to tell her, because she would find out anyway.

'Her name is Isabelle,' he said. 'And yes, you have met her. In France.'

'Her?' she exclaimed. 'The snooty, skinny doctor? And you invited her to our house, to my house, on my holiday, so you could fuck her? The holiday that you fucking ruined by nearly getting yourself fucking killed?'

The taxi moved unsteadily, almost grazing a kerb, as though the cab driver had been disconcerted by what he was overhearing. Iona leant forward and slid the partition open.

'Stop here, please,' she told the driver. Her voice was suddenly pleasant and light again. The cabbie pulled up to the kerb. Iona turned to Martin. 'Get out,' she said.

'What?'

'Get out of the cab. Now.' She wasn't going to brook any argument, but he tried. It was always worth trying.

'Let's talk about this. Don't do anything rash. Let's talk about this properly, in the morning.'

'Get the fuck out of the cab and don't talk to me about doing anything rash. Your whole life you've been rash. I wish you'd died on that fucking mountainside, I really do. I wish we'd fucking left you there. And she could have come and collected your body, if she could be bothered.' Iona's rages, when they came, were usually fierce, short squalls that died away again. He had never seen her look quite like this, her face so red with anger. She wasn't crying, yet, but her eyes were brimming with tears. 'Get out!' she shouted, one last time.

Martin obeyed, bending over to climb out of the cab. As he descended, he felt something hit him in the back. On the pavement next to him was Iona's green hat.

As the cab pulled away, he kicked the hat with its spirals of green straw into the gutter like discarded apple peel.

It took him a moment to get his bearings; he was in Smithfield. He started to walk through the archway of the meat market, beneath the green- and purple-painted ironwork that supported the roof. He tried to walk purposefully, even though he couldn't walk as fast as he wanted, and in any case he wasn't sure where he was going.

Martin paused between the pairs of red phone boxes and went to lean against an ornate sea-green railing. He wanted to find someone to blame for the situation, someone other than himself. To lay the fault with whoever had taken the photo, whoever had decided to give it to that muckraking website. He ran through the suspects in his head, trying to come up with ways he could get revenge, but he knew this was only a diversion. He had already lost control of the story and he had to clutch it back. It wasn't just a story, he reminded himself, it was his life.

He tried to ring Victoria, but her phone rang once and then went dead. Perhaps she was in a meeting and couldn't speak. He tried again and the same thing happened. He would give it a few minutes. A wave of tiredness consumed him, the kind he hadn't felt since he was in hospital.

Martin walked out of the market building again, willing himself on, turned off the main road into a narrower street and found a small pub, etched glass in the doors and a long bar inside. He ordered a pint of lager and carried it to one of the pub's wooden booths. The booth had doors inset with green stained-glass panels. He pulled the door closed behind him, shutting himself and his drink away from the world and the people outside.

He tried Victoria again. For a third time, the call was rejected. Almost as soon as that call was cut off, his phone rang again. It was Anjali Mehta.

'Anjali,' he said. 'Good to hear from you. Funnily enough, I've just been trying to get hold of Victoria.'

'I know,' Anjali said. 'She's – she's not available right now.' Anjali was not a good liar. She was too straightforward. Victoria, he knew, was probably sitting next to her.

'We have a bit of an issue here,' Martin said.

'Yes,' Anjali agreed. 'That's why I was calling. I'm sure you realise we're not going to be able to go ahead with the launch of the campaign. At least, not in its current form. It's just – it's going to raise too many questions.'

Martin took a long sip of the lager.

'I can see where you're coming from,' he said.

'I mean, it's very disappointing,' Anjali continued, 'given all the work that's gone into it. We'd sent the advisory notices out as well.'

'What are you going to say? About why it's off?'

Anjali paused. He thought he could hear her whisper something to someone nearby.

'Diary clash, something like that. Victoria has to be out of the country. Unavoidable international meeting.'

'Don't you think people will spot something a bit odd about it?'

'That's for us to worry about. Sounds like you have your own worries right now.'

Who the hell was she to be speaking to him like that, a self-confident twenty-something who thought she was it, just because she had a Masters and a job in the government? The trouble was, she was and she did and she could consign him to the outer darkness, just like that. She just had. The title might have been his for life, unless he had committed some heinous crime, but the grace and the favour could be gone in an instant.

Martin hesitated before he made the next call. It wasn't something he usually did. Normally he called first and thought later. This was a call he had to make soon, before anyone else did, but he wasn't sure how it would go. Or how he wanted it to go. For a moment, before he made the phone call, he allowed himself to imagine it.

In the scenario he called into being, Isabelle made a sudden, impulsive decision. She would leave Christophe. She would come to London. They would find somewhere to live. He would see the twins at weekends. Martin conjured an image of himself and Isabelle, walking through west London, a new start in a new part of town. He saw the two of them as though through someone else's eyes, taking Maisie and Finn to the playground in Kensington Gardens, standing together hand in hand as they watched the children climb on the wooden pirate ship. It was a picture of contentment and he wanted to hold on to it for as long as possible. They had never talked about the future. It was one of the subjects that had been off limits. One way or the other, they were going to have to.

It was early evening in France – not a time that he would normally call her. Assuming she was in France, of course. He heard the long rings at the other end of the line. He rarely rang her like this, and it was possible that she wouldn't take his call either. Martin willed her to pick up the phone.

'Hello?' There was an anxiety in Isabelle's voice as she answered and Martin was afraid that somehow she had already heard.

'Are you alone?' he asked. 'Can you talk?'

'I'm at work,' she replied. He heard the sound of a door closing. Her voice relaxed a little. 'It's fine. I can talk. How are you?'

'I'm sorry,' he began. 'I've got some bad news.'

'Is this about your health? Are you OK?'

'It's not that. I'm well – physically, at least. It's just that I'm in trouble and I'm afraid you're involved.'

There was a small gasp at the other end of the line, a quiet 'Oh.'

'Your wife has found something out?'

'Yes. And it's worse than that.' He needed to tell her everything, as quickly as possible. In a rush, he explained about the website, the kind of gossip it relayed, what they had shown, what they had written. Isabelle asked what the site was called and as he told her, he could hear her tapping at a keyboard. There was a long silence as she read what must have been on her screen, another 'Oh.'

'Have you read it?'

'I'm reading it now. This is dreadful. I can't believe they can do this. And your wife saw this?'

'I had to tell her. Because all the press here read that site and they were going to start calling us and coming to the house. I couldn't let her find out from them.'

'I see. Where are you?'

'I'm in a pub, drinking on my own in the middle of the afternoon.' As he said it, Martin realised he was close to tears. 'This was supposed to be a great day, one of the best days of my life.' He leant back against the wooden panelling. 'And instead my whole life is falling apart.'

He wanted words of comfort from Isabelle but she was slow to supply them.

'It's not falling apart,' she said, at last. 'You'll get through this.' He noticed that she said 'you'll' get through this. She didn't say 'we' would get through it. She didn't see it as a problem shared.

'What about Christophe?' he asked.

'What about him?'

'Are you going to tell him?' Another of those pauses.

'I don't know.'

'Why not?'

'Because he has so many other problems to deal with at the moment. The arrest, the investigations. It might . . . it might be too much.'

Anger was starting to rise in Martin's chest and he struggled to control it, struggled to breathe and stay calm as everyone kept reminding him to do.

'We've all got problems that are too much. We don't all get to choose how they arrive. Be honest with him. Be brave.'

'How dare you tell me to be brave,' Isabelle said. 'When you barely cared if we got killed, Lawrence and I, that time. When I spend half my life in the kind of places you no longer have to set foot in, where there are diseases and wars, while you sit in a nice air-conditioned office or in the House of Lords.'

'That's a different kind of courage, though, isn't it? You can be out there being a hero, being a saint, and you don't have to worry about all these things, about all these other choices. You can just escape from it.' It was a cheap shot but he wasn't above those when he wanted to use them.

'That isn't fair,' Isabelle said. Her voice was still low and quiet. He remembered she was in the office, even though she was behind a closed door.

'Just leave him,' Martin pleaded. 'You'll do it anyway, won't you, if he ends up in prison? Because that will destroy the image of the kind of life you think you have. What happens, if the fortune goes and the family's reputation goes? What happens to you then? Why wait?'

'But he's – what's the expression – innocent until proven guilty, isn't he?' It was rare that Isabelle was stumped for a term in English. 'I can't just go because he's suspected of something, because maybe his former clients are angry with him, trying to make allegations against him. It's all politically motivated, anyway. Maybe people want to get at him because they want to get at Sylvie. Maybe Kalombo's being blamed by his rivals for things that they're equally guilty of.'

'You believe that?' Martin retorted. 'They could be dangerous, some of those people, not just the ones in Africa, if what the reports say are true.'

'I don't know what I believe,' Isabelle said. 'But I can't simply walk out, just because you say so.'

'Why not?' Martin persisted. 'What's to stop you?'

'I can't throw my whole life in the air, because all of a sudden it suits you that I should. What if I'd said the same thing, yesterday? Before all this changed. When you were about to go to the big ceremony with your family? Would you have given me the same answer?'

Martin could barely remember yesterday. Yesterday was a different world.

'It isn't yesterday,' he said. 'It's today. And you could come here. We could work something out.'

'I'm not coming there,' she said. 'Not now, of all times. Not if there are going to be people chasing you around, chasing me around. I need to stay here. I've got other problems, too. Work, for instance. One project already at risk, others could follow it. I can't let people down.'

Martin was going to let her down on that as well.

'Oh yes,' he said. 'That film, with you, with Lawrence? They don't think it's a good idea to go ahead with a big launch, at the moment. Because of the . . . the unfavourable publicity.'

'It's cancelled, you mean?'

'I wouldn't say cancelled. Postponed, maybe. Until things have quietened down.' He was trying to be diplomatic but she could see through him instantly.

'Martin,' Isabelle insisted, raising her voice, 'tell me the truth.'

'OK,' he said. It was a day for uncomfortable truths so he might as well put all of them out there. 'It's never going to see the light of day. Victoria doesn't want anything more to do with it, so we won't have their backing or their funding. Not in this country, at any rate. You might be able to use some of the material, at some point, but not for a while.'

'That's terrible,' Isabelle said. 'We need the funding. We need the visibility.'

'You don't want that kind of visibility,' Martin said. 'Trust me.'

'I see,' Isabelle said. 'I'll have to tell people here and explain why. I can't see a way around it.'

'Fine,' Martin replied. 'Do what you have to do.' There was a trickle of lager still left at the bottom of the pint glass and he tipped up the glass to drain the last of it into his mouth. 'Please talk to me. Please tell me what's happening. Even if you don't feel you can come here. I could come to you, meet you somewhere. Like we used to.'

That image of the playground, the children, the flat somewhere, the life that worked out, was dissipating. He could no longer conjure it clearly.

'I can't promise,' she said.

'You don't have to promise,' he said. 'Just say it's possible. Anything's possible.'

'It's possible,' Isabelle repeated, but it sounded to him as if it was an infinitely small possibility.

Martin hung up and thought about getting another pint. He decided against it. He had a sudden surge of energy, a belief that he could make things work, despite the odds against him. He would find the cake he had promised Maisie and Finn that morning, he would go home and apologise and maybe he would be able to get his life back, the life that belonged to him.

He emerged from the pub and looked from side to side, as though there was a danger someone had tracked him down. Then he went in search of a bike; one of those clunky hire bikes would have to do. He knew he wasn't supposed to, that it was against doctors' advice and Iona's furious insistence, but there was something consoling about the thought. He would be able to weave through the streets, unnoticed and noiseless, free for a few minutes at least, along familiar back routes, the alleys of the City and the canal towpath. As he yanked the bike out of the rack, it occurred to him that he shouldn't go home, that there might be journalists waiting for him there, as well as whatever awaited him inside the front door. But all he could think about was going home.

23

A SLEEPY LIZARD scuttled across the terrace, changing direction back and forth as Lawrence's shadow fell on it, before escaping into a crack in the wall. Along the edge of the terrace, purple irises were emerging into flower. Beyond, the vineyards were in new, pale-green leaf. The pool was still closed, a green tarpaulin stretched taut over it and held in place by a lattice of elastic ropes. There was something forlorn about the house without the blue of the pool.

As Lawrence approached the house, he could hear high-pitched yells from the far end of the garden. He drew nearer and saw Maisie and Finn chasing each other around the lawn. They didn't notice him and carried on shouting at each other.

He peered in through the windows, trying to find Iona. The glass door that led to the kitchen was ajar and he saw her inside. He tapped on the glass of the window and she beckoned him to come in. She put the knife she had been holding down on a chopping board and held out her arms to welcome him. She was in a royal-blue jumper, which was baggy on her and looked like it must have belonged to Martin, with holes at the elbows where a white shirt showed through. He gave her a long hug.

'For you,' he said, indicating the five-litre box of local wine he'd put on the kitchen island. 'I thought you might need it.'

'I'll try not to drink it all at once,' she said. 'Thank you.'

'Are the twins all right out there?' he asked. 'They were making quite a lot of noise.'

'Too much chocolate,' Iona said, indicating two Easter baskets of coloured straw that sat on the kitchen counter, containing half-eaten chocolate bunnies. 'They always have to have too much of a good thing. Just like . . .' She stopped herself. 'I'm not saying that. I don't want to start blaming him for everything. I don't want to be one of those women.'

She looked, on the surface, as though she was bearing up well. She had lost some weight, that much even Lawrence could tell. Her red hair was scraped back into a messy ponytail. As ever, her fringe was trailing over her eyebrows and brushing against the heavy frames of her glasses. When he looked more closely he could see her eyes were tired, small lines clustering in the corners and dark shadows where the glasses rested on her cheekbones.

'How are you all doing?' he asked.

Iona cast a quick glance at the wine and then shook her head. 'Too early, isn't it?'

Lawrence checked his watch – it was the middle of the afternoon.

'Probably,' he acknowledged.

Iona made tea instead. They went outside to the terrace and sat beneath the metal canopy overhung with pale-purple wisteria. Iona pushed her sleeves up to her elbows, lifted her glasses from her face for a moment and rubbed her eyes.

'It's hard,' she said. 'I've done it before but this is really hard.'

'Because of those two?' Lawrence indicated Maisie and Finn with a waved hand towards the further reaches of the garden.

'Partly that,' Iona agreed, taking a sip of her tea. 'But I had Freya already, last time, and she was much smaller. She was too young to ask questions, which helped. It's more that Martin is determined to make life difficult.'

'In what way?' Lawrence asked. 'I'd have thought he doesn't have a leg to stand on.'

'Morally, of course he doesn't and he knows it. But legally, financially – he's using every trick in the book.' She put her glasses back on, the better to inspect Lawrence. 'I need to know that none of this is going to get back to him.'

Lawrence held up a palm as if he was saying an oath. 'Of course not.'

'Have you spoken to him much – since it all happened?'

Lawrence had almost given up on Martin ever calling him back. He had been bombarding him with messages, supportive ones at first, ones of encouragement and sympathy. There were questions that Lawrence needed answers to and he wasn't getting them.

'It's hard to get hold of him, these days. I left him a message, that day. I think he texted me back, a few days later. When the story had started to die down. At first I thought he was deliberately ignoring me, but he must have had dozens of messages, if not hundreds.'

'And since then?'

'I can't get any sense out of him. There was this project we were working on, this film. It could have been really good. It was powerful stuff. But no one wanted to hear about it any more, let alone pay for it.' Lawrence realised that he was talking about himself, that he was, even if only by implication, mentioning Isabelle. 'But no, I won't talk to him. Anything you say stays right here.'

Iona stood up and walked towards the edge of the terrace, staring out at the distant hills.

'You must have known,' she said, not looking back at him. 'Last summer, you must have known about her.'

'I didn't, at first. But later, yes.'

'When?'

'When we found him, after the accident. When he was in hospital. He didn't tell me exactly, but I knew.'

'And you didn't tell me because?' Iona whirled around. She was silhouetted against the sky and Lawrence had to shield his eyes with his hand in order to see her face.

'Because that was the last thing you needed, at that point. You'd been through enough. And I imagined that you'd have had him dropped from the air ambulance back onto the mountain, from a great height, if you knew.' She almost managed to laugh. 'I thought he'd see sense,' Lawrence continued. 'He'd had a close call and I thought he would appreciate what he had, not want to put it all at risk. That's what I told him, anyway.'

'But this is Martin we're talking about,' Iona said. 'He rolls the dice again. He always takes chances.'

'That's true. I should have known him better.'

'People rarely do tell you, though, do they?' Iona said. 'I mean, even with my ex – my last ex – everyone knew he was up to no good and I didn't know the half of it.'

There was an anguished howl from the end of the garden, beyond the statue. It didn't sound like the excited screams that the twins had been emitting until now. Iona thumped her mug of tea down on the table and ran in the direction of the yelling. Lawrence followed behind her. They were met by Maisie, who was running to fetch her mother.

'Finn's fallen out of the tree,' she announced, her fists on her hips. 'He says it was my fault, but it isn't.' Her father's daughter, Lawrence thought, getting her own exculpation in first.

'I don't care whose fault it is,' Iona told her. 'Is he all right?'

If he's screaming, he's all right, Lawrence remembered a paramedic once saying to him. It's the ones who aren't screaming you have to worry about. Finn was lying under a fig tree, wailing theatrically.

'Can you get up?' Iona asked.

'My ankle hurts,' he howled. 'And Maisie wobbled the branches.'

Iona was brisk; she had seen that the branch he pointed out was quite near the ground. 'I'm sure it does,' she said. 'But I think you can probably get up.'

Lawrence willed the little boy to stand up.

Maisie fixed Lawrence with a forbidding stare.

'Why are you here?' she asked. 'Because you're Daddy's friend and Daddy isn't here any more.'

'Because I'm your mummy's friend too,' he told her. 'And I

live near here, so when you came here on holiday I thought I'd come and say hello.'

'Are you French?' Maisie said. 'Because you don't sound French.'

'No,' he replied. 'I just live here. I like it here. It's warm and sunny.'

Maisie shrugged, accepting his answer as adequate, and went to stand over her brother. Iona lifted Finn to his feet and he put his weight tentatively on his injured ankle.

'I think I can walk,' he said. He wrapped one small arm around Iona and hobbled along towards the house.

'Well done,' Lawrence said. 'That's very brave.' Finn scowled back at him and didn't reply. He looked to Iona instead.

'Can I have some more chocolate now?' he asked. 'Since I'm hurt?'

'No.' Iona was firm. Finn screwed up his face again as though he was preparing to cry. She ushered him into the living room, lifted him onto the sofa and picked up some DVDs from the table. 'Which one of these do you want to watch?' Finn picked a cartoon and Iona switched on the TV, set the film playing. Maisie trailed behind and sat down alongside her brother.

'Where's Freya?' Lawrence asked.

'She's on an art course, in London, staying with a friend. She didn't want to come. She's taking all this quite badly.'

On the far wall of the room, the Patrick Caulfield print had been taken down, leaving a faint dusty outline. It was leaning against the wall below, the wine bottles and the vines in shadow. The other picture was still in place: a tourist poster from the 1930s, advertising excursions to Mont Ventoux. The mountain, etched in grey and white, loomed against a clear blue sky. The caption exhorted visitors not to miss the chance to see it: '*Ne quittez pas la Provence sans faire l'excursion.*'

Iona saw him looking.

'He can keep that one,' she said, pointing towards the poster. 'I don't want it. I don't ever want to see a picture of that mountain again. But the other one, the Caulfield, that's mine and I love it.'

She walked towards the silkscreen print and stroked a hand along the edge of the frame. 'It makes me sad, at the moment.' Iona crouched down, inspecting the bright, photographic labels on the wine bottles, the pile of red plates with white polka dots. 'This is what I imagined – what we imagined – it would be like. Visitors, food, drink. A place where people would be happy.'

She got up again and took a professional step back, to look from a greater distance. There was a bright diagonal strip across the image, a shaft of sunlight hitting the table, where the vine leaves of the background were yellow against pale blue, the grapes ovals of cobalt, the same shade as her sweater. 'Maybe I'll be able to see it like that again, one day.' She turned her back on the print and headed towards the kitchen. 'And if I can't, then it's valuable, it's a limited edition and he certainly can't have it.'

'It's like that, is it?' Lawrence observed.

'It is like that,' she replied. They walked back out onto the terrace, where the children would not hear them. 'He's moving out, this week, while we're here. I mean, he's gone, he's not living with us anyway, but I just want all of his stuff gone as well. His clothes, his books, his bloody bikes, all of that.'

Lawrence returned from the village with a pile of three square pizza boxes. He brought them into the kitchen. Iona picked up the wine box and turned it on its side, fiddling with the card-board until she could release the plastic spigot that would allow her to pour the wine. She fetched two tumblers from a cupboard and pushed the tap to release a stream of red wine into each glass. They clinked their glasses together.

'I don't know what we're toasting,' Iona said.

'The future?'

'The future.' She took a long sip of the wine and sighed. She called the twins and handed her glass back to Lawrence so that she could carry the pizzas to the terrace. She flipped open the lid of one of the boxes and handed a couple of slices to each child.

'It's cold,' Maisie complained.

'The pizza?' Lawrence asked.

'No, the wind. It's not like the summer. I don't like it here when we can't go in the swimming pool.'

'It's fine,' Iona insisted. 'Eat your pizza.'

Once the twins were intent on their food, Lawrence asked Iona, in a low voice, what was happening with the houses, how were they dividing them up?

'We're keeping the London house,' she said. 'Me and the children.' She lowered her voice to a near-whisper. 'Because even he realises it's better for them to stay where they are, because of schools and everything.'

Iona had done well to get that, though he wasn't surprised. It was the same thing he had done, after all. He had not even put up an argument when Harriet had made the same case. The Elliots' house was a lovely place, he remembered. It was a huge, double-fronted Victorian villa in Islington that Iona had gutted, modernised, filled with elegant flower arrangements and carefully chosen art. Lawrence wondered how much it was worth these days: two million, three million, five? He had lost touch with the exorbitant cost of property in London, except to know that he would never again be able to afford it.

'This one, however,' she said, 'we're still arguing about. Well, the lawyers are still arguing.'

'Why are you arguing?'

Iona sighed again and checked that the twins were not listening. 'It's to do with what it's worth. Get me some more wine and I'll explain.'

Lawrence found a carafe in the kitchen and filled it with Côtes du Rhône. He refilled Iona's glass.

'He got a good deal on this place. He got a *very* good deal.' She washed down a bite of pepperoni pizza with a swig of wine. 'You know we bought it from – them, right?' She couldn't bring herself to even say the family's name.

'I knew that.'

'It was in a terrible state when we got it. You should have

seen it. The roof was leaking, the plaster was falling off, the shutters were warped. The pool wasn't really a pool, it was more like a cross between a pond and a water tank, full of green stagnant water. Someone had died, the old lady, and they couldn't agree on dividing the inheritance. At least, that's what he told me. I'm not sure what to believe any more. I wanted to bring it back to life. If I'd known then what I know now . . .' Iona mused. She paused, reluctant to finish her thought.

'Then what?'

'I'd have bought something else, somewhere else. As far away from them as I could. Not in a place like this, a place where everyone knows everyone else, where everyone knows your business.'

'Small towns are small towns everywhere. But why does this affect the legal stuff, the divorce?'

Iona was topping up her glass again. Maisie and Finn said that they had finished their pizza and asked to leave the table, pleading for ice creams. Iona waved them in the direction of the kitchen and told them to help themselves.

'He paid a lot less for it than he should have. He told me it was because it was a private sale, he dealt with the family directly. We didn't have to go through the estate agents. One less person to take their cut was how he put it. So now he's saying that what he paid for it was the true value, that his assets are not worth as much as my side says they are; even though my lawyers are arguing that all the work I did on it meant it's worth a lot more now anyway. But none of it seems to quite stack up how it should.'

'How much less did he pay?'

'I don't know. It was into the hundreds of thousands of euros, I know that much. But he'd never tell me exactly. There was a lot I didn't know. I'm only starting to realise that now.'

Lawrence sat silently for a while. It wasn't going to be that simple, he realised. Iona seemed to realise only half the problems there were.

'He bought it from Christophe, didn't he?'

'Her husband, yes.' She almost spat out the words, still avoiding using their names. 'I can't believe he didn't think one of us would find out.'

'And you know about Christophe? I mean, about what's been happening to him?'

'Not really. I know what I read on that stupid website. To be honest I couldn't face reading all of it.'

'He's under investigation, he's been arrested once but then they had to release him. The inquiry's still going on. They're looking into all his property deals, because they know he hasn't been paying all the tax he should, that he hasn't declared all his income. They caught him going across the border to pay money into his Swiss bank account. And it's pretty certain that he's been laundering money for some very, very nasty people. One of them's been indicted for war crimes, had his assets frozen. Taking their ill-gotten money and turning it into nice clean French villas like this one, a place they can go shopping and buy wine and all that. Retire to if things go wrong for them at home. Which meant that Christophe should have run a mile from him.'

'But that's not Martin's fault, is it? I mean, whatever I think of him right now, he wouldn't necessarily have known all that.'

'That's the question, though, isn't it? Your problem is going to be that the French taxman, the French police, are looking through every single deal Christophe's done in the last few years, as evidence. And if they think Martin was complicit, that he knew more than he's telling you, any suspicion that there was money passed under the table, then . . .'

'Then what?'

'Then Martin won't only need a divorce lawyer.'

'Oh shit,' Iona said. She leant back in the chair and stared at the sky. 'You haven't got any of those sneaky cigarettes you sometimes have, by any chance?' He had, and he lit one for her. 'I mean it's not actually a crime, is it?'

Lawrence nodded. 'Well, it could be.'

'Why? I mean, if I give someone ten per cent off a picture,

because I like them, or to make a sale, then that's just business, isn't it? There's no victim.'

'True. But if you declared the sale price, with the discount, and paid your taxes on the basis of the sale price and your buyer gives you the other ten per cent in cash, no questions asked, then that's tax dodging. You're right, everyone does it, up to a point.' Lawrence had collected enough blank taxi receipts in his time. 'It's just that once they find there's something to investigate, they don't let it go. You must know how hot they are on money-laundering these days.'

'Tell me about it. Every time someone buys a piece of art, half our time is spent filling in forms, checking their identity and their bank details. Art's nice and portable – well, most of it – if you have to get out of somewhere in a hurry.'

Iona flicked ash onto the terrace. She rested her chin in the palm of her hand, her elbow on the table. She was deep in thought.

'But we don't know that, do we? That Martin was paying Christophe anything in return, anything off the books? So it might just have been a bargain?'

'It doesn't have to be cash. It could be anything. Presents. Services. In Martin's case, advice. How much does he charge?'

'For what?'

'For his advice. Professional advice.'

Iona shrugged and shook her head. 'I have no idea what he charges these days.'

'But he talks to Christophe, right? And Sylvie. And Is . . . and her? I know he was working with her. I was working with them.'

'Yes. All the bloody time. And I don't even want to talk about her.'

'I know you don't. But on the face of it, if it's not all going through the books, it looks dodgy.'

'Oh fuck.' Iona blew smoke out with one long exhale. 'That's going to make things difficult.'

'Do you have the documents?' Lawrence asked. 'The sale and purchase of the house?'

'They're around somewhere. Not here, I don't think. Probably in London. Why?'

'Because you might need them. Your lawyers might need them, whatever happens.' Lawrence had another thought. 'Maybe, since you're here, you should see if you can get some copies from the local notary. Whatever you decide to do. In case it comes down to it.'

'I can't think about this all now,' Iona protested. 'It's late and I'm tired. Maybe in the morning.'

'Did you go with Martin? When he signed the documents? Is the place in joint names?'

'It's in his.'

'And did he buy it direct from Christophe, from the Vernets, or some other way – through a company?'

Iona shrugged.

'It was another thing I should have asked, and didn't. A family trust, I think he might have said.'

'I imagine the authorities are all over it,' Lawrence said. 'It can take them ages. Particularly if the trust's based offshore, in some tax haven. It's as if there are boxes within boxes. You could help them,' Lawrence suggested. 'Tell them what you know. Drop a hint to the Revenue. It might help you, in the long run.'

Iona's expression flickered and changed. At first, she looked horrified, then intrigued. Then her face seemed to settle somewhere between the two.

'I could do that, couldn't I?' She weighed up the possibility for a moment, then ground the cigarette butt out on the flagstones. 'No, I couldn't. I do hate him right now, but I'm not sure I hate him that much.'

'I'm not going to say whether you should or you shouldn't. Only you can decide that. But it'll come out anyway, in the end. One way or another.'

'I hate all this,' she said. She put her head in her hands. 'I hate how it ends. I hate it all coming down to lawyers and arguments and dividing everything up. I thought we were happy, I really did. I hate having to put a price on all of it.'

She stood up and Lawrence saw that there were tears in her eyes that she was blinking back. He picked up the empty pizza boxes and carried them into the kitchen. It was strangely quiet in the rest of the house and he realised they hadn't heard from the twins in a while. They found the two of them curled up on the sofa, heads to each other's feet.

'And now I'm a neglectful single mother as well,' Iona said when she saw them. 'They didn't even brush their teeth.' She bent down, lifted Maisie from beneath her armpits in a practised gesture and hoisted the sleeping child onto her shoulder in a fireman's lift. 'Can you get the other one, please?'

Lawrence looked at Finn, who had one leg bent up, one arm outstretched above his head, his mouth agape. He leant over and tried to work out how to pick the boy up. It was so long since he had done this, so long since Josh was small enough to carry. He put his hands on either side of Finn's chest, caught hold of him and lifted. He was a solid little boy, heavier than Lawrence expected. He raised him up and the boy's head drooped onto his shoulder. His eyes flickered and opened for a moment. Lawrence stood still and hoped that he would fall asleep again. He walked carefully across the terracotta tiles and out to the hallway.

Iona was ahead of him on the stairs. Lawrence trod heavily, each step an effort.

'In here,' Iona said, just loud enough for him to hear. She had put Maisie down on one of the twin beds and was unstrapping her shoes, taking off her socks. Lawrence heaved Finn down and put him on the bed. He opened the Velcro straps of the boy's shoes and lined the shoes up. He hesitated, unsure what else to do, so stepped back and waited in the doorway while Iona took off some of the children's clothes. She kissed each sleeping twin on the forehead and then turned to leave the room.

'I don't know how he can do it,' Lawrence said, almost to

himself. 'When they're so small. When they need you so much.'

'It's hard work, on your own,' she said. She switched off the light in the children's room and pulled the door half closed behind her. 'But if I can't trust him any more . . .'

'I know,' Lawrence reassured her. 'I mean, who am I to talk? I did the same thing, I left – well, Harriet threw me out – and they're bigger now. You think they don't take the same amount of looking after, but they do.'

Iona walked into the large white bedroom with the heavy armoire. She crossed her arms and pulled off her blue jumper, throwing it onto the bed. It dislodged her glasses from her face and they fell on the floor. Lawrence bent down to pick them up and handed them back to her. Iona sat on the edge of the bed and put her face in her hands, ignoring the glasses he was holding out. She was sobbing, her shoulders shaking, large sobs that welled into howls of grief.

He sat down on the edge of the bed beside her.

'Ssshh,' he soothed, putting his arm around her shoulders.

'I'm sorry,' Iona stammered through her tears. 'It's just – I can't do this. I can't do all this on my own.'

'You can,' he reassured her. 'You're doing an amazing job. You're an amazing woman.' He rubbed her shoulder, the top of her arm. With his other hand, he held out the glasses again. She took them but placed them on the bedside table. 'You really are. You've always amazed me.'

She turned her face back to him, her eyes red and puffy with tears. Lawrence wiped one of the large round tears from her cheek with his thumb. 'Don't cry,' he said. 'Please don't cry.'

They both leant in towards each other at the same time, his hand moving away from her face to stroke her hair. Iona's mouth was soft and warm as he kissed her and he wrapped his arms around her. It was so long since he had kissed anyone like this and the forgotten pleasure came back to him, something he had no longer expected to feel.

*

It must have been early in the morning when the phone woke him. He was disorientated, trying to place himself in this strange room where the early light was streaming through half-open shutters. Then he saw Iona asleep beside him, her hair spread out on the pillow like sunrays. He found the phone, buried inside the pocket of his trousers, on the floor, and answered it in a whisper.

'Who is it?' He would have gone into the corridor but he remembered that he was naked and the twins were liable to wake up. As he held the phone to his ear, he rummaged in the pile of clothes for his boxer shorts.

'It's me, Dad.' Lizzie's voice sounded anxious. 'Where are you?'

'Lizzie,' he almost exclaimed, before remembering that he should be quiet.

'I thought you'd be here, but you're not here.' Lawrence was struggling into his boxers while holding the phone in one hand. He wasn't sure what day it was, let alone why Lizzie was expecting to find him. 'You are in France, aren't you?' she continued.

'I'm in France, yes. Sorry, Lizzie, I'm really confused but where are you exactly?'

'I'm at your house. I rang the doorbell but there is no answer. I thought maybe you didn't hear me.'

'You're in Saint Barthélemy? Now? Listen, I'm really sorry but did I make a mistake? Did you try to email me?'

'You didn't know,' Lizzie said. 'I just came. Are you upstairs, because I'll wait for you to come down.'

'I'm — not upstairs,' Lawrence admitted. 'I'm just — I stayed over at a friend's house.' Iona stirred in her sleep.

'Oh,' Lizzie said.

'What time is it?'

'Nearly eight.'

'Do you have money? Go to the cafe in the square. Get yourself some breakfast. I'll see you there in ten minutes.' Lizzie was about to ring off when he remembered something else. 'Lizzie?'

'Yes, Dad?'

'Doesn't term start this week? Aren't you supposed to be back at college?'

'Er, yes. It did. I mean, I am. But I've changed my mind about it all. That's why I came. I wanted to discuss things with you. Can you hang up now, because this is costing me a fortune. I'll tell you everything when we meet.'

'Lizzie,' he asked, before she could hang up. There was an evasion in her voice that he recognised from when she was little. 'Does Mum know you're here?'

'No,' she confessed. 'I couldn't face telling her.' She cut off the call before he could shout out in exasperation. Lawrence put the phone on the bedside table, pulled on the rest of yesterday's clothes. He was torn between waking Iona and not waking her. He shook her by the shoulder and whispered that he had to leave, that his daughter had arrived, out of the blue and that he'd call her later. She muttered something in a sleep-filled voice that might have been 'OK.'

He tied the grey sweater that had been Martin's around his shoulders and crept down the stairs, willing the ancient wood not to creak. As he padded across the hallway, he heard high-pitched French voices, children's voices, in the living room. The television was on and cartoons were blaring. He saw the back of one tousled head protruding above the linen of the sofa. Maisie or Finn, he couldn't tell which, was awake. He walked as softly as he could, then turned the door handle to open the patio door. As he walked away he tried not to look back, in case he saw a small, scowling face following his progress. He reached the car and the church clock began to chime eight.

24

THE EARLY MORNING clatter of activity in the streets on the edge of the City reassured him: the huge lorries, doors thrown open to reveal great red-and-white carcasses of meat hanging from racks; the white-clad porters heaving them into the Smithfield halls; the City workers in suits passing between them; the jostle of trade. London felt festive that week; some shops and houses already had bunting fluttering in anticipation of the Royal Wedding. It was like an early summer, an interlude full of holiday weekends.

It was all going to work out, Martin told himself. He liked waking up amid all of this. It gave him energy, it gave him his edge back. He had a flat in a glorious, curved art deco building looking over a square. He had swum in the indoor pool that morning, beating down the lengths with determination at six o'clock, as soon as it opened. He was going to get fit again. He was meeting Lucy Fox for breakfast two minutes' walk away and he could walk to the office in ten minutes.

Lucy was already there when he arrived, dressed in gym gear, black Lycra leggings and neon-green trainers. She was perched on a wooden stool at a small round red table. She had a large cup of coffee in front of her and was digging into a huge glass bowl of fruit-dotted granola with her spoon while checking emails on her BlackBerry. It was typical of Lucy to handle so many tasks at once. She swallowed down a mouthful of breakfast before she spoke.

'Thanks for coming,' she said as he sat down on the stool

opposite. Martin had an uncomfortable sense of having been summoned, though he was her boss. This was her agenda. The cafe was full of other people her age, hunched over silver laptops at long tables.

He summoned a waitress and ordered a double espresso. He looked at Lucy's granola before deciding, instead, that he could murder a bacon sandwich.

'Bacon sandwich?' Lucy observed as the waitress turned her back. 'I thought you were off all that?'

'Some days, nothing else will do,' he replied, trying to make light of it. Lucy gulped at her latte and launched into something she had obviously been planning.

'This is something I needed to say in person, and I thought it was best to do it out of the office.' He wondered why the urgency and Lucy, efficient as ever, answered the question before he had even asked it. 'And I'm sorry about the short notice, but they want to make an announcement as soon as possible. So it doesn't get completely buried under all the bloody bunting and the rest of the hoo-ha.'

'What announcement is this, Lucy?' She should already have known that no announcements of any kind were going to get a hearing in the next few weeks. It was even a bad time for announcements you wanted to slip out unnoticed; people were wise to the burying of bad news these days..

'I've been offered a job, back in Westminster. And it's one I really want to take.'

'Working for whom?'

'The leader's team. The opposition, obviously.' It was where she had come from and it was always likely at some point that she'd go back, but Martin hadn't expected her to go so soon, not when power was still a distant prospect at best.

'You're wasted on them,' Martin observed.

'You would say that, wouldn't you?' His acceptance of the peerage had been something Lucy had teased him about, but this time it was more needling.

'No, it's not about being tribal. You know I'm not tribal. It's just that I can't see why you would waste the next four years in opposition, doing stuff that doesn't matter, for less money.'

'It does matter. Someone's got to be in opposition. You have to lay the groundwork. I can't just stroll back in there in four years' time and expect it all to be done.'

Martin shrugged.

'Well, if you feel like that about it there's not much to say. How much are they paying you? Because you'll be losing out on a lot, if you don't stay until the deal's signed. Enough to set you up for the future. Enough that you can afford to work for as many hopeless causes as you want.' He needed her to stay, in truth. She was an asset. He was on the point of signing the deal to sell the company and he needed his key people in place. He couldn't afford to lose her now; people were paying him good money to tie her in to her contract.

'It's not about the money,' she replied. 'It's the kind of offer you don't get more than once.'

'That's not true.' Martin said. 'They'll keep asking. They need you more than you need them. Stay until the deal's done here, stay another year or two and they'll be begging for you.' He went on, aware of how needy he sounded. 'I know I say this all the time,' he continued, 'but you have such a great future with us. I really mean that. You bring in business. That matters, too.'

'Thank you,' Lucy said, sipping her coffee. 'I've really enjoyed working with you. I've learned a lot. It's been a great experience. But it's time for me to move on. And if the choice is between going now and signing up to stay with you long-term, then it's only honest to tell you and not sign anything I can be held to.' She dug her long spoon into the granola and heaved it out, piled with yoghurt. After she'd swallowed her mouthful, she continued. 'And I'm going to be honest with you, because you've always been good to me and I owe it to you. I was looking around anyway. I've not been happy, not for a while. I was starting to feel – a bit uncomfortable.'

'Is this about the Isabelle thing?'

'Well, that came into it. On the margin.'

'You've got to be able to put up with a bit of adverse publicity in this business. It goes with the territory.'

'I know that. Believe me I know that. It's all got a bit too close for comfort. I'm not happy with it.' Martin was crestfallen. He thought Lucy was on his side, would take his part.

'So you're going back from the dark side to the even darker side? People don't play nicely there either. They don't always abide by the rules. They don't have your scruples. You'll be happy back doing that?'

'I've drafted something for you,' she said, not answering his question. She picked up her BlackBerry and held it out to Martin so he could read the screen. 'If you need some words to say why I'm going.' He glanced at the screen for a moment and then waved it away, hardly bothering to read the words about Lucy's exciting opportunity and her key role and how delighted he supposedly was to wish her all the best for her continued success.

'Send it out. I'm sure it's fine.'

'So they can go ahead and announce, from their side? Because we need to coordinate on this.'

'They can announce what they like, when they like. And I'll need you to go, straight away. You'll get whatever's in your contract.'

It was Lucy's turn to look dejected.

'Don't be like this,' she said.

'Like what?'

'As though you don't care. As though I should just take a cardboard box and clear out my stuff. I'm being straight with you, that's all. Don't get all huffy about it.'

Martin muttered a 'Sorry' that he didn't really mean.

'Thanks. I mean, I know you're going through a difficult patch at the moment, so I'm sorry if my timing's not great for you.'

Martin was struck by an awful thought. He considered not

voicing it aloud, but if Lucy was going to be painful in her honesty then so was he.

'Did you put someone up to it?'

'What do you mean?'

'The photo. The one that got onto the website. The one that started all of this, all the stories in the papers, all the people hanging around outside my house. The one that meant that my wife has thrown me out and my government job has been kicked into long grass from which it will never emerge.'

'I can't believe you're seriously suggesting that. I'm not even going to dignify that with an answer.'

'You could have done. I mean, you weren't there but you know plenty of people who were. Someone could have come to you and you could have nudged them in the right direction.'

'Martin, you're completely paranoid. And I can't believe that you would think that of me.'

'Dark arts. You know about dark arts. That's probably what they're getting you in to do. It's probably what got you the job.'

'I'm not going to listen to this any more, Martin. It's not worthy of you.'

'They could have been listening to my phone messages. You could have tipped someone off.'

Lucy stood up, tugged a ten-pound note from her wallet and tucked it under the coffee cup.

'I'm not going to sit here and listen to you spouting this sort of fucking nonsense.'

'I notice you're not saying that you didn't, are you? You're not denying it.'

'I'm not playing some stupid non-denial denial game with you, if you're not believing anything that I say. I said I refuse to answer a fucking insulting question.'

Lucy stuck out a hand for him to shake, defying him to ignore it, to snub her. Martin stood up and grudgingly shook her hand.

'Goodbye, Martin. You'll get through this. But you're better than this.' She was out of the door in moments, almost at a run, off in pursuit of the better offer, the next step. Martin watched her go as he ate the rest of his bacon sandwich. He was reminded of a piece of advice he had been given by an old boss once. 'Be nice to people on their way up,' he had counselled Martin, 'because you'll meet them again on your way down.' Well, he had singularly failed to observe that today.

The cab dropped him off on St James's Square. Martin was early for the meeting and he bought another coffee at a coffee shop where everyone seemed to be a headhunter or a prospective client, pairs of people who didn't know each other having stilted conversations over sheaves of printed papers. He carried the coffee into the square and slurped scalding foam through the hole in the plastic lid as he waited for David Crichton to join him.

David was punctual, as ever. He was Martin's finance director and he suited the job. His was a presence that reassured people. He was thickset, with a broad, open face and a bluff manner. He marched into the square, stopped as he came through the gate and turned around to look for Martin. Together, they paced the path around the edge of the square, beneath the lime trees.

'This is it, isn't it?' David seemed on edge. 'Make or break.' He was never this ill at ease, even before important meetings like this one.

'It's fine,' Martin assured him. 'We'll just go in there, like we've done with all the other meetings before this one. They've heard the big picture; this is just to go over the details. You're good with the details. You know the drill.'

They started to walk towards the private equity firm, Ormonds, on the Pall Mall edge of the square. These meetings with potential investors were all much the same; Martin knew all the questions they asked, the answers that they wanted to hear. They were so close to signing the deal, only a few legal documents away from an investment that would buy a large chunk of the company. He would be set up for life. He would have to skirt around Lucy Fox's departure; he could almost make out that he had an agent in place now, an influential contact who would be bound to come back. Martin took a last draught of the coffee, threw the paper cup towards the bin by the gate, and missed. Milk froth spattered over the pathway. His heart was racing but he put that down to the extra caffeine.

A young woman in a dark suit showed them into the board-room. There was already a tray with jugs, cups and biscuits on the lustrous mahogany table in front of them. Two of the Ormonds team entered the room. Martin would have found it hard to tell one from the other, if Anders Malmgren hadn't been Swedish. He and Rupert Squire had the same blond hair, similar expensive suits, cold handshakes. Malmgren released the elastic from his Moleskine notebook as he sat down and took out a slim fountain pen; he deferred to Squire. The squat grey starfish of the conference phone on the table squawked into life.

'We're just bringing in Ramesh, from New York,' Malmgren said as he leant over to speak into the machine.

Ramesh Choudhury introduced himself. He was legal counsel, he said, rattling off the long list of names of his prestigious white-shoe firm.

'It must be early, over there,' Martin observed. Choudhury didn't respond; his time was too expensive for small talk about the time of day.

'Ramesh has a few questions for you – Martin, David. If you don't mind.' Rupert Squire's politeness was unnerving.

'Of course,' Martin said. 'How can we help you, Ramesh?'

Choudhury's disembodied, New York-accented voice came through the speakerphone.

'Yes, we have to ask you a few questions about some of your clients.'

'Go ahead.'

'You've advised Christophe Vernet, a director of Vernet Patrimoine?'

'Yes.'

'And Sylvie Barroux, currently environment minister in the French government, his sister?'

'Well, informally. On an ad hoc basis. But, yes.'

'And also the non-governmental organisation which employs the wife of Christophe Vernet, Isabelle Reynaud – Vision Internationale?'

'That's correct, yes.'

Ramesh paused before he asked his next question.

'As you may be aware, Mr Vernet has recently been arrested in connection with an investigation into a suspected breach of international sanctions.'

'I am aware of that, yes.'

'As a result, his bank accounts and those of his family companies have been frozen.'

'I didn't know that,' Martin said.

'We have also been alerted to a transfer of funds between your own personal account and that of a company controlled by the Vernet family.'

'Yes, I bought a house.'

'A house?' There was disbelief in Ramesh's voice.

'The family's old house. As a holiday home. But that was personal. Nothing to do with the business. And it was a while ago, before any of this came up.'

'But a personal financial relationship does exist between yourself and the family?'

'I suppose so, yes.' Martin hadn't thought of it in such stark terms.

There was a pause at the end of the line. Anders and Rupert exchanged glances with one another that they had not intended Martin to see. Anders plucked the black elastic of his notebook and strapped it closed again.

Ramesh appeared to be addressing Malmgren and Squire, now, as though Martin were no longer in the room.

'We have to advise you that this transaction could potentially incur a significant risk under the terms of the FCPA.'

'The FCPA?' Martin asked. He had a feeling that he should already know what that was.

'Foreign Corrupt Practices Act,' Malmgren explained. 'It's very rigorous. Concerns the payment of bribes to foreign officials outside the United States.'

'Bribes?'

'It's very broadly defined,' Squire continued. He leaned towards the speakerphone, his finger hovering over a button. 'Thank you, Ramesh. We'll refer back to you later.' Squire addressed Martin again. 'The Americans are very jumpy about that sort of thing. There have been several prosecutions. As you know, we operate in both jurisdictions.'

'Which means what, as far as the deal's concerned?'

Martin glanced across at David Crichton, in the seat next to him. His shoulders had slumped down and he was gazing at his own reflection in the surface of the boardroom table. Martin stared at the two men opposite. They looked at each other again before Squire turned back to him.

'We need to confer, to take a view on this, as to where we are, going forward. We'll loop back to you shortly, if we may.' Rupert Squire stood up and started to move towards the door. He held the door open and showed Martin and David out.

'What the hell did that all mean?' Martin asked, as they found themselves back in St James's Square.

'You tell me,' David replied in an unusually sullen tone.

'It's nonsense,' Martin protested. 'The Americans and their ridiculous rules. It's not as if there's anything dodgy about it.'

'They don't seem to think it's nonsense.'

'Lawyers,' Martin continued. 'Always telling you the reasons that things can't be done.'

'But that's it, isn't it?' David said. 'It's off. The deal's off. If New York vetoes it then that's the last we'll hear.'

'Squire said he'd get back to us.'

'That's just what they say. It's over, as far as they're concerned.'

Martin pressed his fingertips into the edges of his eye sockets, hoping it would make his head feel clearer.

'It's not over,' he insisted. 'Nothing's ever over. If not these guys, then there are plenty of others.'

'I'm not sure,' David said. 'Our position's getting worse. The longer this goes on, the less enticing a prospect we are.'

'Why do you say that?'

'You know as well as I do that our financial position's looking less favourable by the day. We've lost clients. We're starting to have cashflow issues. I had a message this morning saying that HMRC might want to launch an investigation. I presume it's related to the Vernet case.'

'And you didn't think to tell me that, before we went into the meeting?'

'I was going to tell you. I just didn't get the chance. And I couldn't raise it in there.'

Martin shook his head.

'You did have the chance. You just decided, for whatever stupid reason you may have had, not to tell me.'

David stuck out an arm and hailed a passing taxi. As it pulled up, he turned to Martin.

'Are you coming back to the office?'

'I'll catch you up.'

It was around half past seven when he left the office. Martin crossed Paternoster Square and made his way out towards the bombed-out church that stood as a monument, the spaces once occupied by pews now filled with beds of roses. It all seemed different that evening. The memorials that he always took to be signs of resurgence – the ball of gold fire that topped the column in Paternoster Square that remembered the Great Fire, this church that had been destroyed in the Blitz – seemed just to remind him of destruction. He sometimes stopped in the old church, but not today. He walked on, cutting behind Bart's hospital and into Smithfield.

At first, he didn't notice the man standing in the doorway of the apartment building. Martin was preoccupied. Everything was pressing on him, weighing him down. It seemed that all the choices were being made for him and he hated that. He rummaged in a pocket for his keys, his eyes cast down. There was a flicker of movement at the edge of his field of vision and he looked up.

He wished he had seen him before. He wasn't sure if there was a back way into the building but he could have looked for one. The man was about his own height and age and had close-cropped blond hair, a freckled face; he wore a waterproof jacket. There was something in his hand that looked like several sheets of paper.

'Lord Elliot?' the man said. He was standing close to him, far too close. Martin ignored him and tried to walk on past. The man moved to block his way through the front door. 'Lord Elliot?' he repeated. 'Martin Elliot?'

'Yes?' Martin snapped. 'What do you want? I'm not saying anything.' It wasn't on, you didn't block people's way into their own home. Every hack knew that. 'Where are you from? Because I'll be making a complaint to your editor.'

The man thrust the sheaf of papers into Martin's hand and, surprised, Martin took them.

'Lord Elliot, I'm serving you with an international letter of request from the French judiciary to cooperate with their investigations. You have now been formally served with the said documents.'

Martin looked down at the folded papers in his hands. He wanted to drop them, as if they were on fire.

'Thank you, sir,' the man said. His job done, he turned and

walked away. Martin managed to climb the steps to the glass front doors, gained the entrance hall. The lift doors opened ahead of him; he stepped in and waited until they closed again. It wasn't until he was out of sight, alone in the lift as it rose, that he collapsed against the inside wall of the lift, grasping on to the handrail to try to stay on his feet.

25

LIZZIE HAD CHOSEN the same table he always chose. As he arrived, she was spreading butter onto a chunk of baguette. Her hair was unwashed and tousled and she was wearing jeans with a hole at the knee, an old grey fleece jacket that was unzipped to show a souvenir T-shirt from Cambodia beneath. Her rucksack was propped against the cafe wall. Lizzie spotted him across the square and waved.

As he reached her table, she stood up and wrapped him in a huge hug, holding him tight.

'How did you get here?' he asked. What she was doing here could wait until he'd had a cup of coffee.

'A plane,' she said, 'then a bus. Then a taxi for the last bit of the way.'

'You look shattered,' he said.

'I am shattered,' Lizzie agreed. 'And I won't ask where you've been.'

Elodie approached the table as Lawrence sat down.

'Ah,' she exclaimed, as though she had solved a mystery that had been puzzling her. She had spotted the resemblance. Lawrence made the introductions and the two young women kissed each other on the cheek. Elodie fetched Lawrence's usual coffee and a croissant that he hadn't requested. Because it was a special day, she told him. Because his daughter was here. It was a special day, though Lawrence's delight at seeing her was mixed with concern.

'OK,' he said, putting the coffee cup back in the saucer. 'So what's all this about?'

'I didn't want to go back,' Lizzie said. She flicked her hair out of her face. 'It's the other students, mostly. The work is easy – it's too easy – but I haven't found anyone I fit in with. I say things to them and they look at me as though I'm speaking a different language.'

All the things that Lawrence thought of to say were the obvious ones.

'Have you tried joining things? Clubs? Activities?'

'That's what Mum said,' Lizzie replied, rolling her eyes. 'But I don't want to do – drama, or tennis, or whatever she suggested.'

'Well, she has a point. I know everyone thinks you meet your best friends for life in the first week but it doesn't always happen like that.'

'The whole place just seems so small,' Lizzie complained. 'No one can see anything beyond their corridors. They sit in their rooms and stare at their computer screens and don't know or care anything about the world outside. I thought it would be different. You always said that at college you used to sit and debate with people, argue into the night about everything, that you thought you were setting the world to rights. I haven't met anyone who even thinks the world needs to be set right.'

Lawrence was starting to understand.

'Maybe you need to change subjects. They might let you do that. Politics? History? Something that involves debates, argument?' Lizzie chewed at the end of her baguette before replying.

'Maybe,' she said. 'I'm not sure. I need to take some time, think about it.'

'You can't just quit,' Lawrence declared. 'You have to do something. You're going to need a degree. It's tough out there.'

Lizzie threw back her head and tilted back on the chair, the way he recognised that he did himself. She laughed a dismissive laugh.

'You can talk!'

'That's not fair,' Lawrence protested.

'Pot. Kettle. You quit everything. You split up with Mum. You quit your job. And here you are – doing what, exactly? You're only fifty-one. You're too young to be retired and wasting your time.'

'That's not the point. We're talking about you now, not me. And I quit things after trying, really hard, for a long time, not to quit them. I was with your mum for the best part of twenty years. And I wouldn't have left if she hadn't thrown me out. And I spent twenty-five years working before they decided I was past it. So that doesn't justify you turning around and quitting before you've even started.'

'You can't blame other people for everything, Dad. All these things aren't just things that happened to you. You can't just be a spectator in your own life. Sometimes you have to take responsibility for your decisions.'

'Did you come all this way just to tell me off? Because you could have done it over the phone.'

'No, but I didn't come all this way to take lectures, either.'

'You came in order to avoid going to lectures is what I gathered.' Lizzie managed a smile at his weak joke. 'We have to tell your mother,' Lawrence continued. 'I'll call her, if you like. Take the flak.'

Lizzie groaned. 'Do we have to tell her?'

'Yes,' Lawrence insisted. 'Because think what will happen if we don't.'

'On one condition.'

'What's that?'

'She's not allowed to write about it.'

'Oh, I see. Fair enough. Does that bother you?'

Lizzie started to speak with her mouth still full of baguette.

'It's awful. I've always hated it. I hate it even more now. The worst one was when I'd just got to college. She wrote this whole piece about how traumatic it was for her, all about empty-nest syndrome and ageing and death. About how she'd cried the whole way home and nearly crashed the car because she couldn't see clearly. As though it was all about her, nothing to do with me.'

'Did she name you in it? At least you don't have the same name.'

'She didn't. But the thing is, everyone knew anyway. She said which university I was at, said something about studying languages. So everyone was laughing about this dreadful clingy mother in the paper, posting the article on Facebook and making all these comments. And then I was in the bar one evening and someone started a conversation about it, one of those guys who thinks they're so cool and acts as though they don't have parents, as though they were brought up on the mean streets when you know they really come from Basingstoke or somewhere. Everyone was laughing about it. And there must have been a look on my face that they could read. And the Basingstoke guy – I mean, his name's Gabriel, for Christ's sake – Gabriel looked straight at me and said: 'You look as if we're talking about your own mother.' I didn't say anything, but he knew.'

'He's a bully, by the sound of it.'

'He is. And I've coped with that before but I thought people would have grown out of it by now. Anyway I'm fed up with it, fed up with Mum seeing my life as material for her, as good copy.'

'I understand,' Lawrence said. 'I'll tell her.'

'You know the worst thing?' Lizzie said. Lawrence shook his head. 'It's that it's not even true. It's this exaggerated version of her, the way she thinks the readers want her to be. I asked Josh about that crying episode when I left for college and he said she hardly cried at all, at least not that he could see. It's all "my darling little girl is leaving home" and actually she's quite calm about it, but she can't write a column just saying it's fine, I'm proud, she'll be OK, because that's not what people will pay money to read.' Lizzie's impression of a self-dramatising Harriet was accurate, the fingertips to the forehead, the overemphatic hand gestures.

'She does care,' Lawrence reassured her. 'I'm sure she does miss you.'

'I know that. But it's that she knows she has to make everything more dramatic, to make it a better story. And sometimes that's not the fair thing to do.'

'OK,' Lawrence said. 'We'll tell her. We'll go back to the house and we'll call her, before she has a chance to make all this even more dramatic than it needs to be. Lizzie hoisted her rucksack onto one shoulder with the ease of an experienced traveller. 'Do you want me to take that?' Lawrence offered.

'It's fine,' Lizzie said as they set off across the square. They were about to pass through the archway that led to the house when Lawrence noticed the British car parked on a corner of the square, a big black four-wheel drive that he recognised. He saw the two small, protesting faces of children strapped into child seats in the back. He scanned the square again to see if he could see her. She must have gone to the bakery, he realised.

'Can you wait a moment?' he asked Lizzie. 'I'll be right back. Do you want anything from the bakery?' Lizzie swung the rucksack down again and leant it against a stone wall. Lawrence crossed the road, swerving to avoid a cyclist in an orange jersey who swung past at speed. Through the shop window he could see Iona handing over money and taking a paper bag of pastries and a couple of baguettes in return. She opened the door, the bell tinkling behind her as it closed. She almost jumped when she saw him.

'You left,' she said. She held the baguettes across her body protectively. She kept her distance from him, not kissing him hello.

'I'm sorry,' Lawrence said. 'I had to go. I told you but I think you were still half asleep.'

'Why?'

'I had a call. From Lizzie. She's turned up here. She didn't tell me she was coming.'

'Your daughter?'

'She's over there. Come and say hello, or she'll think it's odd.'

'This is odd, though, isn't it?'

'I suppose so,' Lawrence said. As long as she didn't say, straight

232

away, that it had been a mistake. They were both too old to be making that kind of mistake.

'Did you say anything to her?'

'No, but she knows I wasn't at home last night. And she's not stupid.'

'Are you sure I should say hello? I have to get back to the twins. They're in the car.'

'I saw them. You've got to come this way, anyway.' Iona followed him back across the square. 'Lizzie, you remember Iona Fairfax, don't you?'

'Oh, yes,' Lizzie said, scrutinising Iona's face, trying to place her. 'You have that gallery, don't you? I remember.'

'Lizzie's on an impromptu holiday,' Lawrence explained.

'They're the best kind,' Iona said. 'Are you at university now?'

'I started in the autumn,' Lizzie answered, avoiding a straight response. 'And you're on holiday down here?'

'We – I – well, we bought a house down here. The children and I are here for the holidays.' Another partial answer. Iona turned towards Lawrence. 'It's our last day.'

'Will we get a chance to see you, before you go?' Lawrence asked, continuing the pretence that this was all just small talk.

'Probably not,' Iona said. 'I have to pack. Sort these two out.' She gestured towards the twins in the back of the car, who were getting increasingly frustrated at being left out.

'Safe journey home, in that case,' Lawrence said. He kissed her once on each cheek, her scent mingling with the smell of fresh bread. 'Take care,' he said gently.

'I will,' she replied. There was a loud yell of 'Mummy' from inside the car. 'I'm sorry, I'd better get these kids back.'

'You didn't get any bread for us,' Lizzie observed. She picked the rucksack up again, one strap over her shoulder. There was a silence as they both walked through the archway, turned down the narrow lane that led to Lawrence's house. Lizzie gazed around at the small houses, the potted geraniums that stood on the windowsills of the houses opposite, the cracked paint on the front doors. 'It hasn't changed,' she said. 'It's so long since I've been here but it hasn't changed.'

She didn't speak again until they were inside the house and Lawrence had closed the front door behind them.

'She's Martin's wife, isn't she?'

'Yes. Well, she was. They've split up.' Lawrence walked to the far side of the room to open the doors onto the courtyard. The air in the house was stale.

'I saw something about it.' Lizzie was pacing the room, apparently still hungry. She took an apple from the fruit bowl and started to eat it. 'And that's where you were?' she asked. 'Last night?'

Lawrence kept his back towards her, not wanting Lizzie to see his face. He combed his fingers through the back of his hair, suddenly aware that it was unbrushed.

'I'll call your mother for you,' he said. 'On one condition.'

'Yes?'

'That she doesn't hear a word about this. Because otherwise she will write about it, and it won't just be in the opinion pages. We'll all be her material.'

'Deal,' Lizzie replied, crunching the apple.

Lawrence turned, smiled at his daughter and picked up the phone.

26

THE COURTROOM WAS smaller than he had expected, far too confined a space for the scale of the questions it addressed. The building backed onto a railway line and a motorway, the wrong side of the Hague's tracks, far from the embassies and the art galleries. The only sign that it was not an ordinary office block was the high electrified wire fence around it, the array of security cameras. Inside, it was clean and modern, the walls lined with blond wood. The lawyers sat at ranks of desks, staring into their computer screens, occasionally consulting paper files beside them, listening to the proceedings through headphones. Lawrence felt as though he had been sealed away in this box of a room. Even the public gallery was separated from the courtroom by thick glass windows that could be screened off with blinds when a witness's identity was to be protected. At intervals during the proceedings the judge would order the sound feed to the public area to be cut, so that they could be seen but not heard. A viewer outside would have watched them goldfishing and gesticulating and not known what was being said. Not that there were many of them, from what Lawrence could see. The journalists came for the big names, the war criminals whose crimes people remembered.

Lawrence took his place in the witness stand. He made his solemn undertaking that he would speak the truth, the whole truth and nothing but the truth. Ahead of him sat a row of clerks and officials in black robes with white jabots; behind them, the judges, in similar robes with blue facings.

If he looked to his left, he could see the man that he assumed to be Faustin Kalombo. Kalombo sat in the back row of the defence's side of the courtroom. His chunky frame was squeezed into a black office chair and he leant back, away from the desk in front of him. He scarcely seemed to notice Lawrence's arrival as he conferred with his lawyer in the seat next to him. He was wearing a shiny navy suit, a white shirt and a blue silk tie with a huge knot. His left hand rested on the pale wood of the desk, as though the weight of his vast watch was weighing his arm down. He must have been the same man. Lawrence stared at him, as though Kalombo might look up and recognise him. Lawrence tried to picture him as he had been before, in the sweaty fatigues and the mirrored sunglasses. He could form the image well enough; the stocky man before him transformed into the angry commander on the road, the man whose gesture ordered Olly's death. They could have been one and the same man. But here, in a court of law, where he had given his word that he would tell only the truth, the uncertainty crept in.

They had asked Lawrence whether he would prefer to be screened from view, so that he didn't have to see the accused, but Lawrence had told them there was no need for that. Marieke, the young woman who had been assigned to take care of him, had soon stopped worrying much about his welfare, because he resisted all her attempts to look after him. Unlike the other witnesses, he was not in need of her help. He could travel by himself, knew his way around, didn't want his hand held. He couldn't see what Kalombo could do to him now, here in the safety of Europe.

The prosecution counsel, a young, bespectacled woman with a New Zealand accent, stood up to question Lawrence. Lawrence had imagined it would be his chance to tell the whole story, from beginning to end, as far as he remembered it, but instead, almost every time he spoke, he was interrupted. This closed, hermetic court was not the public stage he wanted.

When Lawrence had prepared for his appearance, he was

shocked by how little he really remembered, how little he really knew. Although the events of that day were fixed in his mind, the precise date on which it happened was not. It was not an anniversary he had marked; his memories of Olly were prompted in other ways. Several phone calls to Harriet – once she had calmed down about Lizzie's unscheduled departure from university – had established that she no longer had his old diaries. Nor would they have told him much; Lawrence used to write little more in them than flight departure numbers and long arrows down the page that only indicated the name of the country he was due to travel to. Birthdays were there, wedding anniversaries, too often overwritten by the long lines, the trips with no set end date, where he would stay until it was decided that the story was over.

Now he had to sound confident, like a man who remembered precise places, dates and names. He had to sound like Martin. Martin would have been the better witness. He remembered that sort of thing. Lawrence was the prosecution's witness and they treated him gently, asking him to expand on what he remembered of the place he had filmed, what he had seen. The prosecutor was building up Lawrence and the importance of his evidence.

'The court will be shown some shocking video footage,' she began. 'It will be analysed by an expert who will show that this is the original material, which has not been tampered with.' Lawrence could have told them that, though presumably they needed someone else's word for it. She explained how Lawrence's evidence fitted in with the case that she was making.

'Tell me,' the trial lawyer began in a soft, flat voice, 'who were the members of your team?' The dialogue was interspersed with pauses as she spoke into a microphone and flicked through documents on a stand.

'Myself,' Lawrence began, 'the producer, Martin Elliot, and the cameraman, Oliver Dawson. We also had a local driver and a fixer.' The lawyer paused after his reply, to allow the translator to finish.

'And this material is the original, unedited material that Mr . . .' She paused to check the name against her papers again. 'That Mr Dawson filmed?' Lawrence nodded. 'Mr Leith, can you speak that into the record, please?'

'Yes, it is,' Lawrence said.

He had tried to prepare himself for the moment the film would play on a screen in the courtroom. Lawrence inhaled slowly through his nose as the lawyers fussed about with the screening, calling through to someone behind the scenes who was failing to play the tape out correctly. He blew the breath out again slowly through his lips, counting as he did so.

He had to give grudging credit to Ed Blake; for once in his career he had done something that might conceivably be controversial. His protests had become gradually weaker as Lawrence had persisted and eventually Lawrence and others had persuaded him that doing nothing, on this rare occasion, had the potential to be more damaging than acting.

What Lawrence had not been prepared for was hearing Olly's voice again. He didn't intrude often, just an occasional word of direction to Lawrence, an 'OK, we're rolling' from behind the camera. He was startled to hear the Australian accent, the voice that always had a laugh in it, even when Olly was being critical.

Lawrence saw himself squat down in the encampment to talk to the boy soldier.

'Can you tell me your name?' he began, 'your name, and how old you are?'

He was Benjamin, though he didn't give his surname, and he was nine years old. He told them which class he had been in at school, before he admitted, with regret, that he didn't go to school any more. Lawrence had just asked him to tell his own story, in his own way, of how he had turned from a schoolboy to a soldier. He had not asked what the prosecutors asked the other witnesses: precisely who had told them to do what, for the names of the people in charge or the names of villages. There were good reasons for that at the time; the boy had been risking enough as it was, talking to them. Asking him to provide more information wouldn't have done him any good.

The prosecutor talked Lawrence through what he remembered of the place and the children he had met there. He was hazy on some of the details and he worried that his evidence was not precise enough. He could not tell them how many children there had been, but he was adamant that these soldiers were the age they said they were. There had been both boys and girls, children who should have been at home or at school. He remembered their terrible misplaced pride in doing things they should not have done and seeing things they should never have seen.

The defence lawyer, standing on the opposite side of the courtroom, was a tall Englishman with a quiff of salt-and-pepper hair that flopped forwards as he spoke. He turned the pages of the document in front of him before he looked in Lawrence's direction.

'Mr Leith,' he began. 'One of your colleagues was killed, shortly after the filming of the footage the court has just been shown.' Lawrence wasn't sure whether this was a statement or a question that required a response. 'Is that correct?' the lawyer prompted.

'Yes. Our cameraman, Oliver Dawson.'

'Can you describe the incident?'

One of the judges on the bench interrupted the lawyer, telling Lawrence that he didn't need to answer the question, that it wasn't relevant to the matter at hand. The lawyer protested and rephrased his question.

'I'm suggesting, Mr Leith, that your memories of what you saw that day are inevitably coloured by the sad incident that occurred shortly afterwards.'

'No,' Lawrence replied, hoping that the microphone in front of him would not pick up the pounding of his heart. 'We saw what we saw. We filmed what we saw. We didn't distort it or misrepresent it. Our only motivation – my only motivation –

then and now, was to tell the rest of the world what was going on, to tell the truth.'

'But if one of your colleagues was killed, and you and your other colleague escaped with your lives, then I suggest that you have a reason to pursue revenge against those you hold responsible?'

Lawrence looked towards the bench, wondering whether the judges would say that this question too was out of order, but there was no objection.

'I am quite capable of separating the incidents. This court isn't considering the case of my colleague, Mr Dawson. This is not about revenge for me, nor for my other surviving colleague, Mr – Lord – Elliot.'

'Although Martin Elliot is not giving evidence to this court?'

'That's a matter for him. But I can tell you that Martin Elliot saved my life. He hid the tapes that you have just seen presented in evidence, so that the militiamen who killed Oliver Dawson couldn't find them, and so that the world could see them. He tried to save Oliver Dawson, even at the risk of his own life. And then he knew when to stop trying, before both of us were killed too, meaning I'm here today to give evidence. Whatever you say—'

Lawrence saw the judge move to interrupt him and he stopped speaking. It may not have been a direct answer to the line of questioning, but it was what he had needed to say. He needed to let the record show what had really happened. He wanted some transcript, somewhere, to show that Martin had been capable of behaving well, under the greatest of pressure and when it really mattered.

The defence lawyer pushed him further on what he had known about the chain of command of the child soldiers; what Lawrence recalled seemed too little. He had often been the kind of reporter who flew in and flew out again, brief visits to conflicts whose origins he barely understood, to places where he didn't speak the language. The defence tried to make that criticism to undermine him, that he was not someone who had a deep knowledge of anywhere in Africa, let alone the history of Congo and its people. The more he persisted, the more Lawrence kept explaining that he understood what he had seen, and that was all that mattered. He told the truth, as far as he could see it; he bore witness. It was a frustrating process, full of interruptions and pauses that seemed designed to break his concentration. The judge asked him to speak more slowly, so that the translators could keep pace with what Lawrence was saying.

'And you are no longer working for your news organisation?' the lawyer asked. Lawrence could sense an affected disdain in his voice and he tried to ignore it. It was a tactic, the same as the others, to make him doubt himself and the value of what he was saying.

'I retired, two years ago.'

'You're young to have retired, if you don't mind me saying.'

'It's a job for a young person,' Lawrence said, trying not to sound too facetious.

'Did you *retire* because you were no longer a reliable employee?' The counsel put a drawled emphasis on Lawrence's supposed retirement, as if to suggest it was nothing but a euphemism.

'No,' Lawrence insisted. He drove his right thumbnail hard into the palm of his left hand, reminding himself to keep his emotions under control. 'I chose to pursue other avenues. It was my own decision to leave.' The lawyer looked down and flicked through a page or two.

'And now?'

'I am pursuing a freelance career. I am semi-retired.' The lawyer nodded as though there was little that could usefully be said about such a lack of success. The presiding judge hurried him to a close, saying that the time allotted for Lawrence's testimony was running out. Lawrence had little sense of how long he had been in the room; there was no natural light and the outside world was far removed. He stood down from the witness stand and he was free to go.

*

Lawrence had noticed the young man before, sitting on one of the chairs in the waiting room, in a new-looking padded coat that was a size too big for him. The sleeves of the coat hung down over his hands. He was waiting at the bus stop outside the court.

'Excuse me, sir, do you speak English?' His voice was polite but hesitant. Lawrence said that he did. 'Can you help me find the right bus for the city centre, please?'

'Of course,' Lawrence said, drawing nearer and examining the timetable. He pointed to the number of the bus that would take the man to the Central Station.

'Thank you, sir,' the young man replied. 'It's hard to understand it. I'm not used to – a place like this.' He gestured towards the buildings around them, the lanes of busy traffic going by, the train passing them on the embankment above. 'You've been in the court, as well, sir,' he observed. It was a statement, rather than a question.

'Yes, I have.'

'You are a lawyer, then?'

Lawrence shook his head. He had never thought he looked like a lawyer, but he could see how he could be taken for one. He was an older man in a suit and the raincoat that he rarely had need of in France.

'I'm a witness.'

The young man looked confused. 'An expert witness?'

'No, just a witness. Like you?'

He nodded in reply. For a moment, Lawrence wondered what the chances were that he was Benjamin, but he corrected himself. There were hundreds of victims, many witnesses, young men and young women who were testifying about the childhoods that had been stolen from them. Lawrence worried that he was doing something wrong. He was pretty sure he wasn't supposed to talk to other witnesses in the case. He might be in contempt of court. What if it undermined the whole thing? Lawrence started to move away. 'I'm sure the bus will be here in a minute. I'm going to walk.'

'I don't want to talk about the case,' the young man insisted. He held out a hand to Lawrence, who took a step backwards. As he did so, a bus drew up at the stop. He could have walked away then, allowed the doors to shut and his fellow witness to be driven away, but he climbed onto the bus alongside him. 'My name's Fidèle,' he said.

'Lawrence.' Lawrence held out his hand for Fidèle to shake. Fidèle insisted that Lawrence take the seat next to him.

'Can you help me, Lawrence?' Fidèle asked. Lawrence felt a sinking reluctance to be drawn in any further. Coming here in itself was as close to being involved as he had ever imagined he could be.

'What kind of help?' Lawrence ventured.

'I don't want to go home,' Fidèle said. 'Back to Congo. They say I can stay here as long as I'm needed, at the trial. But then I have to go back. I want to stay in Europe.'

Lawrence shrugged and gestured with his hands open, as if to say he had nothing to offer.

'I don't know,' he replied. 'It's difficult. They don't let many people stay here.'

'But what can I do?' Fidèle pleaded. 'It's dangerous for me to go home. After saying what I said in there, in the court, about the criminals from back home. People will be angry with me. They say they protected my identity, but that means nothing. Everyone at home knows where I went. Most people never get to go to Europe and suddenly I was leaving on a plane.'

'I'm sorry,' Lawrence said. 'I'm sure there are people you can ask, but I don't know who they are. Do you have family here? Friends?' In the court, he had seen that witnesses like Fidèle appeared only as a kaleidoscope of pixellated squares, their voices distorted and the translation overlaid, addressed by the lawyers only as 'Mr Witness'. Fidèle shook his head again.

'I finished school,' Fidèle continued. 'I have my diploma. I could work. I would work hard, start a business maybe. I can speak English, French. I could go to England or to France. Where do you live?'

'Well – France. France and England.' Lawrence was uncomfortable with explaining how easy it was for him to move between one and the other. 'I can't really help you. I don't have any power to do that. But maybe you should ask the authorities here, in Holland. Tell them why it would be dangerous for you to go home. I don't know what they'll say. What did the people from the court office say?'

'They said the same as you, that they couldn't do anything to help. They said their responsibility was to make sure I could give my evidence, then to make sure that I went home.' An electronic voice on the bus announced its final destination, City Hall.

'Come with me,' Lawrence said. 'You can try, at least. We'll find where to ask. I can't promise you anything more.'

City Hall was another pristine white office block, with a cafe on the ground floor and trams coming and going outside. Fidèle looked uncertain as they walked into the atrium of the building.

'Here?' It looked more like a shopping centre than a government building. Lawrence went up to the information desk to ask if there was somewhere they could enquire about asylum matters. The receptionist pointed them in the right direction.

'Do you have papers?' Lawrence asked. Fidèle tapped the chest of his padded jacket to indicate an inside pocket. 'I'm going to leave you here,' Lawrence said. 'It's the office over there. Tell them what you told me. Tell them about everything that happened to you, before, what you told the court.' Fidèle looked smaller again, younger, afraid. 'Are you sure?' Lawrence asked. 'Sure you don't want to go home? Because it could be a long wait, here, probably staying somewhere that's not great. Far from your family. And then they might send you back anyway.'

'It can't be worse than what happened to me at home,' Fidèle said.

'Then good luck,' Lawrence said. He clapped a hand onto

Fidèle's shoulder, turned him and sent him away in the direction of the office. Lawrence soon lost sight of him and he walked back out of City Hall, back to the luxury of being able to go where he wanted to go, to cross the borders that he chose.

27

MARTIN TOOK OFF the fluorescent cycling jacket with its splatter of mud down the back and hung it carelessly on one of the brass hooks. He unzipped his backpack and pulled a folded navy jacket from inside, shaking it out to get rid of the creases. He smoothed the jacket on, straightening the shoulders, and pulled a rolled-up tie from the bottom of his bag. Then raised his collar and slipped the tie around his neck. This place demanded that you be correctly dressed, even though it was stuffily hot.

A couple of pegs away, he heard a woman muttering under her breath, complaining about something as she hung her coat on her labelled coathanger. She was short, with dyed dark hair set in waves. Martin straightened the knot of his tie, zipped his bag closed again and swung it up to his shoulder.

'Is something the matter?' he asked her. She looked at him as though she had not noticed him until that moment. Martin didn't recognise her, though he probably should have done. He was still getting to know people and it was proving harder than he had imagined.

'Too many,' she muttered. 'Far too many, these days.'

'Too many what?' he asked.

'Too many like you, I'm afraid.' He wondered which offending group he was perceived to belong to. 'Newcomers. Not knowing how we do things. It's got too crowded. It used to be so calm and orderly up this end. These days, you can barely hear yourself think.'

It wasn't crowded that morning; most of the hangers in the cloakroom were empty. The place seemed calm and orderly, as far as Martin could tell. They prided themselves on their politeness, their civility to one another, yet this Lady could still manage to be extraordinarily rude.

'Sometimes, change is a good thing,' Martin said. She didn't reply except to huff, shaking her head and shuffling off towards the exit. She disliked him already, regardless of any hint of scandal. Well, to hell with her.

It seemed as though he had just got in under the wire, Martin thought as he found his way down the wood-panelled corridors. He made a couple of wrong turnings before he found the right direction.

He had started to dread the buzz of his BlackBerry. Every message seemed to bring worse news. Will Haywood, one of his expensive lawyers, had started out confident, assuring Martin that it was Christophe who was the source of the problems, that his own involvement was at worst incidental. The more Haywood discovered, the less reassuring he became, the more terse and formal the tenor of his messages. Martin's whole life was being turned inside out, by everyone. Iona's lawyers kept demanding documents, financial statements; so did the French investigators, so did the tax investigators.

'What is Mistral?' Haywood asked in one meeting. Martin had looked at him, confused.

'The wind?' he ventured. 'It's a kind of wind. In France.'

Haywood shook his head. 'Not in this context.'

'I'm not sure what you mean.'

Haywood shoved a sheet of paper across a polished wood desk towards him.

'It appears to be a company, a holding company. Registered offshore. In Panama.'

Martin shrugged. 'Nothing to do with me.'

'It is,' Haywood insisted. 'You seem to have bought your house from them. Do you not remember?'

'Oh,' Martin said, scanning through the document written in French. 'It must be to do with the Vernet company, one of the family's holdings. It had slipped my mind.'

'This is important,' the lawyer said in a slow voice that suggested Martin did not fully comprehend his situation. 'As far as you are aware, this was a Vernet family company?'

'I bought the house from the Vernets, yes.'

Martin was losing what little patience he had with the way the lawyers worked. They seemed so literal-minded, so pedantic, going through every piece of paper and every email line by line. This wasn't, in Martin's experience, how the world was supposed to work. In this new domain, everything was questioned, nothing was assumed to be true, everything was being held up to the light.

'You're sure?' Will Haywood stared at him again. 'Because what I'm being told is that Mistral was a vehicle used to shield other assets, ones that didn't belong to the family. Client assets.'

'Which means what?'

'Which means that Faustin Kalombo's money was put through that company. That, effectively, you bought your house from him.'

Martin sat back in the office chair, holding on to his wrist in case his hand started to tremble. He could feel the blood start to rush through his temples in the way that now frightened him.

'That can't be the case,' he protested. There was no way Christophe would have done something like that to him. He had known Christophe for years. He had done enough to help him, to help Sylvie when they both needed it. He put Isabelle out of his mind, because she didn't quite fit with the story he was telling himself.

'It seems to be the case,' Haywood repeated. 'But you're telling me you had no idea whatsoever about this?'

'None at all,' Martin said. 'I simply don't believe it.' Haywood made a note on the pad beside him on his desk, then typed something on a keyboard.

Martin had managed to find himself an office – well, a share of an office with Lady Gray. She had lined her bookcases with photographs showing the highlights of her career, alongside former presidents and prime ministers. He was about to sit at the desk, below the latticed window with its dingy strip of net curtain, to try to get on with some work, when the phone rang.

He was surprised to see Victoria Loxton's name come up. She hadn't spoken to him since the day of his introduction. He had tried, once or twice, when things seemed to have calmed down, but the calls and texts went unanswered, the emails unacknowledged. He would have called Julian too, but they hadn't spoken since Julian had told him that Heathcote's was taking their PR account elsewhere. He had claimed it wasn't personal, though Martin knew that to be a lie.

When Victoria rang, he started to pace the office.

'Victoria,' he said, with all the cheerfulness he could muster. 'Good to hear from you.'

'I can't really talk,' she said. 'But I need to see you. Where are you?' He told her he was in the House and she seemed relieved.

'Central Lobby?' he suggested. 'I can be there in five minutes.'

'Not there,' she said. She explained where she wanted to meet, gave him a hurried series of directions to take him through the maze of corridors, and rang off.

She was already waiting there when he arrived, after wrong turns and backtracking, a route that had led him through car parks and past kitchens. Victoria stood in a narrow passageway between buildings, barely wide enough for two people to pass. There was an open door to a storeroom where old gilt chairs with velvet seats were stacked, waiting to be fixed. From somewhere above, Martin could hear a choir singing, their voices carrying on the air from a chapel he hadn't known existed.

Victoria was in a navy suit, her face stern.

'What is it?' he asked.

'I need to talk to you. But I need people not to know that I've talked to you.'

'OK. What's happened?'

'People are starting to ask questions, about the summer.'

'What about it?'

'About the fact that we came to stay with you.'

'Well, you did,' Martin said. 'There's nothing wrong with that, is there? It was a holiday, that's all.'

'Yes, but they seem to be putting two and two together and making dozens.'

'Who are these people?'

'I've had a couple of calls, Anjali's had calls. Katie Meredith's sniffing around it.'

For Katie Meredith to be onto a story was bad news; she had a great ability to get stories in the paper, no matter how flimsy their substance. Martin knew that a Katie Meredith story was one that made other journalists roll their eyes in a mixture of envy and dismissiveness. Even though others would knock it down eventually, it was the Meredith version of a story that people would remember.

'How did Katie Meredith hear about it?'

'It can't have been that hard. There were plenty of people who knew. Other friends who we went on to stay with after you. It's the kind of thing we mentioned in passing. It didn't seem to matter, then.'

'And it doesn't matter now, does it? We discussed this before.'

'It's starting to matter. I called people about you, when you were missing. I tried to pull strings, call in favours. Your friend Lawrence insisted that I get half the Foreign Office involved. I called Patrick Chambers, for instance. Got him to get on to the embassy in Paris.'

'And what's wrong with that? It was an emergency. You were doing everything you could to help. Surely that's a good thing to have done?'

'Patrick doesn't seem to think so. He's worried about it. He's being very stand-offish with me. Cancelled a visit he was supposed to make to my constituency.'

Martin didn't have much time for Victoria's complaints about people cutting her dead. She had done it herself when it suited her.

'What should I say? If Katie Meredith asks?'

So this was what it was about, this meeting behind the workshops and the dustbins, all the skulking among the chairs with wonky legs and the defunct photocopiers.

'Tell her the truth. Tell her that yes, you visited me. For a couple of days, with the family. That I had an accident and you helped in the search, which was a kind and generous thing to do and exactly what anyone would have done, under the circumstances.'

'And what about the Vernets? The whole family was there. Sylvie, Christophe, Isabelle. It looks bad. It all looks really bad.'

'But you haven't had any financial dealings with Christophe, have you?' Victoria shook her head. A workman came by, carrying an old computer that he put into a pile for recycling. She fell silent for a moment as the man passed, mistrustful of anyone who might overhear their discussion.

'Of course not,' she continued, once he was out of earshot. It was better if she didn't know about the requests from the French authorities, Martin decided. No one seemed to know, so far, but it was only a matter of time. These things had a way of leaking, by fair or unfair means. What Victoria genuinely did not know was going to be less harmful to her. When it came out, as it would, it was better that she could show genuine shock and disbelief. As far as she was concerned, Christophe was involved in a scandal that was of little concern in Britain, that involved questionable business dealings in far-flung countries.

'So as long as you've declared everything, you're in the clear, aren't you?'

'Declared everything?'

'The hospitality. Just to be on the safe side. It's hard to put a value on it, I know.' Victoria slapped a hand to her mouth. She closed her eyes as if in the hope that when she opened them again, Martin would have disappeared. She grabbed hold of the back of a stack of chairs.

'I forgot. I didn't think.' There was little that Martin could say to reassure her. She should have known. Everyone should know by now. Expenses were fair game. You had to be cleaner than clean, now that everyone knew the cost of each paper clip and each chocolate bar that MPs put on their expenses. 'It was just a couple of days.'

'I know,' Martin said. 'But work it out. Add it up. Look at it the way Katie Meredith will look at it. What was it – three, four nights in a villa in the south of France? Meals, drinks.'

'But it wasn't for gain, was it? We're friends, aren't we? I know you've worked with Julian – the friendship's really with him. You didn't just invite us because I was an MP. That's allowed, in the rules.'

'You could argue that,' Martin said. 'You probably will have to argue that. But look at it from the other side. Someone – Katie Meredith or anyone else who brings a complaint – could see it differently. That we're connected, politically. That I was inviting you to secure an advantage.'

'Is that what it was?'

Martin really didn't know any more. He found it difficult to disentangle his own motives. What had he wanted in inviting Julian and Victoria to France? It had been a casual invitation, at first, an offhand remark. Come and stay, if you're in the area. The kind of thing people said to each other all the time without really meaning it; well, the few people who had something like that to offer. He thought how rarely, though, he invited people without, in some way or other, wanting something from them. They were clients or potential clients, people who were useful or influential to know. Those were just the terms of trade. They all wanted something from him, too. Julian was an important client – had been an important client.

'It wasn't, but that hardly matters. It's what it looks like that counts. It looks like we were trading favours: a holiday in France for a peerage, a few meals and drinks for the Heathcote's account. It will all be weighed up and whatever we thought at the time will count for nothing.'

'But anything to do with expenses is toxic. I had enough trouble last time and it was only over a couple of lampshades and some tree surgery. If this gets out, I'm finished.' Victoria leant against the stack of chairs and they creaked. 'What can I do?' she asked Martin, almost begging.

'You could declare it now,' he suggested. 'But then if someone's looking at it — and Katie Meredith will be — they'll notice that you didn't declare the hospitality until nine months after the fact. And they'll draw their own conclusions from that. If she's smart, and she is, Meredith will be getting some rent-a-quote MP to make a complaint about you.'

'And that means there'll be an investigation.'

'Exactly. Once someone's made a formal complaint, it stands the story up for all the other hacks who would normally pour cold water on a Katie Meredith story. There's a formal investigation, there's a committee looking into it. It's all news. And you can fight it all you want but all that people will remember is the allegation, the idea that you took a freebie holiday, even though you and Julian can perfectly well afford your own.'

'I'm going to have to tell people,' Victoria said at last. 'The whips. Try to manage this before it gets out.'

'That's what I'd advise you to do,' Martin said. 'If I were advising you. Which of course I'm not.' Victoria was now restless, looking ready to leave. 'You'll come back from this,' Martin said. 'They can't afford to lose people like you, in the long run. They need smart, articulate women and they don't have enough of you. You'll have a decent resignation, an honourable one as they go, you'll wait out your time and then you'll be back.'

Victoria shrugged, her mouth twisted up into a rueful expression.

'You think so?'

'I'm sure. Just ride it out.'

She turned and walked briskly away, her heels echoing down the alleyway. Martin followed the passageway in the opposite direction. As he crossed the courtyard that served as a car park, he checked his messages. There was one from David Crichton: *Call urgently. Bank threatening to pull plug. May need to call in administrators.*

He was just about to press David's number when the phone rang and he answered the withheld number without checking.

'Yes?'

'Is that Lord Elliot? I'm so sorry to trouble you.' A light, deceptively gentle voice. 'This is Katie Meredith.'

In the chapel above, the choir was still singing, somewhere behind the stained glass.

28

LAWRENCE WHISTLED ALONG to Charles Aznavour as he pulled the stopper from the half-full bottle of red wine. He poured himself a large glass and swirled the wine around, watching the movement of the liquid against the curve of the glass, inhaling its aroma. He kept the music on low, so as not to disturb Lizzie. She was somewhere upstairs, reading something about international politics and development. Harriet had calmed down, after a while. They were trying to work something out with the university, a deal that would allow her to take a break and go back next year. Lizzie was persuading all of them that it was best for her to be in France. She would keep up her studies, she said, get a job. As he crossed the room and opened the glass doors, he allowed himself to sing along to 'Mes Emmerdes'.

À corps perdu, j'ai couru, assoiffé, obstiné, vers l'horizon . . .

It was a song about striving and it seemed to suit his mood. The phone rang and he intended to ignore it. The phone had been ringing more, over the last few weeks. There had been quite a few emails from people he used to know, former colleagues who had taken little interest in him over the last year or two, keen to get back in touch. The conversations all went along the same lines: first, an eager enquiry about his new life; a wistful comment or two about how lovely it must be to have got away from it all; a wish that the caller, too, could give it all up and move to the sunshine. The caller would proffer a bit of gossip, some news about mutual friends. Then they would move on to the real reason they had called: had he heard about Martin Elliot?

Lawrence would feign a degree of ignorance, say that he knew there was something going on – an affair, wasn't it? They'd fill him in on some of the details, then casually ask whether he knew much about Martin's house. Wasn't it somewhere nearby? Lawrence would acknowledge that it was in the area, but not be drawn any further. He didn't know much about it, he would tell them. He said he wasn't the best person to ask. Who was the best person to ask? they would enquire, pen poised at the other end of the line. Sorry, he would say, I can't help you. Most of them would lose interest at that point, wish him well, say that if he happened to be in London he should look them up for a pint. Lawrence would ring off, knowing that the promised pint would never happen and he would be unlikely to hear from them again.

This time, the phone kept ringing. He thought he had better answer it, before the noise bothered Lizzie. She seemed to have found something she enjoyed doing and he didn't want to break her concentration. He picked up the phone and took it outside to the little table in the courtyard. It was Iona. He had not expected that. They had spoken once since she went home; he had called her to check that she had got back safely. It had been a strange conversation, warm but awkward, where much went unsaid. She apologised, saying that the children could overhear her. They promised each other that they would talk about what had happened properly, another time, but they had not done so yet. Lawrence braced himself for all the honesty that was prob- ably about to come his way with a sip of wine.

'How are you?' he asked.

'I've been better,' she said. 'Where have you been? I've been trying to get hold of you.' He saw the light blinking on the answer machine; Lizzie had evidently decided not to answer his phone either.

'Sorry. I was out in town. I didn't have the mobile with me. What's the matter?'

'It's Martin,' she began. Lawrence felt his stomach drop, his throat tighten. What had she told him? He hoped Iona hadn't had one of her moments of disarming honesty, told him everything. 'You haven't heard from him, have you? He hasn't said where he is?'

'No,' Lawrence said. He hadn't expected to. 'Why?' He walked back indoors and tried to find where he had left his mobile, in case Martin had called him on that. Three missed calls from Iona, none from anyone else. Iona's voice sounded panicked, the way it had last time.

'The police came to the house this morning. My first thought was that he'd been killed on his bike.'

'He's back on his bike?'

'As far as I know. I told him not to, I told him it wasn't worth the risk, but he doesn't have to listen to me any more, so I know he goes out on the bike. It made me feel sick. I want to be divorced from him but I don't want to be widowed.'

'But it wasn't that?'

'No. At least it wasn't that. But the police said they were looking for him, that he had failed to turn up to an arranged interview in the morning. I told them they'd come to the wrong place and that he didn't live here any more. I gave them the other address, told them to try the office as well. This very polite young officer gave me his card and said to call if I heard from him. Then he called me back this afternoon and he said he didn't want to worry me unduly but that they hadn't managed to find him at his current address either and that no one in the office had seen him today.'

'Why are the police looking for him?' Lawrence asked. 'What was it they wanted to talk to him about?'

'They wouldn't really tell me. But I think it's to do with Christophe Vernet. All they would say was some police-speak, you know, that they wanted to talk to him in connection with an ongoing inquiry.'

'He could be anywhere,' Lawrence said. 'Did they try the House of Lords?'

'I don't know. I've tried all his numbers but they just ring out. The BlackBerry doesn't answer at all. The Lords number just goes to a person on a switchboard who takes a message. Nadia, his PA at the office, was in a complete state. She said they'd all been told yesterday that the company was going into administration and that they might be losing their jobs.'

'And Martin wasn't there to tell them?'

'He told them, but now he hasn't turned up again. They're furious with him. She said that people were walking out of the office, not doing any work, going to the pub.'

'Where do you think he might be?'

'I don't know. He might be hiding out somewhere, until all these stories about Victoria blow over, about her staying at the house and not declaring it. Did you see that she had to resign?' Lawrence had heard. She paused before continuing. 'Well, I have one idea. That's why I need your help.'

'You think he's in France?'

'He might have gone there. To look for . . . her.' She still couldn't say Isabelle's name.

'She might be in Paris,' Lawrence said. 'She might be anywhere in the world, knowing her. If he's followed her to − I don't know, Darfur − there's not an awful lot either of us can do.'

'That's no reason not to try, Lawrence. You can call her, I can't. You can ask her if she knows where he is. Tell her why. Tell her he's in more trouble if he doesn't come back. If he's run away it makes everything look worse.'

'He must know that, mustn't he? That's everything he's about, everything he's spent years telling other people. How to manage a crisis. How things are going to look.'

'He can't be thinking straight. Everything's gone wrong for him. First us, then the business. Then all of this with the police, everyone's all over the holiday with Victoria. At least the bit about the police doesn't seem to have got into the papers yet, but it will do. It will now, if he's run away. They'll make sure of that. They might issue an arrest warrant for him or something. I don't know how it all works.'

Iona's was talking so fast that Lawrence could barely understand her.

'When did you last speak to him?'

'It was a couple of days ago. He called in the middle of the night. He sounded like he'd been drinking. He was crying and said he wanted to see the children, that he missed them terribly.'

'And what did you say?'

'I said that it was gone midnight and I wasn't going to discuss it when he was in such a state. I said we needed to sort something out, through the lawyers. I told him he could still see them, of course, but that he wasn't helping himself by behaving like this. That it would only upset them more.'

'Try not to worry, Iona. I'll do everything I can, I promise. We did it before. We can do it again.'

'I hope so,' she said. Lawrence wished that she was nearer so that he could console her, and then wondered whether that was a purely selfish thought.

'How are you bearing up?' he asked.

'Not great,' she admitted. 'There's all of this, and then I've had the Revenue wanting to go through all the books at the gallery. They seem to think that because Martin might have had dodgy connections, then so might I. That I might have been selling art to people who wanted to launder their money through me. And if it's true that Martin's business has gone under then I don't know how that's going to affect us. He had been saying to the lawyers that basically there was no money left, but I don't believe that's true. I'm worried his creditors will come after the house. And the children are difficult; fractious, unsettled.'

'Are you going to be OK?'

'I have to be,' Iona said. 'I don't have the luxury of not being OK. I have to get the children up in the morning and check that there's milk in the fridge and get them to school and make enough money to pay for it all. They rely on me. *I* can't run away. I have to keep going, whatever happens.'

'You'll get through this,' Lawrence assured her. Iona was resilient.

Even if it came to the very worst. Though he wasn't going to think about that just yet.

When he put the phone down, he realised he had drunk the whole glass of wine without having noticed it. He picked up his mobile and searched for Isabelle's number. It was a long shot, but he had promised Iona he would try. The *Affaire Barroux*, as they called it in the French papers, seemed to rumble on without conclusion, vying for attention with other scandals. If Lawrence mentioned it to people he met here, in the village, they seemed to shrug and move on.

'Everyone knows these things,' was the considered view of Gilles and Kévin in the bar. 'Everyone knows that politicians get up to things like that. Money in brown envelopes. It's normal.' Lawrence would protest that it wasn't normal, that it was appalling. 'What can you do?' the reply would come. 'They're all the same.'

Isabelle's phone rang, at least. The longer it rang, the less hopeful he was that she would answer. The line went dead and he picked up his reading glasses so that he could write a text message. He started to compose it, tapping the letters out laboriously with his index finger. Lawrence couldn't do that thing his children did, writing with two thumbs at the same time. But then, they couldn't do shorthand. There were skills you had that became obsolete without you ever noticing.

As he typed, the phone rang. It was Isabelle.

'Lawrence?' she began. 'I think I missed a call from you. Did you mean to call me?'

'I did,' he said. 'Where are you?'

'Why?' She sounded suspicious of him. He wasn't surprised. They had hardly spoken since they had come back from Africa. He'd had a couple of angry calls from her, asking what he'd heard about the film they had made. He'd referred her back to Martin, saying he knew almost as little as she did.

'It's about Martin. Have you seen him? Heard from him?'

'I've heard from him, but I haven't seen him.' Lawrence could detect a gap between what she was telling him and what she knew.

'Where are you? Are you in Paris?'

'No. I'm at the Barroux house. The one you came to.'

'And where was Martin, when you heard from him?'

'He said he had left Paris, on the train. That he was coming down here. That he had looked for me in Paris but he couldn't find me.'

'Did you tell him where you were?' There was a long silence at the other end of the phone.

'I wouldn't. He asked and asked but I didn't say. He's behaving very erratically. Almost crazy.'

'How long ago was it that he called you?'

'Earlier this afternoon. A few hours ago now.'

'I need your help,' Lawrence said. 'Please. I'm worried about him – his family are worried about him. I'm going to come down there to you, in case he turns up.'

He could tell that Isabelle was reluctant, but it was somewhere to start. Lawrence went upstairs to Lizzie's room. She put down her book as he entered and stretched out her long legs.

'What's up?' she said. 'What should we have for supper?' They had been enjoying cooking together; it was a pleasure they shared.

'I'm not going to be able to have supper. Not yet. Something's come up.'

Lizzie was bemused. He explained who he'd been speaking to and what was going on. Lizzie got up from her chair, a quick youthful movement. She picked up her hoodie from the end of the bed.

'I'm coming with you,' she declared.

'Are you sure?'

'Of course. You might need help.'

As Lawrence sped down the straight roads that led through the vineyards towards the town, he filled Lizzie in on who Isabelle was. He realised how little he had told her until now, in the months since she had encouraged him to go on the trip to

Africa. Lizzie plied him with questions as he tried to keep his eye on the road.

'She sounds amazing,' Lizzie observed. 'The work she's doing, I mean.'

'The work is amazing,' Lawrence agreed. 'I'm not so sure about her.'

'Does it matter, though, if she does good things?'

It was a bigger question than Lawrence could manage to answer as he negotiated a busy roundabout.

'It depends, I suppose,' he said as he took the turning that led to the house. He drove slowly, trying to recall which of the villas was the right one.

'Do you think she knew?'

'Knew what?'

'That her husband was doing deals with those guys in Congo? That she maybe had to deal with them, to be able to work there?'

'She would never answer that.'

'Must mean she did.' Lizzie could be pithy. 'Sometimes you have to do deals with people like that . . . unpleasant people.' She had a knack for seeing through the delusions of others. It was what Lawrence himself had assumed, when he thought about it. He wondered, a thought he had long since consigned to the back of his mind, what had happened to Celestine. He thought of her restored eyesight, her stationery shop, her hopes for her son Patrice to go to college. He hoped Celestine was doing OK; he resolved to find out. People like Celestine mattered, and they were the ones who suffered for things that were far beyond their control.

He rolled down the car window and buzzed the intercom. The gates ground open and he eased forward up the gravel drive. Isabelle came out onto the terrace at the front of the house and watched the two of them get out of the car.

'Any sign of him?' Lawrence asked. Isabelle shook her head. She cast an enquiring look towards Lizzie. 'This is my daughter,' he said. 'She's staying with me.'

'Do you want to come in?' Isabelle asked. They followed her through the door into the gloomy house. She had a glass of wine already on the table and she fetched two more glasses, pouring wine for them both without asking. Lawrence took a sip, out of politeness.

'What time did he call you, exactly?' he enquired.

Isabelle checked her watch. 'Three, maybe?'

'Did he say what time his train arrived?'

'No, because I didn't ask. It would have let him know I was in the area.'

'Does he know this house?'

'He might do. When he was buying the house, maybe. I wasn't there. He's never mentioned it.' Lawrence noticed that there were suitcases heaped in a corner of the room, beneath the shelves full of ornaments; rugged, well-travelled bags out of place in this fussy house.

'Are you heading off again?' he asked Isabelle.

'I'm moving to Cairo,' she said.

'Cairo?' Lizzie asked.

'There's a lot of work to do. Libya. Syria. Iraq. People are going to need help.'

'For good? I mean, are you going permanently?' Lawrence asked.

'For as long as I need to,' she said.

Something occurred to Lawrence. 'If he were coming here, he'd be here by now. We should look for him at his own house.' Lawrence put his glass back on the table. He wasn't sure why, but he had a sense that something was wrong. It was the same sense he'd had on the drive up Mont Ventoux, when the storm came down; the same sense he'd had on the road in Congo, years before. He tried to get his rational mind to override it before it overwhelmed him, before he started getting the physical reactions he knew might follow. 'We should go and look for him, straight away.'

'Should I come?' Isabelle was hesitant.

'Definitely.' Lawrence was going to insist on it, if it came down to it. They would need her help, one way or another. He got up and ushered the two women out of the house, towards the car. Lizzie climbed into the back seat.

As they approached the roundabout on the edge of town, the traffic slowed.

'Turn down there,' Isabelle said, indicating a narrow turning off to the right.

'Why?' Lawrence asked.

'Can you see it?' Isabelle said. 'There's a police car, up there, stopping the traffic.'

'What for?'

'Anything they can,' she shrugged. 'Usually drinking and driving. They've got strict on it, all of a sudden. They do it on market day, when they think everyone will have been out having a few drinks. Or to check you've got your seat belt on. It's worth avoiding them, if you think we're in a hurry.'

'Dad,' Lizzie piped up from the back seat. 'You've had a couple of glasses already.'

'One and a half,' Lawrence protested, but he swung the car into the turning anyway. 'Where do I go from here?' he asked as they carried on down a road that ran between high hedges and concrete walls and which narrowed the further they went. They came to a junction that would have led them back to the main road, far past the police controls.

'No, keep going,' Isabelle said. 'Straight over.' She pointed towards an unmade road that continued ahead of them.

'Are you sure?' Lawrence hesitated at the crossing. A tractor passed along the wider road, in front of the car.

'Go on. Trust me.'

As the tractor moved away, Lawrence went forward and jolted onto the rutted track. Clouds of dust flew up and a farm cat dashed away into a field nearby.

'It's the back route,' Isabelle insisted. 'It'll get us there quicker.'

He felt a stone hit the car's undercarriage and he wasn't sure

Isabelle's secret way would get them there at all. The track started to wind up the side of a hill, a high crumbling bank topped with oak trees to the left of them.

'We used to come this way,' Isabelle explained. 'Visiting Christophe's mother, when she lived there. Once we're over the ridge of this hill, you'll see it.'

They crested the hill and Lawrence could see the house below them; its newly repaired roof, the driveway with its row of trees, a blue-green corner of the pool. Lawrence pulled up by the closed gates and climbed out to press the buzzer on the gatepost. He waited a while, but there was no answering click or buzz, no voice at the other end. He tried to push the gates, to see if they would give, but they wouldn't.

He peered through the bars of the gate, looking at the house. He couldn't be sure, but he thought he saw a light in an upstairs window. It was a light, or else a glint of the sun catching on a pane of glass.

He turned back to Lizzie and Isabelle in the car.

'I think I saw a light, in the house.'

'Have you tried his phone again?' Lizzie suggested. Lawrence reached back for his phone and rang Martin's number. There was no ring; it cut out and went straight to a brusque message. He tried once more with the same result.

'We should go in,' he announced.

'How?' they asked, with one voice.

He put an experimental foot on the gate to see if he could climb it but his shoe wouldn't fit into the gaps between the bars at the top of the metal panel. It was too high to pull himself over. The two women got out of the car and examined the walls to either side.

'Here, give me a lift,' Isabelle said, pointing to a section of the wall and the laurel hedge above it. Lawrence interlaced his fingers and held out his hands for her to put a foot onto, then lifted her up so that she could gain the top of the wall. She was as light as he had expected. Isabelle scrambled through the hedge.

He did the same for Lizzie. Lizzie stood on the top of the wall, waiting to see if he needed help. He hauled himself up beside her. He shoved the laurel branches away as he pushed through the hedge. As he jumped down on the other side, Lawrence wondered, for a moment, what the hell he was doing breaking into Martin's house.

29

THE SUN WAS beginning to lower towards the horizon, edging down over the hills. He could see cars and bikes on the roads that traversed the plain, between the trees and the vines. There were people who still had places to go and things to do, people who were needed, who were expected home. The place had looked different on the road up, bright yellow broom sprouting at the roadsides and scarlet poppies beneath the olive trees. He had seen apricots ripening in the trees. Even the new growth and the warmth weren't enough to make him feel any optimism.

When the taxi dropped him at the house, he felt like an impostor again. All this ochre plaster, these lavender shutters, that swimming pool; they couldn't possibly be his. True, he had pressed in the code that enabled the gates to open, he had the keys in his hand, but the whole place felt tainted.

There was such a thing as a deal that was too good to be true, after all. He knew he should not have come, but he had to see the place one more time, whatever happened. It was all he had left and he doubted he would have it for long.

It had all seemed straightforward, at the time. He had known Christophe for years, though never well. The more he thought about it, the more he thought that no one knew Christophe well. Not even Isabelle. Perhaps not even Sylvie. Christophe had always seemed to glide through life, untroubled, entitled. His first memory of Christophe was of him turning up his nose at the dining-hall food in the first week of their MBA course, loudly proclaiming the superiority of French cuisine. He had quickly gained a reputation as snooty, was teased for his old-world attitudes. He was never going to pull all-nighters, he declared, unlike his classmates who expected to have to work ridiculous hours in return for ridiculous sums of money. As Martin discovered, Christophe would never have to. He had money already and that made it easy to make more. Studying in America was another luxury, like his handmade shoes. He didn't need to do it, but it gave him those extra contacts, that extra edge. He had no desire to go into politics – he had left that to Sylvie, who wanted to emulate their father, although the senator had not expected it of a daughter. 'Property – that's where it's at,' he had once told Martin, over a single malt in a bar, using an idiom that sounded wrong coming from his mouth. 'There are people who have more money than they know what to do with, and I can tell them what to do with it.'

He had rarely seen Christophe in the years that passed. He was a name in a contacts book, a fellow alumnus. Martin dropped him a line, now and then, keeping him posted on his news; business, marriage, children. Christophe had married Isabelle and Martin had always thought she was far too good for him, though never said so. They would cross paths, once in a while, have a drink in a hotel bar in Knightsbridge. They traded favours, because that was a currency they both dealt in. When it came to buying a holiday house, Christophe was the obvious person to call. His timing was perfect, Christophe had told him. He knew just the thing. And while he had him, there were a couple of issues he could do with Martin's advice on. Perhaps they could come to some arrangement.

And yet, Martin wondered, you could think that you knew people, knew their lives and their stories, that their lives could be entangled with yours, but then you could find out that you really knew nothing about them at all.

Martin tried to tell himself that he could not have known

the nature of the people Christophe was doing deals with, but he couldn't convince himself of that narrative. And if he couldn't persuade himself, then he would never be able to persuade anyone else.

When he agreed to meet Faustin Kalombo, at Christophe's request, he knew it was the same man. At the time Olly died, they hadn't been sure of his name, but the investigations into his killing had confirmed it. Although Martin had not had much cause to think of it in recent years, he never forgot names. He knew well enough the story that Faustin Kalombo wanted to tell, the story that he was merely a businessman who had been unfairly hounded by his political opponents, had only the tiniest sliver of truth. 'Winner's justice,' Isabelle had called it, and because he wanted to believe everything she told him, he had listened to her. 'Terrible things were done by people on all sides,' she had said once, 'and we are all quite prepared to forget half of them, because they were the half done by the people who won, the people we now have to trust to keep order, if not peace.' Olly's death was one death among many thousands. Perhaps, he told himself, people had to be allowed to show they could change. The past could remain in the past.

The thing was, he had decided to refuse to represent Kalombo's interests. Martin wasn't averse to representing governments that were trying to reform, but Kalombo wasn't in a position of legitimate power. Martin didn't yet have the right team to handle that kind of business and this wasn't where he wanted to start. It was going to be a purely practical calculation, not an ethical one, and he had still been working out the best way to tell a former warlord, politely, that he didn't want his money, thank you. Martin had left that conversation to Christophe, telling him he didn't feel his was the right firm to represent Mr Kalombo at that time. Christophe, Martin had thought, could be relied upon to be discreet. What Christophe might have been doing with Kalombo's money fell under the cloak of that confidenti- ality and he had, quite deliberately, never asked Christophe any difficult questions. By then, after all, he had his own secrets to keep from Christophe. By then, there was Isabelle.

When Martin had seen reports that Kalombo had been indicted and then arrested by the ICC, he'd thought that was the end of the matter – at least, until he was asked to testify himself. That was a conflict of interest too far.

He had unlocked the doors, wandered around inside the house. No one had been here since Iona and the children had come in the holidays, except for the gardener and the man he'd instructed to open the swimming pool ahead of the summer. Iona had taken the Caulfield picture but she had left him the Mont Ventoux. He wasn't sure if that was a calculated insult, leaving him with that reminder of the mountain. Martin opened the sideboard and rummaged through the collection of bottles that they had left there; crème de cassis, pastis, calvados. Holiday drinks, the kind you didn't drink anywhere else. There was a half-full bottle of cognac near the back. That would do. He pulled it out of the cupboard and didn't bother with a glass.

He ambled out of the house, down the steps, towards the pool. He was surprised that no one had found the house so far, that there were no reporters waiting at the gates. They were slacking. He took his shoes off and sat at the water's edge. The pool guy hadn't finished the job, he noticed. The water was green-tinged and dirty. Pine needles and flies floated on the surface. He pulled the cork from the bottle and tilted the cognac into his mouth. The warmth of the alcohol flooded into him.

Again, he had broken all the rules that he normally explained to others at great cost per hour. Don't get into trouble in the first place, he would have said. Be transparent and be fair and play by the rules. That way there's nothing to get caught for. Mistake one. Then, at first, he had stuck his head in the sand, hoped that if he ignored it, it would all go away. Mistake two. And now here he was, running away from it all instead of facing up to it. Mistake three. There was no point in counting all the mistakes. It was just that this time, when faced with the adrenalin surge that gave him the option of fight or flight, he chose flight, on some flawed instinct, and there was no knowing why.

All the things he should have done, he had not done. He should have stood up in public, made an apology, shown contrition. He should have sat down with the police and told them everything he knew, even though it wasn't much. Sat down with the administrators who would be finding someone to buy whatever was left of the business, trying to put a value on something that was a collection of people and of experience already dissipating and therefore hard to put a price on. It was easy to say, now that he had made the final mistake of running away. He knew that it made him look worse and because it looked worse, it was worse.

Everyone was better off without him. Iona was better off; she would find someone else. There were people in her world, the art world, who swarmed about her already. They loved her, her openness, her irreverence, her wide welcoming smile, her uproarious and inappropriate laughter. Maisie and Finn would do just fine without him. He saw them more often asleep than awake, anyway, when he went in after getting home to kiss them good night, tucking their protruding legs back under the covers and stroking their hair. Freya would be fine; more distrustful still, perhaps, but then maybe that would serve her well, in the long run. As for Isabelle – well, it seemed she wanted to be without him, anyway. At the thought of her, he took another slug of brandy. She could go to wherever in the world she was going, save all those nameless people who meant more to her than anyone she really knew. She could even keep up the pretence of her marriage to Christophe, if she didn't feel his disgrace outweighed the family's reputation. Good for her.

On the way from Avignon, he had asked the taxi driver to stop at the hunting shop at the edge of town. Although it was too early for the season, there were a few huntsmen in the car park, bearded men in caps with dogs in the boots of their cars.

He had walked in and examined the racks of shotguns that lined the walls, the shelves of cartridges, the cases of hunting knives. He had even asked a man behind the counter if it was possible to buy a gun. Of course it is, the man had said, asking him which sort he wanted. Martin looked at the selection as though he knew what he was talking about, as though he had any idea how to use a gun, in real life. I just need to see your permit, the man had continued. Your hunting permit, he had explained. Martin had shrugged and walked away. He didn't know what he was doing. He climbed back into the taxi empty-handed and told the driver to carry on to the house.

In the distance, further around to the east, he could see the mountain. The view of the mountain was one of the reasons he wanted the house; to be able to wake up and look at it in the mornings, see how it caught the light at different times of the day. He had imagined seeing it covered with snow in the winter, cycling up it in the summer. He hated its presence now. He lifted the brandy bottle again, holding its awkward wide base in two hands and trying to direct the narrow neck towards his mouth. He had drunk enough to make everything start to blur and his movements were becoming more clumsy. If he hadn't gone up the mountain that morning, the image of his life as he wanted it might have been preserved. No one would have known about Isabelle, for a start. Lawrence would not have known about Isabelle. He himself would have cycled into Paris with the others on the bike ride and she would have greeted him with them. There would have been nothing out of the ordinary about it, nothing for anyone to have suspected.

His BlackBerry was becoming uncomfortable in his pocket as he sat on the edge of the pool. He had switched it off when he left Paris, after he had called Isabelle and she had refused to tell him where to find her. That was another image he had grasped at, as the TGV hummed southwards over its viaducts. He could have lived here, in the village. He would have found something to do. Isabelle could have lived here too. She could have travelled to anywhere in the world and come back to this place. Martin had imagined living out his disgrace here until he was forgotten about, then starting to make his way back. He wasn't sure what he could do, but he would do something. Something small, even. Open a bar. Set up a shop, a bike shop even. People who came here wanted bike shops.

As the train had drawn into Avignon, unpleasant notes of reality had intruded into the story he had been telling himself. He was the former owner of a business that had gone bust. He had liabilities; no one would lend him money, not even enough to buy the lease on a small provincial cycle shop. He was a bad risk. That was before the French authorities finished finding out whatever they were trying to find out; they would get Christophe on some count or other, no matter how well placed his friends and relations were. And if they got Christophe, there was always the chance they would get him too.

He picked up the BlackBerry and turned it over in his hands. For a moment, he considered switching it back on, to see who had been trying to get hold of him. He decided against it. It could only be bad news. The police, demanding to know where he was. His colleagues − former colleagues − likewise. The administrators; there were bound to be documents he was supposed to have signed, meetings he was supposed to have attended. Martin picked it up and hurled it, as hard as he could, into the dirty green water. He watched it sink beneath the surface once more, giving out a few pathetic bubbles. His arm was weak again, his throw had been feeble. He tried to stretch the arm out, spread his fingers and contract them, but they wouldn't obey his commands. It was as if he had been sleeping heavily with his arm beneath him and the nerves were failing to respond. He rubbed his arm with his other hand to try to bring the sensation back, but it was like rubbing a limb that belonged to someone else. He pressed down with his good hand onto the stone flags, hoping that he would be able to move and to get his circulation going again. Even the good arm lacked its usual power. Martin got to his feet but his balance was going. He blamed the brandy. He stumbled and the bottle beside him fell over. There was an explosion of lights behind his eyes, bright flashes of red and green and white that seemed to streak across the inside of his skull. He closed his eyes, as though that would help him to see the brilliant lights better. He felt himself toppling over, towards the pool. Martin's last conscious thought was to wonder why there were fireworks, when it wasn't even Bastille Day.

30

THEIR FEET CRUNCHED on the gravel as they walked along in the shade of the trees. The neat lavender bushes beneath the pines were just about to come into bloom.

'Are you sure he's here?' Lizzie asked. 'It doesn't look like there's anyone around.'

Lawrence wasn't sure which of them should go first, which of them Martin would be the least unhappy to see. It was probably Lizzie, but he couldn't send her out ahead.

'There's something about this place,' Isabelle said. 'I don't know what it is . . .' She left the sentence unfinished. There was a sound from around the side of the house that sounded like a splash.

'Martin?' Lawrence called out. 'Martin, are you here?'

He continued up the driveway and got no reply. He stopped and listened and could hear nothing. There were no more splashes; perhaps he had imagined it. The three of them stepped onto the terrace. Isabelle was right, there was something uncanny about this place when it was empty. It needed people, the shouting of children and the chatter of guests. The last time he was here there had been life, the twins, Iona. Lawrence saw there was a light in the living room, downstairs. As he peered in through the doors, calling out for Martin again, Lizzie grabbed him by the shoulder.

'Dad!' she yelled. 'Look! There!'

There was a shape floating in the pool, face down. It could only have been Martin. At the edge of the pool was an empty brandy bottle, lying on its side. Isabelle was already running down the steps to the poolside and he chased after her, Lizzie following. Without thinking, Lawrence kicked off his shoes and jumped in. The water was deep and he sank below the surface, struggling to get his head above water. His clothes were weighing him down. He trod water and worked his way over to Martin's head. He thought that if he could flip Martin over, he would be able to drag him to the edge, but flipping him proved hard. He grabbed Martin by the armpit and tried to pull him around. He was so heavy, a dead weight. He could have been there for hours, Lawrence thought. It could be too late, far too late.

He towed Martin to the side of the pool. Isabelle was kneeling on the tiles, crouched over.

'Can you lift him?' Lawrence sputtered. He was out of breath with the exertion. Lizzie knelt alongside Isabelle as he pushed Martin's body so that it was parallel to the edge of the pool. The two women tried to reach down to pull him up, but the level of the water was too low. They could grasp at his clothes but not haul him out.

'It's no use,' Lizzie said. 'If we try from here, we'll fall in too.'

'You've got to take him down to the shallow end,' Isabelle said. 'Then we can get him from there.'

'Turn him over,' Lizzie suggested.

'I'm trying that,' Lawrence said as he paddled. Isabelle managed to raise one of Martin's arms so that he rolled over onto his back. His eyes were closed and Lawrence couldn't hear whether he was breathing. Lawrence kicked and tugged and Martin's weight started to shift as he towed him. With a huge effort, Lawrence reached the shallow end. He laid Martin's head on the first step of the pool as Isabelle and Lizzie waded into the water to help him.

Lawrence coughed up some of the water he had swallowed, bent over to catch his breath. Isabelle had already reached forward, her hands under Martin's armpits to pull him out of the water.

'Hold his head,' she instructed. 'So that I don't hit it on the steps.'

Lizzie had walked down towards Martin's legs and was preparing to hoist them. Lawrence slid his hand under Martin's scalp and felt the bristles pressing into his palm. He felt warm, he thought. He still felt warm. He couldn't have been in the water for long. Isabelle bent her knees and called out to lift on a count of three. They heaved him from the water and laid him on the side of the pool. The water, pouring out of his clothes, spread out around Martin.

Lawrence knelt, helping to put Martin into the recovery position. He looked across at Isabelle to see if he was doing the right thing and she nodded. He put his fingers into Martin's mouth, pulled his tongue forward and then ran a finger around the inside of his cheeks, trying to get the water out, removing a pine needle. He bent in close to try to hear if he was still breathing, wanting to feel the breath on his wet cheek. There was no coughing yet, no splutter of life.

'Is he . . .?' he asked Isabelle, moving back to give her more space. 'Is he alive?'

'Call the *pompiers*,' Isabelle directed Lizzie, before she answered him. 'Go to the house and open the gates, so that they can get in. Tell them we're in Saint Barthélemy, the Chemin des Lauriers. Anything else they need to know, give the phone to me.'

Lawrence handed his phone over to Lizzie and she rang. There was a fearful expression on her face but she spoke fluently and clearly.

'There's a pulse,' Isabelle said. 'Not much, but there's something there.' She rolled Martin onto his back and started to pump his chest. She was intent on the task and she saw no one else. Tucking her hair away behind her ears, she bent over Martin's face, pinched his nose shut, lifted his chin up and breathed into his mouth. Her mouth separated from his for a second and then she inhaled, tried again, another breath. Still nothing.

'Do you want me to try?' Lawrence offered. He was sitting there, watching, not doing enough.

Isabelle shook her head. 'I can do it,' she insisted.

'I know you can. But I can help. We can both try. Until the ambulance comes. Or until . . .' They both knew what he meant.

'We keep trying.' Isabelle repeated the actions. She sat back on her heels for a moment to catch her own breath and Lawrence insisted that he take over. He compressed Martin's chest, his hands on Martin's wet, solid torso, counted the pumps until Isabelle told him it was enough. She told him he had to press hard, not to worry about it, not to worry about the bones. Lawrence remembered how Martin's collarbone had been rebuilt with metal pins.

'Breathe,' she said. 'Now.'

He put his own mouth over Martin's, grasped his fingers on Martin's nose to hold it shut and exhaled as far as he could, pushing the breath out and imagining it entering Martin's lungs. Then he lifted his head, took a long breath in, tried once again. He felt an answering pressure, a quick movement of Martin's body under his hands. The chest shook and Lawrence could feel him try to take his own breath. There was a short, wet cough from his throat.

'He's breathing!' Lawrence exclaimed. The two of them put him onto his side again and he groaned as they rolled him. Water dribbled from his mouth.

'We're here,' he told Martin. His eyes flickered slightly and opened part way. 'We're here with you. It's Lawrence. Isabelle is here. The ambulance is coming. We're going to get you to hospital and you're going to be fine.'

Lawrence kept talking. He didn't know the right thing to say but it didn't matter, he just needed to reassure him, to let him know he was not on his own. Martin didn't like to be alone.

Martin tried to speak, his words just about intelligible. 'Let me go.'

'I'm not letting you go,' Lawrence said in a soft voice. 'I'm here and I'm not letting you go.' It occurred to him that this was what Martin wanted, that he didn't want to be rescued after all. Perhaps he had thrown himself in and they had not come too late, for Martin, but too early. 'It's going to be all right,' he insisted. 'I'm not going to let you go. We're going to get you back home, to Maisie and to Finn.' Lawrence remembered someone else. 'To your Mum,' he said. 'We need to get you back to your Mum. Don't let me have to tell your Mum.'

Martin's eyes widened for a second and Lawrence knew that he had heard him. It was an old line they used to exchange, a long time ago, whenever they were getting into a tricky situation. It had become a shorthand between them, a codeword that meant they were doing something that would either win them an award or get them killed. Then they had had to do it, to tell Olly's mum, over a crackly long-distance phone line to Brisbane, and after that they had never said it again. This time, Lawrence meant it in earnest.

He had not noticed that Isabelle had moved away, now that Martin had started to breathe, and was speaking on the phone that Lizzie had passed over to her. She started to walk up the steps towards the drive.

'The ambulance is coming,' Lawrence repeated. 'They're going to be here any second now. They're going to look after you.' He reminisced about places the two of them had been together. He described an evening they had spent in Istanbul, covering a story long forgotten, when they had sat in a floating restaurant on the Bosphorus, eating fresh fish as the water lapped against the restaurant's walls, the sun low over the water, the view of the great suspension bridge beyond. Lawrence retold the anecdote that he had told so many times, about how Martin had insisted on going into a belly-dancing club, lured in by a man standing on the street who promised them beautiful girls, only to discover there was more than belly-dancing on offer. He kept talking, though he scarcely knew what he was talking about any longer. He kept his hand on Martin's wrist, checking that the pulse was still there. Martin was still breathing, but he was no longer speaking. Lawrence started to feel cold, sitting in his wet clothes at the poolside, but he kept talking.

He heard the crunch of wheels on gravel, the opening of car

doors. The *sapeurs-pompiers* came down the flight of steps towards the pool, with Isabelle and Lizzie ahead of them, showing them the way.

'They're here now,' Lawrence told Martin. 'They're big guys, look like the French second row. They'll have no trouble with you.' The rescue team carried a stretcher between them, which they placed by the edge of the pool. Lawrence stood back to let them get to Martin.

'Make sure they know,' he said to Isabelle. 'Tell them about what happened last time, his last accident. The warning stroke. Do you think this was another one?'

Isabelle nodded. 'I've already told them that. They're going to take him to hospital, the best one, the place he was before.'

They lifted Martin onto the stretcher and hoisted it up between them with ease, then made their way up the steps towards the waiting ambulance. Lawrence and Lizzie followed them. They put Martin inside the ambulance and Isabelle asked to climb in with him. Lawrence stepped forward, wanting to go as well.

One of the crew members held up a finger.

'Just one,' he told Lawrence. There was no room, he explained.

'How is he?' Lawrence asked. 'How is he going to be?'

The paramedic made a tilting gesture with his spread hand. Lawrence recognised it to mean that it would be touch and go.

'Ring me, once you know more,' Lawrence called to Isabelle as they prepared to shut the ambulance doors and drive away. 'We'll follow you.'

Lawrence put his arm around Lizzie's shoulder as the vehicle drove off through the gates, down the track. His car was no longer where he had left it, in front of the gates, but parked up by the house. Lizzie must have moved it there. He was proud of his daughter, how resourceful she had been, how calm.

'I'm sorry,' he said. 'I'm sorry you had to see all that.'

'It's OK,' Lizzie replied. 'I hope he's going to be all right.'

'I don't know,' Lawrence said. 'I really don't know. But we tried. That's all we could do.'

'And you,' Lizzie said. 'Are you going to be all right?'

'What do you mean?'

'I know you sometimes – you have bad reactions to things. To shocks. Loud noises, sudden things happening.'

That was the first time that Lawrence realised what had not happened. He had not run away. He had not collapsed. He had been able to help and if he had not succeeded, he had tried.

'You need to get some dry clothes on,' Lizzie said. 'If we're going to get to the hospital.'

'There'll be some upstairs.'

Lawrence went to pick up his shoes from the poolside. As he picked them up he saw the black oblong at the base of the pool. It was Martin's BlackBerry.

31

'GRADUALLY,' AGATA SAID. 'Take it one step at a time. You've got a programme and you need to stick to it.' She bowed her head over the display on the handlebars of the bike to check what he had done, pressed a few buttons and instructed him to slow down. Martin obeyed her and rotated the pedals at less speed. She was strict, but then she had to be. She had a face that didn't incline to smiles easily and winning a smile from Agata was an aim to be pursued. Martin got a smile, occasionally, when his range of movement increased, when he could show her that his arm moved further than it had before.

He spent much of his time these days on a bike and in a pool, but it was a far cry from what he had been used to. If there was one thing worse than not riding a bike, it was riding a bike that didn't go anywhere. Still, he did it. He had to keep doing it, day after day, week after week. He made himself do it, because there was little else to do. He couldn't accept that he would never be on a real road again, never climb a real hill. He would be able to do it, if he just kept working at it.

The swimming pool was too warm, like a children's pool, and as he carried out his next set of exercises, under Agata's stern guidance, Martin tried not to remember the other pool, the view across the plain, the clock chiming on the tower in the village, the mountains in the distance. There was no view from this pool; it had white walls and not even a window giving onto the outside.

All he thought of, as he moved slowly through the water or

pedalled repetitively on the stationary bike, were his ways back. Counting back, Martin realised it was the first time in over twenty years that he hadn't held a summer party. The parties had started small, as casual gatherings in a small flat where his friends drank beer from the bottle, ate crisps, smoked cigarettes on the tiny balcony. They had become more elaborate as he had moved on. In later years, boxes full of glasses were delivered ahead of the party, the garden was stacked high with crates of wine and champagne, they had hired staff to take coats and hand out canapés. The date had not needed to be saved this year, a blank in the calendar where that late-June weekend was usually blocked out. It was interesting to discover, of all those people who had drunk his beer, years before, and his champagne, more recently, which were the ones he still heard from. Martin had expected that they would be very few and he had been proved right. There were the people he never heard from at all, the ones he knew he would never hear from again. They believed he was toxic, that any contact with him would contaminate them. The Heathcotes, for instance, Victoria and Julian both. He could live without them. He had never really been part of their world.

There were others who managed to distinguish between his public disgrace and his private suffering, who expressed their sympathy for the latter while deliberately avoiding the former. Martin could understand that; it was probably what he would have done as well. A few, he realised, were merely curious, the people who thrived on ill-fortune and relished hearing bad news. Iona kept them at bay. The leeches, she called them. She despised them even more than he did. Iona had little time for the so-called friends who only called around when things were wrong, who seemed to relish their troubles more than they had been happy for their success.

'If anyone else comes round and expects a cup of tea and looks at me with those awful puppy eyes and that inclined head that says "It must all be so terrible for you" looking like they're Princess bloody Diana visiting an orphanage, I'm going to slap them,' she said. 'I don't want biscuits and I don't want sympathy. I want someone who'll say that it's happy hour at the pub and that we're going whether I like it or not.'

Iona had let him come home. He slept in the spare room, now that he could manage the stairs with less difficulty than before. They agreed that that was the best thing, because he needed rest, because it was still hard for him to get comfortable and he didn't want to disturb her. There were the other reasons, though, that they didn't yet talk about. Martin was aware that he was there on sufferance. They were talking about selling the house, moving somewhere smaller and more manageable, further east. There were places that Iona knew, beyond the gallery in Hackney, that she said were up-and-coming. With the Olympics, she maintained, those areas would be better known before long. They could still get a bargain, relatively speaking. Martin was reluctant, but he knew they would have to do it and he would let Iona make the decisions. He owed her that. At least he would live among people who did not know or care who he was, what he had been, who would not give him knowing glances or talk behind their hands about him. He was still waiting, what seemed like an interminable wait, for the prosecutors to decide whether he had actually done anything that deserved to be taken through the courts.

He had not seen Isabelle since they took him to hospital. She had sat with him in the back of the ambulance, though he had barely been conscious of her presence at the time. Lawrence had told him, after he had asked several times, that she had gone to Egypt. There were more people there who needed to be rescued. Martin tried not to think about her, although it was hard. Sometimes, when Iona was out at work, he would call up the aid agency's website on the laptop, refresh it to search for pictures or for news of her. He would close the website again, delete the browser history in case Iona checked what he had been doing all day. With the agency website went the French news pages where he searched for details of the *Affaire Barroux*, of

Sylvie Barroux and her career that seemed to continue, undamaged.

The house in France would need to be sold as well, assuming that the lawyers and the prosecutors could determine if it was his to sell. In any case, Martin had no desire to see it again. For him, it was a place that no longer existed. He imagined it reverting to the state it had been in before, the roof falling back in, the doors warping, the plaster crumbling away, the garden growing wild. He had heard that Lawrence was selling some kind of story about the whole affair, a tell-all story of his part in Martin's downfall. The lawyers had suggested that he try to block it, threaten legal action against the paper, but he had no reason to do that. It would probably mostly be true, as far as Lawrence saw it, and there was little that could lower his own reputation any further in the estimation of right-thinking people, as the legal expression had it. He had already been exposed to hatred, contempt and ridicule; he was already shunned and avoided. Paying lawyers to take it through the courts would do nothing to help and might only make it worse. Lawrence was free to tell the story as he wanted. It was his story, too.

He was disappointed in Lawrence, but not surprised. It was what he did. He had a grudging respect for the man who had once been his friend. At least he had shown some initiative. It was probably what he would have done in the same situation. Even so, there was a sadness about it all, the knowledge that they would never again sit and have a drink together, share a meal. They shared a history and that history too had gone. There was no one else who shared those memories of his former life and that loss seemed to make the memories vanish.

Martin climbed out of the swimming pool, using the steps, the way he had to these days. It had always seemed such a simple thing, to push himself out of the pool with his hands on the edge, lifting his body from the water and onto land, that he had never thought about it before. Now he knew every muscle that it took, all the strength that he lacked. He shrugged the towel around his shoulders and plodded towards the changing room.

Outside the gym, he waited for the bus. Previously he never used to wait for buses but walked on ahead until the bus caught up with him. In fact, he couldn't remember when he had last taken a bus. The bus pulled up and he climbed on, avoiding going up the stairs but refusing to sit in the seats with the image of the man with a stick. As the bus moved off, he stared out of the window, watched busy people going about their lives. There was a way back, he told himself. He didn't know what it was, yet, but with time it would take shape. He had built a life for himself before and he could do it again. If he kept searching, he would, eventually, be able to find a way back.

32

'THIS WAY,' GEORGE said. 'That's good. Look over there a bit.' He lowered the viewfinder from his eye. 'Can you try to look a bit happier?'

'I'm not supposed to look happy, am I?' Lawrence asked. 'It's not exactly a happy story.'

'I know,' George replied. 'It's just that you've got quite a miserable-looking face. So you can afford to go a bit further in the other direction. Has anyone ever told you that before?'

'Yes,' Lawrence said. 'Plenty of people.' Olly Dawson had always said it, for one. He had always joked about Lawrence being a bloody gloomy-looking bugger, as miserable as a bandicoot. Ed Blake had often told him much the same; Lawrence needed to look more open, more approachable, more friendly. The viewers didn't like it, otherwise. They needed a way in to the story. Lawrence remembered the phone call he'd had the other day. It had been Ed Blake on the line, genial, affable, enquiring after Lawrence's health. Lawrence had asked why he was calling.

'We'd like to talk to you,' Blake had said. 'Some of the programmes are very keen to get hold of you. It's just that you don't seem to be answering their calls. We wondered – is there a studio nearby that you could get to? We'd be happy to send a car.'

Lawrence said that he had to decline Blake's kind offer. He was under contract to someone else, he explained. There was a deal that he couldn't break. Though when the article came out, he'd be happy to speak to people then, under certain conditions.

Though the nearest studio, as far as he knew, was in Marseille, a couple of hours' drive. Ed Blake had sounded affronted but he tried not to let on.

'You've been bought up, is that it?' He said that he understood and that he'd have someone be in touch. Lawrence suggested he get in contact with the paper and they would be able to give him more information about the timings. As he thought about the conversation, he smiled. George's motor drive clicked, a burst of images captured.

'That's more like it,' he said. 'Let's get a couple more, over here. By the fountain. And keep thinking about whatever it was you were thinking about, just then.'

Lawrence got up from the cafe chair and moved towards the fountain.

'I'm not sure about the water being in shot,' he said. 'Given what we're talking about.'

'It won't be,' George said. 'It just gives a good light.'

He took a few more shots as Lawrence stood next to the fountain. He showed Lawrence the results on the screen on the back of the camera.

'See?'

Lawrence agreed that they were good shots. The light was filtered through the leaves of the plane tree. He stood straight, his gaze into the middle distance. The bunting was out of focus behind him. In the earlier images, he was sitting at the cafe table, his arm slung loosely over the back of a chair in his habitual way. He was in one of his good shirts, a dark-pink linen, a cream jacket that he had pulled that morning from its dry-cleaner's plastic wrapper. He'd had his hair cut. It was how he wanted to be seen. It was how he imagined himself.

He had refused to do the portraits against the backdrop of Martin's house, though he had driven with George up the track that Isabelle had showed him to take some photos. George knelt down on the sandy verge and trained a long lens on the house. He could see the empty pool, the untended lawn. There were no parties this year and the house stood empty, a sign on the gate warning that the property was protected by an alarm system.

'Are you happy?' he asked George as they sat down at the table. Happy with the work, he meant, and that was what George understood. George unpacked his laptop from his backpack and started to transfer the pictures from the camera. Lawrence offered him a coffee while he worked.

'Yup,' George said, holding a hand over his computer screen to shield it from the sunlight. 'Looks good. You happy?'

It was a bigger question than Lawrence could answer. His phone rang and saved him from having to answer it.

'How's it coming?' Harriet asked.

'Nearly done.'

'Really?' she chided him.

'Really nearly.'

'You've got George Miller with you, is that right? He's good.'

'He's done an excellent job,' Lawrence agreed.

Harriet knew he was struggling with the piece and had offered him help that he had reluctantly accepted. She had told him he needed to put more of himself into it, after he sent her his first attempts. It needs to be in the first person, she said. You need to make it about you.

'It isn't about me,' he had protested. 'I just happened to be there. I saw it.'

'I know you're uncomfortable with that,' she replied. 'You always have been. You always thought you were just the observer, neutral, objective. But this time you aren't. This is a story about you and about what happened. And that's the way you have to tell it. That's the top line: how I saved disgraced peer. My ringside seat at his downfall, to be brutal.'

'It's more complicated than that.'

'I know it is. But you have to simplify it, make it easier to understand.'

Back at the house, Lawrence brought up the document on his screen again, before he pressed Send.

Martin Elliot capped his glittering career with the purchase of a luxury villa in the South of France and the offer of a peerage from the Prime Minister. His successful and well-connected friends were happy to enjoy his generous hospitality. Little did any of us know that within a year he would be facing ruin.

It was pretty dreadful stuff, Lawrence readily admitted, but that was what they said they wanted. He had sat up late with Lizzie, discussing whether he should accept the offer from Harriet or not. Lizzie was sceptical.

'You know how I feel about this,' she said. 'Turning your own life into copy. It makes you fair game for everyone.'

'I'm not planning to do it for ever,' Lawrence replied. 'Just this once. It's a big story.'

'That's what you say now,' she said. 'But what about the next time, and the next time?'

'Well, I hope there isn't going to be a next time. Also, your mum made a good point.'

'Which was what?'

'That it's better, coming from me. That they'd do the story anyway and if it was someone else, someone who didn't know him, they'd go harder on him.'

Lizzie shook her head. 'She's just saying that. Because it's good for her if you do it, makes her look better. She's just waiting to do her "the Martin Elliot I knew" piece, if she hasn't done it already.'

Lizzie was right. It was a turn of phrase he'd heard before, a journalistic good cop/bad cop routine.

'The Martin I know,' Lawrence corrected. 'He's not in the past tense.'

Friends say that Lord Elliot is continuing his recovery at home in London. His company, Elliot Associates, has been placed into administration. Lord Elliot faces an inquiry into whether he has broken any parliamentary rules. The Crown Prosecution Service

*refused to comment on whether they had received a file and whether
Lord Elliot could face charges.*

He had written those bits from force of habit, the facts that
he thought needed to be included. Harriet told him that those
would be taken out, would go somewhere else. That was for the
news story, she said. This is something different.

*Lady Elliot is better known by her own name, Iona Fairfax. She
is the owner of the Fairfax Gallery in Hackney, east London, and
is a charming, vibrant woman who is also a great hostess. She
makes all her guests feel at ease, whether they come from the
worlds of art, business or politics. The couple have twin children,
Maisie and Finn, five years old, and Martin Elliot is stepfather
to Freya, sixteen, her daughter from a previous relationship with
the artist Seb Anderson. Iona Fairfax was deeply upset by the
revelation that her husband had been conducting a long-standing
affair with Dr Isabelle Reynaud, the wife of property tycoon
Christophe Vernet.*

There were parts of the story he wasn't going to tell. Parts
he hadn't even told Harriet, because if she knew, she would
insist that he included them. He hadn't told her about Iona.
Telling Iona about his decision had been one of the hardest
phone calls he'd had to make, harder even than the call he had
made from outside Martin's hospital room, the night they'd
rescued him. At least that night he had done the right thing,
had some slight prospect of hope to hold out to her. He had
stood in the white hospital corridor under a flickering strip light
and explained then that they had found Martin, but he wasn't
in a good state. He gave Iona all the platitudes that people used
in those circumstances, because they were the words that came
most easily. That they would have to wait and see, that the
doctors were doing everything that they could. She wanted to
know exactly what had happened and he had told her, as best

he could at that point. The doctors still weren't sure of the order of events – whether he had fallen in the water first, and then had an attack, or the other way around. Martin, at that stage, hadn't been able to tell them. Either way, there was a long road to his recovery. The last time he had seen her was when she had come to take him home.

'I know it seems strange,' Iona said to Lawrence, 'after everything that has happened. But what else could I do? I can't leave him on his own.'

'I understand,' Lawrence said.

'We'll see how we go,' she continued. 'Once he's better. If he's better.'

When he had rung her to tell her that he was going to write the story for Harriet's paper, she went silent. At first he had thought she was going to hang up on him straight away. Instead, he heard her footsteps, the sliding of a door, a change in the atmosphere from indoors to outdoors.

'I've gone into the garden,' she said. 'Away from Martin.'

'It's going to be sympathetic,' Lawrence had said.

'Really?' Iona snapped back, incredulous. 'You think that will help him, help us, dragging us all through it again? How much are they paying you?'

They were paying him enough. More than enough. More than the money that Martin still owed him, which he knew that he would never get back. He was on the list of creditors, he had been told, but the biggest debts had to be paid first, the ones to the taxman for instance, and his was a very long way down.

'I won't say anything about you,' he promised her. 'Nothing that isn't already known. Nothing about – the last holiday.'

'So this is all about you looking heroic, is that it? Brave foreign correspondent leaps to the rescue, that sort of thing?'

'It's not like that,' he protested.

'It is like that,' Iona insisted. 'And you know it is. Just admit it. I'd have more respect for you if you could be honest about it.'

'OK, if you insist. It is like that. It's all about me. It's all about me being over the hill and unemployed and trying to make a bit of money, trying to get people to remember who I once was. Playing on my old contacts and trying to get some sympathy. Happy now?'

'No, not happy. But at least it's true.'

She said she would make sure not to look out for it, when it was published. She didn't read that paper, anyway.

'How's he doing?' Lawrence asked.

'Better, thanks. He'll never be completely back to full strength, they don't think, but he refuses to believe it. He won't let go. He can't.'

'He'll find his way back, somehow. I know him.'

'That's exactly what he says. The trouble is, he hasn't got the patience.' Iona paused. 'Go easy on him. I try to keep the papers away from him but he will insist on knowing what's going on. He'll find it online. So he'll read it, whatever you say.'

Harriet had emailed him a scan of a picture she had found in one of their albums, the ones she had kept. She wanted to ask him if the paper could use it. Lawrence had clicked on the image to enlarge it. The colours in the picture had faded and it was an overexposed photo, taken in bright unforgiving light. The two of them, him and Martin, were standing on an airfield, next to a small plane. It was somewhere hot, with a clear sky. From the picture, he couldn't tell where they were. There were no signs he could read, no familiar landmarks, just a few low buildings at the edge of the airfield and the plane next to them, the runway stretching away to the horizon. There were a couple of flight cases at their feet that must have contained equipment. At first, Lawrence could still not remember where the picture had been taken, which story they had been covering. Some people remembered everything like that, all the places they had travelled to, every story. At least, they claimed they did. Some of the stories grew embellished in the retelling of them. The further away that part of his life was, the more Lawrence realised how much he had forgotten, how little of it stayed with him. There were moments of your life that stuck with you but there were far longer stretches of time that disappeared, went blank. He and Martin had their arms around each other, his hand on Martin's shoulder. They were wearing almost matching outfits, the on-the-road uniform of pale-blue shirt and beige chinos. Martin still had hair, then, a dark boyish quiff above a widow's peak, only just beginning to recede. Lawrence's hair was still blond, swept back from his face, brushing his collar. They were both laughing; whoever had taken the photo must have said something to amuse them both. Before he replied to Harriet with the finished piece, he opened up the picture one more time, saved it to his desktop so that he could find it again easily. He knew it then, knew who had made them laugh. It was so vivid that he could almost feel the hot wind across the airfield. He saw the face of the person taking the photo. It had been Olly Dawson. Martin had said 'Make sure you don't cut our heads off' just to wind him up, as he was taking the picture, with Lawrence's tiny pocket camera.

'With this piece of crap,' Olly replied as he snapped, 'you'll be lucky if the picture comes out at all. Stand still.'

They all looked optimistic, then, looking forward, not knowing what lay ahead. Lawrence closed the photo and sent the article.

The picturesque village of Saint Barthélemy is full of traditions. I have owned a cottage there for almost twenty years. Every year the villagers celebrate their saint's day and toast the coming wine harvest. There is a procession to the church and a feast that goes on late into the night. The villagers dress in traditional costumes and are watched by locals and tourists alike. It has been popular with British visitors in recent years, in part because of the excellent local wine and the increasing enthusiasm for cycling holidays.

He woke early on Sunday morning. It was going to be another hot day. He checked his email; there were offers of work coming in, interview requests, commissions, an approving message from

Harriet saying that people in the office loved the piece. He would work through the messages later in the day. Lizzie had already left for work. The square was busy with people.

Lawrence made his way beneath the plane trees, hoping that his table was still free. It was always tricky in August, when the tourists came, the cyclists filling their water bottles from the fountain, the families pushing tables together for more space. His article might have the unwelcome effect of bringing more of them. He glanced towards the bakery, as he did every morning, hoping that he might glimpse someone who would never come. Occasionally, he thought he saw her − a dark-haired, slender woman with big sunglasses and a straw shopping basket. There were many women who looked like Isabelle, who could have been her, but they were not. His table was vacant and he claimed it. Lizzie emerged from the cafe with her tray and smiled at him.

'Your usual, Dad?' she said, before moving along to take an order from a grey-haired English couple who spoke to her in painstaking, badly accented French. Lizzie brought him out a *cafe crème*. The clock was starting to chime ten and he clenched his fist, digging his nails into his palm. He knew what to expect. He heard the sound of gunshots from the direction of the church. He looked across and watched the English couple flinch as they heard it, stare at each other in alarm. They looked around at him for reassurance and he gave them a smile. They did a double take when they recognised him. The mayor, Pascal, led the procession down the hill and into the square. The saint was carried through on his platform. Pascal took out a large red handkerchief and wiped the sweat from his brow, slung the shotgun over his shoulder and accepted the traditional glass to raise a toast. As he did so, Lawrence raised his own coffee cup in echo and drank from it, an offering to the year to come.

Acknowledgements

With grateful thanks to my agent, Rebecca Carter of Janklow and Nesbit, to my editor at John Murray, Mark Richards, and his team including Becky Walsh.

I would also like to thank those who helped me with research questions, in particular Olly Grender and Paul Swallow, as well as others who have been generous with their time and answers.

The friendship and moral support of the Prime Writers authors has been invaluable – thanks to you all.

From Byron, Austen and Darwin

to some of the most acclaimed and original
contemporary writing, John Murray takes pride in
bringing you powerful, prizewinning, absorbing
and provocative books that will entertain you
today and become the classics of tomorrow.

We put a lot of time and passion into what we
publish and how we publish it, and we'd like to
hear what you think.

Be part of John Murray – share your views with us at:

www.johnmurray.co.uk

 johnmurraybooks

@johnmurrays

johnmurraybooks